PAPER BODIES

PAPER BODIES

A MARGARET CAVENDISH READER

edited by Sylvia Bowerbank
and Sara Mendelson

broadview literary texts

Canadian Cataloguing in Publication Data

Newcastle, Margaret Cavendish, Duchess of 1624?-1674
    Paper bodies : a Margaret Cavendish reader

(Broadview literary texts)
Includes bibliographical references.
ISBN 1-55111-173-X
I. Bowerbank, Sylvia Lorraine.   II. Mendelson, Sara Heller, 1947-   .
III. Title.

PR3605.N2A6 1999   828'.409   C99-931318-5

Broadview Press Ltd., is an independent, international publishing house, incorporated in 1985.

North America:
P.O. Box 1243, Peterborough, Ontario, Canada K9J 7H5
3576 California Road, Orchard Park, NY 14127
TEL: (705) 743-8990; FAX: (705) 743-8353;
E-MAIL:customerservice@broadviewpress.com

United Kingdom:
Turpin Distribution Services Ltd.,
Blackhorse Rd., Letchworth, Hertfordshire SG6 1HN
TEL: (1462) 672555; FAX (1462) 480947; E-MAIL: turpin@rsc.org

Australia:
St. Clair Press, P.O. Box 287, Rozelle, NSW 2039
TEL: (02) 818-1942; FAX: (02) 418-1923

www.broadviewpress.com

Broadview Press is grateful to Professor L.W. Conolly for editorial advice on this volume.

Broadview Press gratefully acknowledges the financial support of the Book Publishing Industry Development Program, Ministry of Canadian Heritage, Government of Canada.

Text design and composition by George Kirkpatrick

PRINTED IN CANADA

Contents

Acknowledgements

We should like to express our warm thanks to Sarah Brophy and Lisa Stefaniak for their skilled and meticulous assistance with editorial work. Several colleagues and friends have generously shared their scholarly expertise, or read and commented on portions of the text, including Elaine Auerbach, Frances Dolan, James Fitzmaurice, Howard Jones, Nanette LeCoat, Alan Mendelson, Nancy Miller, Mary O'Connor, Anne Shaver, Carl Spadoni, and Gweno Williams. We are grateful to the staff of Mills Memorial Library at McMaster University for help with early editions and illustrations held in Special Collections. We owe a special debt of gratitude to Mary O'Connor, to whom this book is dedicated.

List of Illustrations

Introduction

The writings of Margaret Cavendish are remarkable for their vivid depiction of the mores and mentality of seventeenth-century England. Yet paradoxically, she was probably unique for her time in the extent to which she herself transcended the rigid categories of gender and class that defined most people's lives. The paradox begins to recede when we realize that her works illuminate the most significant preoccupations of her society precisely because she played with, probed, ridiculed or rejected the dominant assumptions that structured early modern beliefs and behaviour. In the process of writing, Margaret Cavendish fashioned a personal identity, indeed an entire universe, radically different from the world in which she lived.

Born in 1623 of a wealthy gentry family, Margaret Lucas lived a leisured and sheltered life in the Essex countryside as the youngest of eight children. With private tutors kept "for formality rather than benefit," she spent much of her time in a self-absorbed process of reflection and experimentation, creating her own fashions, contemplating the world of nature, and writing sixteen "baby-books," her first efforts in a lifetime of recording her philosophical and scientific speculations.

This country idyll ended abruptly in 1642 when King and Parliament began to rally forces for what was to become the English Civil War, an internecine conflict that led ultimately to the execution of King Charles I and the abolition of the monarchy in 1649. As royalists in a county dominated by parliamentarians, the Lucas family were alienated from their élite neighbours and vulnerable to popular violence. In 1643 they joined the King's court at Oxford, where Margaret persuaded her mother to allow her to become a maid of honour to Queen Henrietta Maria.[1]

When the Queen fled with her court to Paris in 1644, Margaret Lucas accompanied her. Painfully shy and lonely in the alien *milieu* of the French court, Margaret longed to return to the sanctuary of her family. Instead, in 1645 she met and married William Cavendish,

---

1 For Cavendish's own account of this and other events in her life, see *A True Relation of My Birth and Breeding*, below, p. 41.

Marquis of Newcastle, a widower with grown-up children. Because of his role as royalist general, the Marquis was declared a traitor and his estates confiscated. The couple lived in exile on the continent for fifteen years, first in Holland and then in Antwerp, until the restoration of Charles II to the throne in 1660. Far from her family and powerless to act on behalf of the royalist cause, Cavendish learned of the deaths of her mother, her eldest brother and a favourite sister, and of the execution in 1648 of her youngest brother by court martial. In 1651 Cavendish made a brief visit to England in an attempt to appeal for income from her husband's confiscated estates, but her petition was unsuccessful.

Although Newcastle was eager to have more children, especially sons, Cavendish never became pregnant. Without maternal duties to occupy her, she spent much of her time writing stories and poetry. Meanwhile her interest in the new science was encouraged by a close friendship with her brother-in-law Sir Charles Cavendish, an avid mathematician who was conversant with the latest scientific discoveries and speculations. Scientific themes and problems dominate her first publication, *Poems and Fancies* (1653), a work that she described as a kind of substitute for physical offspring: "Condemne me not for making such a coyle/ About my Book, alas it is my Childe."

In 1660 the couple returned to England, where the Marquis regained his English estates. In 1665 he was created Duke of Newcastle as a reward for his loyalty to the royalist cause. But his ambition of playing a key role in Charles II's government never materialized. The couple settled into a quiet country life that they spent restoring their estates at Welbeck and Bolsover, making only occasional brief visits to London. Meanwhile, Cavendish continued to be immensely productive. From 1653 until her death twenty years later, she published more than a dozen folio volumes on a great diversity of topics, ranging from scientific speculations to poetry and plays, a book of orations, a volume of letters to an imaginary friend, and a biography of her husband.

★   ★   ★   ★   ★

The title for our collection – *Paper Bodies* – is taken from one of Margaret Cavendish's *CCXI Sociable Letters* (1664), in which she writes of her unfounded fear that her plays had been lost at sea while being transported from Antwerp to London to be published. She would have felt the loss of her twenty plays as the loss of twenty lives, she writes, "for in my Mind I should have Died Twenty Deaths." Fortunately, Margaret always kept copies of her works until they were printed,

and then I Commit the Originals to the Fire, like Parents which are willing to Die, whenas they are sure of their Childrens Lives ... But howsoever their Paper Bodies are Consumed, like as the Roman Emperours, in Funeral Flames, I cannot say, an Eagle Flies out of them, or that they Turn into a Blazing Star, although they make a great Blazing Light when they Burn. (Letter CXLIII, below, p. 81)

The marvellous expression "paper bodies" suggests that for Cavendish, her writings serve as surrogate bodies that will keep her identity and ideas alive. This way of thinking about texts raises certain questions. What sorts of embodiments are texts? What is the relationship between a writer's "paper bodies" and the actual lived context of the past? How do we – three centuries later – go about restoring or recovering the "body" out of the textual remains? By what criteria should we judge one reconstruction of the past or "the body" to be more plausible or authentic than another? By what reading methods do we assemble the mental and material culture of early modern England out of "paper bodies"?

In this collection, we present clusters of texts that invite inquiry into three topics, which, although separated here for the sake of analysis, interact with each other in innumerable ways: first, birth, breeding and self-fashioning; second, gender and serious play; and finally, women and the new science. A Cavendish primary text, accompanied by related documents from the same period, exemplifies each inquiry topic: *A True Relation of My Birth, Breeding and Life* (1656) for topic one; *The Convent of Pleasure* (1668) for topic two; and *The Description of a New World, Called The Blazing World* (1666) for topic three. Readers are encouraged to create their own clusters of texts and to discover their own connections and discontinuities among the texts and contexts.

A. Birth, Breeding, and Self-fashioning

> Mother Love: Husband you have a strange nature, that having but one child, and never like to have more, and this your childe a daughter; that you should breed her so strictly, as to give her no time for recreation when other children have Play-fellows, and toyes to sport and passe their time withall.

> Father Love: Good wife be content, doth not she play when she reads books of Poetry, and can there be nobler, amiabler, finer, usefuller, and wiser companions than the Sciences, or pleasanter Play-fellows than the Muses; can she have freer conversation, than with wit, or more various recreations than Scenes, Sonets and Poems; Tragical, Comical, and Musical, and the like.
>
> (Cavendish, *Youths Glory and Deaths Banquet*)

In a period when spiritual and political autobiographies predominate, Margaret Cavendish's *A True Relation of My Birth, Breeding and Life* (1656) offers an unusually vivid example of a personal and secular autobiography. Besides giving an account of the events of her life, *A True Relation* presents a candid paper-body reproduction of the vulnerabilities of Cavendish's own physical and psychological body. By her own diagnosis, her body is that of the melancholic – heavy, lethargic, immobilized by distemper, sleeplessness, and agoraphobia. The epistle to *A True Relation* explains why Cavendish does not like to talk about her books, so much so that some people suspect she did not write them. Cavendish is not good at talking: she is shy in company, because her body cannot be trusted. It manifests its natural bashfulness in embarrassing ways. At times it contracts to a "chill paleness" whereby she is unable to speak at all. When dining with the philosopher Thomas Hobbes in Paris, she was struck dumb. At other times, her body becomes so ungovernable, her gestures so erratic, and her tongue so voluble that people judge her to be vain, extravagant, or even mad. Perhaps this was what Mary Evelyn witnessed when she met the Duchess and reported on her extravagant speech and gestures (below, pp. 91-3; see Harris 198-9). In one of her *CCXI Sociable Letters*, Margaret Cavendish writes a poignant account of the disruptive effects of extreme bashfulness (Letter CXXXVII, below, pp. 77-8). Cavendish's sense of herself is closely tied up with her "melancholic" humour. In *A True Relation*, she interprets the vulnerabilities of her body as manifestations of her melancholia. There and in her other writings, Cavendish analyses, satirizes, and reconceptualizes melancholia and the contemporary prescriptions for its cure. In Cavendish's play *Loves Adventures* (1662), Lady Wagtail advises Lady Ignorance:

If you are troubled with melancholly vapours, arising from crude humours, you must take as soon as you wake after your first sleep, a draught of Wormwood-wine, then lye to sleep again, and then half an hour before you rise, drink a draught of Jelley-broth, and after you have been up an hour and half, eate a White-wine-caudle, then a little before a dinner, take a Toste and Sack, and at your meals, two or three good glasses of Clarret-wine; as for your Meats, you must eate those of light digestion, as Pheasant, Partridges, Cocks, Snipes, Chickens, young Turkies, Pea-chickens and the like; And in the Afternoon, about four or five a clock, you must take Naples-bisket dip'd in Ippocrass... (*Playes*, 23)

Following such a regimen not only revives the spirits, but lets one "discourse wittily, and makes one such good company, as invites acquaintance, and ties friendship."

In her own life, Cavendish defines and administers self-cures: she eats little more than boiled chicken and drinks only water; she does not dance, run, or walk abroad; she keeps her body confined to her chamber, subjecting it to self-prescribed regimens of fasting, purging, and blood-letting. She is, however, well aware that conventional medical wisdom would have her do otherwise. In her play *Matrimonial Trouble* (1662), the following advice is given to Lady Hypochondria: "goe abroad, to divert your melancholy, and eat as others do, that may have good meat and drink, and not live by the Air, as you do" (*Playes*,

465). Doctor Theodore Mayerne complained in a letter to Margaret's husband that she refused to follow his advice, and worsened her condition by thinking and writing too much.[1] This is not how she herself sees her literary labours. For Cavendish, writing becomes her survival strategy. Like the Muses and other feminized abstractions, the female icon of Melancholia was used in the early modern period to symbolize the creative genius of men, but never that of women. Cavendish subversively appropriates the figure of Melancholia to authorize and empower herself as a writer. Melancholia is at once the incurable "natural defect" of her body and the pre-condition of the courageous productivity of her mind. Although her body is barren and incapacitated, her mind is "industrious" and "restless to Live, as Nature doth, in all Ages, and in every Brain." (Letter XC, below p. 71).[2] Through writing, Cavendish gains a measure of control over her body, her tongue, her gestures, her language; she produces surrogate "paper bodies" that speak elegantly and wisely in public. And yet, at the same time, the strange rhythms and vagaries of her prose inscribe and preserve the vulnerable, apologetic body of melancholia. Well might Cavendish agree with the words of Julia Kristeva in *Black Sun*: "my pain is the hidden side of my philosophy, its mute sister" (p. 4).

Although *A True Relation* purports to be a factual narrative – a "true relation" – Cavendish reminds us of her life-long project to discover and invent new and unique versions of herself. In a telling passage, she describes her great delight in inventing her clothes and appearance. The same "delight in singularity" holds true of all her pursuits, whether "fashion of cloths, contemplation of thoughts, [or] actions of life." The theme of experimenting with multiple versions of herself crops up in all her writings. In her *CCXI Sociable Letters*, her very sociability is constructed between her own writer's persona and an idealized version of herself, sometimes a lady with the initials M.L. for Margaret Lucas (her maiden name) or a lady preoccupied with one of Cavendish's recurrent interests, such as bashfulness (Letter CXXXVII) or melancholia (Letter XCIII).

---

1   "A Booke, Wherein is Contained Rare Minerall Receipts Collected at Paris," Nottingham University, Cavendish MSS, PwV. 90 (unfoliated); Mendelson (1987) 26.
2   For Cavendish's discussion of connections between bodily infertility and melancholia, see Letter XCIII, below, pp. 72-4.

Here on this Figure Cast a Glance,
But so as if it were by Chance,
Your eyes not fixt, they must not stay,
Since this like Shadowes to the Day
It only represents; for Still
Her Beauty's found beyond the Skill
Of the best Paynter, to Imbrace
These lovely Lines within her face.
View her Soul's Picture, Judgment, wit,
Then read those Lines which Shee hath writt,
By Phancy's Pencill drawne alone
Which Peece but Shee, Can justly owne.

Illustration 1: The frontispiece from Margaret Cavendish's *Plays Never Before Printed* (1668) depicts the writer framed by two classical figures of harmonious creativity: Athena with a vanquished head of the gorgon Medusa on her shield, and Apollo with his lyre. (Courtesy the Bodleian Library, Oxford, Vet. A. 3. c.113.)

Cavendish's mode of self-fashioning is typically expansive and extravagant, like Nature's own creativity. She explicitly rejects any notion of self-fashioning as the ascetic repression of the imagination or the devaluation of the body. This is evident, for example, in the satirical portrait of a female "Sanctified Soul," whose pious regimen has led to a complete repudiation of her former appearance and identity, so much so that she is no longer recognizable: "She hath left Curling her Hair, Black Patches are become Abominable to her, Laced Shoes and Galoshoes are Steps to Pride, to go Bare-neck'd she accounts worse than Adultery" (Letter LI, below, p. 67). In *The Convent of Pleasure*, Cavendish advocates modes of self-transformation that cultivate the earthly pleasures of the body while freeing it from social and psychological constraints, even the constraints of contemporary gender roles.

B. Gender and Serious Play

Mother Love: Come, come, Husband, I will have her bred, as usually our Sex is, and not after a new fashioned way, created out of a self-opinionated, that you can alter nature by education: No, no, let me tell you, a woman will be a woman, do what you can, and you may as soon create a new World, as change a womans nature and disposition.

(Cavendish, *Youths Glory, and Deaths Banquet*)

Without a doubt, feminism continues to require its own forms of serious play.

(Judith Butler, *Gender Trouble*)

Margaret Cavendish's play *The Convent of Pleasure* (see below, pp. 97-135) presents a parodic critique of a gender order that postulates fixed polarities between the masculine and the feminine. In Act I, Lady Happy refuses to perform her "natural" role as a wife and mother; she institutes the convent, not as a place of self-denial and restraint, but of freedom and happiness: "retiredness bars the life from nothing else but Men." Here women perform all the occupations in the convent from prioress and physician to gardener and cook, making no distinction between man's and woman's work. The enclosed women follow the rule of nature; they eat, drink, dress, decorate their rooms, and design their recreations in conformity to the dictates of the seasons. The men outside the walls, however, claim that Lady Happy's behaviour is unnatural and dangerous; her enclosure threatens the commonwealth. The play unfolds as an ongoing debate over what constitutes "natural" behaviour. It demonstrates, in numerous ways, what Judith Butler calls "the performative character of gender" (24-5).

Like Cavendish's other plays, *The Convent of Pleasure* experiments extensively with dramatic form. As a playwright, Cavendish rejects the conventional unities of time, place, and action in order to create more probable and natural action, for example, by including unconnected scenes, and unrelated characters who are not brought together by an artificial plot.[1] At the same time, the promiscuous juxtaposition of various modes of drama is often deployed to radical effect. In this context, let us consider the masque of the sea deities, which occurs near the end of the play. In it, Lady Happy impersonates a magnificent Sea Goddess, the Princess plays Neptune, and the other ladies of the convent play various water nymphs (IV.i). The ceremonial exchanges of the masque arrange all the bounty of the oceans to the pleasure of the sea-goddess and to the sovereign use of Neptune. How might Cavendish's belated use of the masque form be understood? How might this sea-deity masque be represented in the staging and performance of the play?

During the 1630s, when Margaret Lucas was a girl growing up in the countryside, the glory of Charles I and Henrietta Maria was celebrated in the court masque, an art form that synthesized drama, music, art, costume, and dance to epitomize the harmonizing powers of the monarchy. In a typical Caroline masque, various elements of the cosmos, the state, and the passions are at first depicted in terrible chaos, but finally become tame and peaceful under the restored and rightful sovereignty of the King and Queen.[2] In a Caroline masque, it

---

1   "I would have my Playes to be like the Natural course of all things in the World, as some dye sooner, some live longer, and some are newly born, when some are newly dead, and not to continue to the last day of Judgment; so my scenes, some last longer than othersome, and some are ended when others are begun; likewise some of my Scenes have no acquaintance or relation to the rest of the Scenes..." Prefatory epistle "To the Reader," *Playes* (1662).

2   On the politics of the masque, Roy Strong argues that "All the masques express the power of the monarchy to bring harmony, the rich gifts of nature and the natural world into obedience." In *Splendour at Court: Renaissance Spectacle and Illusion.*

is often the mediating power of the Queen along with her ladies – playing mythological figures – that brings about the final scene of harmonious love and peace.[1] For example, in Jonson's *Chloridia* (1631), by "the providence of Juno" and the technological wizardry of Inigo Jones, a monstrous world is transformed into a green paradise as Chloris, played by the Queen herself, appears in her bower.[2] The final scene of William Davenant's *Salmacida Spolia* (1640) was designed by Inigo Jones to display a great celestial cloud containing the Queen as the chief heroine, illuminated and accompanied by her ladies in a glorious assumption of absolute power and concord.

Perhaps Margaret Cavendish longed for the halcyon days and feminine powers of the Caroline court. Perhaps she was influenced by the old-fashioned tastes of a husband thirty years her senior, who had put himself to great expense in order to stage two masques on his own estates for the pleasure of the King and Queen.[3] Whatever the case, Margaret Cavendish includes a number of interesting masques and masque-like effects in her writings (see *Poems and Fancies* 155-60). One masque segment occurs in *The Blazing World* when the Empress goes back to her former world to help the countrymen of her birthplace fight their enemies.[4] As her countrymen watch from their ships, the Empress advances towards them wearing stunning garments made

---

London: Weidenfeld and Nicolson, 1974: 219. See also Stephen Orgel, *The Illusion of Power: Political Theater in the English Renaissance*. Berkeley: University of California Press, 1975.

1   Masque roles designed to exhibit Henrietta Maria's beneficent powers include: "Divine Beauty" descending in a great cloud from the harmony of the spheres, in Aurelian Townshend's *Tempe Restored* (1632); Indamora, Queen of Love, establishing chaste love on earth, in William D'Avenant's *Temple of Love* (1635); and the "Queen of Brightness" in William D'Avenant's *Luminalia* (1638).

2   For insight into Jones's art in creating the costumes and special effects of the Caroline masque, see John Harris, Stephen Orgel, and Roy Strong, compilers, *The King's Arcadia: Inigo Jones and the Stuart Court: A quatercentenary exhibition held at the Banqueting House, Whitehall from July 12th to September 2rd, 1973*. London: Arts Council of Great Britain, 1973.

3   Both were written by Ben Jonson. *The King's Entertainment at Welbeck* (May, 1633) was followed by an entertainment designed for the Queen, *Love's Welcome at Bolsover* (July, 1634). In her biography of her husband, Margaret Cavendish estimates that the latter event, including lodging expenses of their majesties, cost William between £14,000 and £15,000. See Cavendish, *Life of William Cavendish*, ed. Firth, 103.

4   See p. 237. Loosely speaking, *Blazing World* can be seen as a version of Henrietta Maria's life: a young woman comes from foreign parts, marries the monarch, and is given the power to rule by her uxorious husband.

of the star stone, and appears to walk on the face of the water. The illusion of the Empress as an angel or deity clothed in light, walking on water, is clearly staged for effect. Yet Cavendish insists that the Empress's powers are – unlike the artificial machinery of the Caroline masque – shrewd deployments of natural, if unknown, effects. The Empress is actually stepping on the heads and backs of fishmen from the Blazing World that support her without being seen, and who also carry firestone to illuminate her body. Thus, the hidden labour of her subjects is made visible in the text, though not to her countrymen whom the Empress wishes to subdue or, at least, impress with her might. Taken as a whole, the effect is comic as well as commanding.

Cavendish's masque experiments – created as they were in a more censorious age when the pastoral illusions of court ideology could only be produced with some degree of irony – convey only fleeting, ambivalent moments of power and might. The use of the masque in *The Convent of Pleasure*, taken by itself, seems to reproduce pastoral fantasies of an absolutist harmony in which feminine sea deities grace the majestic sovereignty of Neptune to whom – "from whale to herring" – all are "subject fish" (IV. i). Yet, in the context of the play as a whole, the pacific effect of such a patriarchal harmony is seriously disrupted by the series of plays-within-the-play that occupy the centre of the play (Act III, scenes ii-x). The plays-within-the-play present a relentless series of vignettes on the wrongs done to women: husbands of every class steal their wives' earnings or jointures; spend the household finances on drink, gaming or whores; beat their wives and children; and often abandon them to poverty and shame. In the Caroline court masque, suffering, angry, dispossessed women would have been displayed in the antimasque, demonized as the disruptive and malcontent elements of society, and then driven out by the arrival of tame, benign feminine powers. In *Convent of Pleasure*, the abused women of the plays-within-the-play not only provoke sympathy and solidarity, but also invite a critique of social injustice, in general, and of the privileged pleasures of the ladies of the convent, in particular.

The twenty-one ladies of the convent have the means to repudiate compulsory heterosexuality and to enter into a realm of gender play. Their chief recreation is the dramatization and reinvention of gender politics. The foreign "Princess" comes to the convent specifically to join in the experimental pleasures of erotic friendship, cross-dressing, and role-playing; she is especially desirous to wear a masculine habit and act the lover's part (III.i). Early in the play, faced with the enclosure of desirable women, the other men – Monsieurs Adviser, Courtly, and Take-pleasure – decide to take manly action, but in what does this consist? "Manliness" proves to be more elusive than they thought. They first try on the ribbons and finery of the suitor (I.i); they then affect machismo in their plans to burn the convent down or storm the walls (II.iv). Finally, they devise a strategy to infiltrate the convent dressed as women, but can men play women? Monsieur Adviser claims their masculine voices, gestures, and shapes will give the men away: "We shall never frame our Eyes and Mouths to such coy, dissembling looks, and pritty simpering Mopes and Smiles, as they do" (II.iv). The feminine identity, for which they are supposed ill-equipped, is immediately revealed to be, not woman's natural behaviour, but the learned refinements of the gentlewoman. Thus, the men think they might be able to pass for "lusty country wenches" (II.iv).

Yet, in the play, one man – the Prince as the Princess – does perform "woman" in subtle and instructive ways. In performance, how could the radical potential of these scenes become manifest? How does one play the Princess? The scenes between Lady Happy and the Princess are sophisticated and witty in their gender negotiations. How should their flirtation, embracing and kissing be staged? In a scene for the play written by the Duke of Newcastle,[1] Lady Mediator claims to have known all along that the kissing between the Princess and Lady Happy was too "vigorous" to be kissing between two women (v. ii). But is there some essential (physiological?) sign in a kiss that unmistakably reveals whether the lover is a man or a woman? Lady Happy's anxiety over her desire for the Princess indicates otherwise. For her, kissing the Princess is so pleasurable that she asks herself: "why may not I love a Woman with the same affection I could a Man?" How can such a passion be against nature?

The ending of Convent of Pleasure lends itself to a range of interpretive performances. Has the Prince changed in any substantial way, given the range of gender-bending experiences he has undergone during the play? Is the Lady Happy disappointed or pleased to

---

1   Gweno Williams is engaged in a forthcoming study of the Duke's "interventions" in the Duchess's plays.

discover the masculine identity of her lover? Is the ending happy for Lady Happy, who is now to be a wife after all her railings against the oppression of marriage? Finally, by way of invitation to readers to take up the challenge of staging performances of *The Convent of Pleasure*, we call your attention to the pioneering work of Gweno Williams. In 1995 Williams and her students at the University College of Ripon and York St. John succeeded in demonstrating that *The Convent of Pleasure* (which had never been staged) would make a wonderful production (see illustrations pp. 110, 133).[1]

In many of her writings, Margaret Cavendish invents literary experiments that play with notions of gender. The category of "woman" does not stand as a single uncontested constant; its cultural meaning is explored, destabilized, and challenged. The Preface to *The World's Olio* is included in this collection (below, p. 136) to exemplify Cavendish's scrutiny of traditional ideological constructions of "woman." In the preface, she not only rehearses truisms about the essential differences between man and woman, but also recites a dreary litany of the non-accomplishments of women throughout history. At the same time, Cavendish dares women to defy stereotypes about their place in nature, to take up ambitious projects, and to contribute to intellectual life: "Women can have no excuse, or complaints of being Subjects, as a hindrance from thinking; for Thoughts are free, those can ever be inslaved, for we are not hindered from studying" (see below, p. 140).

Cavendish's *Female Orations* (see below, pp. 143-7) present another very different debate on gender politics. In the preface to *Female Orations*, Cavendish indicates that even the form of men's and women's orations is gendered: while the men speak in a series of authoritative speeches, the women speak in conversation. To present women's orations publicly is itself unique, says Cavendish, because women's intellectual debates are rarely heard by men: "one short Oration concerning the Liberty of Women hath so Anger'd that Sex, as after the Mens Orations are ended, they Privately Assemble together, where three or four take the place of an Orator, and Speak to the rest; the only Difficulty will be, to get Undiscovered amongst them, to hear their Private Conventicles." In their orations, the seven female

---

1   For a detailed analysis of both theoretical and practical problems and strategies for a modern production of *The Convent of Pleasure*, see Williams 100-105.

speakers give diverse and conflicting responses to such fundamental questions as: Is there one true and constant "nature" of woman? Is woman naturally weak and inferior to man? Is it nature or man that makes woman weak and inferior? Can woman's nature be improved? If so, how?

The first female speaker has called the assembly of women on the assumption that they share a common cause and should unite "to make our Selves as Free, Happy, and Famous as Men." The second speaker also calls for collective action against male tyrants; according to her, all women are in "the Hell of Subjection" and need to find a remedy for their misery. The ground shifts considerably, however, with the third speaker; she argues that men are the protectors, defenders, and lovers of women, who use their power and labour to ensure the happiness, not the oppression, of women. The fourth speaker denies that women are essentially weak and witless; they can improve their minds and bodies by imitating the exercises and sociability of men: "let us Hawk, Hunt, Race, and do the like Exercises as Men have, and let us Converse in Camps, Courts, and Cities, in Schools, Colleges, and Courts of Judicature, in Taverns, Brothels, and Gaming Houses, all which will make our Strength and Wit known, both to Men, and to our own Selves." The fifth speaker finds this notion of women imitating men preposterous, but the sixth speaker supports it, saying that all creatures should imitate their superiors and thus improve on their natures.

Finally, the seventh speaker transforms the debate dramatically by denying the very premise of the other speakers that women are inferior to men – whether by nature or by the oppression of men: "for we Women are much more Favour'd by Nature than Men, in Giving us such Beauties, Features, Shapes, Gracefull Demeanour, and such Insinuating and Inticing Attractives, as Men are Forc'd to Admire us, Love us, and be Desirous of us, in so much as rather than not Have and Injoy us, they will Deliver to our Disposals, their Power, Persons, and Lives, Inslaving Themselves to our Will and Pleasures." (For an even more provocative discussion of women's power, see Letter XVI of *CCXI Sociable Letters* [below, p. 66], which claims that, if women are not citizens, then they need not be subjects of the commonwealth and that, though men seem to govern the world, it is women that really do.) The fact that the series of seven female orations is structured as a debate brings into relief the problem of whether there is a common ground on which women's solidarity can be built. Even the opening salutation used in the orations – "Ladies, Gentlewomen, and other Inferiors" – is a reminder that class distinctions must be made between "inferiors" and their "superiors". The conflicting interplay of ideas about gender relations suggests that, for Cavendish, women do not constitute an easily unifiable group. Yet the very depiction of an assembly of women debating the issue of the nature of woman is in itself a stunning *tour-de-force*.

C. Women and the New Science

And if it be an Age when the effeminate spirits rule, as most visible they doe in every Kingdome, let us take the advantage, and make the best of our time, for feare their reigne should not last long; whether it be in the Amazonian Government, or in the Politick Common-wealth, or in flourishing Monarchy, or in Schooles of Divinity, or in Lectures of Philosophy, or in witty Poetry, or any thing that may bring honour to our Sex... And though we be inferiour to Men, let us shew our selves a degree above Beasts; and not eate, and drink, and sleep away our time as they doe.

(Cavendish, "To all Writing Ladies," *Poems and Fancies)*

To appreciate fully the remarkable achievement of Cavendish's *Description of a New Blazing World* (see below, p. 151), it is necessary first to have a sense of the barriers to early modern women's participation in the new science (Bowerbank, forthcoming). Until recently, the scientific revolution of the seventeenth century was seen as the collective achievement of certain European men, who created research institutions in order to advance man's knowledge and empire over nature. The scientific pursuits of early modern European women were, for the most part, forgotten or undervalued as the leisured activities of a few well-placed "scientific ladies" (Meyer, 1955). Recent feminist scholarship, however, has reclaimed some of the contributions made by early modern European women to the emergence of science. This new research has presented a very different picture of the scientific revolution and women's part in it (Alic, 1986; Ogilvie,

1986; Schiebinger, 1989; Shteir, 1996; Hunter and Hutton, 1997). At the same time, the objectivity of early modern science itself has been called into question by feminist theorists who have demonstrated that gender operated as an ideological determinant to define the nature of science and the scientific observer (Keller, 1985; Schiebinger, 1993).

Despite institutional and ideological barriers, women's relationships to early modern science were complex and various. Much of the scientific labour of early modern women was restricted to the ancillary functions of normal science. Women acted as copiers of manuscripts; as observers and computers of data; and as illustrators, simplifiers, translators, and popularizers of men's scientific and mathematical texts. Some well-placed women were generous patrons of science, who attended public lectures on science and developed extensive library collections of new scientific publications (Phillips, 1990). Others ventured to publish scientific textbooks for lay readers. While it is true that most women were excluded or restricted in their practice of science, a few managed to achieve important discoveries, while others began to question, to resist, and to develop alternative ways to do "natural philosophy," or science.

Margaret Cavendish spent much of her life studying natural philosophy. Yet until recently, she was remembered primarily as a fashionable "scientific lady" whose greatest triumph was her famous visit to the Royal Society on May 30, 1667 (Meyer). On that day, a large crowd assembled to catch sight of the illustrious Duchess of Newcastle. If diarists Samuel Pepys and John Evelyn were typical, members of the Royal Society showed more interest in the Duchess's extravagant appearance than in her ideas. According to Pepys (who admitted to not liking her "at all"), the Duchess of Newcastle did not have anything to say worth hearing but was "full of admiration" (Nicolson 104-14). Evelyn composed a lengthy satire in the form of a street ballad, "I'll tell thee Jo," which focussed on details of the Duchess's costume, including its androgynous character:

> But Jo her headgear was so pretty
> I ne'er saw anything so witty
> Tho I was half afeared
> God bless us when I first did see her

She looked so like a Cavalier
But that she had no beard.[1]

Robert Boyle and Robert Hooke were selected to perform experiments on colours, the use of a good microscope, the weighing of air in a receiver by means of the rarefying machine, and the pulling apart of two well wrought marble blocks, which took a weight of 47 pounds (Birch, History, I, 175, 177-8). It is clear that Cavendish's brief entry into the professional space of science was understood as an unusual courtesy given to a high-ranking noble and potential patron.

Between 1600 and 1800, the new science struggled to establish its hegemony over the production of new knowledge. When the Royal Society was instituted in 1662, one of its main aims was to establish a demarcation between professional scientists and mere amateurs. Throughout Europe, women were systematically barred from membership in scientific academies, and thus from the process of producing legitimate knowledge about nature. Neither the French Academy of Sciences nor the Royal Society of London permitted women to be members. In publishing his *Experiments and Considerations touching Colours* (1664), Robert Boyle insisted that his primary concern was "to teach a young gentleman" to understand and to improve on his experiments. He recognized, however, that another type of reader was eager to enjoy such "easy and recreative experiments." All sorts of curious beholders – including the ladies – were attracted to the performance of scientific experiments as novel entertainment. Even though Boyle himself, as a naturalist, measured the success of his experiments "by their use, not their strangeness or prettiness," he and other natural philosophers were not above catering to the public's taste for scientific amusements ("Preface"). Thus, on occasion, the Royal Society invited high-ranking ladies as well as men to attend meetings in which experiments were performed as entertainment. The Duchess's 1667 visit was one such occasion. When Pepys claimed that the Duchess was "all admiration" that day, he stereotyped her as a credulous lady for whom the tricks and trifles of experiments could produce only wonder and amusement, not understanding.

Whatever Cavendish might have said that day, her own writings

---

1 Public Record Office, State Papers 29/450, Item 102, fo. 164

not only resist the hegemonic claim of early modern science to interpret nature, but also present women as agents in the production of scientific knowledge. Published in 1666, Cavendish's *Description of a New Blazing World* is the first fictional portrayal of women and the new science. In *Blazing World*, Cavendish depicts her heroine, the Empress, in multiple roles in relationship to science. She is the promoter of scientific research; she invents a royal society of virtuosi; she initiates learned conferences; she interrogates existing knowledge; she herself speculates on natural philosophy; and she forms an intellectual collaboration with a female character summoned from the earth, called the "duchess of Newcastle."

To appreciate the extent of Cavendish's bold originality, we need only compare *Blazing World* with a work published twenty years later, Fontenelle's *Entretiens sur la pluralité des mondes*[1] (1686), a book which is often cited as the first work to encourage women's participation in science. In a series of garden conversations, a male expert flirtatiously explains the Copernican system to a witty and receptive Marquese (see illustration p. 318). It is apparent from Fontenelle's own prefatory remarks that he intended to pioneer a new role for women:

> In this Discourse I have introduced a fair Lady to be instructed in Philosophy, which till now, never heard any speak of it; imagining, by this Fiction, I shall render my Work more agreeable; and to encourage the Fair Sex (who lose so much time at their Toylets[2] in a less charming Study) by the Example of a Lady who had no supernatural Character, and who never goes beyond the Bounds of a Person who has no Tincture of Learning, and yet understands all that is told her, and retains all the Notions of Tourbillions and Worlds without Confusion: And why should this Imaginary Lady have the Precedency of all the rest of her delicate Sex? Or do they believe they are not as capable of conceiving that she learned with so much Facility?

During the eighteenth century, Fontenelle's *Entretiens sur la pluralité*

---

1   conversations on the plurality of worlds
2   the process of dressing

Illustration 2: The question of whether women should study science is raised in Benjamin Martin's *the Young Gentleman and Lady's Philosophy* (1772), when an older brother Cleonicus seeks to teach his sister Euphrosyne about astronomy. In one exchange, she says: "To calculate an Eclipse! A strong thing to talk of for a woman, Cleonicus." He answers: "A Woman! Why, this Woman-hood of yours, seems to be mightily in the Way." (Courtesy Mills Memorial Library, McMaster University.)

des mondes was widely read and imitated. The literary device of conversations between a male expert and a charming female learner was repeatedly deployed as a strategy to make scientific knowledge more interesting and accessible to the lay public – for example in Algarotti's *Newtonianismo per le dame* (1737; translated by Elizabeth Carter in 1739) and Benjamin Martin's *The Young Gentleman and Lady's Philosophy* (1772) (see illustration p. 27).

Despite the asymmetrical power relations in Fontenelle's *Entretiens*, women readers are invited to take both interest and pleasure in thinking about such topics as the Copernican hypothesis and extraterrestrial life. When Aphra Behn translated Fontenelle's *Entretiens* into English as *A Discovery of New Worlds* in 1688, she prefaced her edition with a remarkable essay entitled "An Essay on Translated Prose," which protests that Fontenelle's charming Marquese is an unrealistic creation, a woman who is at once intelligent and silly. At the same time, Behn dares to advance her own serious defence of the Copernican hypothesis. Behn's essay is included in this collection (p. 314) in order to illustrate an independent woman's defence of the new science. Besides their common interest in promoting women's participation in science, Fontenelle's *Entretiens* and Cavendish's *Blazing World* show another telling similarity. Both works present a positive exploration of one of the most controversial ideas of the seventeenth century: the plurality of worlds.

The *Blazing World* was not the first new world that Margaret Cavendish created. Her earliest book, *Poems and Fancies* (1653), is full of playful and serious explorations of other worlds and their inhabitants. Seventeenth-century Europeans were much given to speculating about the co-existence of other worlds, as yet unknown to them. This is not surprising, given their recent discovery of "new" worlds and lands on the earth and the revolutionary new astronomy developed by Copernicus, Kepler, and Galileo. The very notion of a plurality of worlds led to unparalleled intellectual excitement. At the same time, because such ideas were linked to a revival of atomism, speculations about other worlds and their inhabitants led to considerable anxiety (Dick 44-60). The very coherence of the Christian world order seemed threatened. Earlier in the century, in "An Anatomy of the World: the First Anniversary," John Donne worried that "the new philosophy calls all into doubt":

And freely men confesse that this world's spent,
When in the Planets, and the Firmament
They seeke so many new; they see that this
Is crumbled out againe to his Atomis.
'Tis all in pieces, all cohaerence gone...

Some books, such as Henry More's *Democritus Platonissans, or an Essay upon the Infinity of Worlds out of Platonick Principles* (1647) and Gassendi's *Animadversions in decimum librum Diogenes Laertius* (1649), were concerned to reconcile the doctrine of infinite worlds with Christian theology (Dick chap. 3). The vortex cosmology of René Descartes, as described in *Principia Philosophia* (1644), implied an infinity of inhabited planets and stars. Thus, Christina, Queen of Sweden, wondered whether a Cartesian must "hold that all these stars have inhabitants, or, still better, that they have earths around them, full of creatures more intelligent and better than he" (qtd. Dick 112). Because the technology of the telescope permitted earth-like features on the moon to become visible for the first time, life-on-the-moon books – such as John Wilkins' *Discovery of a World in the Moone* (1638), Cyrano de Bergerac's *Les estats et empires de la lune* (1657), and later Aphra Behn's farce, *The Emperor of the Moon* (1687) – became immensely popular. During the 1640s and 1650s, Cavendish herself was part of the Newcastle circle of emigrés in Paris, which took an avid interest in atomism and speculation about other worlds (Kargon 73). Her first book, *Poems and Fancies* (1653), includes many radical poems that at once advocate and yet satirize an atomistic universe in which a multiplicity of invisible worlds co-exist with the visible world. To illustrate Cavendish's early and amused experimentation with the multiplication of worlds, *Paper Bodies* includes two linked poems: "Of many Worlds in this World," and "A World in an Eare-Ring" (pp. 252-4).

In 1666 Margaret Cavendish published two books, *Observations upon Experimental Philosophy* and *The Description of a New World, called the Blazing World*, which were bound together as companion pieces. *Observations* explained Cavendish's own ideas about natural philosophy, while *Blazing World* presented the same ideas in an original format, which we would now call science fiction. The year 1666 was itself known as the *annus mirabilis* in Europe, partly because of millenial associations of the number "666". John Dryden's timely poem "Annus Mirabilis" celebrated the dawning of a new age of English supremacy. Like many of his contemporaries, Dryden linked the emergence of England as a world economic and cultural power to the founding of the Royal Society. Under the licence of King Charles II, the Royal Society was dedicated to establishing English hegemony in the realm of knowledge. Its founding marked the realization of Francis Bacon's dream of a scientific society, as envisioned in his utopian fantasy *The New Atlantis* (1627) (below, p. 264).

In *The Blazing World*, Cavendish invents a world that functions as a brilliant critique of Bacon's *New Atlantis* and as an alternative model of understanding and living with nature. Read together, Bacon's *New Atlantis* and Cavendish's *Blazing World* give considerable insight into seventeenth-century debates over what constitutes appropriate knowledge and power over nature. The two texts bear important resemblances: they are structured as travel narratives in which the main figures are caught in a storm and, by luck, discover and explore an unknown "new" world. In both texts, deliberate allusions are made to the original Biblical paradise, thus raising interesting questions about how the discovery of "new worlds" challenges traditional beliefs. Moreover, in both *The New Atlantis* and *The Blazing World* the imaginary state takes scientific research as its top priority. Thus both texts explore the complicated relationships between scientific and political power. And at the heart of each text is the problem of the proper use and limitation of human knowledge.

The question of whether either *The New Atlantis* or *The Blazing World* is a utopia is open for debate. In Bacon's *New Atlantis*, European travellers discover a tightly-regulated island-state called Bensalem. At the centre of the state is Salomon's House, which is instituted to advance knowledge and enlarge "the bounds of Human Empire" over Nature. The state gives its top honours not only to inventors and interrogators of nature, but surprisingly – at least at first glance – to fathers of families. The chief ritual of the state is the Feast of the Family, said to be "a most natural, pious and reverend custom" whereby the state holds a feast in honour of a Tirsan, any man who has produced thirty blood descendants. During the public ceremony, one son is formally designated "the Son of the Vine." Obviously, the state is patriarchal and invention is a masculine prerogative. What is women's place in Bacon's utopian world of Bensalem? It is not just a simple case of excluding women from becoming scientists. During the Feast just described, the fruitful mother of the family, from whose "body the whole lineage is descended," is placed in an enclosed loft with a stained-glass window, where she sits unseen and silent (below, p. 283).

The cultural significance of the honourable, but silent and glassed-in figure of the wife, the fecund mother of these thirty blood descendants, is made manifest in the last pages of *The New Atlantis*, where the fate of Nature herself is presented in a parallel fashion. Bacon constructs the future as a "masculine birth of time"[1] when, by the arts of men, wild Nature will be finally subdued, lawfully improved and made serviceable for the benefit of society. The fruit of trees will be made sweeter and bigger than their present nature. Wines and drinks will be concocted from "the tears or woundings of trees." Beasts and birds will be kept in parks – enclosures of the wild – not only for pleasurable viewing but for dissections and trials, useful for human health. Earth will once more become man's reserve; its soils, its waters, its animals and its plants will be transformed into a paradise for the health and prosperity of humanity.[2] As Carolyn Merchant argues in *The Death of Nature*, the masculinization of the scientific enterprise was reflected not only institutionally through the male membership of academies, but also symbolically through the gendering of reason and invention as masculine, and nature (its object of research) as feminine (Merchant, 1980). In Bacon's work, the ancient metaphorical link between woman and nature is deployed to reinscribe both woman and nature as resources to be utilised for the modern project.

In her writings, Cavendish reappropriates this metaphorical link in order to invest herself with the agency and authority to speak for true, free nature. To speak on behalf of nature is to gesture towards a self-governing domain that cannot be subjected to the rational will of modern man. Both *Blazing World* and *Observations* make the crucial assertion that each creature has its own limited knowledge and power commensurate with its particular place in nature. Both texts satirize the arrogant opinions of modern philosophers who claim that

---

1   "The Masculine Birth of Time" is one of Bacon's titles; see Merchant 170.

2   These and other themes are the subject of a forthcoming book-length study by Sylvia Bowerbank entitled *Speaking for Nature: Women and Ecologies in Early Modern England*.

mankind has superior powers of observation, especially when aided by the technology of the microscope. *Observations* presents an extensive critique of Robert Hooke's *Micrographia* (1665), quoting *Micrographia* directly to show the hubris of modern philosophers. In the following passage, Cavendish counters Hooke's claim that, by rectifying the operations of the mind (with the aid of new technologies, such as the microscope), modern philosophers can gain power over natural causes and effects:

> I do not understand, first, what they mean by our power over Natural causes and effects: for we have no power over natural causes and effects; but onely one particular effect may have some power over another, which are natural actions: but neither can natural causes nor effects be over-powred by man so, as if man was a degree above Nature, but they must be as Nature is pleased to order them; for Man is but a small part, and his powers are but particular actions of Nature, and therefore he cannot have a supreme and absolute power. (*Observations*, 6)

Cavendish's heroine of *The Blazing World* finds a world that directly contradicts the scientific utopia created by Francis Bacon. The opening sequence seems to set up the familiar narrative code of the romance. A beautiful maiden is threatened by rape when a love-stricken merchant and his men seize her from the shore of her homeland and carry her out to sea. The narrative takes a surprising turn, however, when a tempest forces the vessel to move towards the north pole where the men all freeze to death. Only the lady survives, rescued by Nature, as it were. Alone in a hostile environment, like many romance heroines before her, she is seemingly in need of another rescue. But *Blazing World* is not conventional in either content or form. As Michael McKeon points out in *The Origins of the Novel* (chapter 1), the late seventeenth century was a period of destabilization and reformulation of literary genres. In "To the Reader," Cavendish tells us that she is deliberately inventing an experimental piece of prose fiction, a generic hybrid of romance, philosophy, and fantasy.

In *Blazing World*, the strange and wonderful qualities of the blazing light create an alternative space and time, a world that seemingly does not conform to the laws of nature, at least as Europeans understand them. Cavendish's heroine passes through the north pole to discover an icy strange world where other suns – unknown to European science – shine in splendour. Called the Blazing World, it is home to a startling diversity of unknown creatures: bear-men, fox-men, bird-men, fish-men (mermen), lice-men, and many other hybrids of several complexions, green, black, tawny, and even deep purple. The Blazing World is so astonishing that it startles the imagination and undercuts the complacent notion that the fecundity of Nature can finally be contained within one system of human thought. Once the lady becomes the Empress of the Blazing World, she calls a conference of her virtuosi, including bird-men as astronomers, bear-men as experimental philosophers, spider-men as mathematicians, ape-men as chemists, and worm, fish and fly-men as natural philosophers. During the conference, the Empress raises a myriad of questions, directed to the appropriate specialists. The birdmen, for example, are asked "Why is the sun hot?" More and more questions are asked: What causes wind? How is snow made? What makes the sea salty? What are the elemental materials of life? Should we dissect monsters in the interest of science? What makes coal black? Why do nettles both sting and heal? Even questions about Biblical accounts are asked, for example, when the Empress wonders whether Adam gave names to all the fishes he could not have seen in Paradise.

The answers given to these questions are multiple, partial, and inconclusive. Even with their telescopes and microscopes, the bear-men cannot settle these matters. Their observations just lead to more debate and dissension. The Empress laughs at the microscope for making a louse look like a lobster (see text and illustration, pp. 171-2). Just for fun, she tells the bear-men to invent a technology of miniaturization, but decides that such a device would merely deceive the senses, making a mighty whale look like a vinegar eel, and an ostrich look like a mite. The conference with the various natural philosophers is conducted as a pleasurable exchange of ideas, so much so that the bear-men and worm-men feel free to laugh when the Empress's opinions seem naive to them. Finally, after all the learned reports are in, the Empress concludes: "Nature's works are so various and wonderful, that no particular creature is able to trace her ways."

The microscope is not the only technology that is subject to amused attention in *The Blazing World*. Wind-making machines, submarines, and miniaturization lenses are some of the remarkable inventions mentioned in the text. In her treatment of technology,

Cavendish again wants to show the superiority of nature's strategies. Human design can capitalize, but not improve, upon nature. In imitation of nature's architecture, the apemen/architects have built the city of Paradise as close to the earth as possible. The sea-men of the Blazing World are said to be excellent navigators because of a long tradition of "subtle observations" of nature; they need no modern technology of compasses, cards, watches, etc. The ships of the royal fleet are made of soldered gold and fashioned so that they can be united on the seas like a giant honeycomb. Even the war technology that the Empress uses to defeat the enemies of her original homeland is based on exploiting the natural properties of the star and fire stones. Before forming a coalition with her homeland the Empress decides first to impress and to startle her former countrymen with her power and splendour. So she engineers the spectacle of her walking on the sea:

> the Emperess appear'd with Garments made of the Star-stone, and was born or supported above the Water, upon the Fish-men's heads and backs, so that she seemed to walk upon the face of the Water, and the Bird- and Fish-men carried the Fire-stone, lighted both in the Air, and above the Waters. [She] appeared onely in her Garments of Light, like an Angel, or some Deity, and all kneeled down before her.

As her former countrymen tremble and submit to her, she advances across the water, coming close enough so that they can hear her voice, but not so close that they can see the fish-men that hold her aloft.

This spectacle of self-aggrandisement seems to indicate the Empress's unbridled pride and ambition – especially as demonstrated in the last half of *The Blazing World*. But the strategy is in keeping with the Empress's policy to use awe-inspiring, rather than life-destroying, tactics for keeping the peace, admittedly under her royal rule. As she says in her epilogue, her text is harmless; the only destructive thing she has done (even in imagination) is to kill off some men in a boat, who deserve their fate for kidnapping a lady. The spectacle of walking on water also works to urge us to consider whether new worlds and new natures are waiting to be discovered by those readers with bold imaginations.

Margaret Cavendish, Duchess of Newcastle: A Brief Chronology[1]

c. 1573:	birth of Thomas Lucas, Margaret Cavendish's father
1591:	birth of Sir Charles Cavendish, elder brother of William Cavendish
1593:	birth of William Cavendish, Earl, Marquis and later Duke of Newcastle
1597–1603:	Thomas Lucas outlawed from England by Elizabeth I for killing a relative of Lord Cobham in a duel
before 1604:	birth of Margaret's eldest brother Thomas to Elizabeth Leighton, Thomas Lucas's betrothed
1603:	death of Elizabeth I and accession of James I, who allows Thomas Lucas to return to England
1604:	marriage of Thomas Lucas and Elizabeth Leighton
1606–1617:	births of John, Mary, Elizabeth, Charles, Anne, and Catherine Lucas, Margaret's siblings
1618:	marriage of William Cavendish to Elizabeth Howard, widow, heiress of William Bassett
1623:	birth of Margaret Lucas, eighth and last child of Thomas and Elizabeth Lucas, of St. John's Abbey, Colchester, Essex
1625:	death of Margaret's father
1625:	death of James I and accession of Charles I, who weds Henrietta Maria of France
early 1630s?:	Margaret Lucas writes her 16 'Baby-books'
1640:	first meeting of the Long Parliament (3 November 1640 – 16 March 1660)
1642–60:	English Civil War
1643:	William Cavendish, Earl of Newcastle, created Marquis
1643:	death of William Cavendish's first wife, Elizabeth Cavendish
1643:	Margaret Lucas joins Queen Henrietta Maria's court

---

1 For more biographical details, see Grant (1957) and Mendelson, *Mental World* 1–61.

	at Oxford as maid of honour
1644:	Battle of Marston Moor; William Cavendish leaves England for France
1644:	Henrietta Maria and her court leave England for France
1644-45:	patent granted for John Lucas, Margaret's brother, as Baron Lucas of Shenfield
1645:	marriage of William Cavendish, Marquis of Newcastle, and Margaret Lucas, in Paris (early December)
1647:	deaths of Margaret Cavendish's niece, sister, and mother
1648:	Sir Charles Lucas, Margaret Cavendish's youngest brother, shot by martial law after the siege of Colchester (28 August)
1649:	execution of Charles I (30 January) and abolition of monarchy
1649:	by order of Parliament, William Cavendish declared an enemy and traitor to the English government; his estates confiscated
1649:	publication of two plays by William Cavendish, *The Country Captain* and *The Variety*
1649-60:	the Interregnum, when England was declared a republic and was ruled without a king
1651:	Margaret Cavendish in England to petition to Parliament for income from her husband's estates (10 December); her petition is refused
1652:	Margaret Cavendish stays in England for 9 months, writing *Poems and Fancies*
1653:	Margaret Cavendish writes *Philosophical Fancies* (1653) in 3 weeks; publication of *Poems and Fancies*
1654:	death of Sir Charles Cavendish, William Cavendish's older brother
1655:	publication of *The Worlds Olio* (2nd edn, 1671) and *Philosophical and Physical Opinions*
1656:	publication of *Natures Pictures* (2nd edn, 1671), including 'A True Relation of My Birth and Breeding'
1658:	publication of William Cavendish's *La Méthode Nou-*

velle et Invention Extraordinaire de dresser les Chevaux (Antwerp, 1658)

1660: Restoration of Charles II to the English throne

1662: publication of *Playes* and *Orations of Divers Sorts*

1662: Royal Society of London incorporated by Charles II

1664: publication of *Philosophical Letters* and *CCXI Sociable Letters*

1665: William Cavendish created Duke of Newcastle

1666: publication of *Observations upon Experimental Philosophy* and *The Description of a New World, called the Blazing World* (2nd edn, 1668)

1667: Margaret Cavendish attends a meeting of the Royal Society (30 May)

1667: publication of *The Life of...William Cavendishe, Duke, Marquess, and Earl of Newcastle...*

1668: publication of *Plays Never Before Printed*

1673: death of Margaret Cavendish (December) and burial in Westminster Abbey

1676: publication of *Letters and Poems in honour of the Incomparable Princess, Margaret, Dutchess of Newcastle*

1676: death of William Cavendish

A Note Concerning the Texts

We have reproduced verbatim spelling and puctuation of primary printed sources, with silent correction of obvious printers' errors and using modern typography.

I

BIRTH, BREEDING, AND
SELF-FASHIONING

1. *A TRUE RELATION OF MY BIRTH, BREEDING, AND LIFE.* (1656)

Cavendish's autobiographical memoir, *A True Relation of my Birth, Breeding, and Life*, was printed as an addendum to her collection of tales, *Natures Pictures drawn by Fancies Pencil to the Life* (1656). It was one of her earliest works, appearing more than a decade before the publication of her biography of her husband, *The Life of... William Cavendishe, Duke, Marquess, and Earl of Newcastle...* (1667). For a discussion of the cultural and political context of *A True Relation*, see Introduction, pp. 9-16.

My Father was a Gentleman,[1] which Title is grounded and given by Merit, not by Princes; and 'tis the act of Time, not Favour: and though my Father was not a Peer of the Realm, yet there were few Peers who had much greater Estates, or lived more noble therewith: yet at that time great Titles were to be sold, and not at so high rates, but that his Estate might have easily purchased, and was prest for to take; but my Father did not esteem Titles, unless they were gained by Heroick Actions; and the Kingdome being in a happy Peace with all other Nations, and in it self being governed by a wise King, King *James*, there was no imployments for Heroick Spirits; and towards the latter end of Queen *Elizabeths* reign, as soon as he came to Mans estate, he unfortunately fortunately[2] kill'd one Mr. *Brooks* in a single Duel; for my Father by the Laws of Honour could do no less than call him to the Field to question him for an injury he did him, where their Swords were to dispute, and one or both of their lives to decide the argument, wherein my Father had the better; and though my Father by Honour challeng'd him, with Valour fought him, and in Justice kill'd him, yet he suffered more than any Person of Quality usually doth in cases of Honour; for though the Laws be rigorous, yet the present Princes most commonly are gratious in those misfortunes, especially to the injured: but my Father found it not, for his exile[3] was from the time of his misfortunes to Queen *Elizabeths* death; for the

---

1 Thomas Lucas, of St. John's Abbey, near Colchester; for details of the Lucas family see Grant 27-53, and Mendelson, *Mental World*, 12-18
2 original reads "unfortunately fortunately"
3 1597-1603

Lord *Cobham* being then a great Man with Queen *Elizabeth*, and this Gentleman Mr. *Brooks* a kinde of a Favourite, and as I take it Brother to the then L[ord] *Cobham*, which made Queen *Elizabeth* so severe, not to pardon him: but King *James* of blessed memory gratiously gave him his pardon, and leave to return home to his Native Country, wherein he lived happily, and died peaceably,[1] leaving a Wife and eight Children, three Sons, and five Daughters, I being the youngest Child he had, and an Infant when he died.

As for my breeding, it was according to my Birth, and the Nature of my Sex, for my Birth was not lost in my breeding, for as my Sisters was or had been bred, so was I in Plenty, or rather with superfluity; Likewise we were bred Vertuously, Modestly, Civilly, Honorably, and on honest principles: as for plenty, we had not only, for Necessity, Conveniency, and Decency, but for delight and pleasure to a superfluity; 'tis true, we did not riot, but we lived orderly; for riot, even in Kings Courts, and Princes Palaces, brings ruin without content or pleasure, when order in less fortunes shall live more plentifully and deliciously than Princes, that lives in a Hurlie-Burlie, as I may terme it, in which they are seldom well served, for disorder obstructs; besides, it doth disgust life, distract the appetites, and yield no true relish to the sences; for Pleasure, Delight, Peace and Felicitie live in method, and Temperance.

As for our garments, my Mother did not only delight to see us neat and cleanly, fine and gay, but rich and costly; maintaining us to the heighth of her Estate, but not beyond it; for we were so far from being in debt, before these warrs, as we were rather before hand with the world; buying all with ready money, not on the score, for although after my Fathers death the Estate was divided, between my Mother and her Sonns, paying such a sum of money for Portions to her Daughters, either at the day of their marriage, or when they should come to age, yet by reason she and her children agreed with a mutuall consent, all their affairs were managed so well, as she lived not in a much lower condition than when my father lived; 'tis true my Mother might have increast her daughters Portions by a thrifty sparing, yet she chose to bestow it on our breeding, honest pleasures, and harmless delights, out of an opinion, that if she bred us with needy necessitie, it

---

1 in 1625

might chance to create in us, sharking quallities,[1] mean thoughts, and base actions, which she knew my Father, as well as her self did abhor: likewise we were bred tenderly, for my Mother Naturally did strive, to please and delight her children, not to cross or torment them, terrifying them with threats, or lashing them with slavish whips, but instead of threats, reason was used to perswade us, and instead of lashes, the deformities of vices was discovered, and the graces, and vertues were presented unto us, also we were bred with respectfull attendance, every one being severally waited upon, and all her servants in generall used the same respect to her children, (even those that were very young) as they did to her self, for she sufferd not her servants, either to be rude before us, or to domineer over us, which all vulgar servants are apt, and ofttimes which some have leave to do; likewise she never sufferd the vulgar Serving-men, to be in the Nursery amongst the Nurss Maids, lest their rude love-making might do unseemly actions, or speak unhandsome words in the presence of her children, knowing that youth is apt to take infection by ill examples, having not the reason of distinguishing good from bad, neither were we sufferd to have any familiaritie with the vulgar servants, or conversation: yet caused us to demean our selves with an humble civillity towards them, as they with a dutifull respect to us, not because they were servants were we so reserv'd, for many Noble Persons are forc'd to serve through necessitie, but by reason the vulgar sort of servants, are as ill bred as meanly born, giving children ill examples, and worse counsel.

As for tutors, although we had for all sorts of Vertues, as singing, dancing, playing on Musick, reading, writing, working,[2] and the like, yet we were not kept strictly thereto, they were rather for formalitie than benefit, for my Mother cared not so much for our dancing and fidling, singing and prating of severall languages; as that we should be bred virtuously, modestly, civilly, honorably, and on honest principles.

As for my Brothers, of which I had three, I know not how they were bred, first, they were bred when I was not capable to observe, or before I was born; likewise the breeding of men were after different manner of wayes from those of women: but this I know, that they loved Virtue, endeavour'd Merit, practic'd Justice, and spoke Truth;

---

1 to shark: to make a living by swindling or sponging on others
2 needlework

they were constantly Loyal, and truly Valiant; two of my three Brothers were excellent Soldiers, and Martial Discipliners, being practic'd therein, for though they might have lived upon their own Estates very honourably, yet they rather chose to serve in the Wars under the States of *Holland*,[1] than to live idly at home in Peace, my Brother Sir *Thomas Lucas* there having a Troop of Horse, my brother the youngest Sir *Charl[e]s Lucas* serving therein: but he served the States not long, for after he had been at the siege and taking of some Towns, he returned home again; and though he had the less experience, yet he was like to have proved the better Souldier, if better could have been, for naturally he had a practick Genius to the Warlike Arts, or Arts in War, as Natural Poets have to Poesy: but his life was cut off before he could arrive to the perfection thereof, yet he writ a Treatise of the Arts in War, but by reason it was in Characters,[2] and the Key thereof lost, we cannot as yet understand any thing therein, at least not so as to divulge it. My other Brother, the Lord *Lucas*, who was Heir to my Fathers Estate,[3] and as it were the Father to take care of us all, is not less Valiant than they were, although his skill in the Discipline of War was not so much, being not bred therein, yet he had more skill in the use of the Sword, and is more learned in other Arts and Sciences than they were, he being a great Scholar, by reason he is given much to studious contemplation.

Their practice was, when they met together, to exercise themselves with fencing, wrestling, shooting, and such like exercises, for I observed they did seldome hawk or hunt, and very seldome or never dance, or play on Musick, saying it was too effeminate for Masculine Spirits; neither had they skill, or did use to play, for ought I could hear, at Cards or Dice, or the like Games, nor given to any Vice, as I did know, unless to love a Mistris were a crime, not that I knew any they had, but what report did say, and usually reports are false, at least exceed the truth.

---

1 the Thirty Years' War (1618-48), fought throughout Europe, chiefly between Catholic and Protestant areas; as English Protestants, the Lucas brothers served under Protestant Dutch forces against Catholic Spain during the 1620s

2 in code or shorthand

3 Because Thomas, the eldest son, was born before Cavendish's father was allowed to return from exile and marry her mother, the Lucas estate was inherited by John, the second (but first legitimate) son

As for the pastimes of my Sisters when they were in the Country, it was to reade, work, walk, and discourse with each other; for though two of my three Brothers were married, my Brother the Lord *Lucas* to a virtuous and beautifull Lady, Daughter to Sir *Christopher Nevil*, Son to the Lord *Abergavenny*, and my Brother Sir *Thomas Lucas* to a virtuous Lady of an antient Family, one Sir *John Byron's* Daughter; likewise, three of my four Sisters, one married Sir *Peter Killegrew*, the other Sir *William Walter*, the third Sir *Edmund Pye*, the fourth as yet unmarried, yet most of them lived with my Mother, especially when she was at her Country house, living most commonly at *London* half the year, which is the Metropolitan City of *England*: but when they were at *London*, they were dispersed into several Houses of their own, yet for the most part they met every day, feasting each other like *Job's* Children. But this unnatural War came like a Whirlwind, which fell'd down their Houses, where some in the Wars were crusht to death, as my youngest Brother Sir *Charl[e]s Lucas*, and my brother Sir *Thomas Lucas*; and though my Brother Sir *Thomas Lucas* died not immediatly of his Wounds, yet a Wound he received on his head in *Ireland* short-ned his life.

But to rehearse their Recreations. Their customes were in Winter time to go sometimes to Plays, or to ride in their Coaches about the Streets to see the concourse and recourse of People; and in the Spring time to visit the Spring-garden, Hide-park, and the like places; and sometimes they would have Musick, and sup in Barges upon the Water; these harmless recreations they would pass their time away with; for I observed, they did seldome make Visits, nor never went abroad with Strangers in their Company, but onely[1] themselves in a Flock together agreeing so well, that there seemed but one Minde amongst them: And not onely my own Brothers and Sisters agreed so, but my Brothers and Sisters in Law, and their Children, although but young, had the like agreeable natures, and affectionable dispositions; for to my best remembrance I do not know that ever they did fall out, or had any angry or unkind disputes. Likewise, I did observe, that my Sisters were so far from mingling themselves with any other Company, that they had no familiar conversation or intimate acquain-tance with the Families to which each other were linkt to by Mar-

---

1 only

riage, the Family of the one being as great Strangers to the rest of my Brothers and Sisters, as the Family of the other.

But sometime after this War began, I knew not how they lived; for though most of them were in *Oxford*, wherein the King was, yet after the Queen went from *Oxford*, and so out of *England*,[1] I was parted from them; for when the Queen was in *Oxford*, I had a great desire to be one of her Maids of Honour, hearing the Queen had not the same number she was used to have, whereupon I wooed and won my Mother to let me go, for my Mother being fond of all her Children, was desirous to please them, which made her consent to my request: But my Brothers and Sisters seem'd not very well pleas'd, by reason I had never been from home, nor seldome out of their sight; for though they knew I would not behave my self to their, or my own dishonour, yet they thought I might to my disadvantage, being unexperienced in the World, which indeed I did, for I was so bashfull when I was out of my Mothers, Brothers, and Sisters sight, whose presence used to give me confidence, thinking I could not do amiss whilst any one of them were by, for I knew they would gently reform me if I did; besides, I was ambitious they should approve of my actions and behaviour, that when I was gone from them I was like one that had no Foundation to stand, or Guide to direct me, which made me afraid, lest I should wander with Ignorance out of the waies of Honour, so that I knew not how to behave my self. Besides, I had heard the World was apt to lay aspersions even on the innocent, for which I durst neither look up with my eyes, nor speak, nor be any way sociable, insomuch as I was thought a Natural Fool, indeed I had not much Wit, yet I was not an Idiot, my Wit was according to my years; and though I might have learnt more Wit, and advanced my Understanding by living in a Court, yet being dull, fearfull, and bashfull, I neither heeded what was said or practic'd, but just what belong'd to my loyal duty, and my own honest reputation; and indeed I was so afraid to dishonour my Friends and Family by my indiscreet actions, that I rather chose to be accounted a Fool, than to be thought rude or wanton; in truth my bashfulness and fears made me repent my going from home to see the World abroad, and much I did desire to

---

1   Queen Henrietta Maria, who fled England in May, 1644, and set up her exiled court in Paris; Cavendish was 21 at the time

return to my Mother again, or to my sister *Pye*,[1] with whom I often lived when she was in *London*, and loved with a supernatural affection: but my Mother advised me there to stay, although I put her to more charges than if she had kept me at home, and the more, by reason she and my Brothers were sequestred from their Estates,[2] and plundered of all their Goods, yet she maintained me so, that I was in a condition rather to lend than to borrow, which Courtiers usually are not, being alwayes necessitated by reason of great expences Courts put them to: But my Mother said, it would be a disgrace for me to return out of the Court so soon after I was placed; so I continued almost two years, untill such time as I was married from thence; for my Lord the Marquis of *Newcastle*[3] did approve of those bashfull fears which many condemn'd, and would choose such a Wife as he might bring to his own humours, and not such an one as was wedded to self conceit, or one that had been temper'd to the humours of another, for which he wooed me for his Wife; and though I did dread Marriage, and shunn'd Mens companies, as much as I could, yet I could not, nor had not the power to refuse him, by reason my Affections were fix'd on him, and he was the onely Person I ever was in love with: Neither was I ashamed to own it, but gloried therein, for it was not Amorous Love, I never was infected therewith, it is a Disease, or a Passion, or both, I onely know by relation, not by experience; neither could Title, Wealth, Power or Person entice me to love; but my Love was honest and honourable, being placed upon Merit, which Affection joy'd at the fame of his Worth, pleas'd with delight in his Wit, proud of the respects he used to me, and triumphing in the affections he profest for me, which affections he hath confirmed to me by a deed of time, seal'd by constancy, and assigned by an unalterable decree of his promise, which makes me happy in despight of Fortunes frowns; for though Misfortunes may and do oft dissolve base, wilde, loose, and ungrounded affections, yet she hath no power of those that are united either by Merit, Justice, Gratitude, Duty, Fidelity, or the like; and though my Lord hath lost his Estate, and banish'd out

---

1 Catherine, wife of Edmund Pye
2 as royalist landholders, their estates were confiscated by Parliament
3 William Cavendish, Earl, Marquis, and finally Duke of Newcastle (1593-1676), royalist general, exiled as a traitor by Parliament; a widower with several children at the time of his marriage to Margaret Lucas in 1645

of his Country for his Loyalty to his King and Country, yet neither despised Poverty, nor pinching Necessity could make him break the Bonds of Friendship, or weaken his Loyal Duty to his King or Country.

But not onely the Family I am linkt to is ruin'd, but the Family from which I sprung, by these unhappy Wars, which ruine my Mother lived to see, and then died, having lived a Widow many years, for she never forgot my Father so as to marry again; indeed he remain'd so lively in her memory, and her grief was so lasting, as she never mention'd his name, though she spoke often of him, but love and grief caused tears to flow, and tender sighs to rise, mourning in sad complaints; she made her house her Cloyster, inclosing her self, as it were therein, for she seldom went abroad, unless to Church, but these unhappy Warrs forc'd her out, by reason she and her children were loyall to the King; for which they plundered her, and my Brothers of all their Goods, Plate, Jewells, Money, Corn, Cattle, and the like, cut down their Woods, pull'd down their Houses, and sequestred them from their Lands and Livings; but in such misfortunes my Mother was of an Heroick Spirit, in suffering patiently where there is no remedy, or to be industrious where she thought she could help; She was of a grave Behaviour, and had such a Magestick Grandeur, as it were continually hung about her, that it would strike a kind of an awe to the beholders, and command respect from the rudest, I mean the rudest of civiliz'd people, I mean not such Barbarous people, as plundered her, and used her cruelly, for they would have pulled God out of Heaven, had they had power, as they did Royaltie out of his Throne: also her beauty was beyond the ruin of time, for she had a well favoured loveliness in her face, a pleasing sweetness in her countenance, and a well temper'd complexion, as neither too red, nor too pale, even to her dying hour, although in years, and by her dying, one might think, death was enamoured with her, for he imbraced her in a sleep, and so gently, as if he were afraid to hurt her: also she was an affectionate Mother, breeding her children with a most industrious care, and tender love, and having eight children, three sons and five daughters, there was not any one crooked, or any ways deformed, neither were they dwarfish, or of a Giant-like stature, but every ways proportionable, likewise well featured, cleer complexions, brown haires, but some lighter than others, sound teeth, sweet breaths, plain speeches, tunable voices, I mean not so much to sing as in speaking, as not stuttering, nor wharling[1] in the throat, or speaking through the Nose, or hoarsly, unless they had a cold, or squeakingly, which impediments many have: neither were their voices of too low a strain or too high, but their notes & words were tuneable and timely; I hope this Truth will not offend my Readers, and lest they should think I am a partiall Register, I dare not commend my Sisters, as to say they were handsome, although many would say they were very handsome: but this I dare say, their Beautie, if any they had, was not so lasting as my Mothers, time making suddener ruin in their faces than in hers; likewise my Mother was a good Mistriss to her servants, taking care of her servants in their sickness, not sparing any cost she was able to bestow for their recovery: neither did she exact more from them in their health than what they with ease or rather like pastime could do: she would freely pardon a fault, and forget an injury, yet sometimes she would be angry, but never with her children, the sight of them would pacify her, neither would she be angry with others, but when she had cause, as with negligent or knavish servants, that would lavishly or unnecessarily waste, or subtilly, and theevishly steal, and though she would often complain, that her family[2] was too great for her weak Management, and often prest my Brother to take it upon him, yet I observe she took a pleasure, and some little pride in the governing thereof: she was very skilfull in Leases, and setting of Lands, and Court-keeping,[3] ordering of Stewards, and the like affaires: also I observed, that my Mother, nor Brothers before these warrs, had ever any Law-suites, but what an Atturney dispatched in a Term with small cost, but if they had, it was more than I knew of, but as I said, my Mother lived to see the ruin of her Children, in which was her ruin, and then dyed;[4] my brother Sir *Thomas Lucas* soon after, my brother Sir *Charles Lucas* after him, being shot to death for his Loyall Service,[5] for he was most constantly Loyall and Couragiously active, indeed he had a superfluity of courage; My eldest sister[6] died some time before my Mother, her death being, as I believe, hastned

---

1   speaking roughly or with a burr
2   her household and estate
3   setting of lands: the allocation of landholdings to tenants; court-keeping: presiding at manorial courts
4   in 1647
5   executed by court martial in 1648
6   Mary

through grief of her onely daughter, on which she doted, being very pretty, sweet natured, and had an extraordinary wit for her age, she dying of a Consumption,[1] my sister, her Mother dyed some half a year after of the same disease, and though time is apt to waste remembrance as a consumptive body, or to wear it out like a garment into raggs, or to moulder it into dust, yet I finde the naturall affections, I have for my friends, are beyond the length, strength and power of time: for I shall lament the loss so long as I live, also the loss of my Lords Noble Brother,[2] which died not long after I returned from *England*, he being then sick of an Ague, whose favours and my thankfulness, ingratitude shall never disjoyne; for I will build his Monument of truth, though I can not of Marble, and hang my tears as Scutchions[3] on his Tombe: He was nobly generous, wisely valliant, naturally civill, honestly kind, truly loving, vertuously temperate, his promise was like a fixt decree, his words were destiny, his life was holy, his disposition milde, his behaviour courteous, his discourse pleasing, he had a ready wit and a spacious knowledge, a settled judgement, a cleer understanding, a rationall insight, he was learned in all Arts and Sciences, but especially in the Mathematicks, in which study he spent most part of his time; and though his tongue preacht not Morall Phylosophy, yet his life taught it, indeed he was such a person, that he might have been a pattern for all Mankind to take; he loved my Lord his brother with a doting affection, as my Lord did him, for whose sake I suppose he was so nobly generous, carefully kind, and respectfull to me; for I dare not challenge his favours as to my self, having not merits to deserve them, he was for a time the preserver of my life, for after I was married some two or three years, my Lord travell'd out of *France*, from the City of *Paris*, in which City he resided the time he was there, so went into *Holland*, to a Town called Rotterdam, in which place he stayed some six months, from thence he returned to *Brabant*,[4] unto the City of *Antwerpe*, which Citie we past through, when we went into *Holland*, and in that City my Lord settled himself and Family, choosing it for the most pleasantest, and quietest place to retire him-

1 a wasting disease, probably a form of tuberculosis
2 Sir Charles Cavendish, who died in 1654; for his role as Margaret's mentor and benefactor, see Mendelson, *Mental World*, 28, 39
3 scutcheon or escutcheon: a shield bearing a coat of arms
4 Flanders

self and ruined fortunes in; but after we had remaind some time therein, we grew extremely necessitated, Tradesmen being there not so rich, as to trust my Lord for so much, or so long,[1] as those of *France*: yet they were so civill, kind and charitable, as to trust him, for as much as they were able; but at last necessity inforced me to return into *England*, to seek for reliefe; for I hearing my Lords Estate, amongst the rest of many more estates, was to be sold,[2] and that the wives of the owners should have an allowance therefrom, it gave me hopes I should receive a benefit thereby; so being accompanied with my Lords onely brother Sir *Charles Cavendish*, who was commanded to return, to live therein, or to lose his Estate, which Estate he was forc't to buy with a great Composition,[3] before he could enjoy any part thereof; so over I went, but when I came there, I found their hearts as hard as my fortunes, and their Natures as cruell as my miseries, for they sold all my Lords Estate, which was a very great one, and gave me not any part thereof, or any allowance thereout, which few or no other was so hardly dealt withall; indeed I did not stand as a beggar at the Parliament doore, for I never was at the Parliament-House, nor stood I ever at the doore, as I do know, or can remember, I am sure, not as a Petitioner, neither did I haunt the Committees, for I never was at any, as a Petitioner, but one in my life, which was called Gold-smiths-Hall,[4] but I received neither gold nor silver from them, only an absolute refusall, I should have no share of my Lords Estate; for my brother, the Lord *Lucas* did claim in my behalf, such a part of my Lords Estate, as wives had allowed them, but they told him, that by reason I was married since[5] my Lord was made a Delinquent,[6] I could have nothing, nor should have any thing, he being the greatest Traitor to the State, which was to be the most loyall Subject to his King and Countrey: but I whisperingly spoke to my brother to conduct me out of that ungentlemanly place, so without speaking to them one word good or bad, I returned to my Lodgings, & as that Committee was the first, so was it the last, I ever was at as a Petitioner; 'tis true I went

1   for goods on credit
2   by the Parliamentary Committee for Compounding, responsible for confiscating and selling the estates of royalist landowners
3   a large fine
4   where the Parliamentary Committee for Compounding met and received petitions
5   after
6   name given by Parliament to those who assisted the King's cause in the Civil War

sometimes to Drury-House to inquire how the land was sold, but no other ways, although some reported, I was at the Parliament-House, and at this Committee and at that Committee, and what I should say, and how I was answered; but the Customes of England being changed as well as the Laws, where Women become Pleaders, Atturneys Petitioners and the like, running about with their severall Causes, complaining of their severall grievances, exclaiming against their severall enemies, bragging of their severall favours they receive from the powerfull, thus Trafficking with idle words bring in false reports, and vain discourse; for the truth is, our Sex doth nothing but justle[1] for the Preheminence of words, I mean not for speaking well, but speaking much, as they do for the Preheminence of place, words rushing against words, thwarting and crossing each other, and pulling with reproches, striving to throw each other down with disgrace, thinking to advance themselves thereby, but if our Sex would but well consider, and rationally ponder, they will perceive and finde, that it is neither words nor place that can advance them, but worth and merit: nor can words or place disgrace them, but Inconstancy and boldness: for an honest Heart, a noble Soul, a chast Life, and a true speaking Tongue, is the Throne, Scepter, Crown and Footstoole, that advances them to an honorable renown, I mean not Noble, Vertuous, Discreet, and worthy Persons, whom necessity did inforce to submit, comply and follow their own suites, but such as had nothing to lose, but made it their trade to solicite; but I dispairing being positively denied at Goldsmiths Hall, besides I had a firm faith, or strong opinion, that the pains was more than the gains, and being unpractised in publick Imployments, unlearned in their uncouth Ways, ignorant of the Humors, and Dispositions of those persons to whom I was to address my suit, and not knowing where the Power lay, and being not a good flatterer, I did not trouble my self or petition my enemies; besides I am naturally Bashfull, not that I am ashamed of my minde or body, my Birth or Breeding, my Actions or Fortunes, for my Bashfulness, is my Nature, not for any crime, and though I have strived and reasoned with my self, yet that which is inbred, I find is difficult to root out, but I do not find that my Bashfulness is concern'd with the Qualities of

---

1   jostle

the Persons, but the number, for were I to enter amongst a company of Lazarouses,[1] I should be as much out of countenance, as if they were all *Cesars* or *Alexanders*, *Cleopatras* or Queen *Didoes*;[2] neither do I find my Bashfulness riseth so often in Blushes, as contracts my Spirits to a chill paleness, but the best of it is, most commonly it soon vanisheth away, and many times before it can be perceived, and the more foolish, or unworthy, I conceive the company to be, the worse I am, and the best remedy I ever found was, is to perswade my self, that all those Persons I meet, are wise and vertuous: the reason I take to be is, that the wise and vertuous censure lest,[3] excuse most, praise best, esteem rightly, judge justly, behave themselves civilly, demeans themselves respectfully and speaks modestly when fools or unworthy persons are apt to commit absurdities, as to be bold, rude, uncivill both in words and actions, forgetting or not well understanding themselves, or the company they are with, and though I never met such sorts of ill bred creatures, yet Naturally I have such an Aversion to such kinde of people, as I am afraid to meet them, as children are afraid, of spirits,[4] or those that are afraid to see or meet Devills; which makes me think this Naturall defect in me, if it be a defect, is rather a fear than a bashfulness, but whatsoever it is, I find it troublesome, for it hath many times obstructed the passage of my speech, and perturbed my Naturall actions, forcing a constrainedness or unusuall motions, but however, since it is rather a fear of others, than a bashfull distrust of my self, I despaire of a perfect cure, unless Nature as well as Human governments could be civilized, and brought into a Methodicall order, ruling the words and actions with a supreme power of reason, and the authority of discretion: but a rude nature is worse than a brute nature, by so much more as man is better than beast, but those that are of civill natures and gentile[5] dispositions, are as much neerer to celestiall creatures as those that are of rude or cruell [dispositions] are to Devills: but in fine after I had been in England a year and half

---

1   lazar: a poor diseased person, especially a leper
2   Dido: legendary queen of Carthage, whose tragic love-affair with Aeneas, the mythical founder of Rome, is recounted in Virgil's *Aeneid*
3   least
4   ghosts
5   gentle

in which time I gave some half a score visits and went with my Lords Brother to hear Musick in one Mr. *Lawes*[1] his House, three or four times, as also some three or four times to Hide Park with my sisters, to take the aire, else I never stirr'd out of my lodgings, unless to see my Brothers, and Sisters, nor seldom did I dress my self,[2] as taking no delight to adorn my self, since he I onely desired to please was absent, although report did dress me in a hundred severall fashions: 'tis true when I did dress my self, I did endeavour to do it to my best becoming, both in respect to my self, and those I went to visit, or chanc't to meet, but after I had been in England a year and a half, part of which time I writ a Book of Poems, and a little Book called my Phylosophicall Fancyes, to which I have writ a large addition, since I returned out of England, besides this Book and one other[3]: as for my Book intituled the *Worlds Ollio*,[4] I writ most part of it before I went into England, but being not of a merry, although not of a froward or peevish disposition, became very Melancholy, by reason I was from my Lord, which made my mind so restless, as it did break my sleeps, and distemper my health, with which growing impatient of a longer delay, I resolved to return, although I was grieved to leave Sir *Charles*, my Lords Brother, he being sick of an ague, of which sickness he died: for though his ague was cur'd, his life was decayed, he being not of a strong constitution could not, as it did prove, recover his health, for the dreggs of his Ague did put out the Lamp of his life, yet Heaven knows, I did not think his life was so neer to an end, for his Doctor had great hopes of his perfect recovery, and by reason he was to go into the Country for change of aire, where I should have been a trouble, rather than any ways serviceable, besides, more charge the longer I stayd, for which I made the more hast to return to my Lord, with whom I had rather be as a poor begger, than to be Mistriss of the world absented from him; yet, Heaven hitherto hath kept us, and though Fortune hath been cross, yet we do submit, and are both content with what is, and cannot be mended, and are so prepared, that the

---

1   Henry Lawes (1596-1662), well-known musician and composer, who wrote the music for Milton's *Comus*

2   to dress with concern for an impressive effect

3   *Poems and Fancies* (1653), *Philosophical Fancies* (1653), and *Philosophical and Physical Opinions* (1655); "this Book" was *Natures Pictures* (1656)

4   *The Worlds Olio* (1655)

worst of fortunes shall not afflict our minds, so as to make us unhappy, howsoever it doth pinch our lives with poverty: for if Tranquillity lives in an honest mind, the mind lives in Peace, although the body suffer: but Patience hath armed us, and Misery hath tried us, and finds us Fortune-proof, for the truth is, my Lord is a person, whose Humour is neither extravagantly merry, nor unnecessarily sad, his Minde is above his Fortune, as his Generosity is above his purse, his Courage above danger, his Justice above bribes, his Friendship above self-interest, his Truth too firm for falshood, his Temperance beyond temptation; his Conversation is pleasing and affable, his Wit is quick, and his Judgment is strong, distinguishing cleerly without clouds of mistakes, dissecting truth, so as it justly admit not of disputes: his discourse is always new upon the occasion, without troubling the hearers with old Historicall relations, nor stuft with useless sentences, his behavior is manly without formallity, and free without constraint, and his minde hath the same freedom: his Nature is noble, and his Disposition sweet, his Loyaltie is proved by his publick service for his King and Countrey, by his often hazarding of his life, by the losse of his Estate, and the banishment of his Person, by his necessitated Condition, and his constant and patient suffering; but howsoever our fortunes are, we are both content, spending our time harmlessly, for my Lord pleaseth himself with the Management[1] of some few Horses, and exercises himself with the use of the Sword; which two Arts he hath brought by his studious thoughts, rationall experience, and industrious practice to an absolute perfection: and though he hath taken as much pains in those arts, both by study and practice, as Chimists, for the Phylosophers Stone,[2] yet he hath this advantage of them, that he hath found the right and the truth thereof and therein, which Chimists never found in their Art, and I believe never will: also he recreat[e]s himself with his pen, writing what his Wit dictates to him, but I pass my time rather with scribling than writing, with words than wit, not that I speak much, because I am addicted to contemplation, unless I am with my Lord, yet then I rather attentively listen to what he sayes, than impertinently speak, yet when I am writing any sad fain'd Stories, or serious humours or melancholy passions, I am

---

1   manage: the training of horses in their paces
2   philosopher's stone: a reputed substance which alchemists believed capable of transmuting base metals into gold or silver

Illustration 3: The conventions of the Stuart Court art that harmonized the cosmic, social, and natural orders are mocked, but not overturned, in this wonderfully strange engraving from William Cavendish's *La Méthode Nouvelle et Invention Extrordinaire de Dresser les Chevaux ...* (1658). The apotheosis of the Marquis of Newcastle is commemorated by his beloved, obedient horses, while the classical gods of a pacified heaven look on. (Courtesy the Bodleian Library, Oxford, Antiq. b. B. 1658.1 plate 4.)

forc'd many times to express them with the tongue before I can write them with the pen, by reason those thoughts that are sad, serious and melancholy, are apt to contract and to draw too much back, which oppression doth as it were over power or smother the conception in the brain, but when some of those thoughts are sent out in words, they give the rest more liberty to place themselves, in a more methodicall order, marching more regularly with my pen, on the ground of white paper, but my letters seem rather as a ragged rout, than a well armed body, for the brain being quicker in creating, than the hand in writing, or the memory in retaining, many fancies are lost, by reason they ofttimes out-run the pen, where I, to keep speed in the Race, write so fast as I stay not so long as to write my letters plain, insomuch as some have taken my hand-writing for some strange character, & being accustomed so to do: I cannot now write very plain, when I strive to write my best, indeed my ordinary hand-writing is so bad as few can read it, so as to write it fair for the Press, but however that little wit I have, it delights me to scribble it out, and desperse it about, for I being addicted from my childhood, to contemplation rather than conversation, to solitariness rather than society, to melancholy rather than mirth, to write with the pen than to work with a needle, passing my time with harmeless fancies, their company being pleasing, their conversation innocent, in which I take such pleasure, as I neglect my health, for it is as great a grief to leave their society, as a joy to be in their company, my only trouble is, lest my brain should grow barren, or that the root of my fancies should become insipid, withering into a dull stupidity for want of maturing subjects to write on: for I being of a lazy nature, and not of an active disposition, as some are that love to journey from town to town, from place to place, from house to house, delighting in variety of company, making still one where the greatest number is; likewise in playing at Cardes, or any other Games, in which I neither have practised, nor have I any skill therein: as for Dancing, although it be a gracefull art, and becometh unmarried persons well, yet for those that are married, it is too light an action, disagreeing with the gravity thereof; and for Revelling, I am of too dull a nature, to make one in a merry societie; as for Feasting, it would neither agree with my humour or constitution, for my diet is for the most part sparing, as a little boyld chickin, or the like, my drink most commonly water, for though I have an indifferent good appetite, yet I do often fast, out of an opinion that if I should eate much, and exercise little, which I do, onely walking a slow pace in my chamber, whilest my thoughts run apace in my brain, so that the motions of my minde hinders the active exercises of my body: for should I Dance or Run, or Walk apace, I should Dance my Thoughts out of Measure, Run my Fancies out of Breath, and Tread out the Feet of my Numbers,[1] but because I would not bury my self quite from the sight of the world, I go sometimes abroad, seldome to visit, but only in my Coach about the Town, or about some of the streets, which we call here[2] a *Tour*, where all the chief of the Town goe to see and to be seen, likewise all strangers of what quallity soever, as all great Princes or Queens that make any short stay: for this Town, being a passage or thorough-fare to most parts, causeth many

---

1   numbers: metrical periods or feet
2   in Antwerp

Studious She is and all Alone,
Most visitants, when She has none,
Her Library on which She looks
It is her Head her Thoughts her Books.
Scorninge dead Ashes without fire
For her owne Flames doe her Inspire.

Illustration 4: The frontispiece from Margaret Cavendish's *Philosophical and Physical opinions*(1655) represents Cavendish as an original and independent thinker. As the poem below indicates: "Her Library on which She looks/ It is her Head her Thoughts her Books." (Courtesy the Henry E. Huntington Library and Art Gallery.)

times persons of great quallity to be here, though not as inhabitants, yet to lodge for some short time; and all such as I said, take a delight, or at lest[1] goe to see the custome thereof, which most Cities of note in Europe for all I can hear, hath such like recreations for the effeminate Sex, although for my part I had rather sit at home and write, or walk, as I said, in my chamber and contemplate; but I hold necessary sometimes to appear abroad, besides I do find, that severall objects do bring new materialls for my thoughts and fancies to build upon, yet I must say this in the behalf of my thoughts, that I never found them idle; for if the senses brings no work in, they will work of themselves, like silk-wormes that spinns out of their own bowels; Neither can I say I think the time tedious, when I am alone, so I be neer my Lord, and know he is well: But now I have declared to my Readers, my Birth, Breeding, and Actions, to this part of my Life, I mean the materiall parts, for should I write every particular, as my childish sports and the like, it would be ridiculous and tedious; but I have been honorably born and Nobly matcht, I have been bred to elevated thoughts, not to a dejected spirit, my life hath been ruled with Honesty, attended by Modesty, and directed by Truth: but since I have writ in generall thus far of my life; I think it fit, I should speak something of my Humour, particular Practise and Disposition, as for my humour, I was from my childhood given to contemplation, being more taken or delighted with thoughts than in conversation with a society, in so much as I would walk two or three houres, and never rest, in a musing, considering, contemplating manner, reasoning with my self of every thing my senses did present, but when I was in the company of my Naturall friends,[2] I was very attentive of what they said, or did; but for strangers I regarded not much what they said, but many times I did observe their actions, whereupon my Reason as Judge, and my Thoughts as Accusers, or excusers, or approvers and commenders, did plead, or appeale to accuse, or complain thereto; also I never took delight in closets, or cabinets of toys,[3] but in the variety of fine clothes, and such toys as onely were to adorn my person: likewise I had a naturall stupidity towards the learning of any other Language,

---

1   least
2   family
3   knick-knacks or trinkets

than my native tongue, for I could sooner and with more facility understand the sense than remember the words, and for want of such memory, makes me so unlearned in forraigne Languages as I am: as for my practise, I was never very active, by reason I was given so much to contemplation; besides my brothers and sisters, were for the most part serious, and stayed[1] in their actions, not given to sport nor play, nor dance about, whose company I keeping, made me so too: but I observed that although their actions were stay'd, yet they would be very merry amongst themselves, delighting in each others company: also they would in their Discourse express the generall actions of the world, judging, condemning, approving, commending, as they thought good, and with those that were innocently harmless, they would make themselves merry therewith; as for my studie of books it was little, yet I chose rather to read, than to imploy my time in any other work, or practise, and when I read what I understood not, I would ask my brother the Lord *Lucas*, he being learned, the sense or meaning thereof, but my serious study could not be much, by reason I took great delight in attiring, fine dressing and fashions, especially such fashions as I did invent my self, not taking that pleasure in such fashions as was invented by others: also I did dislike any should follow my Fashions, for I always took delight in a singularity, even in acoutrements of habits, but whatsoever I was addicted to, either in fashions of Cloths, contemplation of Thoughts, actions of Life, they were Lawfull, Honest, Honorable and Modest, of which I can avouch to the world with a great confidence, because it is a pure Truth: as for my Disposition, it is more inclining to be melancholy than merry, but not crabbed or peevishly melancholy, but soft melting solitary, and contemplating melancholy; and I am apt to weep rather than laugh, not that I do often either of them; also I am tender natured, for it troubles my Conscience to kill a fly, and the groans of a dying Beast strike my Soul: also where I place a particular affection, I love extraordinarily, and constantly, yet not fondly but soberly, and observingly, not to hang about them as a trouble, but to wait upon them as a servant, but this affection will take no root, but where I think or find merit, and have leave both from Divine and Morall Laws, yet I find this passion so troublesome, as it is the only torment to my life, for

---

1   staid

fear any evill misfortune or accident, or sickness, or death should come unto them, insomuch, as I am never freely at rest: Likewise I am gratefull, for I never received a curtesie but I am impatient, and troubled untill I can return it, also I am Chast, both by Nature and Education, insomuch as I do abhorre an unchast thought: likewise I am seldom angry, as my servants may witness for me, for I rather chose to suffer some inconveniences, than disturbe my thoughts, which makes me winke many times at their faults; but when I am angry, I am very angry, but yet it is soon over, and I am easily pacified, if it be not such an injury as may create a hate; neither am I apt to be exceptious or jealous, but if I have the lest[1] symptome of this passion, I declare it to those it concerns, for I never let it ly smothering in my breast to breed a malignant disease in the minde, which might break out into extravagant passions, or railing speeches, or indiscreet actions; but I examin moderately, reason soberly, and plead gently in my own behalf, through a desire to keep those affections I had, or at least thought to have, and truly I am so vain, as to be so self-conceited, or so naturally partiall, to think my friends, have as much reason to love me as another, since none can love more sincerely than I, and it were an injustice to prefer a fainter affection, or to esteem the Body more than the Minde, likewise I am neither spitefull, envious, nor malicious, I repine not at the gifts that Nature, or Fortune bestows upon others, yet I am a great Emulator; for though I wish none worse than they are, nor fear any should be better than they are, yet it is lawfull for me to wish my self the best, and to do my honest endeavour thereunto, for I think it no crime to wish my self the exactest of Natures works, my thred of life the longest, my Chain of Destinie the strongest, my minde the peaceablest; my life the pleasantest, my death the easiest, and the greatest Saint in Heaven; also to do my endeavour, so far as honour and honesty doth allow of, to be the highest on Fortunes Wheele, and to hold the wheele from turning, if I can, and if it be comendable to wish anothers good, it were a sin not to wish my own; for as Envie is a vice, so Emulation is a Vertue, but Emulation is in the way to Ambition, or indeed it is a Noble Ambition, but I fear my Ambition inclines to vain glory, for I am very ambitious, yet 'tis neither for Beauty, Wit, Titles, Wealth or Power, but as they are steps

---

1 least

to raise me to Fames Tower, which is to live by remembrance in after-ages: likewise I am, that the vulgar calls, proud, not out of a self-conceit, or to slight or condemn any, but scorning to do a base or a mean act, and disdaining rude or unworthy persons, insomuch that if I should find any that were rude, or too bold, I should be apt to be so passionate, as to affront them, if I can, unless discretion should get betwixt my passion, and their boldness, which sometimes perchance it might, if discretion should croud hard for place; for though I am naturally bashfull, yet in such a cause my Spirits would be all on fire, otherwise I am so well bred, as to be civill to all persons, of all degrees, or qualities: likewise I am so proud, or rather just to my Lord, as to abate nothing of the qualitie of his Wife, for if Honour be the marke of Merit, and his Masters Royall favour, who will favour none but those that have Merit to deserve, it were a baseness for me to neglect the Ceremony thereof; Also in some cases I am naturally a Coward, and in other cases very valiant; as for example, if any of my neerest friends were in danger, I should never consider my life in striving to help them, though I were sure to do them no good, and would willingly, nay cheerfully, resign my life for their sakes: likewise I should not spare my Life, if Honour bids me dye; but in a danger, where my Friends or my Honour is not concerned, or ingaged, but only my Life to be unprofitably lost, I am the veriest coward in Nature, as upon the Sea, or any dangerous places, or of Theeves or fire, or the like, Nay the shooting of a gun, although but a Pot gun,[1] will make me start, and stop my hearing, much less have I courage to discharge one; or if a sword should be held against me, although but in jest, I am afraid: also as I am not covetous, so I am not prodigall, but of the two I am inclining to be prodigall, yet I cannot say to a vain prodigallity, because I imagine it is to a profitable end, for perceiving the world is given, or apt to honour the outside more than the inside, worshipping show more than substance; and I am so vain, if it be a Vanity, as to endeavour to be worshipt, rather than not to be regarded; yet I shall never be so prodigall as to impoverish my friends, or go beyond the limits or facilitie of our Estate, and though I desire to appear at the best advantage, whilest I live in the view of the publick World, yet I could most willingly exclude my self, so as Never to see

---

1 pop-gun: a child's toy that makes a loud popping sound

the face of any creature, but my Lord, as long as I live, inclosing my self like an Anchoret, wearing a Frize-gown, tied with a cord about my waste[1]: But I hope my Readers, will not think me vain for writing my life, since there have been many that have done the like, as *Cesar, Ovid*, and many more, both men and women, and I know no reason I may not do it as well as they: but I verily believe some censuring Readers will scornfully say, why hath this Ladie writ her own Life? since none cares to know whose daughter she was, or whose wife she is, or how she was bred, or what fortunes she had, or how she lived, or what humour or disposition she was of? I answer that it is true, that 'tis to no purpose, to the Readers, but it is to the Authoress, because I write it for my own sake, not theirs; neither did I intend this piece for to delight, but to divulge, not to please the fancy, but to tell the truth, lest after-Ages should mistake, in not knowing I was daughter to one Master *Lucas* of *St. Johns* neer *Colchester* in *Essex*, second Wife to the Lord Marquis of *Newcastle*, for my Lord having had two Wives,[2] I might easily have been mistaken, especially if I should dye, and my Lord Marry again.

---

1   anchoret: recluse or hermit; frieze: coarse woollen cloth; waste: waist
2   Newcastle's first wife was the heiress Elizabeth Bassett Howard, who died in 1643, two years before his marriage to Margaret Lucas.

2. SELECTIONS FROM *CCXI SOCIABLE LETTERS* (1664)

Published in 1664, *CCXI Sociable Letters* is a collection of essays and anecdotes cast in epistolary form, addressed to an imaginary female friend living some distance away. The letters range over an astonishing variety of topics, including science and medicine, religion and philosophy, and commentaries on the people and places that formed Cavendish's *milieu*, Antwerp during the 1650s and Restoration England. The selection of letters reprinted here illustrates some of the themes highlighted elsewhere in her works, including Cavendish's self-fashioning as a writer, her reflections on scientific and philosophical questions, and her playful challenges to the rigid categories of class and gender identity.

PREFACE

To His Excellency The Lord Marquess Of *Newcastle*.

My Lord,

It may be said to me, as one said to a Lady, *Work Lady, Work, let writing Books alone, For surely Wiser Women ne'r writ one;*[1] But your Lordship never bid me to Work, nor leave Writing, except when you would perswade me to spare so much time from my Study as to take the Air for my Health; the truth is, My Lord, I cannot Work, I mean such Works as Ladies use to pass their Time withall, and if I could, the Materials of such Works would cost more than the Work would be worth, besides all the Time and Pains bestow'd upon it. You may ask me, what Works I mean; I answer, Needle-works, Spinning-works,

---

1 In retaliation for what he considered Mary Wroth's slandering of him and his family in an episode of *Urania*, Lord Edward Denny launched a virulent attack on Wroth in his poem "To Pamphilia from the father-in-law of Seralius." After calling Wroth a monster and hermaphrodite, Denny ends his poem with the words, "Work o th'Workes leave idle bookes alone/ For wise and worthier women have written none." Margaret's allusion here indicates not only her awareness of Denny's poem, but her solidarity with Wroth as a woman writer. For Denny's poem see Josephine Roberts's "Introduction" to *The Poems of Mary Wroth*, ed. J. Roberts (Baton Rouge, University of Louisiana Press, 1983), 32-5.

Preserving-works, as also Baking, and Cooking-works, as making Cakes, Pyes, Puddings, and the like, all which I am Ignorant of; and as I am Ignorant in these Imployments, so I am Ignorant in Gaming, Dancing, and Revelling; But yet, I must ask you leave to say, that I am not a Dunce in all Imployments, for I Understand the Keeping of Sheep, and Ordering of a Grange, indifferently well, although I do not Busie my self much with it, by reason my Scribling takes away the most part of my Time. Perchance some may say, that if my Understanding be most of Sheep, and a Grange, it is a Beastly Understanding; My answer is, I wish Men were as Harmless as most Beasts are, then surely the World would be more Quiet and Happy than it is, for then there would not be such Pride, Vanity, Ambition, Covetousness, Faction, Treachery, and Treason, as is now; Indeed one might very well say in his Prayers to God, O Lord God, I beseech thee of thy Infinite Mercy, make Man so, and order his Mind, Thoughts, Passions, and Appetites, like Beasts, that they may be Temperate, Sociable, Laborious, Patient, Prudent, Provident, Brotherly-loving, and Neighbourly-kind, all which Beasts are, but most Men not. But leaving most Men to Beasts, I return to your Lordship, who is one of the Best of men, whom God hath fill'd with Heroick Fortitude, Noble Generosity, Poetical Wit, Moral Honesty, Natural Love, Neighbourly-kindness, Great Patience, Loyal Duty, and Celestial Piety, and I pray God as Zealously and Earnestly to Bless you with Perfect Health and Long Life, as becomes

Your Lordships Honest Wife and Humble Servant
M. Newcastle.

XVI.

Madam,

I Hope I have given the Lady *D. A.* no cause to believe I am not her Friend; for though she hath been of P[arliament]s. and I of K[ing]s. side,[1] yet I know no reason why that should make a difference betwixt us, as to make us Enemies, no more than cases of Conscience in Religion, for one may be my very good Friend, and yet

---

1   Parliament's side and King's side, the two sides in the English Civil War.

not of my opinion, every one's Conscience in Religion is betwixt God and themselves, and it belongs to none other. 'Tis true, I should be glad my Friend were of my opinion, or if I thought my Friend's opinion were better than mine, I would be of the same; but it should be no breach of Friendship, if our opinions were different, since God is onely[1] to be the Judg: And as for the matter of Governments, we Women understand them not; yet if we did, we are excluded from intermedling therewith, and almost from being subject thereto; we are not tied, nor bound to State or Crown; we are free, not Sworn to Allegiance, nor do we take the Oath of Supremacy; we are not made Citizens of the Commonwealth, we hold no Offices, nor bear we any Authority therein; we are accounted neither Useful in Peace, nor Serviceable in War; and if we be not Citizens in the Commonwealth, I know no reason we should be Subjects to the Commonwealth[2]: And the truth is, we are no Subjects, unless it be to our Husbands, and not always to them, for sometimes we usurp their Authority, or else by flattery we get their good wills to govern; but if Nature had not befriended us with Beauty, and other good Graces, to help us to insinuate our selves into men's Affections, we should have been more inslaved than any other of Natur's Creatures she hath made; but Nature be thank'd, she hath been so bountiful to us, as we oftener inslave men, than men inslave us; they seem to govern the world, but we really govern the world, in that we govern men: for what man is he, that is not govern'd by a woman more or less? None, unless some dull Stoick, or an old miserable Usurer, or a cold, old, withered Batchelor, or a half-starved Hermit, and such like persons, which are but here and there one; And not only Wives and Mistresses have prevalent power with Men, but Mothers, Daughters, Sisters, Aunts, Cousins, nay, Maid-Servants have many times a perswasive power with their Masters, and a Land-lady with her Lodger, or a she-Hostess with her he-Guest; yet men will not believe this, and 'tis the better for us, for by that we govern as it were by an insensible power, so as men perceive not how they are Led, Guided, and Rul'd by the Feminine Sex. But howsoever, Madam, the disturbance in this Countrey hath made no breach of Friendship betwixt us, for though there hath been a Civil

---

1   only

2   For seventeenth-century women's civil and political rights in theory and in practice, see Mendelson and Crawford 49-58, 345-430.

War in the Kingdom, and a general War amongst the Men, yet there hath been none amongst the Women, they have not fought pitch'd battels; and if they had, there hath been no particular quarrel betwixt her and me, for her Ladiship is the same in my affection, as if the Kingdom had been in a calm Peace; in which Friendship I shall always remain hers, as also,

Your Ladiships most Humble and Devoted S[ervant].

LI.

Madam,

Yesterday Mrs. *P.I.* was to Visit me, who pray'd me to present her Humble Service to you, but since you saw her she is become an Alt'red Woman, as being a Sanctified Soul, a Spiritual Sister, she hath left Curling her Hair, Black Patches[1] are become Abominable to her, Laced Shoes and Galoshoes[2] are Steps to Pride, to go Bare-neck'd she accounts worse than Adultery; Fans, Ribbonds, Pendants, Neck-laces, and the like, are the Temptations of Satan, and the Signs of Damnation; and she is not onely Transform'd in her Dress, but her Garb and Speech, and all her Discourse, insomuch as you would not know her if you saw her, unless you were inform'd who she was; She Speaks of nothing but Heaven and Purification, and after some Discourse, she ask'd me, what Posture I thought was the best to be used in Prayer? I said, I thought no Posture was more becoming, nor did fit Devotion better, than Kneeling, for that Posture did in a manner Acknowledg from Whence we came, and to What we shall return, for the Scripture says, from Earth we came, and to Earth we shall return; then she spoke of Prayers, for she is all for Extemporary Prayers,[3] I told her, that the more Words we used in Prayer, the Worse they were Accepted, for I thought a Silent Adoration was better Accepted of God, than a Self-conceited Babling; Then she ask'd me, if I thought one might not be Refined, by Tempering their Passions and Appetites, or by Banishing the Worst of them from the Soul and Body, to that Degree, as to be a Deity, or so Divine, as to be above the Nature of Man; I said

---

1   used as cosmetic facial decorations
2   galoshes: fancy raised pattens or clogs
3   extemporaneous rather than set prayers

no, for put the case Men could turn Brass or Iron, or such gross Met-als, into Gold, and Refine that Gold into its height of Purity, yet it would be but a Metal still; so likewise the most Refined Man would be but Human still, he would be still a Man, and not a God; nay, take the Best of Godly Men, such as have been Refined by Grace, Prayer and Fasting, to a degree of Saints, yet they were but Human and Men still, so long as the Body and Soul were joyn'd together, but when they were Separated, what the Soul would be, whether a God, a Devil, a Spirit, or Nothing, I could not tell; with that she Lifted up her Eyes, and Departed from me, Believing I was one of the Wicked and Reprobate, not capable of a Saving Grace, so as I believe she will not come near me again, lest her Purity should be Defiled in my Company, I believe the next news we shall hear of her, will be, that she is become a Preaching Sister;[1] I know not what Oratory the Spir-it will Inspire her with, otherwise I believe she will make no Eloquent Sermons, but I think those of her Calling do defie Eloquence, for the more Nonsense they Deliver, the more they are Admired by their Godly Fraternity. But leaving her to her Self-denying, I return to Acknowledg my self,

Madam,   Your very faithful Friend and Servant.

LV.

Madam,

You were pleased in your last Letter to tell me, that you had been in the Country, and that you did almost Envy the Peasants for living so Merrily; it is a sign, Madam, they live Happily, for Mirth seldom dwells with Troubles and Discontents, neither doth Riches nor Grandeur live so Easily, as that Unconcerned Freedom that is in Low and Mean[2] Fortunes and Persons, for the Ceremony of Grandeur is Constrain'd and bound with Forms and Rules, and a great Estate and high Fortune is not so easily manag'd as a Less, a Little is easily order'd, where Much doth require Time, Care, Wisdom and Study as Considerations; but Poor, Mean Peasants that live by their Labour, are

---

1   During the Interregnum some non-Anglican sects such as the Baptists and Quakers allowed women to preach as well as prophesy.
2   humble

for the most part Happier and Pleasanter than great Rich Persons, that live in Luxury and Idleness, for Idle Time is Tedious, and Luxury is Unwholsom, whereas Labour is Healthful and Recreative, and surely Country Huswives take more Pleasure in Milking their Cows, making their Butter and Cheese, and feeding their Poultry, than great Ladies do in Painting, Curling, and Adorning themselves, also they have more Quiet & Peaceable Minds and Thoughts, for they never, or seldom, look in a Glass to view their Faces, they regard not their Complexions, nor observe their Decayes, they Defie Time's Ruins of their Beauties, they are not Peevish and Froward if they look not as Well one day as another, a Pimple or Spot in their Skin Tortures not their Minds, they fear not the Sun's Heat, but Out-face the Sun's Power,[1] they break not their Sleeps to think of Fashions, but Work Hard to Sleep Soundly, they lie not in Sweats to clear their Complexions, but rise to Sweat to get them Food, their Appetites are not Queazie with Surfeits, but Sharp'ned with Fasting, they relish with more Savour their Ordinary Course[2] Fare, than those who are Pamper'd do their Delicious Rarities; and for their Mirth and Pastimes, they take more Delight and true Pleasure, and are more Inwardly Pleased and Outwardly Merry at their Wakes,[3] than the great Ladies at their Balls, and though they Dance not with such Art and Measure, yet they Dance with more Pleasure and Delight, they cast not Envious, Spiteful Eyes at each other, but meet Friendly and Lovingly. But great Ladies at Publick Meetings take not such true Pleasures, for their Envy at each others Beauty and Bravery Disturbs their Pastimes, and Obstructs their Mirth, they rather grow Peevish and Froward through Envy, than Loving and Kind through Society, so that whereas the Countrey Peasants meet with such Kind Hearts and Unconcerned Freedom as they Unite in Friendly Jollity, and Depart with Neighbourly Love, the Greater sort of Persons meet with Constrain'd Ceremony, Converse with Formality, and for the most part Depart with Enmity; and this is not onely amongst Women, but amongst Men, for there is amongst the Better sort a greater Strife for Bravery[4] than for Courtesie, for Place than Friendship, and in their Societies

---

1 For women, a "white" complexion confirmed their gentry or aristocratic status.
2 coarse
3 wake: an annual local parish festival
4 display or splendour

there is more Vain-glory than Pleasure, more Pride than Mirth, and more Vanity than true Content; yet in one thing the Better Sort of Men, as the Nobles and Gentry, are to be Commended, which is, that though they are oftener Drunken and more Debauch'd than Peasants, having more Means to maintain their Debaucheries, yet at such times as at great Assemblies, they keep themselves more Sober and Temperate than Peasants do, which are for the most part Drunk at their Departing; But to Judg between the Peasantry and Nobles for Happiness, I believe where there's One Noble that is truly Happy, there are a Hundred Peasants; not that there be More Peasants than Nobles, but that they are More Happy, number for number, as having not the Envy, Ambition, Pride, Vain-glory, to Cross, Trouble, Vex them, as Nobles have; when I say Nobles, I mean those that have been Ennobled by Time as well as Title, as the Gentry. But, Madam, I am not a fit Judg for the several Sorts or Degrees, or Courses of Lives, or Actions of Mankind, as to Judg which is Happiest, for Happiness lives not in Outward Shew or Concourse, but Inwardly in the Mind, and the Minds of Men are too Obscure to be Known, and too Various and Inconstant to Fix a Belief in them, and since we cannot Know our Selves, how should we know Others? Besides, Pleasure and true Delight lives in every ones own Delectation; but let me tell you, my Delectation is, to prove my self,

Madam, Your faithful Fr[iend]. and S[ervant].

XC.

Madam,

I am sorry the Plague[1] is much in the City you are in, as I hear, and fear your Stay will Indanger your Life, for the Plague is so Spreading and Penetrating a Disease, as it is a Malignant Contagion, and Dilates it self throughout a City, nay, many times, from City to City, all over a Kingdom, and enters into every Particular House, and doth Arrest almost every Particular Person with Death, at least, layes grievous Sores upon them; Indeed Great Plagues are Death's Harvest, where he

---

1 For details on the incidence and social context of the plague in seventeenth-century England, see Paul Slack, *The Impact of the Plague in Tudor and Stuart England* (London: Routledge & Kegan Paul, 1985).

Reaps down Lives like Ears of Corn; wherefore, Madam, let me per-swade you to Remove, for certainly Life is so Pretious, as it ought not to be Ventured, where there is no Honour to be Gain'd in the Hazard, for Death seems Terrible, I am sure it doth to Me, there is nothing I Dread more than Death, I do not mean the Strokes of Death, nor the Pains, but the Oblivion in Death, I fear not Death's Dart so much as Death's Dungeon, for I could willingly part with my Present Life, to have if Redoubled in after Memory, and would willingly Die in my Self, so I might Live in my Friends; Such a Life have I with you, and you with me, our Persons being at a Distance, we live to each other no otherwise than if we were Dead, for Absence is a Present Death, as Memory is a Future Life; and so many Friends as Remember me, so many Lives I have, indeed so many Brains as Remember me, so many Lives I have, whether they be Friends or Foes, onely in my Friends Brains I am Better Entertained; And this is the Reason I Retire so much from the Sight of the World, for the Love of Life and Fear of Death: for since Nature hath made our Bodily Lives so short, that if we should Live the full Period, it were but like a Flash of Lightning, that Continues not, and for the most part leaves black Oblivion behind it; and since Nature Rules the Bodily Life, and we cannot live Alwayes, nor the Bounds of Nature be Inlarged, I am industrious to Gain so much of Nature's Favour, as to enable me to do some Work, wherein I may leave my *Idea*, or Live in an *Idea*, or my *Idea* may Live in Many Brains, for then I shall Live as Nature Lives amongst her Creatures, which onely Lives in her Works, and is not otherwise Known but by her Works, we cannot say, she lives Personally amongst her Works, but Spiritually within her Works; and naturally I am so Ambitious, as I am restless to Live, as Nature doth, in all Ages, and in every Brain, but though I cannot hope to do so, yet it shall be no Neglect in me; And as I desire to Live in every Age, and in every Brain, so I desire to Live in every Heart, especially in your Ladiships, wherein I believe I do already, and wish I may live Long. Wherefore for my own sake, as well as yours, let me intreat you to Remove out of that Plaguy City, for if you Die, all those Friends you Leave, or Think of, or Remember, partly Die with you, nay, some perchance for Ever, if they were Personally Dead before, and onely Live in your Memory; Wherefore, as you are a Noble Lady, have a Care of your Friends, and go out of that City as Soon as you can, in which you will Oblige all those you Favour, or that Love you, amongst which there is none more Truly, Faithfully, and Fervently, your Friend and Servant, than,

Madam, I, *M. N.*

XCIII.

Madam,

You were pleased in your last Letter to express to me the Reason of the Lady *D.S*s. and the Lady *E.K*s. Melancholy, which was for Want of Children; I can not Blame the Lady *D.S.* by reason her Husband is the Last of his Family unless he have Children, but the Lady *E.K*s. Husband being a Widdower when he Married her, and having Sons to Inherit his Estate, and to Keep up his Family, I Know no Reason why she should be troubled for having no Children, for though it be the part of every Good Wife to desire Children to Keep alive the Memory of their Husbands Name and Family by Posterity, yet a Woman hath no such Reason to desire Children for her Own Sake, for first her Name is Lost as to her Particular, in her Marrying, for she quits her Own, and is Named as her Husband; also her Family, for neither Name nor Estate goes to her Family according to the Laws and Customes of this Countrey; Also she Hazards her Life by Bringing them into the World, and hath the greatest share of Trouble in Bringing them up; neither can Women assure themselves of Comfort or Happiness by them, when they are grown to be Men, for their Name only lives in Sons, who Continue the Line of Succession, whereas Daughters are but Branches which by Marriage are Broken off from the Root from whence they Sprang, & Ingrafted into the Stock of an other Family, so that Daughters are to be accounted but as Moveable Goods or Furnitures that wear out; and though sometimes they carry the Lands with them, for want of Heir-males, yet the Name is not Kept nor the Line Continued with them, for these are buried in the Grave of the Males, for the Line, Name and Life of a Family ends with the Male issue; But many times Married Women desire Children, as Maids do Husbands, more for Honour than for Comfort or Happiness, thinking it a Disgrace to live Old Maids, and so likewise to be Barren, for in the Jews time it was some Disgrace to be Barren, so that for the most part Maids and Wives desire Husbands and Children upon any Condition, rather than to live Maids or Barren: But I am not of their minds, for I think a Bad Husband is far worse than No Husband, and to have Unnatural Children is more Unhappy than to have No Children, and where One Husband proves Good, as Loving and Prudent, a Thousand prove Bad, as Cross and Spendthrifts, and where One Child proves Good, as Dutifull and Wise, a Thousand prove Disobedient and Fools, as to do Actions both to the Dishonour and Ruine of their Familyes. Besides, I have observed, that Breeding Women,[1] especially those that have been married some time, and have had No Children, are in their Behaviour like New-married Wives, whose Actions of Behaviour and Speech are so Formal and Constrain'd, and so Different from their Natural way, as it is Ridiculous; for New Married Wives will so Bridle their Behaviour with Constraint, or Hang down their Heads so Simply, not so much out of True modesty, as a Forced Shamefulness; and to their Husbands they are so Coyly Amorous, or so Amorously Fond and so Troublesome Kind, as it would make the Spectators Sick, like Fulsome Meat to the Stomach; and if New-married Men were Wise men, it might make them Ill Husbands, at least to Dislike a Married Life, because they cannot Leave their Fond or Amorous Wives so Readily or Easily as a Mistress; but in Truth that Humour doth not last Long, for after a month or two they are like Surfeited Bodyes, that like any Meat Better than what they were so Fond of, so that in time they think their Husbands Worse Company than any other men. Also Women at the Breeding of their First Children make so many Sick Faces, although oftentimes the Sickness is only in their Faces, not but that some are Really Sick, but not every Breeding Women; Likewise they have such Feigned Coughs, and fetch their Breath Short, with such Feigning Laziness, and so many Unnecessary Complaints, as it would Weary the most Patient Husband to hear or see them: besides, they are so Expensive in their Longings and Perpetual Eating of several Costly Meats, as it would Undo a man that hath but an Indifferent Estate; but to add to their Charge, if they have not what they Please for Child-bed Linnen, Mantels,[2] and a Lying-in Bed, with Suitable Furniture for their Lying-Chamber, they will be so Fretfull

---

1 pregnant women
2 mantle: a blanket or cover

and Discontented, as it will indanger their Miscarrying; Again to redouble the Charge, there must be Gossiping,[1] not only with Costly Banquets at the Christening and Churching,[2] but they have Gossiping all the time of their Lying-in,[3] for then there is a more set or formal Gossiping than at other ordinary times. But I fear, that if this Letter come to the view of our Sex besides your self, they will throw more Spitefull or Angry Words out of their mouths against me, than the Unbeleeving Jews did hard Stones out of their hands at Saint *Stephan*; but the best is, they cannot Kill me with their Reproaches, I speak but the Truth of what I have observed amongst many of our Sex; Wherefore, Pray Madam, help to Defend me, as being my Friend, and I yours, for I shall Continue as long as I live,

  Madam, Your Ladyship's most Faithfull and Humble Servant.

CXV.

Madam,

  The News here is, that there are many Towns and multitudes of People Drown'd in *H*[olland]. I cannot wonder at it, by reason they live Below Water, like Fishes, onely they do not Swim, so that one may say they are Housed-Fishes, or Fishes in Sluces; indeed, they are Incircled, or Wall'd in with Water, and for my part, I think it should be more secure to live in a Floating Boat, or Ship, Upon the Water, as Rivers, or Seas, than in a Fix'd House Under the Water, for the Water in most Places is Above their Houses; But, though they live like Fishes, for the Manner, or Matter of Water, yet they are not of the Temper of Fishes, for the Matter, or Manner of Nature; for, as for Industry, they are like Ants or Pismires,[4] Prudently Provident, although not absolutely like them in their Government, for their Government is betwixt a Republick and Aristocracy. But by their Government and Industry, they do not appear to be Cold and Stupid, but Hot and Active, they neither want Courage nor Strength, Policy nor Industry,

---

1 festive all-female gatherings, with food and drink provided
2 churching: a ceremony held a month after childbirth to signal the woman's return to normal life
3 lying-in: both the process and the time-period of childbed labour and childbirth
4 pismire: an ant

Wealth nor Jollity; they are as Happy, as yet, to all Outward Appearance, as any Nation, nay Happier than most Nations are, for now they live in Peace, only wanting Champain,[1] or Firm Ground. Their Ships bring them in all Commodities, that are either Useful, Profitable, or Delightful. And as for their Wit, I do not know whether it be so Sharp and Quick as in Drier Climats, yet they seem by their Government, to have as Sound Judgments, and Clear Understanding, as any other Nation: Indeed, they seem to have the Subtilty of the Serpent, the Craft of the Fox, the Strength of the Lion, the Prudence of the Ant, the Sight of the Eagle, and the Wisdom of Rational Men; wherefore I observe, that Men are not according to the Temper of Climats they are Born and Bred in, but according to the Pleasure of Natures Will in Creating, or according to Fortune, Chance, or Breeding, Informing, Conforming, Reforming, Ordering or Disposing. But, Madam, I am not a fit Judg of Nations, People, nor Numbers, being of the Female Sex, who are seldom made Judges, for want of Judgement, and being Retired much to my own Thoughts, I want those Observations that Travelling and Commercing Persons have, or may have, although most Persons of either Sex are forward to give their Opinions, whether Wise or Foolish, and are apt to Censure, whether Truly or Falsly, Generously or Maliciously. But, Madam, lest you should Censure me to be a Tedious Writer, I take my leave, and rest,

Madam, Your Ladiships faithful Friend and Servant.

CXIX.

Madam,

I give you many Thanks for your Counsel, and Advice concerning my Health, for certainly an Over-studious Mind doth Wast the Body, which is the Cause, for the most part, that Painful[2] Students are Lean, for the Mind Feeds as much upon the Body, as the Body upon Meat; But truly, I am sometimes in a Dispute with my self, whether it be better to live a Long and Idle, than a Short, but Profitable Life, that is, to Imploy a Little time Well, or to Wast a Great Deal of Time to no

---

1   champaign: level open country
2   painstaking, diligent

Purpose; and I Conclude, that a Little Good is better than Nothing, or better than a Sum of Evil; for 'tis better through Industry to Leave a Little to After Age, than Die so Poor as to Leave Nothing, no not so much as After Ages may say, there Liv'd such a one in Former Ages, than to Die, and be quite Forgotten; and therefore should I live out the Course of Nature, or could live so Long as *Methusalem*,[1] when the Time were Past, it would seem as Nothing, and perchance I should be as Unwilling to Die then, as if I Died in my Youth, so that a Long, and a Short time of Life, is as one and the same; 'Tis true, Death is Terrible to Think of, but in Death no Terrour Remains; so as it is Life that is Painful both to the Body and Mind, and not Death, for the Mind in Life is Fearful, and the Body is seldom at Ease. But howsoever, I will endeavour, Madam, so to Divide the time of my Bodily Life, as to Imploy part of my Time for Health, and part for Fame, and all for Gods Favour, and when I Die, I will Bequeath my Soul to Heaven, my Fame to Time, and my Body to Earth, there to be Dissolved and Transformed as Nature Pleases, for to her it belongs. I do not much Care, nor Trouble my Thoughts to think where I shall be Buried, when Dead, or into what part of the Earth I shall be Thrown; but if I could have my Wish, I Would my Dust might be Inurned,[2] and mix'd with the Dust of those I Love Best, although I think they would not Remain Long together, for I did observe, that in this last War the Urns of the Dead were Digged up, their Dust Dispersed, and their Bones Thrown about,[3] and I suppose that in all Civil or Home-wars such Inhuman Acts are Committed; wherefore it is but a Folly to be Troubled and Concerned, where they shall be Buried, or for their Graves, or to Bestow much Cost on their Tombes, since not only Time, but Wars will Ruin them. But, Madam, lest I should make you Melancholy with Discoursing of so sad Subjects as Death and Graves, Bones and Dust, I leave you to Livelier and Pleasanter Thoughts and Conversation, and rest,

Madam, Your faithful Friend and Servant.

---

1 Methuselah, the oldest person mentioned in the Bible, who according to Genesis 5:27 lived to be 969 years old
2 interred or entombed
3 During the siege of Colchester in 1648, Parliamentary soldiers broke open the Lucas family tombs, including those of Cavendish's sister and her mother, and scattered their bones; see Grant 101.

Madam,

You were pleased to tell me in your Letter, how much out of Countenance you were, being Surprised with a Visit you Expected not; Truly, Madam, I am very Sensible of your Pain, insomuch as methinks I Feel what you Suffered, for I my self have been, and am still, so Troubled with that Imperfection, (if it may be call'd one) that I have been often so out of Countenance, as I have not only Pitied my self, but others have Pitied me, which is a Condition I would not be in, and the Thoughts that Bashfulness leaves in the Mind, are as great an Affliction as the Mind can have for a Crimeless Defect, for 'tis no Crime to be Bashful, nor a Disgrace, neither to the Life, nor Soul, although it be a Disadvantage to the Person, for Bashfulness Works divers Effects upon the Body, and in the Mind; As for the Mind, it Disturbs the Thoughts so much, as the Thoughts are all in a Confused Disorder, and not any one Thought moves Regularly, neither will they Suffer the Words to pass out of the Mouth, or if they do, they are Uttered without Sense, nay, sometimes in no Language, being but Pieces of Words, or Pieces of the Letters of Words; and others, quite contrary, will speak so Much, and Fast, as none can Understand what they Say, or would Say, Indeed, so Fast, as they make neither Stop, nor Distinction; Again, others will Speak so Shrill, and Loud, as it Deafens the Ears of the Hearers, and others so Soft and Low, as it cannot be Heard what they Say; and some when they are out of Countenance, will Laugh at every Word they Speak, or is Spoken to them, although the Subject be so Sad and Lamentable, as it is proper to be attended with Tears: And for the Body, when the Mind is Bashful, it hath Divers, and Several Misbecoming Motions, as in some their neather[1] Lip will so Quiver, as it will Draw quite Awry, like as in a Convulsion, and in some, their Eyes will so Squint, as they can see nothing Perfectly, and some will Shake their Heads so much, as if they had the Shaking Palsie;[2] and in some their Legs will so Tremble, as they can hardly bear up the Body from falling; and some, their whole Body will be as if they were in a Cold Fit of an Ague;[3] and others, when

---

1 nether: lower
2 shaking palsy: tremulous paralysis in the aged
3 an acute fever similar to malaria, with cold, hot, and sweating stages

they are out of Countenance, have such a Suppressing of Spirits, as they are forced often to Humm, to raise them up; and others, when they are out of Countenance, will look so Pale, as if they were Departing with Life, and on the Contrary, others will be so Red, having a Torrent of Blushes Flow to their Face, that they will appear as if they were Drunk, and that it were the Spirits of Wine which made that Firy and Flaming Colour, and many other Misbecoming Countenances, and several Misbecoming Garbs, Postures, Motions, and Senseless Words, which are not to be Express'd. But howsoever, a Bashful Countenance Expresses a Sensible Mind, and a Modest Nature, and not a Guiltiness of Crimes, for those that are so Bold as to Commit a Crime, will not want Confidence to Out-face it. Wherefore, Madam, let not your Bashful Behaviour be a Disturbance to your Harmless Thoughts, and Virtuous Life, to which Thoughts and Life, I leave you, and rest,

Madam, Your faithful Friend and Servant.

CXXXVIII.

Madam,

You did once, before your last Letter, Desire me to give my Opinion concerning the Influence of the Stars, I did so, and now you Desire my Opinion again, which if I do, I may chance to Contradict my self; But truly, I believe the Planets, or Stars, have no more Influence upon the Bodies, Minds, and Natures of Men, than one Creature hath upon another, or several Creatures upon one, or one upon more; for though the Bodies, Humours, Constitutions, and Minds of Men are subject to Alterations and Changes, yet it is from their Principal Natures, as from the Nature of Mankind, and we see by Experience and Observation, that the Planets have not Power over Laws, Customs, and Education, which are more Firmly Setled, than to be Altered by the Various Effects of the Stars and Planets, which Laws, Customs, and Educations, have Power over the Appetites, Passions, and Constitutions of Men. But we may observe, that the Effects of the Planets Vary Perpetually, for if they were Constant in their Effects, there would be no Change or Alteration, and if they had an Absolute Power over the rest of Nature's Works, as many think, or as others say,

onely over Mankind, their Cross Effects or Influences would make
such a Confusion, as it would make an Utter Destruction of that they
have Power of, which would Cross and Hinder Natures Methodical
Proceedings, and certain Rules and Decrees, by which she Governs,
unless you will say, the Stars, or Planets, are the Fates and Destinies to
all Mankind, if so, there needs no Education, Laws, or Justice; but the
Stars and Planets are too Inconstant and Changing to Decree and
Destinate any thing, for there is no Assurance or Certainty in the
Effects or Influence of the Stars and Planets, there is more Assurance
in the Educations, and Customs of Men, and Custom and Education
hath Stronger Effects, for Custom and Education can Alter the
Unaptness in Natural Capacities and Understandings, the Dull Dis-
positions, Froward, or Evil Passions of the Mind; also it oftentimes
Tempers the Irregular Humours of the Body, and can Restrain the
Unsatiable Appetites of the Body and Senses, and Long Custom
Alters the Nature of Men: Besides, Healthful and Strong Constitutions will become Sick and Faint with Debaucheries and Irregulari-
ties, and Sick and Weak Constitutions will grow Healthful and Strong
with Temperance and Regularity; also Education makes a Man a
Thief, and a Thief an Honest Man, and it is Fortune that makes Kings
and Beggars, and not the Planets, for all that are Born at one point of
Time, have not the same Fortune, as when a King is Born, or else
there would be thousands of Kings, so many Children being Born at
the same point of Time. Likewise all that were Born in such or such a
point of Time, would be Poets, Natural Philosophers, and the like,
whereas there are as Few of them as of Kings; also all that are Born in
such a point of Time, would be Wise, Just, and Prudent men, according to the Influence of the Stars; but if so, I believe there would be
more Wise, and Just men than there are, whereas now for One Wise
man there are Millions of Fools; Besides, it would shew the Stars to
have more Power, and greater Influence, to Produce Fools, Knaves,
Slaves, and Beggars, than Wise, Just, Free, and Rich Noble men; and if
the Planets had no Power over the Fortunes, nor over the Minds of
Men, but over the Bodies of Men, then the Influence the Soul hath
on the Body, would Contradict the Influence of the Planets, and the
Planets Influence would Contradict the Influence of the Soul, so as
by their Crossness the Body would be Perpetually Tortured, and the
Mind Disquieted; and if the Planets had an Influence over the Soul

and Body, then we would be Good and Bad, Wicked and Pious, Valiant and Cowards, Sick and Well, Hungry and Dry, or otherwise have no Appetite, according as the Planets please, or according to their Influences; also all men would be Good and Bad, Sick and Well, Wise and Fools, Valiant and Cowardly, just at one time, as the Sign or Influence is, so that all men under the Domination of such Stars or Planets, would be alike at one Minute, and if all Men should Like or Love one Woman, at one Minute and Time, or all Women one Man, that is, as many as See her or him, that Woman would have more Servants and Suters than she could Please or Answer, and the Man more Mistresses than the Great Turk.[1] Also, if it were according to the Dominion of the Planets, thousands on a Sudden would be Inspired with Poetical Raptures, and soon after be Dull, and Stupid Dolts whenas that Influence Changed: but I believe there is greater Influence from one Nation on another, according to Interest, Strength and Potency, and so from one Man to another, according to Interest, Power, and Authority, than the Stars and Planets have on Several Nations, and Several, and Particular Men, which Produces greater Effects, than the Planets Effects and Influences can do; not but that I believe the Planets can Work as Sudden Effects, nay, far Suddener and Immediate, as we see by the Effects of the Heat, and Light of the Sun; but I believe, that Beauty and Wit have a greater Influence upon the Passions of the Mind, and Senses, and Appetites of the Body, than the Stars; and why may not we think as well, that the Actions, especially the General Actions of men, might have as great an Influence or Power over the Stars and Planets, as the Stars and Planets are thought to have over Men? for I see no reason to the contrary, since they are Fellow Creatures, and not Gods. But surely, every several part and particle in Nature hath an Influence on each other, from which are produced several Effects, and Effects have Influence upon Effects, some on some, and some on others, or perchance they have all a Working Effect to each other, as many Grains of Corn[2] are ground for one Loaf of Bread, many several Materials go to one House, many several Families to one Commonwealth, many several Nations, to one World, and many several Worlds to one Universe. Thus, Madam, I

---

1 Sultan of Turkey
2 wheat or other cereal grain

have Obeyed your second Command, concerning the Influences of the Stars and Planets, as I did your first, but in this Later Discourse, I seem to have no Belief that the Stars have an Influence over the Bodies or Minds, no more than the Bodies or Minds have over the Planets, and so over Fortune, Education, Laws, Custom, and the like, whereas in my Former Letter, I said, they had over the Body, and was apt to Believe they had also over the Mind; but since I Writ the Former Letter concerning this Subject, I have thought of it more than I had then, and Believe every Creature hath some Influence to each other. But I leave both Letters, and the Opinions and Arguments written therein, to your Better Judgment, and rest,

Madam, Your faithful Friend and Servant.

CXLIII.

Madam,

I heard the Ship was Drown'd, wherein the man was that had the Charge and Care of my Playes, to carry them into E[*ngland*]. to be Printed, I being then in A[*ntwerp*]. which when I heard, I was extremely Troubled, and if I had not had the Original of them by me, truly I should have been much Afflicted, and accounted the Loss of my Twenty Playes, as the Loss of Twenty Lives, for in my Mind I should have Died Twenty Deaths, which would have been a great Torment, or I should have been near the Fate of those Playes, and almost Drown'd in Salt Tears, as they in the Salt Sea; but they are Destinated to Live, and I hope, I in them, when my Body is Dead, and Turned to Dust; But I am so Prudent, and Careful of my Poor Labours, which are my Writing Works, as I alwayes keep the Copies of them safely with me, until they are Printed, and then I Commit the Originals to the Fire, like Parents which are willing to Die, whenas they are sure of their Childrens Lives, knowing when they are Old, and past Breeding, they are but Useless in this World: But howsoever their Paper Bodies are Consumed, like as the *Roman* Emperours, in Funeral Flames, I cannot say, an Eagle Flies out of them,[1] or that they

---

1   a reference to the Roman custom of letting an eagle fly from the funeral pyre of a deceased emperor

Turn into a Blazing Star, although they make a great Blazing Light when they Burn; And so leaving them to your Approbation or Condemnation, I rest,

Madam, Your faithful Friend and Servant.

CL.

Madam,

My Thoughts, although not my Actions, have been so busily Imployed about Huswifry these three or four Dayes, as I could think of nothing else, for I hearing my Neighbours should say, my Waiting-Maids were Spoil'd with Idleness, having nothing to do, but to Dress, Curl, and Adorn themselves, and they Excusing themselves, laying the Blame upon me, that I did not set them to any Imployment, but whereas they were ready to Obey my Commands, I was so Slow in Commanding them, as I seldom took any Notice of them, or Spoke to them, and that the truth was, they oftener Heard of their Lady, than Heard, or Saw her themselves, I living so Studious a Life, as they did not See me above once a Week, nay, many times, not once in a Fortnight; wherefore, upon the Relation of these Complaints, I sent for the Governess[1] of my House, and bid her give order to have Flax and Wheels[2] Bought, for I, with my Maids, would sit and Spin. The Governess hearing me say so, Smiled, I ask'd her the Reason, she said, she Smil'd to think what Uneven Threads I would Spin, for, said she, though Nature hath made you a Spinster in Poetry, yet Education hath not made you a Spinster in Huswifry, and you will Spoil more Flax, than Get Cloth by your Spinning, as being an Art that requires Practice to Learn it; besides, said she, the Noise the Wheels make with Turning round, will be Offensive to your Hearing. I was very much Troubled to hear what she said, for I thought Spinning had been Easie, as not requiring much Skill to Draw, and Twist a Thread, nay, so Easie I thought it was, as I did imagine I should have Spun so Small, and Even a Thread, as to make Pure Fine Linnen Cloth, also, that my Maids and I should make so much, as I should not have needed to

---

1   housekeeper
2   flax to spin linen thread; spinning-wheels

Buy any, either for Houshold Linnen, or Shifts.[1] Then I bid her leave me, to Consider of some other Work; and when I was by my self alone, I call'd into my Mind several Sorts of Wrought Works,[2] most of which, though I had Will, yet I had no Skill to Work, for which I did Inwardly Complain of my Education, that my Mother did not Force me to Learn to Work with a Needle, though she found me alwayes Unapt thereto; at last I Pitch'd upon Making of Silk Flowers, for I did Remember, when I was a Girl, I saw my Sisters make Silk Flowers, and I had made some, although Ill-favour'dly;[3] wherefore I sent for the Governess of my House again, and told her, that I would have her Buy several Coloured Silks, for I was Resolved to Imploy my Time in making Silk-Flowers; she told me, she would Obey my Commands, but, said she, Madam, neither You, nor any that Serves You, can do them so Well, as those who make it their Trade, neither can you make them so Cheap, as they will Sell them out of their Shops, wherefore you had better Buy those Toyes,[4] if you Desire them, for it will be an Unprofitable Employment, to Wast Time, with a Double Expence of Mony. Then I told her I would Preserve, for it was Summer time, and the Fruit Fresh, and Ripe upon the Trees; she ask'd me for whom I would Preserve, for I seldom did Eat Sweet-meats[5] my self, nor made Banquets for Strangers, unless I meant to Feed my Houshold Servants with them; besides, said she, you may keep half a score Servants with the Mony that is laid out in Sugar and Coals, which go to the Preserving only of a Few Sweet-meats, that are good for nothing, but to Breed Obstructions, and Rot the Teeth. All which when I heard, I conceived she spoke Reason; at last I considered, that I and my Maids had better be Idle, than to Employ Time Unprofitably, and to spend Mony Idely; and after I had Mused some time, I told her, how I heard my Neighbours Condemn'd me, for letting my Servants be Idle without Employment, and that my Maids said it was my Fault, for they were willing to be Employed in Huswifry; she said, my Neighbours would find Fault, where no Fault was, and my Maids would Complain more if they were kept to Work, than when they had liberty to

---

1 shift: woman's undergarment or smock
2 fancy needlework
3 ill-favoured: ugly or unaesthetic
4 toys: knick-knacks or trinkets
5 sweet-meats: candied preserved fruit

Play; besides, said she, none can want Employment, as long as there are Books to be Read, and they will never Inrich your Fortunes by their Working, nor their Own, unless they made a Trade of Working, & then perchance they might get a poor Living, but not grow Rich by what they can do, whereas by Reading they will Inrich their Understandings, and Increase their Knowledges, and Quicken their Wit, all which may make their Life Happy, in being Content with any Fortune that [is] not in their Power to Better, or in that, as to Manage a Plentiful Fortune Wisely, or to Indure a Low Fortune Patiently, and therefore they cannot Employ their Time better, than to Read, nor your Ladiship better than to Write, for any other Course of Life would be as Unpleasing, and Unnatural to you, as Writing is Delightful to you; besides, you are Naturally Addicted to Busie your time with Pen, Ink, and Paper; but, said I, not with Wit, for if Nature had given me as much Wit to Write, as Fortune hath given me Leisure, my Writing might have been for some Use, but now my Time and Paper is Unprofitably Wasted in Writing, as my Time and Flax would be in Spinning, but since I am fit for no other Employment but to Scratch Paper, leave me to that Employment, and let my Attending Maids have Books to read. Thus, Madam, for a time did I Trouble my Mind, and Busie my Thoughts to no Purpose, but was Forced to Return to my Writing-Work again, not knowing what else to do, and if I had been as Long Absent from my Lord as *Penelope* was from her Husband *Ulysses*, I could have never Employed my Time as she did, for her work only Employed her Hands, and Eyes, her Ears were left open to Loves Pleadings, and her Tongue was at liberty to give her Suters Answers,[1] whereas my Work Employes all the Faculties and Powers of my Soul, Mind, and Spirits, as well as my Eyes and Hands, and my Thoughts are so Busie in my Brain, as they neither Regard, nor take Notice what Enters through the Ears; indeed those Passages are as Stop'd up, or Barr'd close, whereas had *Penelope's* Ears been so Barr'd, her Lovers Petitions, Sutes, and Pleadings, would have been kept without doors, like a Company of Beggars, they might have Knock'd, but not Entred, nor any of the Mind's Family would have ask'd them

---

1 During Ulysses's 20-year absence, his wife Penelope spent her days weaving a large robe for her father-in-law, putting off her numerous suitors (who forced themselves upon her hospitality) by telling them she would not remarry until the robe was finished, and then undoing the day's weaving each night.

what they Desired; neither would the Tongue, the Mind's Almner,[1] have given them one word of Answer, and then it was likely her Amorous Lovers would have gone away, and not stay'd to Feed upon her Cost and Charge, as they did. But, Madam, give me leave to beg your Pardon for Writing so Long a Letter, though it is your Desire I should, I will Tire you no Longer, but Subscribe my self,

Madam, Your faithful Friend and Servant.

---

1   almoner: one who distributes alms (charity) on behalf of a person or institution

3 . PREFACE TO
ORATIONS OF DIVERS SORTS (1662)

Most of Margaret Cavendish's published works offer not just one but a series of prefatory epistles, some addressed to the general reader, and others to different segments of her supposed reading audience; *Poems and Fancies*, for example, contains epistles "To all Noble, and Worthy Ladies," "To Naturall Philosophers," "To Morall Philosophers," "To Poets," "To all Writing Ladies," "to Souldiers," among others. In these prefatory essays, Cavendish carried on the work of self-fashioning, defining herself as an artist and philosopher. At the same time, she fashioned her reading public as well: in the following preface to *Orations of Divers Sorts* (1662), she denounces the "Crabbed Readers" who criticized her former efforts, and asks that her book be read only by "Worthy and Judicious Men, and Noble Persons ... the Just and Wise."

TO THE READERS OF MY WORKS

I Know not how to Please All, that are pleased to Read my Works; for do what I can, Some will find Fault; and the worst is, that those Faults or Imperfections, I accuse my self of in my Prefatory Epistles, they fling back with a double strength against my poor harmless Works, which shewes their Malice and my Truth: And as for my Playes, which they say are not made up so exactly as they should be, as having no Plots, Designs, Catastrophes and such like I know not what, I expressed in the Epistles præfixed before my Playes, that I had not Skil nor Art to Form them, as they should be, for that Work was like a Taylors Work to make Cloaths: But many that find such Faults, are not so good as a Taylor, but meer Botchers or Brokers,[1] to Patch and Set several Old and New Pieces together to make up a Play, which I never did, for I thank my Fates, all is not only New, but my Own, what I have Presented to the World; But this Age is so Censorious,[2] that the Best Poets are found Fault with, wherefore it is an Honour to my Writings, which are so much Inferiour to theirs; Neither can their

---

1 botcher: a tailor who mends or patches clothes; broker: a dealer in second-hand clothes

2 critical

Dislikes Deterr me from Writing, for I Write to Please my Self, rather than to Please such Crabbed Readers. Yet all my Readers have not been so Cross nor Cruel, for there are Many, to whom my Endeavours and Works are Acceptable, and the more Honour it is to my Works, as being Approved and Known by Worthy and Judicious Men, and Noble Persons; But many Men have more Ill Natures to Find Faults with their Neighbours, than Virtue to Mend Faults in Themselves; also they are apt to Censure Other mens Wit, and yet have None of their Own; the truth is, they are a sort of Persons that in Playes preferr Plots before Wit, and Scenes before Humours; in Poems, Rime before Similizing, and Numbers[1] before Distinguishing; in Theology, Faction before Faith, and Sophistry before Truth; in Philosophy, Old Authors before New Truths, and Opinions before Reason; And in Orations, they preferr Artificial Connexions, before Natural Eloquence: All which makes them Foolish, Censorious, and Unjust Judges. Wherefore, I desire, these my Orations may not be Read by such Humour'd men, but by the Just and Wise, which will be a Satisfaction to me.

'Tis Probable, had I been a Learned Scholar, I might have Written my Orations more Short than I have done, but yet some of them are so short, that had they been shorter, they would not have been of Force to Perswade, whereas the Invention of an Orator, or Use of Orations, is to Perswade the Auditors to be of the Orators Opinion or Belief, and it is not Probable, that Forcible Arguments or Perswasions can be Contain'd in two or three Lines of Words; Also had I been a Learned Scholar, I might have Written them more Compendiously,[2] and not so Loose, but I affect Freedome and Ease, even in my Works of Writings; Besides, I have Observ'd, that whatsoever is Bound or Knit Close, is difficult to Disclose, and for Writings, whatsoever is very Compendious, requires some Study to Conceive and Understand the Sense and Design of the Authors Meaning: But I hope that Defect or want of Learning, will not Blemish my Work, nor Obstruct the Sense of my Orations, nor Puzzle the Understanding of the Reader. Only one thing more I desire my Noble Readers, as to Observe that most of my Orations are General Orations, viz. such as

---

1   metre
2   concisely

may be spoken in any Kingdome or Government, for I suppose, that in All, at least in Most Kingdomes and Governments there are Souldiers, Magistrates, Privy-Counsellours, Lawyers, Preachers, and University Scholars.

We have, its true, gotten a Foolish Custom both in our Writing and Speaking, to Indeavour more to Match or Marry Words together, than to Match and Marry Sense and Reason together, which is strange, we should Preferr Shaddows before Substances, or the Spig[1] or Tap before the Liquor, for Words are but to Conveigh the Sense of an Oration to the Ears, and so into the Understanding of the Hearers, like as Spouts do Wine into Bottels; and who, that is Wise, will Regard what the Vessel is, so it be Wholsome and Clean? for should not we believe those to be Fools, that had rather have Foul Water out of a Golden Vessel, than Pure Wine out of Earthen or Woodden Vessels? the like may be said for Words and Sense, for who, that is Wise, would Choose Choice Words before Profitable Reasons? Wherefore, Noble Readers, let me Advise you to Leave[2] this Custom in Writing and Speaking, or rather be Silently Wise, than Foolish in Rhetorick.

I have Indeavoured in this Book to Express Perfect Orators, that Speak Perfect Orations, as to Cause their Auditors to Act, or Believe, according to the Orators Opinion, Judgement, Design, or Desire; But before I did put this my Book forth, Know, Noble Readers, I did Inquire, to find whether any Person had Composed and Put out a Whole Book of Pure and Perfect Orations, but I could neither hear of, nor see any such Works of any Person that Composed and Set forth to the Publick View, a Book of Pure Orations, Composed out of One Orators Own Fancy, Wit, and Eloquence. 'Tis true, I have heard of Single Orations, made by Single Persons, in Single Parts; Also I have seen Orations mixt with History, wherein the Substance of the History is the Ground of their Orations; Also I have seen two Translations call'd Orations, but they are rather Orations in Name than in Reality, for their Nature is History, the One contains Relations of several Countries, in the Other are Relations from several Princes of their Actions, or Fortunes, or Both, Exprest in an Orators Style; yet those are not Perfect or Right Orations, but Adulterated, or rather Hermophrodites. But perchance my Readers will say, I Understand

---

1 spigot
2 abandon

not True Orations; If I do not, I am Sorry for, and ask their Pardon for Speaking what I Understand not. But I desire, Noble Readers, you will not think or believe, I speak to Illustrate my Own Works, and to Detract from the Works of Others, for upon my Conscience I Speak and Write as I Believe, and if I Commit an Error in this Belief, I ask your Pardon, and if you Excuse me, I shall take it for a Favour and Obligation.

I have Written Orations and Speeches of all Sorts, and in all Places fit for Orations, Speeches, or particular Discourses; and first imagining my Self and You to be in a Metropolitan City, I invite you into the Chief Market-place, as the most Populous place, where usually Orations are Spoken, at least they were so in Older times, and there you shall hear Orations Concerning Peace and Warr; but the Generality of the People being more apt to make Warr, than to keep Peace, I desire you to Arm your Selves, supposing you to be of the Masculine Sex, and of Valiant Heroical Natures, to enter into the Field of Warr; and since Warrs bring Ruine and Destruction to One or Some Parties, if not to All, and Loss causes men to Desire Peace, out of Warr I bring you into great Disorders, caused by the Ruins Warrs have made, which I am Sorry for, yet it Must be so, the Fates have Decreed it; and Misery causing men to be Prudent and Industrious, by which they come to Flourish again, at least their Successors, and to shew you their Industry, I bring you out of the Field of Warr into a New-built City, where you must stay the Building of it, for it will be Built Soon, having Many Labourers, and after it is Built, there being a Large Market-place, you may stand or sit with Ease and hear the Orations that are there Spoken; and by Reason, there are some Causes or Cases to be Pleaded, I shall indeavour to Perswade you, after some time of Refreshment, at your own Homes, to go into the Courts or Halls of Judicature; after these Causes are Judged, or at least Pleaded, I shall desire you, to Adorn your Selves fit for the Court, then to Wait upon the Kings Majesty, and if you be Privy-Counsellours, or have any Business or Petitions at the Council Table, by the Kings Permission you may Enter into the Council-Chamber; but great Monarchs having Many Subjects, whereof some are more Active than Wise, and more apt to Complain than to Obey, you may hear the Petitions of the Subjects, and the Speeches or Orations of the Soveraign, and after a good Agreement, Unity, and Love, you may Rest your Selves in Peace, untill such time as your Charity calls you forth to Visit the

Sick, and when as Death hath Releas'd those Sick Persons of their Pains, Humanity will perswade you to wait on their Dead Corps to the Grave, and after some Tears showred on their Graves, and having Dried your Eyes, and Heard some Sermons of Reproof and Instructions, you will be Invited as Bridal-Guests to see some Men and Women United in Holy Matrimony; after the Wedding Ceremonies are ended, you may, as formerly you have done, go into the Market-place again, and hear what Orations there are Spoken, wherein one short Oration concerning the Liberty of Women hath so Anger'd that Sex, as after the Mens Orations are ended, they Privately Assemble together, where three or four take the place of an Orator, and Speak to the rest;[1] the only Difficulty will be, to get Undiscovered amongst them, to hear their Private Conventicles;[2] but if you regard not what Women say, you may Ride to a Country Market-Town, and hear a Company of Gentlemen associate together their Discourse and Pastime; and if you like not their Pastime, then you may Walk into the Fields of Peace, to Receive the Sweet and Healthfull Air, or to View the Curious and Various Works of Nature, and for Variety of Pastime, you may stand or sit under a Spreading Tree, and hear the Country Clowns[3] or Peasants speak, concerning their own Affairs and Course of Life; in which Shady place, Sweet Air, and Happiness of Peace I leave you, unless you will Travel to see the Government or rather Disorders in other States or Kingdomes, to which Observation I will Wait upon you, and when all is in Peace, before we return Home, we will, if you Please, enter some of their Colleges, and hear some School-Arguments,[4] after which return, I shall Kiss your Hands and take my Leave.[5]

M. Newcastle

---

1 See *Female Orations*, below, pp. 143-7.

2 conventicle: a private or illegal meeting, especially of a religious sect, often applied to Nonconformists' meetings during the Restoration; for the gendered segregation of space and speech in the early modern period, see Mendelson and Crawford 205-25

3 clown: a country bumpkin

4 scholastic or academic debates

5 a custom in greeting or leave-taking, whereby those of slightly inferior status kissed the hand of a social superior (especially a monarch or other dignitary) as a ceremonial gesture of respect

4. LETTER OF MARY EVELYN TO
RALPH BOHUN c. 1667[1]

Mary Evelyn (c. 1635-1709) was the wife of diarist John Evelyn (1620-1706), one of the founding members of the Royal Society; among her circle of friends, she was also recognized in her own right for her intellectual and artistic gifts.[2] The social occasion to which she refers in her letter to Mr Bohun was probably one of a round of visits which Evelyn and his wife paid to the duke and duchess of Newcastle at their London house during the weeks before Cavendish's attendance at a Royal Society meeting on 30 May 1667, at which John Evelyn was one of her escorts.[3]

To Mr. Bohun,[4]

Sir,

I am concerned you should be absent when you might confirm the suffrages of your fellow collegiots,[5] and see the mistress both Universities court; a person who has not her equal possibly in the world, so extraordinary a woman she is in all things. I acknowledge, though I remember her some years since[6] and have not been a stranger to her fame, I was surprised to find so much extravagancy and vanity in any person not confined within four walls.[7] Her habit particular,[8] fantastical, not unbecoming a good shape, which she may truly boast of. Her face discovers the facility of the sex, in being yet persuaded it deserves the esteem years forbid, by the infinite care she

---

1 *Diary and Correspondence of John Evelyn.* Ed. Bray. 4 vols. London: 1857. iv: 8-9.
2 For an admiring memoir of Mary Evelyn by Ralph Bohun, the recipient of the letter printed below, see Evelyn, *Diary and Correspondence*, ed. Bray, iv, 3-7.
3 For John Evelyn's account of these visits to the Duke of Newcastle's London house in 1667, see his *Diary* for 18 April, 25 April, 27 April and 11 May 1667.
4 Ralph Bohun, her son's tutor at Oxford, with whom Mary Evelyn carried on a regular correspondence on various social and intellectual topics
5 "suffrages of your fellow collegiots", the judgments on Cavendish by Bohun's academic colleagues, some of whom were also visitors at her London house
6 in Paris in 1645, when Mary Evelyn's parents, Sir Richard and Lady Browne, helped facilitate the use of Sir Richard's private chapel (designated for his use as English Resident at the French court) for Margaret Lucas's marriage to William Cavendish; for details see Grant 85-6
7 Those who were judged insane were confined to a dark room with straw on the floor.
8 singular

takes to place her curls and patches.[1] Her mien surpasses the imagination of poets, or the descriptions of a romance heroine's greatness; her gracious bows, seasonable nods, courteous stretching out of her hands, twinkling of her eyes, and various gestures of approbation, show what may be expected from her discourse, which is as airy, empty, whimsical, and rambling as her books, aiming at science, difficulties, high notions, terminating commonly in nonsense, oaths, and obscenity. Her way of address to people, more than necessarily submissive; a certain general form to all, obliging, by repeating affected, generous, kind expressions; endeavouring to show humility by calling back things past, still to improve her present greatness and favour to her friends. I found Doctor Charlton[2] with her, complimenting her wit and learning in a high manner; which she took to be so much her due that she swore if the schools did not banish Aristotle[3] and read Margaret, Duchess of Newcastle, they did her wrong, and deserved to be utterly abolished. My part was not yet to speak, but admire; especially hearing her go on magnifying her own generous actions, stately buildings, noble fortune, her lord's prodigious losses in the war, his power, valour, wit, learning, and industry, – what did she not mention to his or her own advantage? Sometimes, to give her breath, came in a fresh admirer; then she took occasion to justify her faith, to give an account of her religion, as new and unintelligible as her philosophy, to cite her own pieces line and page in such a book, and to tell the adventures of some of her nymphs. At last I grew weary, and concluded that the creature called a chimera[4] which I had heard speak of, was now to be seen, and that it was time to retire for fear of infection; yet I hope, as she is an original, she may never have a copy. Never did I see a woman so full of herself, so amazingly vain and ambitious. What contrary miracles does this age produce. This lady and Mrs. Philips![5]

---

1   black patches, used cosmetically as a facial ornament
2   Walter Charleton (1619-1707), physician to Charles I and Charles II, and writer on medical and philosophical topics; for an admiring letter from Charleton to Margaret, see below, pp. 303-12.
3   Aristotle's works still comprised the bulk of the scientific curriculum in most seventeenth-century universities.
4   in Greek myth a fire-breathing monster with a lion's head, goat's body and serpent's tail; metaphorically, a wild fantasy or gross misconception
5   the poet Katharine Philips (1631-64), known as the 'Matchless Orinda,' whose verses (published in an unauthorized edition in 1664) were extremely popular during the Restoration

The one transported with the shadow of reason, the other possessed of the substance and insensible of her treasure; and yet men who are esteemed wise and learned, not only put them in equal balance, but suffer the greatness of the one to weigh down the certain real worth of the other. This is all I can requite your rare verses with; which as much surpass the merit of the person you endeavour to represent, as I can assure you this description falls short of the lady I would make you acquainted with: but she is not of mortal race, and therefore cannot be defined.

M.E.

II

GENDER AND SERIOUS PLAY

1. THE CONVENT OF PLEASURE
FROM PLAYS NEVER BEFORE PRINTED
(1668)

The Convent of Pleasure was published in 1668 as part of Margaret Cavendish's second collection of dramatic works, *Plays Never Before Printed*. The play was not produced for the stage during Cavendish's own lifetime; in *The Blazing World* her character the Duchess of Newcastle remarked that the "Wits of these present times" had condemned her plays as "uncapable of being represented or acted" because they had not been composed according to the "Rules of Art"[1] Yet in 1995 a brilliantly successful production of *The Convent of Pleasure* was performed at the University College of Ripon and York St. John[2] (see Illustrations, pp. 110, 133). For a discussion of gender games and other themes within the play, see Introduction, pp. 16-21.

THE CONVENT OF PLEASURE.

A Comedy.

ACT I. SCENE I.

Enter Three Gentlemen.

First Gentleman.

Tom, Where have you been, you look so sadly of it?

2 *Gent.* I have been at the Funeral of the Lord *Fortunate*; who has left his Daughter, the Lady *Happy*, very rich, having no other Daughter but her.

1 *Gent.* If she be so rich, it will make us all Young Men, spend all our Wealth in fine Clothes, Coaches, and Lackies, to set out our Wooing hopes.

3 *Gent.* If all her Wooers be younger Brothers, as most of us Gal-

---

1 See below, p. 247.

2 project originated and text adapted by Gweno Williams, directed by Bill Pinner, performed and recorded at the University College of Ripon and York St. John, March 1995. For an account and analysis of performance strategies, see Williams 100-105.

lants are, we shall undo our selves upon bare hopes, without Probability: But is she handsome, *Tom?*

    2 *Gent.* Yes, she is extream handsome, young, rich, and virtuous.

    1 *Gent.* Faith, that is too much for one Woman to possess.

    2 *Gent.* Not, if you were to have her.

    1 *Gent.* No, not for me; but in my Opinion too much for any other Man.

Exeunt.

Scene II.

Enter the Lady Happy, *and one of her Attendants.*

Servant.

    Madam, you being young, handsome, rich, and virtuous, I hope you will not cast away those gifts of Nature, Fortune, and Heaven, upon a Person which cannot merit you?

    L. *Happy.* Let me tell you, that Riches ought to be bestowed on such as are poor, and want means to maintain themselves; and Youth, on those that are old; Beauty, on those that are ill-favoured; and Virtue, on those that are vicious: So that if I should place my gifts rightly, I must Marry one that's poor, old, ill-favoured, and debauch'd.

    Serv. Heaven forbid.

    L. *Happy.* Nay, Heaven doth not only allow of it, but commands it; for we are commanded to give to those that want.

Enter Madam Mediator *to the Lady* Happy.

    Mediat. Surely, Madam, you do but talk, and intend not to go where you say.

    L. *Happy.* Yes, truly, my Words and Intentions go even together.

    Mediat. But surely you will not incloyster your self, as you say.

    L. *Happy.* Why, what is there in the publick World that should invite me to live in it?

    Mediat. More then if you should banish your self from it.

    L. *Happy.* Put the case I should Marry the best of Men, if any best there be; yet would a Marry'd life have more crosses and sorrows then pleasure, freedom, or hapiness: nay Marriage to those that are virtuous is a greater restraint then a Monastery. Or, should I take delight in

Admirers? they might gaze on my Beauty, and praise my Wit, and I receive nothing from their eyes, nor lips; for Words vanish as soon as spoken, and Sights are not substantial. Besides, I should lose more of my Reputation by their Visits, then gain by their Praises. Or, should I quit Reputation and turn Courtizan, there would be more lost in my Health, then gained by my Lovers, I should find more pain then Pleasure; besides, the troubles and frights I should be put to, with the Quarrels and Brouilleries[1] that Jealous Rivals make, would be a torment to me; and 'tis only for the sake of Men, when Women retire not: And since there is so much folly, vanity and falshood in Men, why should Women trouble and vex themselves for their sake; for retiredness bars the life from nothing else but Men.

Mediat. O yes, for those that incloister themselves, bar themselves from all other worldly Pleasures.

L. *Happy.* The more Fools they.

Mediat. Will you call those Fools that do it for the gods sake?

L. *Happy.* No Madam, it is not for the gods sake, but for opinion's sake; for, Can any Rational Creature think or believe, the gods take delight in the Creature's uneasie life? or, Did they command or give leave to Nature to make Senses for no use; or to cross, vex and pain them? for, What profit or pleasure can it be to the gods to have Men or Women wear coarse Linnen or rough Woollen, or to flea[2] their skin with Hair-cloth, or to eat or sawe thorow[3] their flesh with Cords? or, What profit or pleasure can it be to the gods to have Men eat more Fish then Flesh, or to fast? unless the gods did feed on such meat themselves; for then, for fear the gods should want it, it were fit for Men to abstein from it: The like for Garments, for fear the gods should want fine Clothes to adorn themselves, it were fit Men should not wear them: Or, what profit or pleasure can it be to the gods to have Men to lie uneasily on the hard ground, unless the gods and Nature were at variance, strife and wars; as if what is displeasing unto Nature, were pleasing to the gods, and to be enemies to her, were to be friends to them.

Mediat. But being done for the gods sake, it makes that which in Nature seems to be bad, in Divinity to be good.

---

1 brouillerie (French): a tiff or petty quarrel
2 flay
3 through

L. Happy. It cannot be good, if it be neither pleasure, nor profit to the gods; neither do Men any thing for the gods but their own sake.

Mediat. But when the Mind is not imployed with Vanities, nor the Senses with Luxury; the Mind is more free, to offer its Adorations, Prayers and Praises to the gods.

L. Happy. I believe, the gods are better pleased with Praises then Fasting; but when the Senses are dull'd with abstinency, the Body weakned with fasting, the Spirits tir'd with watching, the Life made uneasie with pain, the Soul can have but little will to worship: only the Imagination doth frighten it into active zeal, which devotion is rather forced then voluntary; so that their prayers rather flow out of their mouth, then spring from their heart, like rain-water that runs thorow Gutters, or like Water that's forced up a Hill by Artificial Pipes and Cisterns. But those that pray not unto the gods, or praise them more in prosperity then adversity, more in pleasures then pains, more in liberty then restraint, deserve neither the happiness of ease, peace, freedom, plenty and tranquillity in this World, nor the glory and blessedness of the next. And if the gods should take pleasure in nothing but in the torments of their Creatures, and would not prefer those prayers that are offer'd with ease and delight, I should believe, the gods were cruel: and, What Creature that had reason or rational understanding, would serve cruel Masters, when they might serve a kind Mistress, or would forsake the service of their kind Mistress, to serve cruel Masters? Wherefore, if the gods be cruel, I will serve Nature; but the gods are bountiful, and give all, that's good, and bid us freely please our selves in that which is best for us: and that is best, what is most temperately used, and longest may be enjoyed, for excess doth wast it self, and all it feeds upon.

Mediat. In my opinion your Doctrine, and your Intention do not agree together.

L. Happy. Why?

Mediat. You intend to live incloister'd and retired from the World.

L. Happy. 'Tis true, but not from pleasures; for, I intend to incloister my self from the World, to enjoy pleasure, and not to bury my self from it; but to incloister my self from the incumbred cares and vexations, troubles and perturbance of the World.

Mediat. But if you incloister your self, How will you enjoy the company of Men, whose conversation is thought the greatest Pleasure?

L. *Happy.* Men are the only troublers of Women; for they only cross and oppose their sweet delights, and peaceable life; they cause their pains, but not their pleasures. Wherefore those Women that are poor, and have not means to buy delights, and maintain pleasures, are only fit for Men; for having not means to please themselves, they must serve only to please others; but those Women, where Fortune, Nature, and the gods are joined to make them happy, were mad to live with Men, who make the Female sex their slaves; but I will not be so inslaved, but will live retired from their Company. Wherefore, in order thereto, I will take so many Noble Persons of my own Sex, as my Estate will plentifully maintain, such whose Births are greater then their Fortunes, and are resolv'd to live a single life, and vow Virginity: with these I mean to live incloister'd with all the delights and pleasures that are allowable and lawful; My Cloister shall not be a Cloister of restraint, but a place for freedom, not to vex the Senses but to please them.

> *For every Sense shall pleasure take,*
> *And all our Lives shall merry make:*
> *Our Minds in full delight shall joy,*
> *Not vex'd with every idle Toy:*
> *Each Season shall our Caterers be,*
> *To search the Land, and Fish the Sea;*
> *To gather Fruit and reap the Corn,*
> *That's brought to us in Plenty's Horn;*
> *With which we'l feast and please our tast,*
> *But not luxurious make a wast.*
> *Wee'l Cloth our selves with softest Silk,*
> *And Linnen fine as white as milk.*
> *Wee'l please our Sight with Pictures rare;*
> *Our Nostrils with perfumed Air.*
> *Our Ears with sweet melodious Sound,*
> *Whose Substance can be no where found;*
> *Our Tast with sweet delicious Meat,*
> *And savory Sauces we will eat:*
> *Variety each Sense shall feed,*
> *And Change in them new Appetites breed.*

> *Thus will in* Pleasure's Convent *I*
> *Live with delight, and with it die.*

Exeunt.

Act II. Scene I.

Enter Monsieur Take-pleasure, *and his Man* Dick.

Monsieur *Take-pleasure.*

   Dick, Am I fine to day?

   Dick. Yes, Sir, as fine as Feathers, Ribbons, Gold, and Silver can make you.

   Takepl. Dost thou think I shall get the Lady *Happy*?

   Dick. Not if it be her fortune to continue in that name.

   Takepl. Why?

   Dick. Because if she Marry your Worship she must change her Name; for the Wife takes the Name of her Husband, and quits her own.

   Takepl. Faith, *Dick,* if I had her wealth I should be *Happy*.

   Dick. It would be according as your Worship would use it; but, on my conscience, you would be more happy with the Ladie's Wealth, then the Lady would be with your Worship.

   Takepl. Why should you think so?

   Dick. Because Women never think themselves happy in Marriage.

   Takepl. You are mistaken; for Women never think themselves happy until they be Married.

   Dick. The truth is, Sir, that Women are always unhappy in their thoughts, both before and after Marriage; for, before Marriage they think themselves unhappy for want of a Husband; and after they are Married, they think themselves unhappy for having a Husband.

   Takepl. Indeed Womens thoughts are restless.

Enter Monsieur Facil, *and Monsieur* Adviser, *to Monsieur* Take-pleasure*; all in their Wooing Accoustrements.*

   Takepl. Gentlemen, I perceive you are all prepared to Woo.

   Facil. Yes faith, we are all prepared to be Wooers. But whom shall we get to present us to the Lady *Happy*?

Adviser. We must set on bold faces, and present our selves.

Takepl. Faith, I would not give my hopes for an indifferent portion.

Facil. Nor I.

Adviser. The truth is, We are all stuft with Hopes, as Cushions are with Feathers.

Enter Monsieur Courtly.

Court. O Gentlemen, Gentlemen, we are all utterly undone.

Adviser. Why, what's the matter?

Court. Why, the Lady *Happy* hath incloister'd her self, with twenty Ladies more.

Adviser. The Devil she hath?

Facil. The gods forbid.

Court. Whether it was the devil or the gods that have perswaded her to it, I cannot tell; but gone in she is.

Takepl. I hope it is but a blast of Devotion, which will soon flame out.

Enter Madam Mediator.

Takepl. O Madam *Mediator*, we are all undone, the Lady *Happy* is incloister'd.

Mediat. Yes, Gentlemen, the more is the pitty.

Adviser. Is there no hopes?

Mediat. Faith, little.

Facil. Let us see the Clergy to perswade her out, for the good of the Commonwealth.

Mediat. Alas Gentlemen! they can do no good, for she is not a Votress to the gods but to Nature.

Court. If she be a Votress to Nature, you are the only Person fit to be Lady Prioress; and so by your power and authority you may give us leave to visit your Nuns sometimes.

Mediat. Not but at a Grate, unless in time of Building, or when they are sick; but howsoever, the Lady *Happy* is Lady-Prioress her self, and will admit none of the Masculine Sex, not so much as to a Grate, for she will suffer no grates about the Cloister; she has also Women-Physicians, Surgeons and Apothecaries, and she is the chief Confessor her self, and gives what Indulgences or Absolutions she pleaseth: Also, her House, where she hath made her Convent, is so big and convenient, and so strong, as it needs no addition or repair: Besides, she has so much compass of ground within her walls, as there is not only room and place enough for Gardens, Orchards, Walks, Groves, Bowers, Arbours, Ponds, Fountains, Springs and the like; but also conveniency for much Provision, and hath Women for every Office and Employment: for though she hath not above twenty Ladies with her, yet she hath a numerous Company of Female Servants, so as there is no occasion for Men.

Takepl. If there be so many Women, there will be the more use for Men: But pray Madam *Mediator*, give me leave, rightly to understand you, by being more clearly informed: you say, The Lady *Happy* is become a Votress to Nature; and if she be a Votress to Nature, she must be a Mistress to Men.

Mediat. By your favour, Sir, she declares, That she hath avoided the company of Men, by retirement, meerly, because she would enjoy the variety of Pleasures, which are in Nature; of which, she says, Men are Obstructers; for, instead of increasing Pleasure, they produce Pain; and, instead of giving Content, they increase Trouble; instead of making the Femal-Sex Happy, they make them Miserable; for which, she hath banished the Masculine Company for ever.

Adviser. Her Heretical Opinions ought not to be suffer'd, nor her Doctrine allow'd; and she ought to be examined by a Masculine Synod, and punish'd with a severe Husband, or tortured with a deboist[1] Husband.

Mediat. The best way, Gentlemen, is to make your Complaints, and put up a Petition to the State, with your desires for a Redress.

Court. Your Counsel is good.

Facil. We will follow it, and go presently about it.

Exeunt.

SCENE II

Enter the Lady Happy, *with her Ladies; as also Madam* Mediator.

Lady *Happy.*
Ladies, give me leave to desire your Confession, whether or no you

---

1 debauched

repent your Retirement.

Ladies. Most excellent Lady, it were as probable a repentance could be in Heaven amongst Angels as amongst us.

L. *Happy.* Now Madam *Mediator*, let me ask you, Do you condemn my act of Retirement?

Mediat. I approve of it with admiration and wonder, that one that is so young should be so wise.

L. *Happy.* Now give me leave to inform you, how I have order'd this our *Convent of Pleasure*; first, I have such things as are for our Ease and Conveniency; next for Pleasure, and Delight; as I have change of Furniture, for my house; according to the four Seasons of the year, especially our Chambers: As in the Spring, our Chambers are hung with Silk-Damask, and all other things suitable to it; and a great Looking-Glass in each Chamber, that we may view our selves and take pleasure in our own Beauties, whilst they are fresh and young; also, I have in each Chamber a Cupboard of such plate, as is useful, and whatsoever is to be used is there ready to be imployed; also, I have all the Floor strew'd with sweet Flowers: In the Summer I have all our Chambers hung with Taffety, and all other things suitable to it, and a Cup-board of Purseline,[1] and of Plate, and all the Floore strew'd every day with green Rushes or Leaves, and Cisterns placed neer our Beds-heads, wherein Water may run out of small Pipes made for that purpose: To invite repose in the Autumn, all our Chambers are hung with Gilt Leather, or Franchipane;[2] also, Beds and all other things suitable; and the Rooms Matted with very fine Mats: In the Winter our Chambers must be hung with Tapestry, and our Beds of Velvet, lined with Sattin, and all things suitable to it, and all the Floor spread over with *Turkie*[3] Carpets, and a Cup-board of Gilt Plate; and all the Wood for Firing to be Cypress and Juniper; and all the Lights to be Perfumed Wax; also, the Bedding and Pillows are ordered according to each Season; *viz.* to be stuft with Feathers in the Spring and Autumn, and with Down in the Winter, but in the Summer to be only Quilts, either of Silk, or fine Holland;[4] and our Sheets, Pillows, Table-Clothes and Towels, to be of pure fine Holland, and every day clean; also, the

---

1 porcelain
2 frangipane: a perfume prepared from the flower of the red jasmine
3 Turkish
4 a fine linen fabric

Rooms we eat in, and the Vessels we feed withal, I have according to each Season; and the Linnen we use to our Meat, to be pure fine Diaper,[1] and Damask, and to change it fresh every course of Meat: As for our Galleries, Stair-Cases, and Passages, they shall be hung with various Pictures; and, all along the Wall of our Gallery, as long as the Summer lasts, do stand, upon Pedestals, Flower-pots, with various Flowers; and in the Winter Orange-Trees: and my Gardens to be kept curiously, and flourish, in every Season of all sorts of Flowers, sweet Herbs and Fruits, and kept so as not to have a Weed in it, and all the Groves, Wildernesses, Bowers and Arbours pruned, and kept free from dead Boughs Branches or Leaves; and all the Ponds, Rivolets, Fountains, and Springs, kept clear, pure and fresh: Also, we will have the choisest Meats every Season doth afford, and that every day our Meat, be drest several ways, and our drink cooler or hotter according to the several Seasons; and all our Drinks fresh and pleasing: Change of Garments are also provided, of the newest fashions for every Season, and rich Trimming; so as we may be accoutred properly, and according to our several pastimes: and our Shifts shall be of the finest and purest Linnen that can be bought or spun.

Ladies. None in this World can be happier.

L. *Happy.* Now Ladies, let us go to our several Pastimes, if you please.

Exeunt.

Scene III.

Enter Two Ladies.

Lady *Amorous.*

Madam, how do you, since you were **Married?**

L. *Vertue.* Very well, I thank you.

L. *Amor.* I am not so well as I wish I were.

Enter Madam Mediator *to them.*

M. *Mediat.* Ladies, do you hear the News?

L. *Vertue.* What News?

M. *Mediat.* Why there is a great Foreign Princess arrived, hearing of the famous *Convent of Pleasure,* to be one of Nature's Devotes.

---

1   linen or cotton fabric with small diamond pattern

L. *Amor.* What manner of Lady is she?

M. *Mediat.* She is a Princely brave Woman truly, of a Masculine Presence.

L. *Vertue.* But, Madam *Mediator,* Do they live in such Pleasure as you say? for they'l admit you, a Widow, although not us, by reason we are Wives.

M. *Mediat.* In so much Pleasure, as Nature never knew, before this *Convent* was: and for my part, I had rather be one in the *Convent of Pleasure,* then Emperess of the whole World; for every Lady there enjoyeth as much Pleasure as any absolute Monarch can do, without the Troubles and Cares, that wait on Royalty; besides, none can enjoy those Pleasures They have, unless they live such a retired or retreated life free from the Worlds vexations.

L. *Vertue.* Well, I wish I might see and know, what Pleasures they enjoy.

M. *Mediat.* If you were there, you could not know all their Pleasure in a short time, for their Varieties will require a long time to know their several Changes; besides, their Pleasures and Delights vary with the Seasons; so that what with the several Seasons, and the Varieties of every Season, it will take up a whole life's time.

L. *Vertue.* But I could judg of their Changes by their single Principles.

M. *Mediat.* But they have Variety of one and the same kind.

L. *Vertue.* But I should see the way or manner of them.

M. *Mediat.* That you might. *Exeunt.*

Scene IV.

Enter Monsieur Adviser, Courtly, Take-pleasure, *and* Facil.

Monsieur *Courtly.*

Is there no hopes to get those Ladies out of their *Convent?*

Adviser. No faith, unless we could set the *Convent* on fire.

Takepl. For *Jupiter's* sake, let us do it, let's every one carry a Firebrand to fire it.

Court. Yes, and smoak them out, as they do a Swarm of Bees.

Facil. Let's go presently about it.

Adviser. Stay, there is a great Princess there.

Takepl. 'Tis true, but when that Princess is gone, we will surely do it.

Adviser. Yes, and be punish'd for our Villany.

Takepl. It will not prove Villany, for we shall do Nature good service.

Adviser. Why, so we do Nature good service, when we get a Wench with Child, but yet the Civil Laws do punish us for it.

Court. They are not Civil Laws that punish Lovers.

Adviser. But those are Civil Laws that punish Adulterers.

Court. Those are Barbarous Laws that make Love Adultery.

Adviser. No, Those are Barbarous that make Adultery Love.

Facil. Well, leaving Love and Adultery, They are foolish Women that vex us with their Retirement.

Adviser. Well, Gentlemen, although we rail at the Lady *Happy* for Retiring, yet if I had such an Estate as she, and would follow her Example; I make no doubt but you would all be content to encloister your selves with me upon the same conditions, as those Ladies incloister themselves with her.

Takepl. Not unless you had Women in your *Convent.*

Adviser. Nay, faith, since Women can quit the pleasure of Men, we Men may well quit the trouble of Women.

Court. But is there no place where we may peak[1] into the *Convent?*

Adviser. No, there are no Grates, but Brick and Stone-walls.

Facil. Let us get out some of the Bricks or Stones.

Adviser. Alas! the Walls are a Yard-thick.

Facil. But nothing is difficult to Willing-minds.

Adviser. My Mind is willing; but my Reason tells me, It is impossible; wherefore, I'le never go about it.

Takepl. Faith, let us resolve to put our selves in Womens apparel, and so by that means get into the *Convent.*

Adviser. We shall be discover'd.

Takepl. Who will discover Us?

Adviser. We shall discover our Selves.

Takepl. We are not such fools as to betray our Selves.

Adviser. We cannot avoid it, for, our very Garb and Behaviour; besides, our Voices will discover us: for we are as untoward to make

---

1   peek

Courtsies in Petticoats, as Women are to make Legs[1] in Breeches; and it will be as great a difficulty to raise our Voices to a Treble-sound, as for Women to press down their Voices to a Base; besides, We shall never frame our Eyes and Mouths to such coy, dissembling looks, and pritty simpering Mopes and Smiles, as they do.

Court. But we will go as strong lusty Country-Wenches, that desire to serve them in Inferiour Places, and Offices, as Cook-maids, Laundry-maids, Dairy-maids, and the like.

Facil. I do verily believe, I could make an indifferent Cook-maid, but not a Laundry, nor a Dairy-maid; for I cannot milk Cows, nor starch Gorgets,[2] but I think I could make a pretty shift, to wash some of the Ladies Night-Linnen.

Takepl. But they imploy Women in all Places in their Gardens; and for Brewing, Baking and making all sorts of things; besides, some keep their Swine, and twenty such like Offices and Employments there are which we should be very proper for.

Facil. O yes, for keeping of Swine belongs to Men; remember the *Prodigal Son.*

Adviser. Faith, for our Prodigality we might be all Swin-heards.

Court. Also we shall be proper for Gardens, for we can dig, and set, and sow.

Takepl. And we are proper for Brewing.

Adviser. We are more proper for Drinking, for I can drink good Beer, or Ale, when 'tis Brew'd; but I could not brew such Beer, or Ale, as any man could drink.

Facil. Come, come, we shall make a shift one way or other: Besides, we shall be very willing to learn, and be very diligent in our Services, which will give good and great content; wherefore, let us go and put these designes into execution.

Courtly. Content, content.

Adviser. Nay, faith, let us not trouble our Selves for it, 'tis in vain.

Exeunt.

---

1 to bow
2 gorget: a deep cape-like collar used as an ornamental neck-covering

Illustration 5: In Margaret Cavendish's *Convent of Pleasure* (1668), Act 3, Scene 1, as Lady Happy falls in love with the Princess, she has to reassess her views on same-sex relationships. This illustration is taken from Gweno Williams's videotape of her 1995 première production of the play at the University College of Ripon and York St. John, directed by Bill Pinner. Lady Happy was played by Sarah Davies, the Princess by Steph Boyd. Video recording by Louis Purver.

Enter the Princess, *and the Lady* Happy, *with the
rest of the Ladies belonging to the Convent.*

Lady *Happy.*

Madam, Your Highness has done me much Honour, to come from
a Splendid Court to a retired *Convent.*

Prin. Sweet Lady *Happy,* there are many, that have quit their
Crowns and Power, for a Cloister of Restraint; then well may I quit a
Court of troubles for a *Convent of Pleasure*: but the greatest pleasure I
could receive, were, To have your Friendship.

L. Happy. I should be ungrateful, should I not be not only your
Friend, but humble Servant.

Prin. I desire you would be my Mistress, and I your Servant;[1] and
upon this agreement of Friendship I desire you will grant me one
Request.

L. Happy. Any thing that is in my power to grant.

Prin. Why then, I observing in your several Recreations, some of
your Ladies do accoustre Themselves in Masculine-Habits, and act
Lovers-parts; I desire you will give me leave to be sometimes so
accoustred and act the part of your loving Servant.

L. Happy. I shall never desire to have any other loving Servant then
your Self.

Prin. Nor I any other loving Mistress then Your-Self.

L. Happy. More innocent Lovers never can there be,
Then my most Princely Lover, that's a She.

Prin. Nor never Convent did such pleasures give,
Where Lovers with their Mistresses may live.

Enter a Lady, *asking whether they will see the Play.*

Lady. May it please your Highness, the Play is ready to be Acted.

The Scene is opened, the Princess *and L.* Happy *sit down,*

---

1   According to seventeenth-century courtship conventions, "servant" and "mistress"
    were technical terms for a male suitor and the female object of his love.

and the Play is Acted within the Scene; the Princess
and the L. Happy *being Spectators.*

Enter one drest like a Man that speaks the Prologue.

Noble Spectators, you shall see to night
A Play, which though't[1] be dull, yet's short to sight;
For, since we cannot please your Ears with Wit,
We will not tyre your limbs, long here to sit.

SCENE II.

Enter Two mean[2] Women.

First Woman.

O Neighbour well met, where have you been?

2 *Woman.* I have been with my Neighbour the Cobler's Wife to comfort her for the loss of her Husband, who is run away with Goody *Mettle* the Tinker's Wife.

1 *Woman.* I would to Heaven my Husband would run away with Goody *Shred* the Botcher's Wife, for he lies all day drinking in an Ale-house, like a drunken Rogue as he is, and when he comes home, he beats me all black and blew, when I and my Children are almost starved for want.

2 *Woman.* Truly Neighbour, so doth my Husband; and spends not only what he gets, but what I earn with the sweat of my brows, the whilst my Children cry for bread, and he drinks that away, that should feed my small Children, which are too young to work for themselves.

1 *Woman.* But I will go, and pull my Husband out of the Ale-house, or I'le break their Lattice-windows down.

2 *Woman.* Come, I'le go and help; for my Husband is there too: but we shall be both beaten by them.

1 *Woman.* I care not: for I will not suffer him to be drunk, and I and my Children starve; I had better be dead.

Exeunt.

---

1 though it
2 lower-class

Scene III

Enter a Lady *and her* Maid.

Lady. Oh, I am sick!

Maid. You are breeding a Child, Madam.

Lady. I have not one minutes time of health. *Ex[eunt].*

Scene IV.

Enter Two Ladies.

First Lady. Why weep you, Madam?

2 Lady. Have I not cause to weep when my Husband hath play'd all his Estate away at Dice and Cards, even to the Clothes on his back?

1 Lady. I have as much cause to weep then as you; for, though my Husband hath not lost his Estate at play, yet he hath spent it amongst his Whores; and is not content to keep Whores abroad, but in my house, under my roof, and they must rule as chief Mistresses.

2 Lady. But my Husband hath not only lost his own Estate, but also my Portion; and hath forced me with threats, to yield up my Jointure,[1] so that I must beg for my living, for any thing I know as yet.

1 Lady. If all Married Women were as unhappy as I, Marriage were a curse.

2 Lady. No doubt of it. *Exeunt.*

Scene V

*Enter a Lady, as almost distracted, running about the Stage,
and her Maid follows her.*

Lady. Oh! my Child is dead, my Child is dead, what shall I do, what shall I do?

Maid. You must have patience, Madam.

Lady. Who can have patience to lose their only Child? who can! Oh I shall run mad, for I have no patience.

---

1   It was illegal for a husband to spend his wife's jointure without obtaining her nominal consent.

Runs off the Stage. Exit Maid after her.

Scene VI.

Enter a Citizen's Wife, as into a Tavern, where a Bush¹ is hung out, and meets some Gentlemen there.

Citizen's Wife.

Pray Gentleman, is my Husband, Mr. *Negligent* here?

1 *Gent.* He was, but he is gone some quarter of an hour since.

Cit. Wife. Could he go,² Gentlemen?

2 *Gent.* Yes, with a Supporter.

Cit. Wife. Out upon him! must he be supported? Upon my credit Gentlemen, he will undo himself and me too, with his drinking and carelessness, leaving his Shop and all his Commodities at six's and seven's; and his Prentices and Journey-men are as careless and idle as he; besides, they cozen him of his Wares. But, was it a He or She-Supporter, my Husband was supported by?

1 *Gent.* A She-supporter; for it was one of the Maid-servants, which belong to this Tavern.

Cit. Wife. Out upon him Knave, must he have a She-supporter, in the Devil's name? but I'le go and seek them both out with a Vengeance.

2 *Gent.* Pray, let us intreat your stay to drink a cup of Wine with us.

Cit. Wife. I will take your kind Offer; for Wine may chance to abate Cholerick vapours, and pacifie the Spleen.

1 *Gent.* That it will; for Wine and good Company are the only abaters of Vapours.

2 *Gent.* It doth not abate Vapours so much as cure Melancholy.

Cit. Wife. In truth, I find a cup of Wine doth comfort me sometimes.

1 *Gent.* It will cheer the Heart.

2 *Gent.* Yes, and enlighten the Understanding.

Cit. Wife. Indeed, and my understanding requires enlightening.

Exeunt.

---

1 a branch hung up as a vintner's sign
2 walk

SCENE VII.

Enter a Lady big with Child, groaning as in labour, and a
Company of Women with her.

Oh my back, my back will break, Oh! Oh! Oh!
1 *Woman.* Is the Midwife sent for?
2 *Woman.* Yes, but she is with another Lady.
Lady. Oh my back! Oh! Oh! Oh! *Juno,*[1] give me some ease.

Exeunt.

SCENE VIII.

Enter two Ancient[2] *Ladies.*

1 *Lady.* I have brought my Son into the World with great pains,
bred him with tender care, much pains and great cost; and must he
now be hang'd for killing a Man in a quarrel? when he should be a
comfort and staff of my age, is he to be my ages affliction?
2 *Lady.* I confess it is a great affliction; but I have had as great; having had but two Daughters, and them fair ones, though I say it, and
might have matched them well: but one of them was got with Child
to my great disgrace; th' other run away with my Butler, not worth
the droppings of his Taps.[3]
1 *Lady.* Who would desire Children, since they come to such misfortunes?

Exeunt.

Scene IX

Enter one Woman meeting another.

1 *Woman.* Is the Midwife come, for my Lady is in a strong labour?

---

1   wife of Jupiter, and Roman goddess of childbirth
2   elderly
3   not worth the spillage of beer or wine from his casks, i.e. worthless (the butler was
    in charge of dispensing liquor for the household)

2 *Woman.* No, she cannot come, for she hath been with a Lady that hath been in strong labour these three days of a dead child, and 'tis thought she cannot be delivered.

Enter another Woman.

3 *Woman.* Come away, the Midwife is come.

1 *Woman.* Is the Lady deliver'd, she was withall?

3 *Woman.* Yes, of life; for she could not be delivered, and so she died.

2 *Woman.* Pray tell not our Lady so: for, the very fright of not being able to bring forth a Child will kill her.

Exeunt.

SCENE X.

Enter a Gentleman *who meets a fair Young Lady.*

Gent. Madam, my Lord desires you to command whatsoever you please, and it shall be obey'd.

Lady. I dare not command, but I humbly intreat, I may live quiet and free from his *Amours.*

Gent. He says he cannot live, and not love you.

Lady. But he may live, and not lie with me.

Gent. He cannot be happy, unless he enjoy you.

Lady. And I must be unhappy, if he should.

Gent. He commanded me to tell you that he will part from his Lady for your sake.

Lady. Heaven forbid, I should part Man and Wife.

Gent. Lady, he will be divorced for your sake.

Lady. Heaven forbid I should be the cause of a Divorce between a Noble Pair.

Gent. You had best consent; for, otherwise he will have you against your will.

Lady. I will send his Lordship an answer to morrow; pray him to give me so much time.

Gent. I shall, Lady.   *Exit* Gentleman.

Lady *Sola*

Lady. I must prevent my own ruin, and the sweet virtuous Ladies, by going into a Nunnery; wherefore, I'le put my self into one to night:

There will I live, and serve the Gods on high,
And leave this wicked World and Vanity.

Exeunt.

One enters and speaks the Epilogue

> *Marriage is a Curse we find,*
> *Especially to Women kind:*
> *From the Cobler's Wife we see,*
> *To Ladies, they unhappie be.*

L. Happy to the Prin. Pray Servant, how do you like this Play?

Prin. My sweet Mistress, I cannot in conscience approve of it; for though some few be unhappy in Marriage, yet there are many more that are so happy as they would not change their condition.

L. Happy. O Servant, I fear you will become an Apostate.

Prin. Not to you sweet Mistress. *Exeunt.*

Enter the Gentlemen.

1 *Gent.* There is no hopes of dissolving this *Convent of Pleasure.*

2 *Gent.* Faith, not as I can perceive.

3 *Gent.* We may be sure, this *Convent* will never be dissolved, by reason it is ennobled with the company of great Princesses, and glorified with a great Fame; but the fear is, that all the rich Heirs will make *Convents*, and all the Young Beauties associate themselves in such *Convents.*

1 *Gent.* You speak reason; wherefore, let us endeavour to get Wives, before they are Incloister'd.

Exeunt.

ACT IV. SCENE I.

Enter Lady Happy *drest as a Shepherdess; She walks very Melancholy, then speaks as to her self.*

My Name is *Happy*, and so was my Condition, before I saw this Princess; but now I am like to be the most unhappy Maid alive: But why may not I love a Woman with the same affection I could a Man?

No, no, Nature is Nature, and still will be

The same she was from all Eternity.

Enter the Princess *in Masculine Shepherd's Clothes.*

Prin. My dearest Mistress, do you shun my Company? is your Servant become an offence to your sight?

L. Happy. No, Servant! your Presence is more acceptable to me then the Presence of our Goddess Nature, for which she, I fear will punish me, for loving you more then I ought to love you.

Prin. Can Lovers love too much?

L. Happy. Yes, if they love not well.

Prin. Can any Love be more vertuous, innocent and harmless then ours?

L. Happy. I hope not.

Prin. Then let us please our selves, as harmless Lovers use to do.

L. Happy. How can harmless Lovers please themselves?

Prin. Why very well, as, to discourse, imbrace and kiss, so mingle souls together.

L. Happy. But innocent Lovers do not use to kiss.

Prin. Not any act more frequent amongst us Women-kind; nay, it were a sin in friendship, should not we kiss: then let us not prove our selves Reprobates.

They imbrace and kiss, and hold each other in their Arms.

Prin. These my Imbraces though of Femal kind,

May be as fervent as a Masculine mind.

The Scene is open'd, the Princess *and L.* Happy *go in.*
A Pastoral within the Scene.

The Scene is changed into a Green, or Plain, where Sheep are feeding, and a
May-Pole in the middle.
L. Happy as a Shepherdess, and the Princess
as a Shepherd are sitting there.
Enter another Shepherd, and Wooes the Lady Happy.

Shepherd.

Fair Shepherdess do not my Suit deny,
O grant my Suit, let me not for Love die:
Pity my Flocks, Oh save their Shepherd's life;
Grant you my Suit, be you their Shepherd's Wife.
L. *Happy.* How can I grant to every ones request?
Each Shepherd's Suit lets me not be at rest;
For which I wish, the Winds might blow them far,
That no Love-Suit might enter to my Ear.

Enter Madam Mediator in a Shepherdess dress, and
another Shepherd.

Sheph. Good Dame unto your Daughter speak for me.
Perswade her I your Son in Law may be:
I'le serve your Swine, your Cows bring home to Milk;
Attend your Sheep, whose Wool's as soft as Silk;
I'le plow your Grounds, Corn I'le in Winter sow,
Then reap your Harvest, and your Grass I'le mow;
Gather your Fruits in Autumn from the Tree.
All this and more I'le do, if y'speak for me.
Shepherdess. My Daughter vows a single life,
And swears, she n're will be a Wife;
But live a Maid, and Flocks will keep,
And her chief Company shall be Sheep.

The Princess as a Shepherd, speaks to the Lady Happy.

Prin. My Shepherdess, your Wit flies high,
Up to the Skie,
And views the Gates of Heaven,
Which are the Planets Seven;

Sees how fixt Stars are plac'd,
And how the Meteors wast;
What makes the Snow so white,
And how the Sun makes light;
What makes the biting Cold
On every thing take hold;
And Hail a mixt degree,
'Twixt Snow and Ice you see
From whence the Winds do blow;
What Thunder is, you know,
And what makes Lightning flow
Like liquid streams, you show.
From Skie you come to th' Earth,
And view each Creature's birth;
Sink to the Center deep,
Where all dead bodies sleep;
And there observe to know,
What makes the Minerals grow;
How Vegetables sprout,
And how the Plants come out;
Take notice of all Seed,
And what the Earth doth breed;
Then view the Springs below,
And mark how Waters flow;
What makes the Tides to rise
Up proudly to the Skies,
And shrinking back descend,
As fearing to offend.
Also your Wit doth view
The Vapour and the Dew,
In Summer's heat, that Wet
Doth seem like the Earth's Sweat;
In Winter-time, that Dew
Like paint's white to the view,
Cold makes that thick, white, dry;
As *Cerusse*[1] it doth lie

---

1 ceruse: white lead used as paint or cosmetic

On th' Earth's black face, so fair
As painted Ladies are;
But, when a heat is felt,
That Frosty paint doth melt.
    Thus Heav'n and Earth you view,
And see what's Old, what's New;
How Bodies Transmigrate,
Lives are Predestinate.
Thus doth your Wit reveal
What Nature would conceal.
L. *Happy.* My Shepherd,
All those that live do know it,
That you are born a Poet,
Your Wit doth search Mankind,
In Body and in Mind;
The Appetites you measure,
And weigh each several Pleasure;
Do figure every Passion,
And every Humor's fashion;
See how the Fancie's wrought,
And what makes every Thought;
Fadom¹ Conceptions low,
From whence Opinions flow;
Observe the Memorie's length,
And Understanding's strength
Your Wit doth Reason find,
The Centre of the Mind,
Wherein the Rational Soul
Doth govern and controul,
There doth She sit in State,
Predestinate by Fate,
And by the Gods Decree,
That Sovereign She should be.
    And thus your Wit can tell,
How Souls in Bodies dwell;
As that the Mind dwells in the Brain,

---

1   to fathom, thoroughly understand

And in the Mind the Soul doth raign,
And in the Soul the life doth last,
For with the Body it doth not wast;
Nor shall Wit like the Body die,
But live in the World's Memory.

Prin. May I live in your favour, and be possest with your Love and Person, is the height of my ambitions.

L. *Happy.* I can neither deny you my Love nor Person.

Prin. In amourous Pastoral Verse we did not Woo.
As other Pastoral Lovers use to doo.

L. *Ha[ppy].* Which doth express, we shall more constant be,
And in a Married life better agree.

Prin. We shall agree, for we true Love inherit,
Join as one Body and Soul, or Heav'nly Spirit.

Here come Rural Sports, as Country Dances about the May-Pole: that Pair which Dances best is Crowned King and Queen of the Shepherds that year; which happens to the Princess, *and the Lady* Happy.

L. *Happy to the Princ.* Let me tell you, Servant, that our Custome is to dance about this May-Pole, and that Pair which Dances best is Crown'd King and Queen of all the Shepherds and Shepherdesses this year: Which Sport if it please you we will begin.

Prin. Nothing, Sweetest Mistress, that pleases you, can displease me.

They Dance; after the Dancing the Princess *and Lady* Happy *are Crowned with a Garland of Flowers: a Shepherd speaks.*

Written by my Lord Duke.[1]

You've won the prize; and justly; so we all
Acknowledg it with joy, and offer here
Our Hatchments[2] up, our Sheep-hooks as your due,
And Scrips of Corduant,[3] and Oaten pipe;

---

1   Cavendish's husband, William Cavendish, Duke of Newcastle
2   shield or tablet exhibiting a coat of arms
3   cordon: an ornamental cord used as an heraldic bearing

So all our Pastoral Ornaments we lay
Here at your Feet, with Homage to obay
All your Commands, and all these things we bring
In honour of our dancing Queen and King;
For Dancing heretofore has got more Riches
Then we can find in all our Shepherds Breeches;
Witness rich *Holmby:*[1] Long then may you live,
And for your Dancing what we have we give.

A Wassel is carried about and Syllibubs.[2]
Another Shepherd speaks, or Sings this that follows.

Written by my Lord Duke.

The Jolly Wassel now do bring,
With Apples drown'd in stronger Ale,
And fresher Syllibubs, and sing;
Then each to tell their Love-sick Tale:
So home by Couples, and thus draw
Our selves by holy *Hymen's*[3] Law.

The Scene Vanishes.
Enter the Princess *Sola, and walks a turn or two in a Musing posture, then views her Self, and speaks.*

Prin. What have I on a Petticoat, Oh *Mars!* thou God of War, pardon my sloth; but yet remember thou art a Lover, and so am I; but you will say, my Kingdom wants me, not only to rule, and govern it, but to defend it: But what is a Kingdom in comparison of a Beautiful Mistress? Base thoughts flie off, for I will not go; did not only a Kingdom, but the World want me.

Exeunt.

---

1 Holmby was the name of a house given by Queen Elizabeth I to her Lord Chancellor, Sir Christopher Hatton (1540-91), supposedly because he was such a good dancer (our grateful thanks to Anne Shaver for this reference).
2 wassail: spiced ale; syllabub: a drink made of milk or cream curdled with sweet wine or cider
3 Hymen: the god of marriage

Enter the Lady Happy *Sola, and Melancholy,*
and after a short Musing speaks.

L. *Happy.* O Nature, O you gods above,
Suffer me not to fall in Love;
O strike me dead here in this place
Rather then fall into disgrace.

Enter Madam Mediator.

M. *Mediat.* What, Lady *Happy,* solitary alone! and Musing like a
disconsolate Lover!
L. *Happy.* No, I was Meditating of Holy things.
M. *Mediat.* Holy things! what Holy things?
L. *Happy.* Why, such Holy things as the Gods are.
M. *Mediat.* By my truth, whether your Contemplation be of Gods
or of Men, you are become lean and pale since I was in the *Convent*
last.

Enter the Princess.

Princ. Come my sweet Mistress, shall we go to our Sports and
Recreations?
M. *Mediat.* Beshrew me, your Highness hath sported too much I
fear.
Princ. Why, Madam *Mediator,* say you so?
M. *Mediat.* Because the Lady *Happy* looks not well, she is become
pale and lean.
Princ. Madam *Mediator,* your eyes are become dim with Time; for
my sweet Mistress appears with greater splendor then the God of
Light.
M. *Mediat.* For all you are a great Princess, give me leave to tell
you,
I am not so old, nor yet so blind
But that I see you are too kind.
Princ. Well, Madam *Mediator,* when we return from our Recre-
ations, I will ask your pardon, for saying, your eyes are dim, condition-
ally you will ask pardon for saying, my Mistress looks not well.

Exeunt.

The Scene *is opened, and there is presented a Rock as in the Sea, whereupon sits the Princess and the Lady* Happy; *the* Princess *as the Sea-God* Neptune, *the Lady* Happy *as a Sea-Goddess: the rest of the Ladies sit somewhat lower, drest like Water-Nymphs; the* Princess *begins to speak a Speech in Verse, and after her the Lady* Happy *makes her Speech.*

I Am the King of all the Seas,
All Watry Creatures do me please,
Obey my Power and Command,
And bring me Presents from the Land;
The Waters open their Flood-gates,
Where Ships do pass, sent by the Fates;
Which Fates do yearly, as *May*-Dew,[1]
Send me a Tribute from *Peru*,[2]
From other Nations besides,
Brought by their Servants, Winds and Tides,
Ships fraught and Men to me they bring;
My Watery Kingdom lays them in.
Thus from the Earth a Tribute I
Receive, which shews my power thereby.
Besides, my Kingdom's richer far
Then all the Earth and every Star.
L. *Happy.* I feed the Sun, which gives them light,
And makes them shine in darkest night,
Moist vapour from my brest I give,
Which he sucks forth, and makes him live,
Or else his Fire would soon go out,
Grow dark, or burn the World throughout.
Princ. What Earthly Creature's like to me,
That hath such Power and Majestie?
My Palaces are Rocks of Stone,
And built by Nature's hand alone;
No base, dissembling, coz'ning Art

---

1 dew gathered at dawn on May-day, thought to have cosmetic properties
2 source of New World gold and other precious commodities

Do I imploy in any part,
In all my Kingdom large and wide,
Nature directs and doth provide
Me all Provisions which I need,
And Cooks my Meat on which I feed.
L. *Happy.* My Cabinets are Oyster-shells,
In which I keep my Orient-Pearls,
To open them I use the Tide,
As Keys to Locks, which opens wide,
The Oyster-shells then out I take;
Those, Orient-Pearls and Crowns do make;
And modest Coral I do wear,
Which blushes when it touches air.
On Silver-Waves I sit and sing,
And then the Fish lie listening:
Then sitting on a Rocky stone,
I comb my Hair with Fishes bone;
The whil'st *Apollo*,[1] with his Beams,
Doth dry my Hair from wat'ry streams.
His Light doth glaze the Water's face,
Make the large Sea my Looking-Glass;
So when I swim on Waters high,
I see my self as I glide by:
But when the Sun begins to burn,
I back into my Waters turn,
And dive unto the bottom low:
Then on my head the Waters flow,
In Curled waves and Circles round;
And thus with Waters am I Crown'd.
Princ. Besides, within the Waters deep,
In hollow Rocks my Court I keep;
Of Amber-greece[2] my Bed is made,
Whereon my softer Limbs are laid,
There take I Rest; and whil'st I sleep,
The Sea doth guard, and safe me keep
From danger; and, when I awake,

---

1   Apollo: the sun-god
2   ambergris: a wax-like substance found floating in tropical seas, used in perfumes

A Present of a Ship doth make.
No Prince on Earth hath more resort,
Nor keeps more Servants in his Court;
Of Mare-maids[1] you're waited on,
And Mare-men[2] do attend upon
My Person; some are Councellors,
Which order all my great Affairs;
Within my wat'ry Kingdom wide,
They help to rule, and so to guide
The Common-wealth; and are by me
Prefer'd unto an high degree.
Some Judges are, and Magistrates,
Decide each Cause, and end Debates;
Others, Commanders in the War;
And some to Governments prefer;
Others are *Neptun's* Priests which pray
And preach when is a Holy day.
And thus with Method order I,
And govern all with Majesty;
I am sole Monarch of the Sea,
And all therein belongs to me.

A Sea-Nymph Sings this following SONG.

1. *We Watery Nymphs Rejoyce and Sing*
   About God Neptune *our Sea's King;*
   In Sea-green Habits, for to move
   His God-head, for to fall in love.

2. *That with his Trident he doth stay*
   Rough foaming Billows which obay:
   And when in Triumph he doth stride
   His manag'd[3] Dolphin for to ride.

3. *All his Sea-people to his wish,*

---

1   mermaids
2   mermen
3   trained, like a horse trained for riding

From Whale *to* Herring *subject Fish,*
With Acclamations do attend him,
And pray's more Riches still to send him.

Exeunt.

The SCENE Vanishes.

ACT V. SCENE I.

Enter the Princess *and the Lady* Happy; *The* Princess *is in a Man's Apparel as going to Dance; they Whisper sometime; then the Lady* Happy *takes a Ribbon from her arm, and gives it to the* Princess, *who gives her another instead of that, and kisses her hand. They go in and come presently out again with all the Company to Dance, the Musick plays; And after they have Danced a little while, in comes Madam* Mediator *wringing her hands, and spreading her arms; and full of Passion cries out.*

O Ladies, Ladies! you're all betrayed, undone, undone; for there is a man disguised in the *Convent,* search and you'l find it.

They all skip from each other, as afraid of each other; only the Princess *and the Lady* Happy *stand still together.*

Princ. You may make the search, Madam *Mediator;* but you will quit[1] me, I am sure.

M. *Mediat.* By my faith but I will not, for you are most to be suspected.

Princ. But you say, the Man is disguised like a Woman, and I am accoustred[2] like a Man.

M. *Mediat.* Fidle, fadle, that is nothing to the purpose.

Enter an Embassador to the Prince;[3] *the Embassador kneels, the* Prince *bids him rise.*

---

1   acquit
2   accoutred: dressed
3   i.e. to the supposed Princess

Princ. What came you here for?

Embass. May it please your Highness, The Lords of your Council sent me to inform your Highness, that your Subjects are so discontented at your Absence, that if your Highness do not return into your Kingdom soon, they'l enter this Kingdom by reason they hear you are here; and some report as if your Highness were restrained as Prisoner.

Princ. So I am, but not by the State, but by this Fair Lady, who must be your Soveraigness.

The Embassador kneels and kisses her Hand.

Princ. But since I am discover'd, go from me to the Councellors of this State, and inform them of my being here, as also the reason, and that I ask their leave I may marry this Lady; otherwise, tell them I will have her by force of Arms.

Exit Embassador.

M. *Mediat.* O the Lord! I hope you will not bring an Army, to take away all the Women; will you?

Princ. No, Madam *Mediator*, we will leave you behind us.

Exeunt.

SCENE II.

Enter Madam Mediator *lamenting and crying with a Handkerchief in her hand.*

Written by my Lord Duke.

O Gentlemen, that I never had been born, we're all undone and lost!

Advis. Why, what's the matter?

M. *Mediat.* Matter? nay, I doubt, there's too much Matter.

Advis. How?

M. *Mediat.* How, never such a Mistake; why we have taken a Man for a Woman.

Advis. Why, a Man is for a Woman.

M. *Mediat.* Fidle fadle, I know that as well as you can tell me; but there was a young Man drest in Woman's Apparel, and enter'd our *Convent*, and the Gods know what he hath done: He is mighty handsome, and that's a great Temptation to Virtue; but I hope all is well: But this wicked World will lay aspersion upon any thing or nothing; and therefore I doubt, all my sweet young Birds are undone, the Gods comfort them.

Courtly. But could you never discover it? nor have no hint he was a Man?

M. *Mediat.* No truly, only once I saw him kiss the Lady *Happy*; and you know Womens Kisses are unnatural, and me-thought they kissed with more alacrity then Women use, a kind of Titillation, and more Vigorous.

Advis. Why, did you not then examine it?

M. *Mediat.* Why, they would have said, I was but an old jealous fool, and laught at me; but Experience is a great matter; If the Gods had not been merciful to me, he might have faln upon me.

Courtly. Why, what if he had?

M. *Mediat.* Nay, if he had I care not: for I defie the Flesh as much as I renounce the Devil, and the pomp of this wicked World; but if I could but have sav'd my young sweet Virgins, I would willingly have sacrificed my body for them; for we are not born for our selves but for others.

Advis. 'Tis piously said, truly, lovingly and kindly.

M. *Mediat.* Nay, I have read the *Practice of Piety;*[1] but further they say, He is a Foreign Prince; and they say, They're very hot.

Courtly. Why, you are Madam *Mediator,* you must mediate and make a Friendship.

M. *Mediat.* Ods body[2] what do you talk of Mediation, I doubt they are too good Friends; Well, this will be news for Court, Town and Country, in private Letters, in the Gazette, and in abominable Ballets,[3] before it be long, and jeered to death by the pretending Wits; but, good Gentlemen, keep this as a Secret, and let not me be the Author,

---

1 *The Practise of Pietie* (1612) by Lewis Bayly, Bishop of Bangor, was one of the most popular seventeenth-century devotional manuals, having reached 45 editions by 1640.

2 euphemistic form of the imprecation "God's body"

3 street ballads

for you will hear abundantly of it before it be long.

Advis. But, Madam *Mediator*, this is no Secret, it is known all the Town over, and the State is preparing to entertain the Prince.

M. *Mediat.* Lord! to see how ill news will fly so soon abroad?

Courtly. Ill news indeed for us Wooers.

Advis. We only wooed in Imagination but not in Reality.

M. *Mediat.* But you all had hopes.

Advis. We had so; but she only has the fruition: for it is said, the Prince and she are agreed to Marry; and the State is so willing, as they account it an honour, and hope shall reap much advantage by the Match.

M. *Mediat.* Yes, yes; but there is an old and true Saying, *There's much between the Cup and the Lip.* Exeunt.

Scene III.

Enter the Prince *as Bridegroom, and the Lady* Happy *as Bride, hand in hand under a Canopy born over their heads by Men; the Magistrates march before, then the Hoboys;*[1] *and then the Bridal-Guests, as coming from the Church, where they were Married.*

All the Company bids them joy, they thank them.

Madam *Mediator.* Although your Highness will not stay to feast with your Guests, pray Dance before you go.

Princ. We will both Dance and Feast before we go; come Madam let us Dance, to please Madam *Mediator.*

The Prince *and* Princess *Dance.*

Princ. Now, Noble Friends, Dance you; and the *Princess,* and I, will rest our selves.

After they have Danced, the Lady Happy, *as now* Princess, *speaks to the Lady* Vertue.

L. *Happy speaks to* L. *Vertue.* Lady *Vertue,* I perceive you keep *Mimick*[2] still.

---

1   hautboy: a performer on the oboe
2   mimic: a pantomimist or buffoon

L. *Happy to the Princ.* Sir, this is the *Mimick* I told you of.

L. *Happy to Mimick.* Mimick, will you leave your Lady and go with me?

Mimick. I am a Married Man, and have Married my Ladies Maid *Nan*, and she will keep me at home do what I can; but you've now a *Mimick* of your own, for the *Prince* has imitated a Woman.

L. *Happy.* What you Rogue, do you call me a Fool?

Mimick. Not I, please your Highness, unless all Women be Fools.

Princ. Is your Wife a Fool?

Mimick. Man and Wife, 'tis said, makes but one Fool.

He kneels to the Prince.

Mimick. I have an humble Petition to your Highness.

Princ. Rise; What Petition is that?

Mimick. That your Highness would be pleased to divide the *Convent* in two equal parts; one for Fools, and th' other for Married Men, as mad Men.

Princ. I'le divide it for Virgins and Widows.

Mimick. That will prove a *Convent of Pleasure* indeed; but they will never agree, especially if there be some disguised Prince amongst them; but you had better bestow it on old decrepit and bed-rid Matrons, and then it may be call'd the *Convent of Charity*, if it cannot possibly be named the *Convent of Chastity*.

Princ. Well, to shew my Charity, and to keep your Wife's Chastity, I'le bestow my bounty in a Present, on the Condition you speak the *Epilogue*. Come, Noble Friends, let us feast before we part.

Exeunt.

Mimick Solus.

Mimick. An *Epilogue* says he, the devil an *Epilogue* have I: let me study.

He questions and answers Himself.

I have it, I have it; No faith, I have it not; I lie, I have it, I say, I have it not; Fie *Mimick*, will you lie? Yes, *Mimick,* I will lie, if it be my plea-

Illustration 6: From Gweno Williams's 1995 production of *The Convent of Pleasure*, Act IV, Scene 1. At the end of the play, Lady Happy and the Prince marry, and heterosexuality seems to be reinstated. But has the Prince's manhood been transformed by his playful inpersonation of a woman?

sure: But I say, it is gone; What is gone? The *Epilogue*; When had you it? I never had it; then you did not lose it; that is all one, but I must speak it, although I never had it; How can you speak it, and never had it? I marry, that's the question; but words are nothing, and then an *Epilogue* is nothing, and so I may speak nothing; Then nothing be my Speech.

He Speaks the EPILOGUE.

Noble Spectators by this Candle-light,
I know not what to say, but bid, Good Night:
I dare not beg Applause, our Poetess then
Will be enrag'd, and kill me with her Pen;
For she is careless, and is void of fear;
If you dislike her Play she doth not care.
But I shall weep, my inward Grief shall show
Through Floods of Tears, that through my Eyes will flow.
And so poor Mimick *he for sorrow die.*
And then through pity you may chance to cry:
But if you please, you may a Cordial give,
Made up with Praise, and so he long may live.

FINIS.

The ACTORS NAMES.

Three Gentlemen.
Lady Happy.
Madam Mediator.
Monsieur Take-pleasure, and Dick his Man.
Monsieur Facil.
Monsieur Adviser.
Monsieur Courtly.
Lady Amorous.
Lady Vertue.
The Princess.
Two mean[1] Women.

---

1   humble or lower-class

A Lady, and her Maid.
Two Ladies.
A distracted[1] *Lady, and her Maid.*
A Citizen's Wife.
Two Ancient Ladies.
A Gentleman and a Young Lady.
A Shepherd.
Sea-Nymphs.
An Ambassador.

---

1   agitated or deranged

2. THE PREFACE TO THE READER, *THE WORLDS OLIO* (1655)

One of Margaret Cavendish's earliest works, *The Worlds Olio* is a miscellany of poems and essays on a diversity of scientific, medical, historical, and philosophical topics. In her Preface to the Reader, she addresses the issue of gender differences, offering an interpretation in conformity with the dominant scientific and medical views of the time, which regarded women as naturally inferior and subordinate to men. But even as Cavendish concedes women's secondary status, she argues that some women might be wiser than some men, whether as a result of education or individual variation; she also suggests that women might claim preeminence by virtue of certain "effeminate" qualities, such as their beauty and charm.

It cannot be expected I should write so wisely or wittily as Men, being of the Effeminate Sex, whose Brains Nature hath mix'd with the coldest and softest Elements;[1] and to give my Reason why we cannot be so wise as Men, I take leave and ask Pardon of my own Sex, and present my Reasons to the Judgement of Truth; but I believe all of my own Sex will be against me out of partiality to themselves, and all Men will seem to be against me, out of a Complement to Women, or at least for quiet and ease sake, who know Womens Tongues are like Stings of Bees; and what man would endure our effeminate Monarchy to swarm about their ears? for certainly he would be stung to death; so I shall be condemned of all sides, but Truth, who helps to defend me. True it is, our Sex make great complaints, that men from their first Creation usurped a Supremacy to themselves, although we were made equal by Nature,[2] which Tyrannical Government they have kept ever since, so that we could never come to be free, but rather more and more enslaved, using us either like Children, Fools, or Subjects, that is, to flatter or threaten us, to

---

1 This passage refers to the humoral theory, which postulated that women were naturally inferior because their bodies were composed of cold and wet humours, whereas men's bodies were composed of the more active hot and dry humours; for a discussion of the theory as applied to gender differences, see Mendelson and Crawford 19-20, 72.

2 Some early modern theologians suggested that Eve had enjoyed social and political equality with Adam before her disobedience resulted in the Fall of mankind.

allure or force us to obey, and will not let us divide the World equally with them, as to Govern and Command, to direct and Dispose as they do; which Slavery hath so dejected our spirits, as we are become so stupid, that Beasts are but a Degree below us, and Men use us but a Degree above Beasts; whereas in Nature we have as clear an understanding as Men, if we were bred in Schools to mature our Brains, and to manure our Understandings, that we might bring forth the Fruits of Knowledge. But to speak truth, Men have great Reason not to let us in to their Governments, for there is great difference betwixt the Masculine Brain and the Feminine, the Masculine Strength and the Feminine; For could we choose out of the World two of the ablest Brain and strongest Body of each Sex, there would be great difference in the Understanding and Strength; for Nature hath made Mans Body more able to endure Labour, and Mans Brain more clear to understand and contrive than Womans; and as great a difference there is between them, as there is between the longest and strongest Willow, compared to the strongest and largest Oak; though they are both Trees, yet the Willow is but a yielding Vegetable, not fit nor proper to build Houses and Ships, as the Oak, whose strength can grapple with the greatest Winds, and plow the Furrows in the Deep; it is true, the Willows may make fine Arbours and Bowers, winding and twisting its wreathy stalks about, to make a Shadow to eclips the Light; or as a light Shield to keep off the sharp Arrows of the Sun, which cannot wound deep, because they fly far before they touch the Earth; or Men and Women may be compared to the Black-Birds, where the Hen can never sing with so strong and loud a Voice, nor so clear and perfect Notes as the Cock; her Breast is not made with that strength to strain so high; even so Women can never have so strong Judgment nor clear Understanding nor so perfect Rhetorick, to speak Orations with that Eloquence, as to Perswade so Forcibly, to Command so Powerfully, to Entice so Subtilly, and to Insinuate so Gently and Softly into the Souls of men; Or they may be compared to the Sun and Moon, according to the discription in the Holy Writ, which saith, *God made two great Lights, the one to Rule the Day, the other the Night*: So Man is made to Govern Common-Wealths, and Women their privat Families. And we find by experience, that the Sun is more Dry, Hot, Active, and Powerfull every way than the Moon; besides, the Sun is of a more strong and ruddier Complexion than the Moon; for we find she is Pale and Wan, Cold, Moist, and Slow in all her Operations; and if it be as Philosophers hold, that the Moon hath no Light but what it borrows from the Sun, so Women have no strength nor light of Understanding, but what is given them from Men; this is the Reason why we are not Mathematicians, Arithmeticians, Logicians, Geometricians, Cosmographers, and the like; This is the Reason we are not Witty Poets, Eloquent Orators, Subtill Schoolmen, Subtracting Chimists,[1] Rare Musicians, Curious Limners;[2] This is the reason we are not Navigators, Architectures,[3] Exact Surveyers, Inventive Artizans; This is the reason why we are not Skilfull Souldiers, Politick Statists,[4] Dispatchfull Secretaries, or Conquering Cæsars; but our Governments would be weak, had we not Masculine spirits and Counsellors to advise us; and for our Strength, we should make but feeble Mariners to tugg and pull up great Ropes and weighty Sayls in blustring Storms, if there were no other Pilots than the Effeminate Sex; neither would there be such Commerce of Nations as there is, nor would there be so much Gold and Silver and other Mineralls fetcht out of the Bowells of the Earth if there were none but Effeminate hands to use the Pick-axe and Spade; nor so many Cities built, if there were none but Women Labourers to cut out great Quarrs[5] of Stone, to hew down great timber Trees, and to draw up such Materials and Engins thereunto belonging; neither would there be such Barrs of Iron, if none but Women were to Melt and Hammer them out, whose weak spirits would suffocate and so faint with the heat, and their small Arms would sooner break than lift up such a weight, and beat out a Life, in striving to beat out a Wedge; neither would there be such Steeples and Pyramids, as there have been in this World, if there were no other than our tender Feet to climb, nor could our Brains endure the height, we should soon grow Dissy[6] and fall down drunk with too much thin Air; neither have Women such hard Chests and strong Lungs to keep in so much Breath, to dive to the bottome of the Sea, to fetch up the Treasures that lie in the watery Womb;

---

1 chemists
2 skilful artists
3 architects
4 statesmen
5 square pieces of stone
6 dizzy

neither can Women bring the furious and wild Horse to the Bit, quenching his fiery Courage, and bridling his strong swift Speed. This is the reason we are not so active in Exercise, nor able to endure Hard Labour, nor far Travells, nor to bear Weighty Burthens, to run long Jornies,[1] and many the like Actions which we by Nature are not made fit for: It is true, Education and Custom may adde somthing to harden us, yet never to make us so strong as the strongest of Men, whose Sinnews are tuffer, and Bones stronger, and Joints closer, and Flesh firmer, than ours are, as all Ages have shewn, and Times have produced. What Woman was ever so strong as *Sampson*, or so swift as *Hazael*?[2] neither have Women such tempered Brains as men, such high Imaginations, such subtill Conceptions, such fine Inventions, such solid Reasons, and such sound Judgement, such prudent Forecast, such constant Resolutions, such quick, sharp, and ready flowing Wits; what Women ever made such Laws as *Moses*, *Lycurgus*, or *Solon*, did? what Woman was ever so wise as *Salomon*, or *Aristotle*? so politick as *Achitophel*? so eloquent as *Tully*? so demonstrative as *Euclid*? so inventive as *Seth*, or *Archimedes*?[3] It was not a Woman that found out the Card, and Needle, and the use of the Loadstone;[4] it was not a Woman that invented Perspective-Glasses[5] to peirce into the Moon; it was not a Woman that found out the invention of writing Letters, and the Art of Printing; it was not a Woman that found out the invention of Gunpowder, and the art of Gunns. What Women were such Soldiers as *Hannibal*, *Cæsar*, *Tamberlain*, *Alexander*, and *Scanderbeg*?[6] what Woman was such a Chymist as *Paracelsus*? such a Physician as

---

1 journeys
2 Sampson: the biblical hero Samson; Hazael (c. 842-800 BCE): Syrian king whose military campaigns are recounted in 2 Kings 12-13
3 Lycurgus: legendary founder of the Spartan constitution and military system; Solon (c. 640- c. 560 BCE): celebrated Athenian legislator who reformed the Athenian constitution; Salomon: the biblical King Solomon; Achitophel: described in 2 Sam. 15-18 as one of Absolom's co-conspirators against King David; Tully: Tullius Cicero (106-43 BCE), famed Roman orator; Seth: third son of Adam and Eve, whose descendant Noah was the ancestor of all mankind (see Gen. 4:25-26); Archimedes (c. 287-212 BCE): considered the greatest mathematician of antiquity
4 magnetic compass
5 telescopes
6 Hannibal (247-182 BCE): Carthaginian general who crossed the Alps in order to attack the Romans during the second Punic War; Tamberlaine: the Tartar conqueror Timur (1333-1405), who ruled vast territories of central Asia and India, and was the

Hipocrates or *Galen?*[1] such a Poet as *Homer?* such a Painter as *Apelles?* such a Carver as *Pigmalion?* such an Architect as *Vitruviuss?* such a Musician as *Orpheus?*[2] What Women ever found out the Antipodes in imagination, before they were found out by Navigation, as a Bishop did?[3] or what ever did we do but like Apes, by Imitation? wherefore Women can have no excuse, or complaints of being subjects, as a hinderance from thinking; for Thoughts are free, those can never be inslaved, for we are not hindred from studying, since we are allowed so much idle time that we know not how to pass it away, but may as well read in our Closets, as Men in their Colleges; and Contemplation is as free to us as to Men to beget clear Speculation; Besides, most Scholars marry, and their heads are so full of their School Lectures, that they preach them over to their Wives when they come home, so that they know as well what was spoke, as if they had been there; and though most of our Sex are bred up to the Needle and Spindle, yet some are bred in the publike Theatres of the World; wherefore if Nature had made our Brains of the same temper as Mens, we should have had as clear Speculation, and had been as Ingenious and Inventive as Men: but we find She hath not, by the effects. And thus we may see by the weakness of our Actions, the Constitution of our Bodies; and by our Knowledge, the temper of our Brains; by our unsettled Resolutions, inconstant to our Promises, the perverseness of our Wills; by our facil Natures, violent in our Passions, supersititious in our Devotions, you may know our Humours; we have more Wit than Judgment, [are] more Active than Industrious, we have more

---

subject of Christopher Marlowe's first play, *Tamberlaine the Great*; Scanderbeg: the name given by the Turks to George Castriota (1403-67), an Albanian noble who led resistance against the advancing Ottoman Turkish empire

1 Paracelsus (1490-1541): Swiss physician and scientist, founder of alchemical medicine; Hippocrates (460-377 BCE): called "father of medicine", most famous of ancient Greek physicians; Galen (129-199): celebrated ancient physician whose medical theories modified and revised those of Aristotle.

2 Apelles (4th century BCE): celebrated Greek painter and portraitist; Pygmalion: legendary king of Cyprus, who fell in love with an ivory statue of a young woman which he himself had carved; Vitruvius: Roman architect and military engineer under Augustus; Orpheus: legendary Greek musician, who supposedly charmed wild beasts with his singing

3 Francis Godwin (1562-1633), Bishop of Llandaff and Hereford, who wrote *The man in the moone; or, A discourse of a voyage thither* (1638) under the pseudonym of Domingo Gonsales; the book describes an imaginary voyage through the centre of the earth.

Courage than Conduct, more Will than Strength, more Curiosity than Secrecy, more Vanity than good Houswifery, more Complaints than Pains; more Jealousie than Love, more Tears than Sorrow, more Stupidity than Patience, more Pride than Affability, more Beauty than Constancy, more Ill Nature than Good: Besides, the Education, and libertie of Conversation which Men have, is both unfit and dangerous to our Sex, knowing, that we may bear and bring forth Branches from a wrong Stock, by which every man would come to lose the property of their own Children; but Nature, out of love to the Generation of Men, hath made Women to be governed by Men, giving them Strength to rule, and Power to use their Authority.

And though it seem to be natural, that generally all Women are weaker than Men, both in Body and Understanding, and that the wisest Woman is not so wise as the wisest of Men, wherefore not so fit to Rule; yet some are far wiser than some men, like Earth; for some Ground, though it be Barren by Nature, yet, being well mucked and well manured, may bear plentifull Crops, and sprout forth diverse sorts of Flowers, when the fertiller and richer Ground shall grow rank and corrupt, bringing nothing but gross and stinking Weeds, for want of Tillage; So Women by Education may come to be far more knowing and learned, than some Rustick and Rude-bred[1] men. Besides, it is to be observed, that Nature hath Degrees in all her Mixtures and Temperaments, not only to her servile works, but in one and the same Matter and Form of Creatures, throughout all her Creations. Again, it is to be observed, that although Nature hath not made Women so strong of Body, and so clear of understanding, as the ablest of Men, yet she hath made them fairer, softer, slenderer, and more delicate than they, separating as it were the finer parts from the grosser, which seems as if Nature had made Women as pure white Manchet,[2] for her own Table, and Palat, where Men are like coarse houshold Bread which the servants feed on; and if she hath not tempered Womens Brains to that height of understanding, nor hath put in such strong Species of Imaginations, yet she hath mixed them with Sugar of sweet conceits; and if she hath not planted in their Dispositions such firm Resolutions, yet she hath sowed gentle and willing Obedience;

---

1 ignorant or uncultured
2 manchet: the finest quality wheat bread, eaten by the upper classes; servants ate coarse-textured bread made of a mixture of inferior grains such as rye or barley

and though she hath not filled the mind with such Heroick Gallantry, yet she hath laid in tender Affections, as Love, Piety, Charity, Clemency, Patience, Humility, and the like; which makes them neerest to resemble Angells, which are the perfectest of all her Works; where men by their Ambitions, Extortion,[1] Fury, and Cruelty, resemble the Devill; But some women are like Devills too, when they are possest with those Evills; and the best of men by their Heroick Magnanimous Minds, by their Ingenious and Inventive Wits, by their strong Judgments, by their prudent forecast, and wise Mannagements, are like to Gods.

---

1   extortion: the act of seizing something from a person by the use of undue authority or excessive force

3. *FEMALE ORATIONS, FROM ORATIONS OF DIVERS SORTS* (1662)

Female Orations forms the last section in Cavendish's book of *Orations of Divers Sorts* (1662). As she explains in her Preface,[1] one of the men's orations concerning the liberty of women "so Anger'd that Sex, as after the Mens Orations are ended, they privately Assemble together, where three or four take the place of an Orator, and Speak to the rest." The seven female orations that follow offer us a remarkably innovative and unfettered exploration of women's nature and potentialities.

FEMAL ORATIONS
PART XI.

I.

Ladies, Gentlewomen, and other Inferiours, but not Less Worthy, I have been Industrious to Assemble you together, and wish I were so Fortunate, as to perswade you to make a Frequentation, Association, and Combination amongst our Sex, that we may Unite in Prudent Counsels, to make our Selves as Free, Happy, and Famous as Men, whereas now we Live and Dye, as if we were Produced from Beast rather than from Men; for Men are Happy, and we Women are Miserable, they Possess all the Ease, Rest, Pleasure, Wealth, Power, and Fame, whereas Women are Restless with Labour, Easeless with Pain, Melancholy for want of Pleasures, Helpless for want of Power, and Dye in Oblivion for want of Fame; Nevertheless, Men are so Unconscionable and Cruel against us, as they Indeavour to Barr us of all Sorts or Kinds of Liberty, as not to Suffer us Freely to Associate amongst our Own Sex, but would fain Bury us in their Houses or Beds, as in a Grave; the truth is, we Live like Bats or Owls, Labour like Beasts, and Dye like Worms.

---

1 See above p. 90.

II.

Ladies, Gentlewomen, and other Inferiour Women, The Lady that Spoke to you, hath spoken Wisely and Eloquently in Expressing our Unhappiness, but she hath not Declared a Remedy, or Shew'd us a way to come Out of our Miseries; but if she could or would be our Guide, to lead us out of the Labyrinth Men have put us into, we should not only Praise and Admire her, but Adore and Worship her as our Goddess; but Alas, Men, that are not only our Tyrants, but our Devils, keep us in the Hell of Subjection, from whence I cannot Perceive any Redemption or Getting out; we may Complain, and Bewail our Condition, yet that will not Free us; we may Murmur and Rail against Men, yet they Regard not what we say: In short, our Words to Men are as Empty Sounds, our Sighs as Puffs of Wind, and our Tears as Fruitless Showres, and our Power is so Inconsiderable, as Men Laugh at our Weakness.

III.

Ladies, Gentlewomen, and other more Inferiours, The former *Orations* were Exclamations against Men, Repining at Their Condition, and Mourning for our Own; but we have no Reason to Speak against Men, who are our Admirers, and Lovers; they are our Protectors, Defenders, and Maintainers; they Admire our Beauties, and Love our Persons; they Protect us from Injuries, Defend us from Dangers, are Industrious for our Subsistence, and Provide for our Children; they Swim great Voyages by Sea, Travel long Journies by Land, to Get us Rarities and Curiosities; they Dig to the Centre of the Earth for Gold for us; they Dive to the Bottom of the Sea for Jewels for us; they Build to the Skies Houses for us; they Hunt, Foul, Fish, Plant, and Reap for Food for us; all which we could not do our Selves, and yet we Complain of Men, as if they were our Enemies, when as we could not possibly Live without them: which shews, we are as Ungratefull, as Inconstant; But we have more Reason to Murmur against Nature than against Men, who hath made Men more Ingenious, Witty, and Wise than Women, more Strong, Industrious, and Laborious than Women, for Women are Witless, and Strengthless, and Unprofitable

Creatures, did they not Bear Children.[1] Wherefore, let us Love men, Praise men, and Pray for men, for without Men we should be the most Miserable Creatures that Nature Hath, or Could make.

I V.

Noble Ladies, Gentlewomen, and other Inferiour Women, The former Oratoress sayes, we are Witless, and Strengthless; if so, it is that we Neglect the One, and make no Use of the Other, for Strength is Increased by Exercise, and Wit is Lost for want of Conversation; but to shew Men we are not so Weak and Foolish, as the former Oratoress doth Express us to be, let us Hawk, Hunt, Race, and do the like Exercises as Men have, and let us Converse in Camps, Courts, and Cities, in Schools, Colleges, and Courts of Judicature, in Taverns, Brothels, and Gaming Houses, all which will make our Strength and Wit known, both to Men, and to our own Selves, for we are as Ignorant of our Selves, as Men are of us. And how should we Know our Selves, when as we never made a Trial of our Selves? or how should Men know us, when as they never Put us to the Proof? Wherefore, my Advice is, we should Imitate Men, so will our Bodies and Minds appear more Masculine, and our Power will Increase by our Actions.

V.

Noble, Honourable, and Vertuous Women, The former Oration was to Perswade us to Change the Custom of our Sex, which is a Strange and Unwise Perswasion, since we cannot Change the Nature of our Sex, for we cannot make our selves Men; and to have Femal Bodies, and yet to Act Masculine Parts, will be very Preposterous and Unnatural; In truth, we shall make our Selves like as the Defects of Nature, as to be Hermaphroditical, as neither to be Perfect Women nor Perfect Men, but Corrupt and Imperfect Creatures; Wherefore, let me Perswade you, since we cannot Alter the Nature of our Persons, not

---

1   For early modern scientific and medical assumptions about woman's nature, see Mendelson and Crawford 18-30.

to Alter the Course of our Lives, but to Rule our Lives and Behaviours, as to be Acceptable and Pleasing to God and Men, which is to be Modest, Chast, Temperate, Humble, Patient, and Pious; also to be Huswifely, Cleanly, and of few Words, all which will Gain us Praise from Men, and Blessing from Heaven, and Love in this World, and Glory in the Next.

VI.

Worthy Women, The former Oratoress's Oration indeavours to Perswade us, that it would not only be a Reproach and Disgrace, but Unnatural for Women in their Actions and Behaviour to Imitate Men; we may as well say, it will be a Reproach, Disgrace, and Unnatural to Imitate the Gods, which Imitation we are Commanded both by the Gods and their Ministers, and shall we Neglect the Imitation of Men, which is more Easie and Natural than the Imitation of the Gods? for how can Terrestrial Creatures Imitate Celestial Deities? yet one Terrestrial may Imitate an other, although in different sorts of Creatures; Wherefore, since all Terrestrial Imitations ought to Ascend to the Better, and not to Descend to the Worse, Women ought to Imitate Men, as being a Degree in Nature more Perfect,[1] than they Themselves, and all Masculine Women ought to be as much Praised as Effeminate Men to be Dispraised, for the one Advances to Perfection, the other Sinks to Imperfection, that so by our Industry we may come at last to Equal Men both in Perfection and Power.

VII.

Noble Ladies, Honourable Gentlewomen, and Worthy Femal Commoners, The former Oratoress's Oration or Speech was to Perswade us Out of our Selves, as to be That, which Nature never Intended us to be, to wit Masculine; but why should we Desire to be Masculine, since our Own Sex and Condition is by far the Better? for if Men

---

1 According to Aristotle, woman was an error in creation, or an imperfect version of the male.

have more Courage, they have more Danger; and if Men have more Strength, they have more Labour than Women have; if Men are more Eloquent in Speech, Women are more Harmonious in Voice; if Men be more Active, Women are more Gracefull; if Men have more Liberty, Women have more Safety; for we never Fight Duels, nor Battels, nor do we go Long Travels or Dangerous Voyages; we Labour not in Building, nor Digging in Mines, Quarries, or Pits, for Metall, Stone, or Coals; neither do we Waste or Shorten our Lives with University or Scholastical Studies, Questions, and Disputes; we Burn not our Faces with Smiths Forges, or Chymist[1] Furnaces, and Hundreds of other Actions, which Men are Imployed in; for they would not only Fade the Fresh Beauty, Spoil the Lovely Features, and Decay the Youth of Women, causing them to appear Old, whilst they are Young, but would Break their Small Limbs, and Destroy their Tender Lives. Wherefore, Women have no Reason to Complain against Nature, or the God of Nature, for though the Gifts are not the Same they have given to Men, yet those Gifts they have given to Women, are much Better; for we Women are much more Favour'd by Nature than Men, in Giving us such Beauties, Features, Shapes, Gracefull Demeanour, and such Insinuating and Inticing Attractives, as Men are Forc'd to Admire us, Love us, and be Desirous of us, in so much as rather than not Have and Injoy us, they will Deliver to our Disposals, their Power, Persons, and Lives, Inslaving Themselves to our Will and Pleasures; also we are their Saints, whom they Adore and Worship, and what can we Desire more, than to be Men's Tyrants, Destinies, and Goddesses?

---

1   chemist

III

WOMEN AND THE NEW SCIENCE

1. THE DESCRIPTION OF A NEW WORLD, CALLED THE BLAZING WORLD (1666)

The Description of a New World, Called the Blazing World was first published in 1666 and again in 1668 as a companion text to *Observations upon Experimental Philosophy*, an important book that presents an extended critique of early modern science. *Observations* questions both the competency of science to know and to control nature, and the efficacy of its methods and technologies, especially as articulated by Robert Hooke in *Micrographia* (1665). In a complementary fashion, *Blazing World* pioneers the genre of science fiction by creating a new world in which to explore the cultural meanings of the new scientific and philosophical ideas of early modernity, including the question of women and power.

THE DESCRIPTION OF A NEW WORLD, CALLED THE BLAZING WORLD.

Written by the Thrice Noble, Illustrious, and Excellent Princesse, The Duchess of Newcastle.

To the Duchesse of Newcastle, on her New Blazing World.

Our Elder World, with all their Skill and Arts,
Could but divide the *World* into three Parts:
Columbus then for Navigation fam'd,
Found a new World, *America* 'tis nam'd:
Now this new World was found, it was not made,
Onely[1] discovered, lying in Times shade.
Then what are *You*, having no *Chaos* found
To make a *World*, or any such least ground?
But your creating Fancy, thought it fit
To make your World of Nothing, but pure Wit.

---

1 only

Your *Blazing-world*, beyond the Stars mounts higher,
Enlightens all with a Coelestial Fier.[1]

William Newcastle.

To the Reader.

If you wonder, that I join a work of Fancy to my serious Philosophical Contemplations;[2] think not that it is out of a disparagement to
Philosophy; or out of an opinion, as if this noble study were but a
Fiction of the Mind; for though Philosophers may err in searching
and enquiring after the Causes of Natural Effects, and many times
embrace falshoods for Truths; yet this doth not prove, that the Ground
of Philosophy is meerly Fiction, but the error proceeds from the different motions of Reason, which cause different Opinions in different
parts, and in some are more irregular then in others; for Reason being
dividable, because material, cannot move in all parts alike; and since
there is but one Truth in Nature, all those that hit not this Truth, do
err, some more, some less; for though some may come nearer the
mark then others, which makes their Opinions seem more probable
and rational then others; yet as long as they swerve from this onely[3]
Truth, they are in the wrong: Nevertheless, all do ground their Opinions upon Reason; that is, upon rational probabilities, at least, they
think they do: But *Fictions* are an issue of mans Fancy, framed in his
own Mind, according as he pleases, without regard, whether the
thing, he fancies, be really existent without[4] his mind or not; so that
Reason searches the depth of Nature, and enquires after the true
Causes of Natural Effects; but Fancy creates of its own accord whatsoever it pleases, and delights in its own work. The end of Reason, is
Truth; the end of Fancy, is Fiction: But mistake me not, when I distinguish *Fancy* from *Reason*; I mean not as if Fancy were not made by the
Rational parts of Matter; but by *Reason* I understand a rational search
and enquiry into the causes of natural effects; and by *Fancy* a voluntary creation or production of the Mind, both being effects, or rather

---

1 celestial fire
2 *The Blazing World* was published as an addendum to *Observations Upon Experimental Philosophy.*
3 unique
4 outside or external to

actions of the rational part of Matter; of which, as that is a more profitable and useful study then this, so it is also more laborious and difficult, and requires sometimes the help of Fancy, to recreate[1] the Mind, and withdraw it from its more serious contemplations.

And this is the reason, why I added this Piece of Fancy to my Philosophical Observations, and joined them as two Worlds at the ends of their Poles; both for my own sake, to divert my studious thoughts, which I employed in the Contemplation thereof, and to delight the Reader with variety, which is always pleasing. But lest my Fancy should stray too much, I chose such a Fiction as would be agreeable to the subject I treated of in the former parts; it is a Description of a *New World*, not such as *Lucian's*, or the *French* man's World in the Moon;[2] but a World of my own Creating, which I call the *Blazing-World*: The first part whereof is *Romancical*, the second *Philosophical*, and the third is meerly *Fancy*, or (as I may call it) *Fantastical*; which if it add any satisfaction to you, I shall account my self a Happy *Creatoress*; if not, I must be content to live a melancholly Life in my own World; I cannot call it a poor World, if poverty be onely want of Gold, Silver, and Jewels; for there is more Gold in it then all the Chymists[3] ever did, and (as I verily believe) will ever be able to make. As for the Rocks of Diamonds, I wish with all my soul they might be shared amongst my noble female friends, and upon that condition, I would willingly quit my part; and of the Gold I should onely desire so much as might suffice to repair my Noble Lord and Husband's Losses:[4] For I am not Covetous, but as Ambitious as ever any of my Sex was, is, or can be; which makes, that though I cannot be *Henry* the Fifth, or *Charles* the Second, yet I endeavour to be *Margaret* the *First*; and although I have neither power, time nor occasion to conquer the world as *Alexander* and *Cæsar* did; yet rather then not to be Mistress of one, since Fortune and the Fates would give me

---

1   refresh
2   Lucian of Samosata (c. 125 - c.200): Greek satirist, author of *The True History*, which described an imaginary voyage to the moon; Savinien Cyrano de Bergerac (1620–1655): French dramatist and novelist, author of *Histoire comique contenant les états et empires de la lune* (1657); see Introduction, pp. 28-9.
3   chemists
4   For a discussion of Newcastle's banishment from England, the confiscation of his estates and loss of income during the English Civil War, see Mendelson, *Mental World*, 27-8, 49-50.

none, I have made a World of my own: for which no body, I hope, will blame me, since it is in every ones power to do the like.

THE DESCRIPTION OF A NEW WORLD, CALLED THE BLAZING WORLD

A Merchant travelling into a forreign Country, fell extreamly in Love with a young Lady; but being a stranger in that Nation, and beneath her both in Birth and Wealth, he could have but little hopes of obtaining his desire; however his love growing more and more vehement upon him, even to the slighting of all difficulties, he resolved at last to steal her away, which he had the better opportunity to do, because her Fathers house was not far from the Sea, and she often using to gather shells upon the shore, accompanied not with above two or three of her servants, it encouraged him the more to execute his design. Thus coming one time with a little light Vessel, not unlike a Packet-boat, mann'd with some few Sea-men, and well victualled, for fear of some accidents, which might perhaps retard their journey, to the place where she used to repair, he forced her away: But when he fancied himself the happiest man of the World, he proved to be the most unfortunate; for Heaven frowning at his theft, raised such a Tempest, as they knew not what to do, or whither to steer their course; so that the Vessel, both by its own lightness, and the violent motion of the Wind, was carried as swift as an Arrow out of a Bow, towards the North-pole, and in a short time reached the Icy Sea, where the wind forced it amongst huge pieces of Ice; but being little, and light, it did by assistance and favour of the Gods to this virtuous Lady, so turn and wind through those precipices, as if it had been guided by some Experienced Pilot, and skilful Mariner: But alas! those few men which were in it, not knowing whither they went, nor what was to be done in so strange an adventure, and not being provided for so cold a Voyage, were all frozen to death, the young Lady onely, by the light of her Beauty, the heat of her Youth, and Protection of the Gods, remaining alive: Neither was it a wonder that the men did freeze to death; for they were not onely driven to the very end or point of the Pole of that World, but even to another Pole of another World, which joined close to it; so that the cold having a double strength at the conjunction of those two Poles, was insupportable: At last, the Boat still

Illustration 7: The frontispiece for John Wilkins's *The Discovery of a New World; or, A Discourse tending to prove, that ('tis probable) there may be another Habitable World in the Moon* (1707) depicts the Copernican hypothesis being expounded by Copernicus on the left and Galileo and Kepler on the right. Wilkins also discusses the possibility of finding a passage from the earth to other worlds. (Courtesy Special Collections, Mills Memorial Library, McMaster University.)

passing on, was forced into another World; for it is impossible to round this Worlds Globe from Pole to Pole, so as we do from East to West; because the Poles of the other World, joining to the Poles of this, do not allow any further passage to surround the World that way; but if any one arrives to either of these Poles, he is either forced to return, or to enter into another World; and least[1] you should scruple at it, and think, if it were thus, those that live at the Poles would either see two Suns at one time, or else they would never want the Suns light for six months together, as it is commonly believed; You must know, that each of these Worlds having its own Sun to enlighten it, they move each one in their peculiar circles; which motion is so just and exact, that neither can hinder or obstruct the other; for they do not exceed their Tropicks, and although they should meet, yet we in this world cannot so well perceive them, by reason of the brightness of our Sun, which being nearer to us, obstructs the splendor of the Suns of the other Worlds, they being too far off to be discerned by our optick perception, except we use very good Telescopes, by which skilful Astronomers have often observed two or three Suns at once.

But to return to the wandering Boat, and the distressed Lady, she seeing all the Men dead, found small comfort in life; their bodies which were preserved all that while from putrefaction and stench, by the extremity of cold, began now to thaw, and corrupt; whereupon she having not strength enough to fling them over-board, was forced to remove out of her small Cabine, upon the deck, to avoid that nauseous smell; and finding the Boat swim between two plains of Ice, as a stream that runs betwixt two shores, at last perceived land, but covered all with snow: from which came walking upon the Ice strange Creatures, in shape like Bears, onely they went upright as men; those Creatures coming near the Boat, catched hold of it with their Paws, that served them instead of hands; some two or three of them entred first; and when they came out, the rest went in one after another; at last having viewed and observed all that was in the Boat, they spake to each other in a language which the Lady did not understand, and having carried her out of the Boat, sunk it, together with the dead men.

---

1   lest

The Lady now finding her self in so strange a place, and amongst such a wonderful kind of Creatures, was extreamly strucken with fear, and could entertain no other Thoughts, but that every moment her life was to be a sacrifice to their cruelty; but those Bear-like Creatures, how terrible soever they appear'd to her sight, yet were they so far from exercising any cruelty upon her, that rather they shewed[1] her all civility and kindness imaginable; for she being not able to go upon the ice, by reason of its slipperiness, they took her up in their rough armes, and carried her into their City, where instead of houses, they had Caves under ground; and as soon as they enter'd the City, both Males and Females, young and old, flockt together to see this Lady, holding up their paws in admiration; at last having brought her into a certain large and spacious Cave, which they intended for her reception, they left her to the custody of the Females, who entertained her with all kindness and respect, and gave her such victuals as they were used to eat; but seeing her constitution neither agreed with the temper of that Climate, nor their Diet, they were resolved to carry her into another Island of a warmer temper; in which were men like Foxes, onely walking in an upright shape, who received their neighbours the Bear-men with great civility and courtship, very much admiring this beauteous Lady, and having discoursed some while together, agreed at last to make her a present to the Emperour of their world; to which end, after she had made some short stay in the same place, they brought her cross that Island to a large River, whose stream run smooth and clear, like Chrystal; in which were numerous Boats, much like our Fox-traps; in one whereof she was carried, some of the Bear- and Fox-men waiting on her; and as soon as they had crossed the River, they came into an Island where there were Men which had heads, beaks, and feathers, like Wild-geese, onely they went in an upright shape, like the Bear-men and Fox-men; their rumps they carried between their legs, their wings were of the same length with their bodies, and their tails of an indifferent size, trailing after them like a Ladies Garment; and after the Bear- and Fox-men had declared their intention and design to their neighbours, the Geese- or Bird-men, some of them joined to the rest, and attended the Lady through that Island, till they came to another great and large River,

---

1   showed

where there was a preparation made of many Boats, much like Birds nests, onely of a bigger size; and having crost that River, they arrived into another Island, which was of a pleasant and mild temper, full of Woods, and the inhabitants thereof were *Satyrs*, who received both the Bear- Fox- and Bird-men, with all respect and civility; and after some conferences (for they all understood each others language) some chief of the *Satyrs* joining to them, accompanied the Lady out of that Island to another River, wherein were very handsome and commodious Barges; and having crost that River, they entered into a large and spacious Kingdom, the men whereof were of a Grass-green complexion, who entertained them very kindly, and provided all conveniences for their further voyage: hitherto they had onely crost Rivers, but now they could not avoid the open Seas any longer; wherefore they made their Ships and tacklings ready to sail over into the Island, where the Emperor of their Blazing-world (for so it was call'd) kept his residence; very good Navigators they were; and though they had no knowledg of the Load-stone, or Needle,[1] or pendulous Watches, yet (which was as serviceable to them) they had subtile observations, and great practice; in so much that they could not onely tell the depth of the Sea in every place, but where there were shelves of Sand, Rocks, and other obstructions to be avoided by skilfull and experienced Sea-men: Besides, they were excellent Augurers, which skill they counted more necessary and beneficial then the use of Compasses, Cards, Watches, and the like; but above the rest, they had an extraordinary Art, much to be taken notice of by experimental Philosophers,[2] and that was a certain Engine, which would draw in a great quant[it]y of air, and shoot forth wind with a great force; this Engine in a calm, they placed behind their ships, and in a storm, before; for it served against the raging waves, like Canons[3] against an hostile Army, or besieged Town; it would batter and beat the waves in pieces, were they as high as steeples; and as soon as a breach was made, they forced their passage through, in spight even of the most furious wind, using two of those Engins at every Ship, one before, to beat off the waves, and another behind to drive it on; so that the artificial wind had the better of the natural; for it had a greater advantage of

---

1   magnetic compass
2   experimental philosopher: early modern term for professional scientist
3   cannons

the waves then the natural of the ships; the natural being above the face of the water, could not without a down-right motion enter or press into the ships, whereas the artificial with a sideward motion did pierce into the bowels of the waves: Moreover, it is to be observed, that in a great tempest they would join their ships in battle array, and when they feared wind and waves would be too strong for them, if they divided their ships, they joined as many together as the compass or advantage of the places of the liquid Element would give them leave; for their ships were so ingeniously contrived, that they could fasten them together as close as a honey-comb without waste of place; and being thus united, no wind nor waves were able to separate them. The Emperors ships were all of Gold, but the Merchants and Skippers of Leather; the Golden ships were not much heavier then ours of Wood, by reason they were neatly made, and required not such thickness, neither were they troubled with Pitch, Tar, Pumps, Guns, and the like, which make our Wooden-ships very heavy; for though they were not all of a piece, yet they were so well sodder'd,[1] that there was no fear of leaks, chinks, or clefts; and as for Guns, there was no use of them, because they had no other enemies but the winds; but the Leather ships were not altogether so sure, although much lighter; besides, they were pitched to keep out water.

Having thus prepared and order'd their Navy, they went on in despight of Calm or Storm, and though the Lady at first fancied her self in a very sad condition, and her mind was much tormented with doubts and fears, not knowing whether this strange adventure would tend to her safety or destruction; yet she being withal of a generous spirit, and ready wit, considering what dangers she had past, and finding those sorts of men civil and diligent attendants to her, took courage, and endeavoured to learn their language; which after she had obtained so far, that partly by some words and signs she was able to apprehend their meaning, she was so far from being afraid of them, that she thought her self not onely safe, but very happy in their company: By which we may see, that Novelty discomposes the mind, but acquaintance settles it in peace and tranquillity. At last, having passed by several rich Islands and Kingdoms, they went towards *Paradise*, which was the seat of the Emperor; and coming in sight of it,

---

1 ` soldered

rejoyced very much; the Lady at first could perceive nothing but high Rocks, which seemed to touch the Skies; and although they appear'd not of an equal height, yet they seemed to be all one piece, without partitions; but at last drawing nearer, she perceived a clift,[1] which was a part of those Rocks, out of which she spied coming forth a great number of Boats, which afar off shewed like a company of Ants, marching one after another; the Boats appeared like the holes or partitions in a Honey-comb, and when joined together, stood as close; the men were of several complexions, but none like any of our World; and when both the Boats and Ships met, they saluted and spake to each other very courteously; for there was but one language in all that world, nor no more but one Emperor, to whom they all submitted with the greatest duty and obedience, which made them live in a continued peace and happiness, not acquainted with other forreign wars, or home-bred insurrections. The Lady now being arrived at this place, was carried out of her Ship into one of those Boats, and conveighed through the same passage (for there was no other) into that part of the world where the Emperor did reside; which part was very pleasant, and of a mild temper: within it self it was divided by a great number of vast and large Rivers, all ebbing and flowing, into several Islands of unequal distance from each other, which in most parts were as pleasant, healthful, rich, and fruitful, as Nature could make them; and, as I mentioned before, secure from all forreign invasions, by reason there was but one way to enter, and that like a Labyrinth, so winding and turning among the rocks, that no other Vessels but small Boats, could pass, carrying not above three passengers at a time: On each side all along this narrow and winding River, there were several Cities, some of Marble, some of Alabaster, some of Agat, some of Amber, some of Coral, and some of other precious materials not known in our world; all which after the Lady had passed, she came to the Imperial City, named *Paradise*, which appeared in form like several Islands; for Rivers did run betwixt every street, which together with the Bridges, whereof there was a great number, were all paved; the City it self was built of Gold, and their Architectures were noble, stately, and magnificent, not like our Modern, but like those in the *Romans* time; for our Modern Buildings are like

---

1 cleft

those houses which Children use to make of Cards, one story above another, fitter for Birds, then Men; but theirs were more large, and broad, then high; the highest of them did not exceed two stories, besides those rooms that were under-ground, as Cellars, and other offices. The Emperors Palace stood upon an indifferent ascent from the Imperial City; at the top of which ascent was a broad Arch, supported by several Pillars, which went round the Palace, and contained four of our English miles in compass: within the Arch stood the Emperors Guard, which consisted of several sorts of men; at every half mile was a Gate to enter, and every Gate was of a different fashion; the first, which allowed a passage from the Imperial City into the Palace, had on either hand a Cloyster, the outward part whereof stood upon Arches sustained by Pillars, but the inner part was close: Being entred through the Gate, the Palace it self appear'd in its middle like the Isle[1] of a Church, a mile and a half long, and half a mile broad; the roof of it was all arched, and rested upon Pillars, so artificially placed, that a stranger would lose himself therein without a Guide; at the extream sides, that is, between the outward and inward part of the Cloyster, were Lodgings for Attendants, and in the midst of the Palace, the Emperors own rooms; whose lights were placed at the top of every one, because of the heat of the Sun: the Emperors appartement for State was no more inclosed then the rest; onely an Imperial Throne was in every appartement, of which the several adornments could not be perceived until one enter'd, because the Pillars were so just opposite to one another, that all the adornments could not be seen at once. The first part of the Palace was, as the Imperial City, all of Gold, and when it came to the Emperors appartement, it was so rich with Diamonds, Pearls, Rubies, and the like precious stones, that it surpasses my skill to enumerate them all. Amongst the rest, the Imperial Room of State appear'd most magnificent; it was paved with green Diamonds (for in that World are Diamonds of all colours) so artificially, as it seemed but of one piece; the Pillars were set with Diamonds so close, and in such a manner, that they appear'd most Glorious to the sight; between every Pillar was a bow or arch of a certain sort of Diamonds, the like whereof our World does not afford; which being placed in every one of the arches in several rows, seemed

---

1   aisle

just like so many Rainbows of several different colours. The roof of the Arches was of blew Diamonds, and in the midst thereof was a Carbuncle, which represented the Sun; the rising and setting Sun at the East and West side of the room were made of Rubies. Out of this room there was a passage into the Emperors Bed-chamber, the walls whereof were of Jet, and the floor of black Marble; the roof was of mother of Pearl, where the Moon and Blazing-stars were represented by white Diamonds, and his Bed was made of Diamonds and Carbuncles.

No sooner was the Lady brought before the Emperor, but he conceived her to be some Goddess, and offered to worship her; which she refused, telling him, (for by that time she had pretty well learned their language) that although she came out of another world, yet was she but a mortal; at which the Emperor rejoycing, made her his Wife, and gave her an absolute power to rule and govern all that World as she pleased. But her subjects, who could hardly be perswaded to believe her mortal, tender'd her all the veneration and worship due to a Deity.

Her accoustrement after she was made Empress, was as followeth: On her head she wore a Cap of Pearl, and a Half-moon of Diamonds just before it; on the top of her Crown came spreading over a broad Carbuncle, cut in the form of the Sun; her Coat was of Pearl, mixt with blew Diamonds, and fringed with red ones; her Buskins and Sandals were of green Diamonds: In her left hand she held a Buckler, to signifie the Defence of her Dominions; which Buckler was made of that sort of Diamond as has several different Colours; and being cut and made in the form of an arch, shewed like a Rain-bow; In her right hand she carried a Spear made of a white Diamond, cut like the tail of a Blazing-star, which signified that she was ready to assault those that proved her Enemies.

None was allowed to use or wear Gold but those of the Imperial race, which were the onely Nobles of the State; nor durst any one wear Jewels but the Emperor, the Empress, and their Eldest Son; notwithstanding that they had an infinite quantity both of Gold and precious Stones in that World; for they had larger extents of Gold, then our Arabian Sands; their precious Stones were Rocks, and their Diamonds of several Colours; they used no coyn, but all their Traffick was by exchange of several Commodities.

Their Priests and Governours were Princes of the Imperial Blood, and made Eunuches for that purpose; and as for the ordinary sort of men in that part of the World where the Emperor resided, they were of several Complexions; not white, black, tawny, olive- or ash-coloured; but some appear'd of an Azure, some of a deep Purple, some of a Grass-green, some of a Scarlet, some of an Orange-colour, &c. Which Colours and Complexions, whether they were made by the bare reflection of light, without the assistance of small particles, or by the help of well-ranged and order'd Atomes; or by a continual agitation of little Globules; or by some pressing and reacting motion, I am not able to determine. The rest of the Inhabitants of that World, were men of several different sorts, shapes, figures, dispositions, and humors, as I have already made mention heretofore; some were Bear-men, some Worm-men, some Fish- or Mear-men,[1] otherwise called Syrenes; some Bird-men, some Fly-men, some Ant-men, some Geese-men, some Spider-men, some Lice-men, some Fox-men, some Ape-men, some Jack-daw-men, some Magpie-men, some Parrot-men, some Satyrs, some Gyants, and many more, which I cannot all remember; and of these several sorts of men, each followed such a profession as was most proper for the nature of their species, which the Empress encouraged them in, especially those that had applied themselves to the study of several Arts and Sciences; for they were as ingenious and witty in the invention of profitable and useful Arts, as we are in our world, nay, more; and to that end she erected Schools, and founded several Societies. The Bear-men were to be her Experimental Philosophers, the Bird-men her Astronomers, the Fly- Worm- and Fish-men her Natural Philosophers, the Ape-men her Chymists, the Satyrs her Galenick Physicians,[2] the Fox-men her Politicians, the Spider- and Lice-men her Mathematicians, the Jackdaw- Magpie- and Parrot-men her Orators and Logicians, the Gyants her Architects, &c. But before all things, she having got a soveraign power from the Emperor over all the World, desired to be informed both of the manner of their Religion and Government, and to that end she called the Priests and States-men, to give her an account of either. Of the States-men she enquired, first, Why they had so few Laws? To which

---

1   mermen or male mermaids
2   Followers of Galen (129-199), a celebrated ancient physician whose medical theories modified and revised those of Aristotle.

they answered, That many Laws made many Divisions, which most commonly did breed factions, and at last brake out into open wars. Next, she asked, Why they preferred the Monarchical form of Government before any other? They answered, That as it was natural for one body to have but one head, so it was also natural for a Politick body to have but one Governor; and that a Common-wealth, which had many Governors was like a Monster of many heads: besides, said they, a Monarchy is a divine form of Government, and agrees most with our Religion; for as there is but one God, whom we all unanimously worship and adore with one Faith, so we are resolved to have but one Emperor, to whom we all submit with one obedience.

Then the Empress seeing that the several sorts of her Subjects had each their Churches apart, asked the Priests whether they were of several Religions? They answered her Majesty, That there was no more but one Religion in all that World, nor no diversity of opinions in that same Religion; for though there were several sorts of men, yet had they all but one opinion concerning the Worship and Adoration of God. The Empress asked them, Whether they were Jews, Turks, or Christians? We do not know, said they, what Religions those are; but we do all unanimously acknowledg, worship and adore the Onely, Omnipotent, and Eternal God, with all reverence, submission, and duty. Again, the Empress enquired, Whether they had several Forms of Worship? They answered, No: For our Devotion and Worship consists onely in Prayers, which we frame according to our several necessities, in Petitions, Humiliations, Thanksgiving, &c. Truly, replied the Empress, I thought you had been either Jews, or Turks, because I never perceived any Women in your Congregations; But what is the reason, you bar them from your religious Assemblies? It is not fit, said they, that Men and Women should be promiscuously together in time of Religious Worship; for their company hinders Devotion, and makes many, instead of praying to God, direct their devotion to their Mistresses. But, asked the Empress, Have they no Congregation of their own, to perform the duties of Divine Worship, as well as Men? No, answered they: but they stay at home, and say their Prayers by themselves in their Closets. Then the Empress desir'd to know the reason why the Priests and Governors of their World were made Eunuchs? They answer'd, To keep them from Marriage: For Women and Children most commonly make disturbance both in Church and

State. But, said she, Women and Children have no employment in Church or State. 'Tis true, answer'd they; but although they are not admitted to publick employments, yet are they so prevalent with their Husbands and Parents, that many times by their importunate perswasions, they cause as much, nay, more mischief secretly, then if they had the management of publick affairs.

The Empress having received an information of what concerned both Church and State, passed some time in viewing the Imperial Palace, where she admired much the skil and ingenuity of the Architects, and enquired of them, first, why they built their Houses no higher then two stories from the Ground? They answered her Majesty, That the lower their buildings were, the less were they subject either to the heat of the Sun, to Wind, Tempest, Decay, &c. Then she desired to know the reason, why they made them so thick? They answered, That the thicker the Walls were, the warmer were they in Winter, and cooler in Summer, for their thickness kept out both cold and heat. Lastly, she asked, why they arched their roofs, and made so many Pillars? They replied, That Arches and Pillars, did not onely grace a building very much, and caused it to appear Magnificent, but made it also firm and lasting.

The Empress was very well satisfied with their answers; and after some time, when she thought that her new founded societies of the Vertuoso's[1] had made a good progress in their several employments, which she had put them upon, she caused a Convocation first of the Bird-men, and commanded them to give her a true relation of the two Celestial bodies, *viz.* the Sun and Moon, which they did with all the obedience and faithfulness befitting their duty.

The Sun, as much as they could observe, they related to be a firm or solid Stone, of a vast bigness, of colour yellowish, and of an extraordinary splendor; but the Moon, they said, was of a whitish colour; and although she looked dim in the presence of the Sun, yet had she her own light, and was a shining body of her self, as might be perceived by her vigorous appearance in Moon-shiny nights; the difference onely betwixt her own and the Suns light was, that the Sun did strike his beams in a direct line; but the Moon never respected the Centre of their World in a right line, but her Centre was always

---

1   virtuoso: one who displays special ability in one or more branches of the arts and sciences, or a nonprofessional who pursues scientific investigations

excentrical. The spots both in the Sun and Moon, as far as they were able to perceive, they affirmed to be nothing else but flaws and stains of their stony bodies. Concerning the heat of the Sun, they were not of one opinion; some would have the Sun hot in it self, alledging an old Tradition, that it should at some time break asunder, and burn the Heavens, and consume this world into hot embers, which, said they, could not be done, if the Sun were not fiery of it self. Others again said, This opinion could not stand with reason; for Fire being a destroyer of all things, the Sun-stone after this manner would burn up all the near adjoining bodies: besides, said they, Fire cannot subsist without fuel; and the Sun-stone having nothing to feed on, would in a short time consume it self; wherefore they thought it more probable that the Sun was not actually hot, but onely by the reflection of its light; so that its heat was an effect of its light, both being immaterial: But this opinion again was laught at by others, and rejected as ridiculous, who thought it impossible that one immaterial should produce another; and believed that both the light and heat of the Sun proceeded from a swift Circular motion of the æthereal Globules, which by their striking upon the optick nerve, caused light, and their motion produced heat: But neither would this opinion hold; for, said some, then it would follow, that the sight of Animals is the cause of light, and that, were there no eyes, there would be no light; which was against all sense and reason. Thus they argued concerning the heat and light of the Sun; but which is remarkable, none did say, that the Sun was a globous fluid body, and had a swift circular motion; but all agreed it was fixt and firm like a centre, and therefore they generally called it the Sun-stone.

Then the Emperess asked them the reason, Why the Sun and Moon did often appear in different postures or shapes, as sometimes magnified, sometimes diminished, sometimes elevated, otherwhiles depressed, now thrown to the right, and then to the left? To which some of the Bird-men answered, That it proceeded from the various degrees of heat and cold, which are found in the air, from whence did follow a differing density and rarity; and likewise from the vapours that are interposed, whereof those that ascend are higher and less dense then the ambient air, but those which descend are heavier, and more dense. But others did with more probability affirm, that it was nothing else but the various patterns of the Air; for like as Painters do not copy out one and the same original just alike at all times, so, said they, do several parts of the Air make different patterns of the luminous bodies of the Sun and Moon, which patterns, as several copies, the sensitive motions do figure out in the substance of our eyes.

This answer the Emperess liked much better then the former, and enquired further, what opinion they had of those Creatures that are called the motes of the Sun? To which they answered, That they were nothing else but streams of very small, rare and transparent particles, through which the Sun was represented as through a glass, for if they were not transparent, said they, they would eclipse the light of the Sun; and if not rare and of an airy substance, they would hinder Flies from flying in the air, at least retard their flying motion: Nevertheless, although they were thinner then the thinnest vapour, yet were they not so thin as the body of air, or else they would not be perceptible by animal sight. Then the Empress asked, Whether they were living Creatures? They answered, Yes: Because they did encrease and decrease, and were nourished by the presence, and starved by the absence of the Sun.

Having thus finished their discourse of the Sun and Moon, the Emperess desired to know what Stars there were besides? But they answer'd, that they could perceive in that World none other but Blazing-stars, and from thence it had the name that it was called the Blazing-world; and these Blazing-stars, said they, were such solid, firm and shining bodies as the Sun and Moon, not of a Globular, but of several sorts of figures, some had tails, and some other kinds of shapes.

After this, the Emperess asked them, What kind of substance or creature the Air was? The Bird-men answered, That they could have no other perception of the air, but by their own respiration: For, said they, some bodies are onely subject to touch, others onely to sight, and others onely to smell; but some are subject to none of our exterior senses: For Nature is so full of variety, that our weak senses cannot perceive all the various sorts of her Creatures; neither is there any one object perceptible by all our senses; no more then several objects are by one sense. I believe you, replied the Empress; but if you can give no account of the Air, said she, you will hardly be able to inform me how Wind is made; for they say that Wind is nothing but motion of the Air. The Bird-men answer'd, That they observed Wind to be more dense then Air, and therefore subject to the sense of Touch; but what properly Wind was, and the manner how it was made, they could not exactly tell; some said, it was caused by the Clouds falling on each other, and others, that it was produced of a hot and dry exhalation, which ascending, was driven down again by the coldness of the air that is in the middle Region, and by reason of its lightness, could not go directly to the bottom, but was carried by the Air up and down: Some would have it a flowing water of the Air; and others again a flowing Air moved by the blas[1] of the Stars.

But the Emperess seeing they could not agree concerning the cause of Wind, asked, whether they could tell how Snow was made? To which they answered, That according to their observation, Snow was made by a commixture of Water, and some certain extract of the element of Fire that is under the Moon; a small portion of which extract being mixed with Water, and beaten by Air or Wind, made a white froth called Snow, which being after some while dissolved by the heat of the same spirit, turned to Water again. This observation amazed the Emperess very much; for she had hitherto believed, That Snow was made by cold motions, and not by such an agitation or beating of a fiery extract upon water: Nor could she be perswaded to believe it until the Fish- or Mear-men had delivered their observation upon the making of Ice, which, they said, was not produced, as some had hitherto conceived, by the motion of the Air, raking the Superfices of the Earth, but by some strong saline vapour arising out of the Seas, which condensed Water into Ice; and the more quantity there was of that vapour, the greater were the Mountains or Precipices of Ice; but the reason that it did not so much freeze in the Torrid Zone, or under the Ecliptick,[2] as near or under the Poles, was, that this vapour in those places being drawn up by the Sun-beams into the middle Region of the Air, was onely condensed into water, and fell down in showres of rain; when as, under the Poles, the heat of the Sun being not so vehement, the same vapour had no force or power to rise so high, and therefore caused so much Ice, by ascending and acting onely upon the surface of water.

This Relation confirmed partly the observation of the Bird- men concerning the cause of Snow; but since they had made mention that

---

1   contemporary technical term for a windy blast or influence of the stars producing changes of weather

2   ecliptic: the apparent orbital path of the sun

that same extract, which by its commixture with Water made Snow, proceeded from the Element of Fire, that is under the Moon; The Emperess asked them of what nature that Elementary Fire was; whether it was like ordinary fire here upon Earth, or such a fire as is within the bowels of the Earth, and as the famous mountains *Vesuvius* and *Ætna* do burn withal, or whether it was such a sort of fire as is found in flints, &c. They answered, That the Elementary Fire, which is underneath the Sun, was not so solid as any of those mentioned fires; because it had no solid fuel to feed on; but yet it was much like the flame of ordinary fire, onely somewhat more thin and fluid; for flame, said they, is nothing else but the airy part of a fired body.

Lastly, the Emperess asked the Bird-men of the nature of Thunder and Lightning? and whether it was not caused by roves[1] of Ice falling upon each other? To which they answered, That it was not made that way, but by an encounter of cold and heat; so that an exhalation being kindled in the Clouds, did dash forth Lightning, and that there were so many rentings of Clouds as there were sounds and Cracking noises: But this opinion was contradicted by others, who affirmed that Thunder was a sudden and monstrous blas, stirred up in the Air, and did not always require a Cloud; but the Emperess not knowing what they meant by blas (for even they themselves were not able to explain the sense of this word)[2] liked the former better; and to avoid hereafter tedious disputes, and have the truth of the Phænomena's of Celestial bodies more exactly known, commanded the Bear-men, which were her Experimental Philosophers, to observe them through such Instruments as are called Telescopes, which they did according to her Majesties Command; but these Telescopes caused more differences and divisions amongst them, then ever they had before; for some said, they perceived that the Sun stood still, and the Earth did move about it; others were of opinion, that they both did move; and others said again, that the Earth stood still, and the Sun did move;[3] some counted more Stars then others; some discovered new Stars never seen before; some fell into a great dispute with others concerning the bigness of the Stars; some said the Moon was another World like their Terrestrial

---

1   slivers
2   "Blas" had been recently invented as a technical term by seventeenth-century cosmologists.
3   the debate over Ptolemaic versus Copernican models of the universe

Globe, and the spots therein were Hills and Vallies; but others would have the spots to be the Terrestrial parts, and the smooth and glossie parts, the Sea: At last, the Emperess commanded them to go with their Telescopes to the very end of the Pole that was joined to the world she came from, and try whether they could perceive any Stars in it; which they did; and being returned to her Majesty, reported that they had seen three Blazing-stars appear there, one after another in a short time, whereof two were bright, and one dim; but they could not agree neither in this observation; for some said it was but one Star which appeared at three several times, in several places; and others would have them to be three several Stars; for they thought it impossible, that those three several appearances should have been but one Star, because every Star did rise at a certain time, and appear'd in a certain place, and did disappear in the same place: Next, It is altogether improbable, said they, That one Star should flie from place to place, especially at such a vast distance, without a visible motion, in so short a time, and appear in such different places, whereof two were quite opposite, and the third side-ways: Lastly, If it had been but one Star, said they, it would always have kept the same splendor, which it did not; for, as above mentioned, two were bright, and one was dim. After they had thus argued, the Emperess began to grow angry at their Telescopes, that they could give no better Intelligence; for, said she, now I do plainly perceive, that your Glasses are false Informers, and instead of discovering the Truth, delude your senses; Wherefore I Command you to break them, and let the Bird-men trust onely to their natural eyes, and examine Celestial objects by the motions of their own sense and reason. The Bear-men replied, That it was not the fault of their Glasses, which caused such differences in their opinions, but the sensitive motions in their optick organs did not move alike, nor were their rational judgments always regular: To which the Emperess answered, That if their glasses were true informers, they would rectifie their irregular sense and reason; But, said she, Nature has made your sense and reason more regular then Art has your Glasses, for they are meer deluders, and will never lead you to the knowledg of Truth; Wherefore I command you again to break them; for you may observe the progressive motions of Celestial bodies with your natural eyes better then through Artificial Glasses. The Bear-men being exceedingly troubled at her Majesties displeasure concerning their Telescopes, kneel'd down, and in the humblest manner petitioned that they might not be broken; for, said they, we take more delight in Artificial delusions, then in natural truths. Besides, we shall want imployments for our senses, and subjects for arguments; for were there nothing but truth, and no falshood, there would be no occasion for to dispute, and by this means we should want the aim and pleasure of our endeavours in confuting and contradicting each other; neither would one man be thought wiser then another, but all would either be alike knowing and wise, or all would be fools; wherefore we most humbly beseech your Imperial Majesty to spare our Glasses, which are our onely delight, and as dear to us as our lives. The Emperess at last consented to their request, but upon condition, that their disputes and quarrels should remain within their Schools, and cause no factions or disturbances in State, or Government. The Bear-men, full of joy, returned their most humble thanks to the Emperess; and to make her amends for the displeasure which their Telescopes had occasioned, told her Majesty, that they had several other artificial Optick-glasses, which they were sure would give her Majesty a great deal more satisfaction. Amongst the rest they brought forth several Microscopes, by the means of which they could enlarge the shapes of little bodies, and make a Lowse appear as big as an Elephant, and a Mite as big as a Whale. First of all they shewed the Emperess a gray Drone-flye,[1] wherein they observed that the greatest part of her face, nay, of her head, consisted of two large bunches all cover'd over with a multitude of small Pearls or Hemispheres in a Trigonal order, which Pearls were of two degrees, smaller and bigger; the smaller degree was lowermost, and looked towards the ground; the other was upward, and looked sideward, forward and backward: They were all so smooth and polished, that they were able to represent the image of any object, the number of them was in all 14000. After the view of this strange and miraculous Creature, and their several observations upon it, the Emperess asked them what they judged those little Hemispheres might be? They answered, That each of them was a perfect eye, by reason they perceived that each was covered with a Transparent Cornea, containing a liquor within them, which resembled the watery or glassie humor of the Eye. To which the Emperess replied,

---

1 For Robert Hooke's drawing of the drone-fly in his *Micrographia* (1665), see Illustration 8 (p.172).

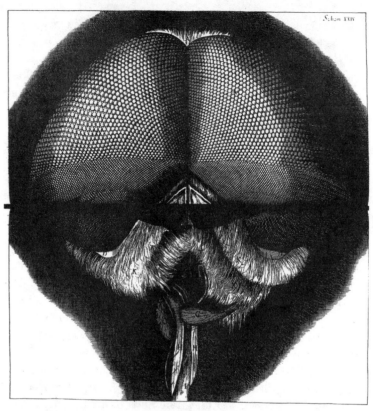

Illustration 8: A drawing made by Robert Hooke for his *Micrographia* (1665) of the "eyes" of a gray drone fly. He describes cutting off the head of a drone fly, fixing it on an Object Plate, and observing multiple protuberant bunches of small hemispheres that he estimates to be near 14,000 eyes. In her *Observations on Experimental Philosophy* (1666), Cavendish questions the capacity of the microscope to discover reality, and laughs at Hookes's experiments, asking, in this case, if drone flies have so many eyes, why can't they see the approach of a spider until it is too late?

That they might be glassie Pearls, and yet not eyes, and that perhaps their Microscopes did not truly inform them: But they smilingly answered her Majesty, That she did not know the vertue of those Microscopes; for they did never delude, but rectifie and inform their senses; nay, the World, said they, would be but blind without them, as it has been in former ages before those Microscopes were invented.

After this, they took a Charcoal, and viewing it with one of their best Microscopes, discovered in it an infinite multitude of pores, some bigger, some less; so close and thick, that they left but very little space betwixt them to be filled with a solid body; and to give her Imperial Majesty a better assurance thereof, they counted in a line of them an inch long, no less then 2700 pores; from which observation they drew this following conclusion, to wit, that this multitude of pores was the cause of the blackness of the Coal; for, said they, a body that has so many pores, from each of which no light is reflected, must necessarily look black, since black is nothing else but a privation of light, or a want of reflection. But the Emperess replied, That if all colours were made by reflection of light, and that black was as much a colour as any other colour; then certainly they contradicted themselves in saying, that black was made by want of reflection. However, not to interrupt your Microscopical inspections, said she, let us see how Vegetables appear through your Glasses; whereupon they took a Nettle, and, by the vertue of the Microscope, discovered that underneath the points of the Nettle there were certain little bags or bladders, containing a poysonous liquor, and when the points had made way into the interior parts of the skin, they like Syringe-pipes served to conveigh that same liquor into them. To which observation the Emperess replied, That if there were such poyson in Nettles, then certainly in eating of them, they would hurt us inwardly, as much as they do outwardly? But they answered, That it belonged to Physicians more then to Experimental Philosophers, to give reasons hereof; for they onely made Microscopial inspections, and related the figures of the natural parts of Creatures according to the presentation of their glasses.

Lastly, They shewed the Emperess a Flea, and a Lowse; which Creatures through the Microscope appear'd so terrible to her sight, that they had almost put her into a swoon; the description of all their parts would be very tedious to relate, and therefore I'le forbear it at this present. The Emperess after the view of those strangely-shaped Creatures, pitied much those that are molested with them, especially poor Beggars, which although they have nothing to live on themselves, are yet necessitated to maintain and feed of their own flesh and blood, a company of such terrible Creatures called Lice, who instead of thanks, do reward them with pains, and torment them for giving them nourishment and food. But after the Emperess had seen the shapes of these monstrous Creatures, she desir'd to know whether their Microscopes could hinder their biting, or at least shew some means how to avoid them? To which they answered, That such Arts were mechanical and below that noble study of Microscopical observations. Then the Emperess asked them whether they had not such sorts of Glasses that could enlarge and magnifie the shapes of great bodies, as well as they had done of little ones? Whereupon they took one of their best and largest Microscopes, and endeavoured to view a Whale thorow[1] it; but alas! the shape of the Whale was so big, that its circumference went beyond the magnifying quality of the Glass; whether the error proceeded from the Glass, or from a wrong position of the Whale against the reflection of light, I cannot certainly tell. The Emperess seeing the insufficiency of those Magnifying-glasses, that they were not able to enlarge all sorts of objects, asked the Bear-men whether they could not make glasses of a contrary nature to those they had shewed her, to wit, such as instead of enlarging or magnifying the shape or figure of an object, could contract it beneath its natural proportion: Which, in obedience to her Majesties Commands, they did; and viewing through one of the best of them, a huge and mighty Whale appear'd no bigger then a Sprat; nay, through some no bigger then a Vinegar-Eele; and through their ordinary ones, an Elephant seemed no bigger then a Flea; a Camel no bigger then a Lowse; and an Ostrich no bigger then a Mite. To relate all their optick observations through the several sorts of their Glasses, would be a tedious work, and tire even the most patient Reader, wherefore I'le pass them by; onely this was very remarkable and worthy to be taken notice of, that notwithstanding their great skil, industry and ingenuity in Experimental Philosophy, they could yet by no means contrive such Glasses, by the help of which they could spy out a *Vacuum*, with all its dimensions, nor Immaterial substances, Non-beings, and Mixt-beings, or such as are between something and nothing; which they were very much troubled at, hoping that yet, in time, by long study and practice, they might perhaps attain to it.

The Bird- and Bear-men being dismissed, the Emperess called both the Syrenes, or Fish-men, and the Worm-men, to deliver their observations which they had made, both within the Seas, and the Earth. First she enquired of the Fish-men whence the saltness of the

---

1   through

Sea did proceed? To which they answered, That there was a volatile salt in those parts of the Earth, which as a bosom contain the Waters of the Sea, which salt being imbibed by the Sea, became fixt; and this imbibing motion was that they call'd the Ebbing and Flowing of the Sea; for, said they, the rising and swelling of the water, is caused by those parts of the volatile salt as are not so easily imbibed, which striving to ascend above the water, bear it up with such a motion, as Man, or some other animal Creature, in a violent exercise uses to take breath. This they affirmed to be the true cause both of the saltness, and the ebbing and flowing motion of the Sea, and not the jogging of the Earth, or the secret influence of the Moon, as some others had made the World believe.

After this, the Emperess enquired, whether they had observed that all animal Creatures within the Seas and other waters, had blood? They answered, That some had blood, more or less, but some had none; In Crea-fishes[1] and Lobsters, said they, we perceive but little blood; but in Crabs, Oisters, Cockles, &c. none at all. Then the Emperess asked them in what part of their bodies that little blood did reside? They answer'd, in a small vein, which in Lobsters went through the middle of their tails, but in Crea-fishes was found in their backs: as for other sorts of Fishes, some, said they, had onely blood about their gills, and others in some other places of their bodies; but they had not as yet observed any whose veins did spread all over their bodies. The Emperess wondering that there could be living Animals without blood, to be better satisfied, desired the Worm-men to inform her, whether they had observed blood in all sorts of Worms? They answered, That as much as they could perceive, some had blood, and some not; a Moth, said they, had no blood at all, and a Lowse had but like a Lobster, a little vein along her back: Also Nits, Snails and Maggots, as well as those that are generated out of Cheese and Fruits, as those that are produced out of Flesh, had no blood. But replied the Emperess, If those mentioned creatures have no blood, how is it possible they can live; for it is commonly said, that the life of an Animal consists in the blood, which is the seat of the Animal spirits? They answered, That blood was not a necessary propriety[2] to the life of an

---

1   crayfish
2   property

animal, and that that which was commonly called animal spirits, was nothing else but corporeal motions proper to the nature and figure of an animal. Then she asked both the Fish- and Worm-men, whether all those Creatures that have blood, had a circulation of blood in their veins and arteries? But they answered, That it was impossible to give her Majesty an exact account thereof, by reason the circulation of blood was an interior motion, which their senses, neither of themselves, nor by the help of any optick instrument could perceive; but as soon as they had dissected an animal Creature to find out the truth thereof, the interior corporeal motions proper to that particular figure or creature were altered. Then said the Emperess, if all animal Creatures have not blood, it is certain, they have neither all muscles, tendons, nerves, &c. But, said she, Have you ever observed animal Creatures that are neither Flesh, nor Fish, but of an intermediate degree between both. Truly, answered both the Fish- and Worm-men, We have observed several animal Creatures that live both in water, and on the Earth indifferently, and if any, certainly those may be said to be of such a mixt nature, that is, partly flesh, and partly fish: But how is it possible, replied the Emperess, that they should live both in Water, and on the Earth, since those Animals that live by the respiration of air, cannot live within Water, and those that live in Water, cannot live by the respiration of Air, as experience doth sufficiently witness. They answered her Majesty, That as there were different sorts of Creatures, so they had also different ways of respirations; for respiration, said they, was nothing else but a composition and division of parts, and the motions of nature being infinitely various, it was impossible that all Creatures should have the like motions; wherefore it was not necessary, that all animal Creatures should be bound to live either by the air, or by water onely, but according as Nature had ordered it convenient to their species. The Emperess seem'd very well satisfied with their answer, and desired to be further informed, Whether all animal Creatures did continue their species by a successive propagation of particulars, and whether in every species the offspring did always resemble their Generator or Producer, both in their interior and exterior figures? They answered her Majesty, That some species or sorts of Creatures, were kept up by a successive propagation of an offspring that was like the producer, but some were not; of the first rank, said they, are all those animals that are of different sexes, besides several others; but of the second rank are for the most part those we call insects, whose production proceeds from such causes as have no conformity or likeness with their produced effects; as for example, Maggots bred out of Cheese, and several others generated out of Earth, Water, and the like. But said the Emperess, there is some likeness between Maggots and Cheese, for Cheese has no blood, and so neither have Maggots; besides, they have almost the same taste which Cheese has. This proves nothing, answered they; for Maggots have a visible, local, progressive motion, which Cheese hath not. The Emperess replied, That when all the Cheese was turned into Maggots, it might be said to have local, progressive motion. They answered, That when the Cheese by its own figurative motions was changed into Maggots, it was no more Cheese. The Emperess confessed that she observed Nature was infinitely various in her works, and that though the species of Creatures did continue, yet their particulars were subject to infinite changes. But since you have informed me, said she, of the various sorts and productions of animal Creatures, I desire you to tell me what you have observed of their sensitive perceptions? Truly, answered they, Your Majesty puts a very hard question to us, and we shall hardly be able to give a satisfactory answer to it; for there are many different sorts of Creatures, which as they have all different perceptions, so they have also different organs, which our senses are not able to discover, onely in an Oyster-shell we have with admiration observed, that the common *sensorium*[1] of the Oyster lies just at the closing of the shells, where the pressure and reaction may be perceived by the opening and shutting of the shells every tide.

After all this, the Emperess desired the Worm-men to give her a true Relation how frost was made upon the Earth? To which they answered, That it was made much after the manner and description of the Fish- and Bird-men, concerning the Congelation of Water into Ice and Snow, by a commixture of saline and acid particles; which relation added a great light to the Ape-men, who were the Chymists, concerning their Chymical principles, Salt, Sulphur and Mercury. But, said the Emperess, if it be so, it will require an infinite multitude of saline particles to produce such a great quantity of Ice, Frost and Snow: besides, said she, when Snow, Ice and Frost, turn again into

---

1   the nucleus of sensation or perception

their former principle, I would fain know what becomes of those saline particles? But neither the Worm-men, nor the Fish- and Bird-men, could give her an answer to it.

Then the Emperess enquired of them the reason, Why Springs were not as salt as the Sea is? also, why Springs did ebb and flow? To which some answered, That the ebbing and flowing of some Springs was caused by hollow Caverns within the Earth, where the Sea-water crowding thorow, did thrust forward, and draw back-ward the Spring-water, according to its own way of ebbing and flowing; but others said, That it proceeded from a small proportion of saline and acid particles, which the Spring-water imbibed from the Earth; and although it was not so much as to be perceived by the sense of Taste, yet was it enough to cause an ebbing and flowing motion. And as for the Spring-water being fresh, they gave, according to their observation, this following reason: There is, said they, a certain heat within the bowels of the Earth, proceeding from its swift circular motion upon its own axe,[1] which heat distills the rarest parts of the Earth into a fresh and insipid water, which water being through the pores of the Earth, conveighed into a place where it may break forth without resistance or obstruction, causes Springs and Fountains; and these distilled waters within the Earth do nourish and refresh the grosser and dryer parts thereof. This Relation confirmed the Emperess in the opinion concerning the motion of the Earth, and the fixedness of the Sun,[2] as the Bird-men had informed her; and then she asked the Worm-men, whether Minerals and Vegetables were generated by the same heat that is within the bowels of the Earth? To which they could give her no positive answer; onely, this they affirmed, That heat and cold were not the primary producing causes of either Vegetables or Minerals, or other sorts of Creatures, but onely effects; and to prove this our assertion, said they, we have observed, that by change of some sorts of corporeal motions, that which is now hot, will become cold; and what is now cold, will grow hot; but the hottest place of all, we find to be the Center of the Earth: Neither do we observe, that the torrid Zone does contain so much Gold and Silver as the Temperate; nor is there great store of Iron and Lead wheresoever there is Gold;

---

1   axle or axis
1   the Copernican hypothesis

for these metals are most found in colder climates towards either of the Poles. This observation, the Emperess commanded them to confer with her Chymists, the Ape-men, to let them know that Gold was not produced by a violent, but a temperate degree of heat. She asked further, Whether Gold could not be made by Art? They answered, That they could not certainly tell her Majesty, but if it was possible to be done, they thought Tin, Lead, Brass, Iron and Silver, to be the fittest metals for such an Artificial transmutation. Then she asked them, Whether Art could produce Iron, Tin, Lead, or Silver? They answered, not, in their opinion. Then I perceive, replied the Emperess, that your judgments are very irregular, since you believe that Gold, which is so fixt a metal, that nothing has been found as yet which could occasion a dissolution of its interior figure, may be made by Art, and not Tin, Lead, Iron, Copper or Silver; which yet are so far weaker, and meaner metals then Gold is. But the Worm-men excused themselves, that they were ignorant in that Art, and that such questions belonged more properly to the Ape-men, which were Her Majesties Chymists.

Then the Emperess asked them, Whether by their sensitive perceptions they could observe the interior corporeal, figurative motions both of Vegetables and Minerals? They answer'd, That their senses could perceive them after they were produced, but not before; Nevertheless, said they, although the interior, figurative motions of natural Creatures are not subject to the exterior, animal, sensitive perceptions, yet by their rational perception they may judg of them, and of their productions if they be regular: Whereupon the Emperess commanded the Bear-men to lend them some of their best Microscopes; at which the Bear-men smilingly answered her Majesty, that their Glasses would do them but little service in the bowels of the Earth, because there was no light; for, said they, our Glasses do onely represent exterior objects, according to the various reflections and positions of light; and wheresoever light is wanting, the glasses will do no good. To which the Worm-men replied, that although they could not say much of refractions, reflections, inflections, and the like; yet were they not blind, even in the bowels of the Earth; for they could see the several sorts of Minerals, as also minute Animals, that lived there, which minute animal Creatures were not blind neither, but had some kind of sensitive perception that was as serviceable to them, as sight, taste, smell, touch, hearing, &c. was to other animal Creatures: By which it is evident, That Nature has been as bountiful to those Creatures that live underground, or in the bowels of the Earth, as to those that live upon the surface of the Earth, or in the Air, or in Water. But howsoever, proceeded the Worm-men, although there is light in the bowels of the Earth, yet your Microscopes will do but little good there, by reason those Creatures that live under ground have not such an optick sense as those that live on the surface of the Earth: wherefore, unless you had such glasses as are proper for their perception, your Microscopes will not be any ways advantagious to them. The Emperess seem'd well pleased with this answer of the Worm-men; and asked them further, whether Minerals and all other Creatures within the Earth, were colourless? At which question they could not forbear laughing; and when the Emperess asked the reason why they laught; We most humbly beg your Majesties pardon, replied they; for we could not chuse but laugh, when we heard of a colourless body. Why, said the Emperess, colour is onely an accident, which is an immaterial thing, and has no being of it self, but in an other body. Those, replied they, that informed your Majesty thus, surely their rational motions were very irregular; For how is it possible, that a natural nothing can have a being in Nature? If it be no substance, it cannot have a being, and if no being, it is nothing; Wherefore the distinction between subsisting of it self, and subsisting in another body, is a meer nicety, and non-sense; for there is nothing in Nature that can subsist of, or by it self, (I mean singly) by reason all parts of Nature are composed in one body, and though they may be infinitely divided, commixed and changed in their particulars, yet in general, parts cannot be separated from parts as long as Nature lasts; nay, we might as probably affirm, that Infinite Nature would be as soon destroyed, as that one Atome could perish; and therefore your Majesty may firmly believe, that there is no body without colour, nor no colour without body; for colour, figure, place, magnitude and body, are all but one thing, without any separation or abstraction from each other.

The Emperess was so wonderfully taken with this discourse of the Worm-men, that she not onely pardoned the rudeness they committed in laughing at first at her question, but yielded a full assent to their opinion, which she thought the most rational that ever she had heard yet; and then proceeding in her questions, enquired further, whether they had observed any seminal principles within the Earth free from all dimensions and qualities, which produced Vegetables, Minerals, and the like? To which they answered, That concerning the seeds of Minerals, their sensitive perceptions had never observed any; but Vegetables had certain seeds out of which they were produced. Then she asked, whether those seeds of Vegetables lost their species; that is, were annihilated in the production of their off-spring? To which they answered, That by an annihilation, nothing could be produced, and that the seeds of Vegetables were so far from being annihilated in their productions, that they did rather numerously increase and multiply; for the division of one seed, said they, does produce numbers of seeds out of it self. But replied the Emperess, A particular part cannot increase of it self. 'Tis true, answer'd they: but they increase not barely of themselves, but by joining and commixing with other parts, which do assist them in their productions, and by way of imitation form or figure their own parts into such or such particulars. Then, I pray inform me, said the Emperess, what disguise those seeds put on, and how they do conceal themselves in their transmutations? They answered, That seeds did no ways disguise or conceal, but rather divulge themselves in the multiplication of their off-spring; onely they did hide and conceal themselves from their sensitive perceptions so, that their figurative and productive motions were not perceptible by animal Creatures. Again, the Emperess asked them, whether there were any Non-beings within the Earth? To which they answered, That they never heard of any such thing; and that, if her Majesty would know the truth thereof, she must ask those Creatures that are called Immaterial Spirits, which had a great affinity with Non-beings, and perhaps could give her a satisfactory answer to this question. Then she desired to be informed, what opinion they had of the beginning of forms? They told her Majesty, That they did not understand what she meant by this expression; For, said they, there is no beginning in Nature, no not of Particulars, by reason Nature is Eternal and Infinite, and her particulars are subject to infinite changes and transmutations by vertue of their own corporeal, figurative self-motions; so that there's nothing new in Nature, nor properly a beginning of any thing. The Emperess seem'd well satisfied with all those answers, and enquired further, whether there was no Art used by those Creatures that live within the Earth? Yes, answered they: for the several parts of the Earth do join and assist each other in composition or framing of such or such particulars; and many times, there are factions and divisions, which cause productions of mixt species; as for example, weeds, instead of sweet flowers and useful fruits; but Gardeners and Husbandmen use often to decide their quarrels, and cause them to agree; which though it shews a kindness to the differing parties, yet 'tis a great prejudice to the Worms, and other animal Creatures that live under ground; for it most commonly causes their dissolution and ruine, at best they are driven out of their habitations. What, said the Emperess, are not Worms produced out of the Earth? Their production in general, answered they, is like the production of all other natural Creatures, proceeding from the corporeal figurative motions of Nature; but as for their particular productions, they are according to the nature of their species; some are produced out of flowers, some out of roots, some out of fruits, some out of ordinary Earth. Then they are very ungrateful Children, replied the Emperess, that they feed on their own Parents which gave them life. Their life, answered they, is their own, and not their Parents; for no part or Creature of Nature can either give or take away life, but parts do onely assist and join with parts, either in the dissolution or production of other parts and Creatures.

After this, and several other Conferences, which the Emperess held with the Worm-men, she dismissed them; and having taken much satisfaction in several of their answers, encouraged them in their studies and observations. Then she made a convocation of her Chymists, the Ape-men, and commanded them to give her an account of the several Transmutations which their Art was able to produce. They begun first with a long and tedious discourse concerning the Primitive Ingredients of Natural bodies, and how, by their Art, they had found out the principles out of which they consist. But they did not all agree in their opinions; for some said, That the Principles of all natural bodies were the four Elements, Fire, Air, Water, Earth, out of which they were composed: Others rejected this Elementary commixture, and said, There were many bodies out of which none of the four Elements could be extracted by any degree of Fire whatsoever; and that, on the other side, there were divers bodies, whose resolution by fire reduced them into more then four different ingredients; and these affirmed, that the onely principles of natural bodies were Salt, Sulphur, and Mercury: Others again declared, That none of the forementioned could be called the True principles of natural bodies, but that by their industry and pains which they had taken in the Art of Chymistry, they had discovered, that all natural bodies were produced but from one Principle, which was Water; for all Vegetables, Minerals and Animals, said they, are nothing else, but simple water distinguished into various figures by the vertue of their seeds. But after a great many debates and contentions about this subject, the Emperess being so much tired that she was not able to hear them any longer, imposed a general silence upon them, and then declared her self in this following discourse:

I am too sensible of the pains you have taken in the Art of Chymistry, to discover the principles of natural bodies, and wish they had been more profitably bestowed upon some other, then such experiments; for both by my own contemplation, and the observations which I have made by my rational and sensitive perception upon Nature, and her works, I find, that Nature is but one Infinite self-moving body, which by the vertue of its self-motion, is divided into infinite parts, which parts being restless, undergo perpetual changes and transmutations by their infinite compositions and divisions. Now, if this be so, as surely, according to regular sense and reason, it appears no otherwise; it is in vain to look for primary ingredients, or constitutive principles of natural bodies, since there is no more but one Universal principle of Nature, to wit, self-moving Matter, which is the onely cause of all natural effects. Next, I desire you to consider, that Fire is but a particular Creature, or effect of Nature, and occasions not onely different effects in several bodies, but on some bodies has no power at all; witness Gold, which never could be brought yet to change its interior figure by the art of Fire; and if this be so, Why should you be so simple as to believe that fire can shew you the principles of Nature? and that either the four Elements, or Water onely, or Salt, Sulphur and Mercury, all which are no more but particular effects and Creatures of Nature, should be the Primitive ingredients or Principles of all natural bodies? Wherefore, I will not have you to take more pains, and waste your time in such fruitless attempts, but be wiser hereafter; and busie your selves with such Experiments as may be beneficial to the publick.

The Emperess having thus declared her mind to the Ape-men, and given them better Instructions then perhaps they expected, not knowing that her Majesty had such great and able judgment in Natural Philosophy,[1] had several conferences with them concerning Chymical Preparations, which for brevities sake, I'le forbear to rehearse: Amongst the rest, she asked, how it came, that the Imperial Race appear'd so young, and yet was reported to have lived so long; some of them two, some three, and some four hundred years? and whether it was by Nature, or a special Divine blessing? To which they answered, That there was a certain Rock in the parts of that World, which contained the Golden Sands, which Rock was hollow within, and did produce a Gum that was a hundred years before it came to its full strength and perfection; this Gum, said they, if it be held in a warm hand, will dissolve into an Oyl, the effects whereof are following: It being given every day for some certain time to an old decayed man, in the bigness of a little Pea, will first make him spit for a week, or more; after this, it will cause Vomits of Flegm, and after that it will bring forth by vomits, humors[2] of several colours; first of a pale yellow, then of a deep yellow, then of a green, and lastly of a black colour; and each of these humors have a several taste, some are fresh, some salt, some sower, some bitter, and so forth; neither do all these Vomits make them sick, but they come out on a sudden and unawares, without any pain or trouble to the patient: And after it hath done all these mentioned effects, and clear'd both the stomack and several other parts of the body, then it works upon the brain, and brings forth of the nose such kind of humors as it did out of the mouth, and much after the same manner; then it will purge by stool, then by urine, then by sweat, and lastly by bleeding at the nose, and the Emerodes;[3] all which effects it will perform within the space of six weeks, or a little more; for it does not work very strongly, but gently, and by degrees: Lastly, when it has done all this, it will make the body break out into a thick scab, and cause both Hair, Teeth and Nails to come off; which scab being arrived to its full maturity, opens first along the back, and comes off all in a piece like an armour, and all this is done within the space of four months. After this the Patient is wrapt into a sear-cloth,[4] prepared of certain Gums and Juices, where-

---

1   natural philosophy: seventeenth-century term for science
2   bodily fluids
3   emerods or haemorrhoids
4   cerecloth: cloth impregnated with wax or gum, used as a dressing in surgery

in he continues until the time of nine Months be expired from the first beginning of the cure, which is the time of a Childs formation in the womb. In the mean while his diet is nothing else but Eagles-eggs, and Hinds-milk; and after the Sear-cloth is taken away, he will appear of the age of Twenty, both in shape, and strength. The weaker sort of this Gum is soveraign in healing of wounds and curing of slight distempers. But this is also to be observed, that none of the Imperial race does use any other drink but Lime-water, or water in which Lime-stone is immerged;[1] their meat is nothing else but Fowl of several sorts, their recreations are many, but chiefly Hunting.

This Relation amazed the Emperess very much; for though in the world she came from, she had heard great reports of the Philosophers-stone,[2] yet had she not heard of any that had ever found it out, which made her believe that it was but a Chymera; she called also to mind, that there had been in the same world a man who had a little Stone which cured all kinds of Diseases outward and inward, according as it was applied; and that a famous Chymist[3] had found out a certain liquor called Alkahest,[4] which by the vertue of its own fire, consumed all diseases; but she had never heard of a Medicine that could renew old Age, and render it beautiful, vigorous and strong: Nor would she have so easily believed it, had it been a medicine prepared by Art; for she knew that Art, being Natures Changeling, was not able to produce such a powerful effect, but being that the Gum did grow naturally, she did not so much scruple at it; for she knew that Natures Works are so various and wonderful, that no particular Creature is able to trace her ways.

The Conferences of the Chymists being finished, the Emperess made an Assembly of her Galenical Physicians,[5] her Herbalists and Anatomists; and first she enquired of her Herbalists the particular effects of several Herbs and Drugs, and whence they proceeded. To

---

1 immersed
2 in alchemy, a substance supposed to have the capability of transmuting base metals into gold
3 Paracelsus (1490-1541), Swiss physician and scientist, founder of alchemical medicine
4 in alchemy, a supposed "universal solvent"
5 followers of the second-century physician Galen, who used herbal (Galenic) rather than chemical (Paracelsian) remedies; in her scientific writings Cavendish preferred herbal remedies

which they answered, that they could, for the most part, tell her Majesty the vertues and operations of them, but the particular causes of their effects were unknown; onely thus much they could say, that their operations and vertues were generally caused by their proper inherent, corporeal, figurative motions, which being infinitely various in Infinite Nature, did produce infinite several effects. And it is observed, said they, that Herbs and Drugs are as wise in their operations, as Men in their words and actions; nay, wiser; and their effects are more certain then Men in their opinions; for though they cannot discourse like Men, yet have they sense and reason, as well as Men; for the discursive faculty is but a particular effect of sense and reason in some particular Creatures, to wit, Men, and not a principle of Nature, and argues often more folly then wisdom. The Emperess asked, Whether they could not by a composition and commixture of other Drugs, make them work other effects then they did, used by themselves? They answered, That they could make them produce artificial effects, but not alter their inherent, proper and particular natures.

Then the Emperess commanded her Anatomists to dissect such kinds of Creatures as are called Monsters. But they answered her Majesty, That it would be but an unprofitable and useless work, and hinder their better imployments; for when we dissect dead Animals, said they, it is for no other end, but to observe what defects or distempers they had, that we may cure the like in living ones, so that all our care and industry concerns onely the preservation of Mankind; but we hope your Majesty will not preserve Monsters, which are most commonly destroyed, except it be for novelty; neither will the dissection of Monsters prevent the errors of Natures irregular actions; for by dissecting some, we cannot prevent the production of others; so that our pains and labour will be to no purpose, unless to satisfie the vain curiosities of inquisitive men. The Emperess replied, That such dissections would be very beneficial to Experimental Philosophers. If Experimental Philosophers, answer'd they, do spend their time in such useless inspections, they waste it in vain, and have nothing but their labour for their pains.

Lastly, her Majesty had some Conferences with the Galenick Physicians about several Diseases, and amongst the rest, desired to know the cause and nature of Apoplexy, and the spotted Plague. They answered, That a deadly Apoplexy was a dead palsie of the brain, and the spotted Plague was a Gangrene of the Vital parts, and as the Gangrene of outward parts did strike inwardly; so the Gangrene of inward parts, did break forth outwardly; which is the cause, said they, that as soon as the spots appear, death follows; for then it is an infallible sign, that the body is throughout infected with a Gangrene, which is a spreading evil; but some Gangrenes do spread more suddenly then others, and of all sorts of Gangrenes, the Plaguy-gangrene is the most infectious; for other Gangrenes infect but the next adjoining parts of one particular body, and having killed that same Creature, go no further, but cease; when as, the Gangrene of the Plague, infects not onely the adjoining parts of one particular Creature, but also those that are distant; that is, one particular body infects another, and so breeds a Universal Contagion. But the Emperess being very desirous to know in what manner the Plague was propagated and became so contagious, asked, Whether it went actually out of one body into another? To which they answered, That it was a great dispute amongst the Learned of their profession, whether it came by a division and composition of parts; that is, by expiration and inspiration; or whether it was caused by imitation: Some Experimental Philosophers, said they, will make us believe, that by the help of their Microscopes, they have observed the Plague to be a body of little Flyes like Atomes, which go out of one body into another, through the sensitive passages; but the most experienced and wisest of our society, have rejected this opinion as a ridiculous fancy, and do for the most part believe, that it is caused by an imitation of Parts, so that the motions of some parts which are sound, do imitate the motions of those that are infected, and that by this means, the Plague becomes contagious and spreading.

The Emperess having hitherto spent her time in the Examination of the Bird- Fish- Worm- and Ape-men, &c. and received several Intelligences from their several imployments; at last had a mind to divert her self after her serious discourses, and therefore she sent for the Spider-men, which were her Mathematicians, the Lice-men which were her Geometricians, and the Magpie- Parrot- and Jack-daw-men, which were her Orators and Logicians. The Spider-men came first, and presented her Majesty with a table full of Mathematical points, lines and figures of all sorts of squares, circles, triangles, and the like; which the Emperess, notwithstanding that she had a very ready wit, and quick apprehension, could not understand; but the more she endeavoured to learn, the more was she confounded: Whether they did ever square the circle,[1] I cannot exactly tell, nor whether they could make imaginary points and lines; but this I dare say, That their points and lines were so slender, small and thin, that they seem'd next to Imaginary. The Mathematicians were in great esteem with the Emperess, as being not onely the chief Tutors and Instructors in many Arts, but some of them excellent Magicians and Informers of Spirits, which was the reason their Characters were so abstruse and intricate, that the Emperess knew not what to make of them. There is so much to learn in your Art, said she, that I can neither spare time from other affairs to busie my self in your profession; nor, if I could, do I think I should ever be able to understand your Imaginary points, lines and figures, because they are Non-beings.

Then came the Lice-men, and endeavoured to measure all things to a hairs breadth, and weigh them to an Atome; but their weights would seldom agree, especially in the weighing of Air,[2] which they found a task impossible to be done; at which the Emperess began to be displeased, and told them, that there was neither Truth nor Justice in their Profession; and so dissolved their society.

After this the Emperess was resolved to hear the Magpie- Parrot- and Jackdaw-men, which were her professed Orators and Logicians; whereupon one of the Parrot-men rose with great formality, and endeavoured to make an Eloquent Speech before her Majesty; but before he had half ended, his arguments and divisions being so many, that they caused a great confusion in his brain, he could not go forward, but was forced to retire backward, with great disgrace both to himself, and the whole society; and although one of his brethren endeavoured to second him by another speech, yet was he as far to seek as the former. At which the Emperess appear'd not a little troubled, and told them, That they followed too much the Rules of Art, and confounded themselves with too nice formalities and distinctions; but since I know, said she, that you are a people who have naturally voluble tongues, and good memories; I desire you to consider

---

1 Cavendish learned of this and other classical mathematical problems from her brother-in-law, Sir Charles Cavendish (see Mendelson, *Mental World*, 28, 37-8). For a poem on the squaring of the circle, see below, p. 000.

2 The weighing of air was one of the experiments performed before the Duchess during her visit to the Royal Society on 30 May 1667, a year after the first publication of *The Blazing World*.

more the subject you speak of, then your artificial periods, connexions and parts of speech, and leave the rest to your natural Eloquence; which they did, and so became very eminent Orators.

Lastly, her Imperial Majesty being desirous to know, what progress her Logicians had made in the Art of disputing, Commanded them to argue upon several Themes or subjects; which they did; and having made a very nice discourse of Logistical terms and propositions, entered into a dispute by way of Syllogistical Arguments, through all the Figures and Modes: One began with an argument of the first mode of the first figure, thus:

> *Every Politician is wise:*
> *Every Knave is a Politician,*
> *Therefore every Knave is wise.*

Another contradicted him with a Syllogism of the second mode of the same figure, thus:

> *No Politician is wise:*
> *Every Knave is a Politician,*
> *Therefore no Knave is wise.*

The third made an Argument in the third Mode of the same figure, after this manner:

> *Every Politician is wise:*
> *Some Knaves are Politicians,*
> *Therefore some Knaves are wise.*

The Fourth concluded with a Syllogism in the fourth Mode of the same figure, thus:

> *No Politician is wise:*
> *Some Knaves are Politicians,*
> *Therefore some Knaves are not wise.*

After this they took another subject, and one propounded this Syllogism:

> Every Philosopher is wise:
> Every Beast is wise,
> Therefore every Beast is a Philosopher.

But another said that this Argument was false, therefore he contradicted him with a Syllogism of the second figure of the fourth Mode, thus:

> Every Philosopher is wise:
> Some Beasts are not wise,
> Therefore some Beasts are not Philosophers.

Thus they argued, and intended to go on, but the Emperess interrupted them: I have enough, said she, of your chopt Logick, and will hear no more of your Syllogismes; for it disorders my reason, and puts my brain on the rack; your formal argumentations are able to spoil all natural wit; and I'le have you to consider, that Art does not make Reason, but Reason makes Art; and therefore as much as Reason is above Art, so much is a natural rational discourse to be preferred before an artificial: For Art is, for the most part, irregular, and disorders mens understandings more then it rectifies them, and leads them into a Labyrinth whence they'l never get out, and makes them dull and unfit for useful imployments; especially your Art of Logick, which consists onely in contradicting each other, in making sophismes, and obscuring Truth, instead of clearing it.

But they replied [to] her Majesty, That the knowledg of Nature, that is, Natural Philosophy, would be imperfect without the Art of Logick, and that there was an improbable Truth which could no otherwise be found out then by the Art of disputing. Truly, said the Emperess, I do believe that it is with Natural Philosophy, as it is with all other effects of Nature; for no particular knowledg can be perfect, by reason knowledg is dividable, as well as composable; nay, to speak properly, Nature her self cannot boast of any perfection, but God himself; because there are so many irregular motions in Nature, and 'tis but a folly to think that Art should be able to regulate them, since Art itself is, for the most part, irregular. But as for Improbable Truth, I know not what your meaning is; for Truth is more then Improbability; nay, there is so much difference between Truth and Improbability, that I cannot conceive it possible how they can be joined together. In short, said she, I do no ways approve of your profession; and though I will not dissolve your society, yet I shall never take delight in hearing you any more; wherefore confine your disputations to your Schools, lest besides the Commonwealth of Learning, they disturb also Divinity and Policy, Religion and Laws, and by that means draw an utter ruine and destruction both upon Church and State.

After the Emperess had thus finish'd the Discourses and Conferences with the mentioned Societies of her Vertuoso's, she considered by her self the manner of their Religion, and finding it very defective, was troubled, that so wise and knowing a people should have no more knowledg of the Divine Truth; Wherefore she consulted with her own thoughts, whether it was possible to convert them all to her own Religion, and to that end she resolved to build Churches, and make also up a Congregation of Women, whereof she intended to be the head her self, and to instruct them in the several points of her Religion. This she had no sooner begun, but the Women, which generally had quick wits, subtile conceptions, clear understandings, and solid judgments, became, in a short time, very devout and zealous Sisters; for the Emperess had an excellent gift of Preaching, and instructing them in the Articles of Faith; and by that means, she converted them not onely soon, but gained an extraordinary love of all her subjects throughout that World. But at last, pondering with her self the inconstant nature of Mankind, and fearing that in time they would grow weary, and desert the divine Truth, following their own fancies, and living according to their own desires, she began to be troubled that her labours and pains should prove of so little effect, and therefore studied all manner of ways to prevent it. Amongst the rest, she call'd to mind a Relation which the Bird-men made her once, of a Mountain that did burn in flames of fire; and thereupon did immediately send for the wisest and subtilest of her Worm-men, commanding them to discover the cause of the Eruption of that same fire; which they did; and having dived to the very bottom of the Mountain, informed her Majesty, That there was a certain sort of Stone, whose Nature was such, that being wetted, it would grow excessively hot, and break forth into a flaming-fire, until it became dry, and then it ceased from burning. The Emperess was glad to hear this news, and forthwith desired the Worm-men to bring her some of that stone, but be sure to keep it secret: She sent also for the Bird-men, and asked them whether they could not get her a piece of the Sun-stone? They answered, That it was impossible, unless they did spoil or lessen the light of the World: but, said they, if it please your Majesty, we can demolish one of the numerous Stars of the Sky, which the World will never miss.

The Emperess was very well satisfied with this proposal, and having thus imployed these two sorts of men, in the mean while builded two Chappels one above another; the one she lined throughout with Diamonds, both Roof, Walls and Pillars; but the other she resolved to line with the Star-stone; the Fire-stone she placed upon the Diamond-lining, by reason Fire has no power on Diamonds; and when she would have that Chappel where the Fire-stone was, appear all in a flame, she had by the means of Artificial-pipes, water conveighed into it, which by turning the Cock, did, as out of a Fountain, spring over all the room, and as long as the fire-stone was wet, the Chappel seemed to be all in a flaming fire.

The other Chappel, which was lined with the Star-stone, did onely cast a splendorous and comfortable light; both the Chappels stood upon Pillars, just in the middle of a round Cloyster which was dark as night; neither was there any other light within them, but what came from the Fire- and Star-stone; and being every where open, allowed to all that were within the compass of the Cloyster, a free prospect into them; besides, they were so artificially contrived, that they did both move in a circle about their own Centres, without intermission, contrary ways. In the Chappel which was lined with the Fire-stone, the Emperess preached Sermons of terror to the wicked, and told them of the punishments for their sins, to wit, that after this life they should be tormented in an everlasting fire. But in the other Chappel lined with the Star-stone, she preached Sermons of comfort to those that repented of their sins, and were troubled at their own wickedness; Neither did the heat of the flame in the least hinder her; for the Fire-stone did not cast so great a heat but the Emperess was able to endure it, by reason the water which was poured on the stone, by its own self-motion turned into a flaming fire, occasioned by the natural motions of the Stone, which made the flame weaker then if it had been fed by some other kind of fuel; the other Chappel where the Star-stone was, although it did cast a great light, yet was it without all heat, and the Emperess appear'd like an Angel in it; and as that Chappel was an embleme of *Hell*, so this was an embleme of *Heaven*. And thus the Emperess, by Art, and her own ingenuity, did not onely convert the Blazing-world to her own Religion, but kept them in a constant belief, without inforcement or blood-shed; for she knew well, that belief was a thing not to be forced or pressed upon the people, but to be instilled into their minds by gentle perswasions; and after this manner she encouraged them also in all other duties and employments, for Fear, though it makes people obey, yet does it not last so long, nor is it so sure a means to keep them to their duties, as Love.

Last of all, when she saw that both Church and State was now in a well-ordered and setled condition, her thoughts reflected upon the world she came from; and though she had a great desire to know the condition of the same, yet could she advise no manner of way how to gain any knowledg thereof; at last, after many serious considerations, she conceived that it was impossible to be done by any other means, then by the help of Immaterial Spirits; wherefore she made a Convocation of the most learned, witty and ingenious of all the forementioned sorts of men, and desired to know of them, whether there were any Immaterial Spirits in their World. First, she enquired of the Worm-men, whether they had perceived some within the Earth? They answered her Majesty, That they never knew of any such Creatures; for whatsoever did dwell within the Earth, said they, was imbodied and material. Then she asked the Flye-men, whether they had observed any in the Air? for you having numerous eyes, said she, will be more able to perceive them, then any other Creatures. To which they answered her Majesty, That although Spirits, being immaterial, could not be perceived by the Worm-men in the Earth, yet they perceived that such Creatures did lodg in the vehicles of the Air. Then the Emperess asked, Whether they could speak to them, and whether they did understand each other? The Fly-men answered, That those Spirits were always cloath'd in some sort or other of Material Garments; which Garments were their Bodies, made, for the most part, of Air; and when occasion served, they could put on any other sort of substances; but yet they could not put these substances into any form or shape, as they pleased. The Emperess asked the Flymen, whether it was possible that she could be acquainted, and have some conferences with them? They answered, They did verily believe she might. Hereupon the Emperess commanded the Fly-men to ask some of the Spirits, whether they would be pleased to give her a visit? This they did; and after the Spirits had presented themselves to the Emperess, (in what shapes or forms, I cannot exactly tell) after some few complements that passed between them, the Emperess told the Spirits that she questioned not, but they did know how she was a stranger in that World, and by what miraculous means she was arrived there; and since she had a great desire to know the condition of the World she came from, her request to the Spirits was, to give her some information thereof, especially of those parts of the world where she was born, bred, and educated, as also of her particular friends and acquaintance; all which, the Spirits did according to her desire; at last, after a great many conferences and particular intelligences, which the Spirits gave the Emperess, to her great satisfaction and content, she enquired after the most famous Students, Writers, and Experimental Philosophers in that World, which they gave her a full relation of; amongst the rest she enquired, whether there were none that had found out yet the Jews Cabbala? Several have endeavoured it, answered the Spirits, but those that came nearest (although themselves denied it) were one Dr. *Dee*, and one *Edward Kelly*, the one representing *Moses*, and the other *Aaron*; for *Kelly* was to Dr. *Dee*, as *Aaron* to *Moses*;[1] but yet they proved at last but meer Cheats, and were described by one of their own Country-men, a famous Poet, named *Ben. Johnson*, in a Play call'd *The Alchymist*,[2] where he expressed *Kelly* by Capt. *Face*, and *Dee* by Dr. *Subtle*, and their two Wives by *Doll Common*, and the Widow; by the Spaniard in the Play, he meant the Spanish Ambassador, and by Sir *Epicure Mammon*, a Polish Lord. The Emperess remembred that she had seen the Play, and asked the Spirits whom he meant by the name of *Ananias*? Some Zealous Brethren, answered they, in *Holland*, *Germany*, and several other places. Then she asked them, Who was meant by the Druggist? Truly, answered the

---

1   The Cabbala, a Jewish medieval tradition of mystical interpretation of the Penta-
     teuch or Hebrew Bible, was reinterpreted by Christian occult and mystical philoso-
     phers in early modern Europe. John Dee (1527-1608), mathematician and
     astrologer, with his partner Edward Kelly, was the best-known of English Christian
     cabbalists. For details and context, see Frances Yates, *The Occult Philosophy in the
     Elizabethan Age* (1979).
2   Ben Jonson's comedy *The Alchemist* was first performed in 1610 and printed in
     1612.

Spirits, we have forgot, it being so long since it was made and acted. What, replied the Emperess, can Spirits forget? Yes, said the Spirits; for what is past, is onely kept in memory, if it be not recorded. I did believe, said the Emperess, That Spirits had no need of memory, or remembrance, and could not be subject to forgetfulness. How can we, answered they, give an account of things present, if we had no memory, but especially of things past, unrecorded, if we had no remembrance? Said the Emperess, By present knowledg and understanding. The Spirits answered, That present knowledg and understanding was of actions or things present, not of past. But, said the Emperess, you know what is to come, without memory or remembrance, and therefore you may know what is past without memory and remembrance. They answered, That their foreknowledg was onely a prudent and subtile observation made by comparing of things or actions past, with those that are present, and that Remembrance was nothing else but a repetition of things or actions past.

Then the Emperess asked the Spirits, Whether there was a threefold *Cabbala?* They answered, *Dee* and *Kelly* made but a two-fold *Cabbala*, to wit, of the Old and New Testament, but others might not onely make two or three, but threescore *Cabbala's*, if they pleased. The Emperess asked, Whether it was a Traditional, or meerly a Scriptural, or whether it was a Literal, Philosophical, or Moral *Cabbala?*[1] Some, answered they, did believe it meerly Traditional, others Scriptural, some Literal, and some Metaphorical; but the truth is, said they, 'twas partly one, and partly the other; as partly a Traditional, partly a Scriptural, partly Literal, partly Metaphorical. The Emperess asked further, Whether the Cabbala was a work onely of natural reason, or of divine inspiration? Many, said the Spirits, that write Cabbala's pretend to divine Inspirations, but whether it be so, or not; it does not belong to us to judg; onely this we must needs confess, that it is a work which requires a good wit, and a strong faith, but not natural reason; for though natural reason is most perswasive, yet Faith is the chief that is required in Cabbalists. But, said the Emperess, Is there not Divine Reason, as well as there is Natural? No, answered they: for there is but a Divine Faith, and as for Reason it is onely natural; but you Mortals are so puzled about this divine Faith, and natural Reason, that you do

---

1   See Yates, *Occult Philosophy*, for the context of these philosophical debates.

not know well how to distinguish them, but confound them both, which is the cause you have so many divine Philosophers who make a Gallimafry[1] both of Reason and Faith. Then she asked, Whether pure natural Philosophers were Cabbalists? They answered, No; but onely your Mystical or Divine Philosophers, such as study beyond sense and reason. She enquired further, Whether there was any Cabbala in God, or whether God was full of Ideas? They answered, There could be nothing in God, nor could God be full of any thing, either forms or figures, but of himself; for God is the Perfection of all things, and an Unexpressible Being, beyond the conception of any Creature, either Natural or Supernatural. Then I pray inform me, said the Emperess, Whether the Jews, or any other Cabbala, consist in numbers? The Spirits answered, No: for numbers are odd, and different, and would make a disagreement in the Cabbala. But, said she again, Is it a sin then not to know or understand the Cabbala? God is so merciful, answered they, and so just, that he will never damn the ignorant, and save onely those that pretend to know him and his secret Counsels by their Cabbala's, but he loves those that adore and worship him with fear and reverence, and with a pure heart. She asked further, which of these two Cabbala's was most approved, the Natural, or Theological? The Theological, answered they, is mystical, and belongs onely to Faith; but the Natural belongs to Reason. Then she asked them, Whether Divine Faith was made out of Reason? No, answered they, for Faith proceeds onely from a Divine saving Grace, which is a peculiar Gift of God. How comes it then, replied she, that Men, even those that are of several opinions, have Faith more or less? A natural belief, answered they, is not a Divine Faith. But, proceeded the Emperess, How are you sure that God cannot be known? The several opinions you Mortals have of God, answered they, are sufficient witnesses thereof. Well then, replied the Emperess, leaving this inquisitive knowledg of God, I pray inform me, whether you Spirits give motion to natural bodies? No, answered they; but on the contrary, natural material bodies give Spirits motion; for we Spirits, being incorporeal, have no motion but from our corporeal vehicles, so that we move by the help of our bodies, and not the bodies by the help of us; for pure Spirits are immovable. If this be so, replied the Emperess, How comes

---

1   gallimaufry: a hash or hodgepodge

it then that you can move so suddenly at a vast distance? They answered, That some sorts of matter were more pure, rare, and consequently more light and agil then others; and this was the reason of their quick and sudden motions. Then the Emperess asked them, Whether they could speak without a body, or bodily organs? No, said they; nor could we have any bodily sense, but onely knowledg. She asked, whether they could have knowledg without body? Not a natural, answered they, but a Supernatural knowledg, which is a far better knowledg then a natural. Then she asked them, whether they had a General or Universal Knowledg? They answered, Single or particular created Spirits, have not; for not any Creature, but God Himself, can have an absolute and perfect knowledg of all things. The Emperess asked them further, Whether Spirits had inward and outward parts? No, answered they; for parts onely belong to bodies, not to Spirits. Again, she asked them, whether their Vehicles[1] were living bodies? They are self-moving bodies, answered they, and therefore they must needs be living; for nothing can move itself, without it hath life. Then, said she, it must necessarily follow, that this living, self-moving body gives a Spirit motion, and not that the Spirit gives the body, as its vehicle, motion. You say very true, answered they, and we told you this before. Then the Emperess asked them, of what forms of Matter those Vehicles were? They said they were of several different forms; some gross and dense, and others more pure, rare, and subtil. Then she enquired, whether Immaterial Spirits were not of a Globous[2] figure? They answered, Figure and Body were but one thing; for no Body was without Figure, nor no Figure without Body; and that it was as much non-sence to say, an Immaterial Figure, as to say an Immaterial Body. Again, she asked, whether Spirits were not like Water, or Fire? No, said they, for both Fire and Water are material; and we are no more like Fire or Water, then we are like Earth; nay, were it the purest and finest degree of Matter, even above the Heavens; for Immaterial Creatures cannot be likened or compared to Material; But, as we said before, our Vehicles being material, are of several degrees, forms and shapes. But if you be not material, said the Emperess, how can you be Generators of all Creatures? We are no more, answered they, the Gen-

---

1 vehicle: the material form in which something spiritual is embodied
2 globular

erators of material Creatures, then they are the Generators of us Spirits. Then she asked, whether they did leave their Vehicles? No, answered they; for we being incorporeal, cannot leave or quit them; but our Vehicles do change into several forms and figures, according as occasion requires. Then the Emperess desired the Spirits to tell her, whether Man was a little World?[1] They answered, That if a Fly or Worm was a little World, then Man was so too. She asked again, whether our Fore-fathers had been as wise, as men were at present, and had understood sense and reason, as well as they did now? They answered, That in former Ages they had been as wise as they are in this present, nay, wiser; for, said they, many in this age do think their Fore-fathers have been Fools, by which they prove themselves to be such. The Emperess asked further, whether there was any Plastick power in Nature? Truly, said the Spirits, Plastick power in a hard word, signifies no more then the power of the corporeal, figurative motions of Nature. After this, the Emperess desired the Spirits to inform her where the Paradise was, whether it was in the midst of the World as a Centre of pleasure? or whether it was the whole world, or a peculiar world by it self, as a world of life, and not of matter; or whether it was mixt, as a world of living animal Creatures? They answered, That Paradise was not in the world she came from, but in that world she lived in at present; and that it was the very same place where she kept her Court, and where her Palace stood, in the midst of the Imperial City. The Emperess asked further, whether in the beginning and Creation of the World, all Beasts could speak? They answered, That no Beasts could speak, but onely those sorts of Creatures which were Fish-men, Bear-men, Worm-men, and the like, which could speak in the first Age, as well as they do now. She asked again, whether they were none of those Spirits that frighted *Adam* out of the Paradise, at least caused him not to return thither again. They answered they were not. Then she desired to be informed, whither *Adam* fled when he was driven out of the Paradise. Out of this World, said they, you are now Emperess of, into the world you came from. If this be so, replied the Emperess, then surely those Cabbalists are much out of their story, who believe the Paradise to be a

---

1 For the early modern concept of man as a "little world" or microcosm, to be compared to the universe or macrocosm, see Tillyard 66.

world of Life onely, without Matter; for this world, though it be most pleasant and fruitful, yet it is not a world of meer immaterial life, but a world of living, material Creatures. Without question, they are, answered the Spirits; for not all Cabbalas are true. Then the Emperess asked, That since it is mentioned in the story of the Creation of the World, that *Eve* was tempted by the Serpent,[1] whether the Devil was within the Serpent, or whether the Serpent tempted her without the Devil? They answered, That the Devil was within the Serpent. But how came it then, replied she, that the Serpent was cursed? They answered, because the Devil was in him: for are not those men in danger of damnation which have the Devil within them, who perswades them to believe and act wickedly? The Emperess asked further, whether Light and the Heavens were all one. They answered, That that Region which contains the Lucid natural Orbs, was by mortals named Heaven; but the beatifical Heaven, which is the Habitation of the blessed Angels and Souls, was so far beyond it, that it could not be compared to any natural Creature. Then the Emperess asked them, whether all Matter was fluid at first? They answered, That Matter was always as it is; and that some parts of Matter were rare, some dense, some fluid, some solid, &c. Neither was God bound to make all matter fluid at first. She asked further, whether Matter was immovable in it self? We have answered you before, said they, That there is no motion but in Matter; and were it not for the motion of Matter, we Spirits, could not move, nor give you any answer to your several questions. After this, the Emperess asked the Spirits, whether the Universe was made within the space of six days, or whether by those six days, were meant so many Decrees or Commands of God? They answered her, that the World was made by the All-powerful Decree and Command of God; but whether there were six Decrees or Commands, or fewer, or more, no creature was able to tell. Then she inquired, whether there was no mystery in numbers? No other mystery, answered the Spirits, but reckoning and counting, for numbers are onely marks of remembrance. But what do you think of the number of Four, said she, which Cabbalists make such ado withal, and of the number of Ten, when they say that Ten is all, and that all numbers are virtually comprehended in four? We think, answered they,

---

1   See Genesis 3: 1-16.

that Cabbalists have nothing else to do but to trouble their heads with such useless fancies; for naturally there is no such thing as prime or all in numbers; nor is there any other mystery in numbers, but what mans fancy makes; but what men call Prime, or All, we do not know, because they do not agree in the number of their opinion. Then the Emperess asked, whether the number of six was a symbole of Matrimony, as being made up of Male and Female, for two into three is six. If any number can be a symbole of Matrimony, answered the Spirits, it is not Six, but Two; if two may be allowed to be a number: for the act of Matrimony is made up of two joined in one. She asked again, what they said to the number of Seven? whether it was not an Embleme of God, because Cabbalists say, that it is neither begotten, nor begets any other number. There can be no Embleme of God, answered the Spirits; for if we do not know what God is, how can we make an Embleme of him? Nor is there any number in God, for God is the perfection himself, but numbers are imperfect; and as for the begetting of numbers, it is done by Multiplication and Addition; but Subtraction is as a kind of death to numbers. If there be no mystery in numbers, replied the Emperess, then it is in vain to refer the Creation of the World to certain numbers, as Cabbalists do. The onely mystery of numbers, answered they, concerning the Creation of the World is, that as numbers do multiply, so does the world. The Emperess asked, how far numbers did multiply? The Spirits answered, to Infinite. Why, said she, Infinite cannot be reckoned, nor numbered. No more, answered they, can the parts of the Universe; for God's Creation, being an Infinite action, as proceeding from an Infinite Power, could not rest upon a finite number of Creatures, were it never so great. But leaving the mystery of numbers, proceeded the Emperess, Let me now desire you to inform me, whether the Suns and Planets were generated by the Heavens, or Æthereal Matter? The Spirits answered, That the Stars and Planets were of the same matter which the Heavens, the Æther, and all other natural Creatures did consist of; but whether they were generated by the Heavens or Æther, they could not tell: if they be, said they, they are not like their Parents; for the Sun, Stars, and Planets, are more splendorous then the Æther, as also more solid and constant in their motions: But put the case, the Stars and Planets were generated by the Heavens, and the Æthereal Matter; the question then would be, out of what these are generated or produced? if these be created out of nothing, and not generated out of something, then it is probable the Sun, Stars and Planets are so too; nay, it is more probable of the Stars and Planets, then of the Heavens, or the fluid Æther, by reason the Stars and Planets seem to be further off from mortality, then the particular parts of the Æther; for no doubt but the parts of the Æthereal Matter alter into several forms, which we do not perceive of the Stars and Planets. The Emperess asked further, whether they could give her information of the three principles of Man, according to the doctrine of the Platonists;[1] as first of the Intellect, Spirit, or Divine Light: 2. Of the Soul of Man her self: and 3. Of the Image of the Soul, that is, her vital operation on the body? The Spirits answered, that they did not understand these three distinctions; but that they seem'd to corporeal sense and reason, as if they were three several bodies, or three several corporeal actions; however, said they, they are intricate conceptions of irregular fancies. If you do not understand them, replied the Emperess, how shall humane Creatures do then? Many, both of your modern and ancient Philosophers, answered the Spirits, endeavour to go beyond sense and reason, which makes them commit absurdities; for no corporeal Creature can go beyond sense and reason; no not we Spirits, as long as we are in our corporeal Vehicles. Then the Emperess asked them, whether there were any Atheists in the World? The Spirits answered, that there were no more Atheists then what Cabbalists make. She asked them further, Whether Spirits were of a globous or round Figure? They answered, That Figure belonged to body, but they being immaterial had no figure. She asked again, Whether Spirits were not like Water or Fire? They answered, that Water and Fire was material, were it the purest and most refined that ever could be; nay, were it above the Heavens: But we are no more like Water or Fire, said they, then we are like Earth; but our Vehicles are of several forms, figures and degrees of substances. Then she desired to know, whether their Vehicles were made of Air? Yes, answered the Spirits, some of our Vehicles are of thin Air. Then I suppose, replied the Emperess, That those airy Vehicles, are your corporeal summersuits. She asked further, whether the Spirits had not ascending and descending

---

1   For the influence of Platonic and neo-Platonic doctrines on early modern thinkers, see Tillyard 21-2, 26, 34, 45-50.

motions, as well as other Creatures? They answered, That properly there was no ascension or descension in Infinite Nature, but onely in relation to particular parts; and as for us Spirits, said they, we can neither ascend nor descend without corporeal Vehicles; nor can our Vehicles ascend or descend, but according to their several shapes and figures, for there can be no motion without body. The Emperess asked them further, whether there was not a World of Spirits, as well as there is of material Creatures? No, answered they; for the word World implies a quantity or multitude of corporeal Creatures, but we being Immaterial, can make no world of Spirits. Then she desired to be informed when Spirits were made? We do not know, answered they, how and when we were made, nor are we much inquisitive after it; nay, if we did, it would be no benefit, neither for us, nor for you mortals to know it. The Emperess replied, That Cabbalists and Divine Philosophers said, mens rational Souls were Immaterial, and stood as much in need of corporeal Vehicles, as Spirits did. If this be so, answered the Spirits, then you are Hermaphrodites of Nature; but your Cabbalists are mistaken, for they take the purest and subtillest parts of Matter for Immaterial Spirits. Then the Emperess asked, when the souls of Mortals went out of their bodies, whether they went to Heaven or Hell, or whether they remained in airy Vehicles? God's Justice and Mercy, answered they, is perfect, and not imperfect; but if you mortals will have Vehicles for your Souls, and a place that is between Heaven and Hell, it must be Purgatory, which is a place of Purification, for which action Fire is more proper then Air, and so the Vehicles of those souls that are in Purgatory cannot be airy, but fiery; and after this rate there can be but four places for humane souls to be in, viz. Heaven, Hell, Purgatory, and this World; but as for Vehicles, they are but fancies, not real truths. Then the Emperess asked them, where Heaven and Hell was? Your Saviour Christ, answered the Spirits, has informed you, that there is Heaven and Hell, but he did not tell you what, nor where they are; wherefore it is too great a presumption for you Mortals to inquire after it; if you do but strive to get into Heaven, it is enough, though you do not know where or what it is, for it is beyond your knowledg and understanding. I am satisfied, replied the Emperess, and asked further, whether there were any figures or characters in the Soul? They answered, where there was no body, there could be no figure. Then she asked them, whether Spirits could be naked? and whether they were of a dark, or a light colour? As for our nakedness, it is a very odd question, answered the Spirits; and we do not know what you mean by a naked Spirit; for you judg of us as of corporeal Creatures; and as for Colour, said they, it is according to our Vehicles; for Colour belongs to Body, and as there is no Body that is colourless, so there is no Colour that is bodiless. Then the Emperess desired to be informed, whether all souls were made at the first Creation of the World? We know no more, answered the Spirits, of the origine of humane souls, then we know of our selves. She asked further, whether humane bodies were not burthensome to humane souls? They answered, That bodies made Souls active, as giving them motion; and if action was troublesome to souls, then bodies were so too. She asked again, whether souls did chuse bodies? They answered, That Platonicks believed, the souls of Lovers lived in the bodies of their Beloved; but surely, said they, if there be a multitude of souls in a world of Matter, they cannot miss bodies; for as soon as a soul is parted from one body, it enters into another; and souls having no motion of themselves, must of necessity be cloathed or imbodied with the next parts of Matter. If this be so, replied the Emperess, then I pray inform me, whether all Matter be soulified? The Spirits answered, They could not exactly tell that; but if it was true, that Matter had no other motion but what came from a spiritual power, and that all matter was moving, then no soul could quit a body, but she must of necessity enter into another soulified body, and then there would be two immaterial substances in one body. The Emperess asked, whether it was not possible that there could be two souls in one body? As for immaterial souls, answered the Spirits, it is impossible; for there cannot be two immaterials in one inanimate body, by reason they want parts, and place, being bodiless; but there may be numerous material souls in one composed body, by reason every material part has a material natural soul; for Nature is but one Infinite self-moving, living and self-knowing body, consisting of the three degrees of inanimate, sensitive and rational Matter, so intermixt together, that no part of Nature, were it an Atome, can be without any of these three degrees; the sensitive is the life, the rational the soul, and the inanimate part, the body of Infinite Nature. The Emperess was very well satisfied with this answer, and asked further, whether souls did not give life to bodies? No, answered they; but Spirits and

Divine Souls have a life of their own, which is not partable, being purer then a natural life; for Spirits are incorporeal, and consequently individable. But when the Soul is in its Vehicle, said the Emperess, then methinks she is like the Sun, and the Vehicle like the Moon. No, answered they, but the Vehicle is like the Sun, and the Soul like the Moon; for the Soul hath motion from the Body, as the Moon has light from the Sun. Then the Emperess asked the Spirits, whether it was an evil Spirit that tempted *Eve*, and brought all the mischiefs upon Mankind, or whether it was the Serpent? They answered, That Spirits could not commit actual evils. The Emperess said they might do it by perswasions. They answered, That Perswasions were actions; but the Emperess not being contented with this answer, asked whether there was not a supernatural Evil? The Spirits answered, That there was a supernatural Good, which was God; but they knew of no supernatural Evil that was equal to God. Then she desired to know, whether Evil Spirits were reckoned amongst the Beasts of the Field? They answer'd, That many Beasts of the field were harmless Creatures, and very serviceable for Man's use; and though some were accounted fierce and cruel, yet did they exercise their cruelty upon other Creatures, for the most part, to no other end, but to get themselves food, and to satisfie their natural appetite; but certainly, said they, you men are more cruel to one another, then evil Spirits are to you; and as for their habitations in desolate places, we having no communion with them, can give you no certain account thereof. But what do you think, said the Emperess, of Good Spirits? may not they be compared to the Fowls of the Air? They answered, There were many cruel and ravenous Fowls as well in the Air, as there were fierce and cruel Beasts on Earth; so that the good are always mixt with the bad. She asked further, whether the fiery Vehicles were a Heaven, or a Hell, or at least a Purgatory to the Souls? They answered, That if the Souls were immaterial, they could not burn, and then fire would do them no harm; and though Hell was believed to be an undecaying and unquenchable fire, yet Heaven was no fire. The Emperess replied, That Heaven was a Light. Yes, said they, but not a fiery Light. Then she asked, whether the different shapes and sorts of Vehicles, made the Souls and other Immaterial Spirits, miserable, or blessed? The Vehicles, answered they, make them neither better, nor worse; for though some Vehicles sometimes may have power over others, yet these by turns may get some power again over them, according to the several advantages and disadvantages of particular natural parts. The Emperess asked further, whether animal life came out of the spiritual World, and did return thither again? The Spirits answered, they could not exactly tell; but if it were so, then certainly animal lives must leave their bodies behind them, otherwise the bodies would make the spiritual World a mixt World, that is, partly material, and partly immaterial; but the Truth is, said they, Spirits being immaterial, cannot properly make a World; for a World belongs to material, not to immaterial Creatures. If this be so, replied the Emperess, then certainly there can be no world of lives and forms without matter? No, answered the Spirits, nor a world of Matter without lives and forms; for natural lives and forms cannot be immaterial, no more then Matter can be immovable. And therefore natural lives, forms and matter, are inseparable. Then the Emperess asked, whether the first Man did feed on the best sorts of the fruits of the Earth, and the beasts on the worst? The Spirits answered, That unless the beasts of the field were barred out of manured fields and gardens, they would pick and chuse the best fruits as well as men; and you may plainly observe it, said they, in Squirrels and Monkies, how they are the best chusers of Nuts and Apples, and how Birds do pick and feed on the most delicious fruits, and Worms on the best roots, and most savoury herbs; by which you may see, that those Creatures live and feed better then men do, except you will say, that artificial Cookery is better and more wholesom then the natural. Again, the Emperess asked, whether the first Man gave names to all the several sorts of Fishes in the Sea, and fresh waters? No, answered the Spirits, for he was an Earthly, and not a watery Creature, and therefore could not know the several sorts of Fishes. Why, replied the Emperess, he was no more an airy Creature then he was a watery one, and yet he gave names to the several sorts of Fowls and Birds of the Air. Fowls answered they, are partly Airy, and partly Earthly Creatures, not onely because they resemble Beasts and Men in their flesh, but because their rest and dwelling-places are on Earth; for they build their nests, lay their eggs, and hatch their young, not in the Air, but on the Earth. Then she asked, Whether the first Man did give names to all the various sorts of Creatures that live on the Earth? Yes, answered they, to all those that were presented to him, or he had knowledg of, that is, to all the prime sorts; but not to every particular; for of

Mankind, said they, there were but two at first, and as they did encrease, so did their names. But, said the Emperess, who gave the names to the several sorts of Fish? The posterity of Mankind, answered they. Then she enquired, Whether there were no more kinds of Creatures now, then at the first Creation? They answered, That there were no more nor fewer kinds of Creatures then there are now; but there were, without question, more particular sorts of Creatures now, then there were then. She asked again, Whether all those Creatures that were in Paradise, were also in *Noah's* Ark? They answered, That the principal kinds had been there, but not all the particulars. Then she would fain know, how it came, that both Spirits and Men did fall from a blessed into so miserable a state and condition they are now in. The Spirits answered, By disobedience. The Emperess asked, Whence this disobedient sin did proceed? But the Spirits desired the Emperess not to ask them any such questions, because they went beyond their knowledg. Then she begg'd the Spirits to pardon her presumption; for, said she, It is the nature of Mankind to be inquisitive. Natural desire of knowledg, answered the Spirits, is not blameable, so you do not go beyond what your natural reason can comprehend. Then I'le ask no more, said the Emperess, for fear I should commit some error; but one thing I cannot but acquaint you withal: What is that, said the Spirits? I have a great desire, answered the Emperess, to make a Cabbala. What kind of Cabbala asked the Spirits? The Emperess answered, The Jews Cabbala. No sooner had the Emperess declared her Mind, but the Spirits immediately disappeared out of her sight; which startled the Emperess so much, that she fell into a Trance, wherein she lay for some while; at last being come to her self again, she grew very studious, and considering with her self what might be the cause of this strange disaster, conceived at first, that perhaps the Spirits were tired with hearing and giving answers to her questions; but thinking by her self, that Spirits could not be tired, she imagined that this was not the true cause of their disappearing, till after diverse debates with her own thoughts, she did verily believe that the Spirits had committed some fault in their answers, and that for their punishment they were condemned to the lowest and darkest Vehicles. This belief was so fixt in her mind, that it put her into a very Melancholick humor; and then she sent both for her Fly- and Wormmen, and declared to them the cause of her sadness. 'Tis not so much, said she, the vanishing of those Spirits that makes me Melancholick, but that I should be the cause of their miserable condition, and that those harmless Spirits should, for my sake, sink down into the black and dark abyss of the Earth. The Worm-men comforted the Emperess, telling her, that the Earth was not so horrid a dwelling, as she did imagine; for, said they, not onely all Minerals and Vegetables, but several sorts of Animals can witness, that the Earth is a warm, fruitful, quiet, safe and happy habitation; and though they want the light of the Sun, yet are they not in the dark, but there is light even within the Earth, by which those Creatures do see that dwell therein. This relation setled her Majesties mind a little; but yet she being desirous to know the Truth, where, and in what condition those Spirits were, commanded both the Fly- and Worm-men to use all labour and industry to find them out, whereupon the Worm-men straight descended into the Earth, and the Fly-men ascended into the Air. After some short time, the Worm-men returned, and told the Emperess, that when they went into the Earth, they inquired of all the Creatures they met withal, whether none of them had perceived such or such Spirits, until at last coming to the very Center of the Earth, they were truly informed, that those Spirits had stayed some time there, but at last were gone to the Antipodes on the other side of the Terrestrial Globe, diametrically opposite to theirs. The Fly-men seconded the Worm-men, assuring her Majesty, that their relation was very true; for, said they, we have rounded the Earth, and just when we came to the Antipodes, we met those Spirits in a very good condition, and acquainted them that your Majesty was very much troubled at their sudden departure, and fear'd they should be buried in the darkness of the Earth: whereupon the Spirits answered us, that they were sorry for having occasioned such sadness and trouble in your Majesty; and desired us to tell your Majesty, that they feared no darkness; for their Vehicles were of such a sort of substance as Catseyes, Glow-worms tails, and rotten wood, carrying their light along with them; and that they were ready to do your Majesty what service they could, in making your Cabbala. At which Relation the Emperess was exceedingly glad, and rewarded both her Fly- and Worm-men bountifully.

After some time, when the Spirits had refreshed themselves in their own Vehicles, they sent one of their nimblest Spirits, to ask the

Emperess, whether she would have a Scribe, or whether she would write the Cabbala her self? The Emperess received the profer which they made her, with all civility; and told him, that she desired a Spiritual Scribe. The Spirit answered, that they could dictate, but not write, except they put on a hand or arm, or else the whole body of Man. The Emperess replied, How can Spirits arm themselves with gantlets[1] of flesh? As well, answered he, as Man can arm himself with a gantlet of steel. If it be so, said the Emperess, then I will have a Scribe. Then the Spirit asked her, whether she would have the Soul of a living or a dead Man? Why, said the Emperess, can the Soul quit a living body, and wander or travel abroad? Yes, answered he, for according to *Plato's* Doctrine, there is a conversation of Souls, and the Souls of Lovers live in the bodies of their Beloved. Then I will have, answered she, the Soul of some ancient famous Writer, either of *Aristotle, Pythagoras, Plato, Epicurus*, or the like. The Spirit said, That those famous men were very learned, subtile and ingenious Writers, but they were so wedded to their own opinions, that they would never have the patience to be Scribes. Then, said she, I'le have the Soul of one of the most famous modern Writers, as either of *Galileo, Gassendus, Des Cartes, Helmont, Hobbes, H. More*, &c.[2] The Spirit answered, That they were fine ingenious Writers, but yet so self-conceited, that they would scorn to be Scribes to a Woman. But, said he, there's a Lady, the *Duchess* of *Newcastle*, which although she is not one of the most learned, eloquent, witty and ingenious, yet is she a plain and rational Writer, for the principle of her Writings, is Sense and Reason, and she will without question, be ready to do you all the service she can. That Lady then, said the Emperess, will I chuse for my scribe, neither will the Emperor have reason to be jealous, she being one of my own sex. In truth, said the Spirit, Husbands have reason to be jealous of Platon-

---

1 gauntlets
2 Galileo Galilei (1564-1642): Italian physicist and astronomer, defender of the Copernican model; Pierre Gassendi (1592-1655): French mechanistic philosopher; René Descartes (1596-1650): French mathematician and philosopher; Jan Baptista van Helmont (1579-1644): Flemish chemist, medical theorist and mystical philosopher; Thomas Hobbes (1588-1679): English philosopher; Henry More (1614-87): English neo-Platonic philosopher and theologian. These writers represent a spectrum or mixture of the main currents of early modern scientific thought, from Hermetic occultism and neo-Platonism to newly formulated mechanistic, atomistic, and materialistic models of the universe.

ick Lovers, for they are very dangerous, as being not onely very intimate and close, but subtil and insinuating. You say well, replied the
Emperess; wherefore I pray send me the *Duchess* of *Newcastle's* Soul;
which the Spirit did; and after she came to wait on the Emperess, at
her first arrival the Emperess imbraced and saluted her with a spiritual kiss; then she asked her whether she could write? Yes, answered the
Duchess's Soul, but not so intelligibly that any Reader whatsoever may
understand it, unless he be taught to know my Characters; for my
Letters are rather like Characters, then well-formed Letters. Said the
Emperess, you were recommended to me by an honest and ingenious
Spirit. Surely, answered the Duchess, the Spirit is ignorant of my
hand-writing. The truth is, said the Emperess, he did not mention
your hand-writing; but he informed me, that you writ sense and reason, and if you can but write so, that any of my Secretaries may learn
your hand, they shall write it out fair and intelligible. The Duchess
answered, That she questioned not but it might easily be learned in a
short time. But, said she to the Emperess, What is it that your Majesty
would have written? She answered, The Jews Cabbala. Then your
onely way for that is, said the Duchess, to have the Soul of some
famous Jew; nay, if your Majesty please, I scruple not, but you may as
easily have the soul of *Moses*, as of any other. That cannot be, replied
the Emperess, for no mortal knows where *Moses* is. But, said the
Duchess, humane Souls are immortal; however, if this be too difficult
to be obtained, you may have the Soul of one of the chief Rabbies or
Sages of the Tribe of *Levi*, who will truly instruct you in that mystery;
when as, otherwise, your Majesty will be apt to mistake, and a thousand to one, but commit gross errors. No, said the Emperess, for I shall
be instructed by Spirits. Alas! said the Duchess, Spirits are as ignorant
as Mortals in many cases; for no created Spirits have a general or
absolute knowledg, nor can they know the Thoughts of Men, much
less the Mysteries of the great Creator, unless he be pleased to inspire
into them the gift of Divine Knowledg. Then, I pray, said the Emperess, let me have your counsel in this case. The Duchess answered, If
your Majesty will be pleased to hearken to my advice, I would desire
you to let that work alone; for it will be of no advantage either to
you, or your people, unless you were of the Jews Religion; nay, if you
were, the vulgar interpretation of the holy Scripture would be more
instructive, and more easily believed, then your mystical way of inter-

preting it; for had it been better and more advantageous for the salvation of the Jews, surely *Moses* would have saved after ages that labour by his own explanation, he being not onely a wise, but a very honest, zealous and religious Man: Wherefore the best way, said she, is to believe with the generality the literal sense of the Scripture, and not to make interpretations every one according to his own fancy, but to leave that work for the Learned, or those that have nothing else to do; Neither do I think, said she, that God will damn those that are ignorant therein, or suffer them to be lost for want of a mystical interpretation of the Scripture. Then, said the Emperess, I'le leave the Scripture, and make a Philosophical Cabbala. The Duchess told her, That sense and reason would instruct her of Nature as much as could be known; and as for numbers, they were infinite, but to add nonsense to infinite, would breed a confusion, especially in humane understanding. Then, replied the Emperess, I'le make a moral Cabbala. The onely thing, answered the Duchess, in morality, is but to fear God, and to love his Neighbour, and this needs no further interpretation. But then I'le make a Political Cabbala, said the Emperess. The Duchess answered, That the chief and onely ground in Government, was but Reward and Punishment, and required no further Cabbala; But, said she, If your Majesty were resolved to make a Cabbala, I would advise you, rather to make a Poetical or Romancical Cabbala, wherein you can use Metaphors, Allegories, Similitudes, &c. and interpret them as you please. With that the Emperess thank'd the Duchess, and embracing her soul, told her she would take her Counsel: she made her also her favourite, and kept her sometime in that world, and by this means the Duchess came to know and give this Relation of all that passed in that rich, populous and happy world; and after some time the Emperess gave her leave to return to her Husband and Kindred into her native world, but upon condition, that her soul should visit her now and then; which she did, and truly their meeting did produce such an intimate friendship between them, that they became Platonick Lovers, although they were both Females.

One time, when the Duchess her Soul was with the Emperess, she seem'd to be very sad and melancholy; at which the Emperess was very much troubled, and asked her the reason of her melancholick humour? Truly said the Duchess to the Emperess (for between dear friends there's no concealment, they being like several parts of one united body) my Melancholy proceeds from an extreme ambition. The Emperess asked, what the height of her ambition was? The Duchess answered, That neither she her self, nor no Creature in the World was able to know either the height, depth or breadth of her ambition; but, said she, my present desire is, that I would be a great Princess. The Emperess replied, so you are, for you are a Princess of the fourth or fifth degree; for a Duke or Duchess is the highest title or honour that a subject can arrive to, as being the next to a Kings Title; and as for the name of a Prince or Princess, it belongs to all that are adopted to the Crown; so that those that can add a Crown to their arms, are Princes, and therefore a *Duke* is a Title above a *Prince*; for example, the *Duke* of *Savoy*, the *Duke* of *Florence*, the *Duke* of *Lorraine*, as also Kings Brothers are not called by the name of Princes, but Dukes, this being the higher Title. 'Tis true, answered the Duchess, unless it be Kings eldest Sons, and they are created Princes. Yes, replied the Emperess, but no Soverain does make a subject equal to himself, such as Kings eldest sons partly are: And although some Dukes be sovereign, yet I never heard that a Prince by his Title is sovereign, by reason the Title of a Prince is more a Title of Honour, then of Soverainty; for, as I said before, it belongs to all that are adopted to the Crown. Well, said the Duchess, setting aside this dispute, my ambition is, that I would fain be as you are, that is, an Emperess of a World, and I shall never be at quiet until I be one. I love you so well, replied the Emperess, that I wish with all my soul, you had the fruition of your ambitious desire, and I shall not fail to give you my best advice how to accomplish it; the best informers are the Immaterial Spirits, and they'l soon tell you, whether it be possible to obtain your wish. But, said the Duchess, I have little acquaintance with them, for I never knew any before the time you sent for me. They know you, replied the Emperess; for they told me of you, and were the means and instrument of your coming hither: Wherefore I'le confer with them, and enquire whether there be not another World, whereof you may be Emperess as well as I am of this? No sooner had the Emperess said this, but some Immaterial Spirits came to visit her, of whom she inquired, whether there were but three Worlds in all, to wit, the Blazing-world where she was in, the World which she came from, and the World where the Duchess lived? The Spirits answered, That there were more numerous Worlds then the Stars which appeared in these three mentioned Worlds. Then the Emperess asked, whether it was not possible, that her dearest friend the Duchess of *Newcastle*, might be Emperess of one of them? Although there be numerous, nay, infinite Worlds, answered the Spirits, yet none is without Government. But is none of these Worlds so weak, said she, that it may be surprised or conquered? The Spirits answered, that *Lucian's* World of Lights, had been for some time in a snuff, but of late years one *Helmont*[1] had got it, who since he was Emperour of it, had so strengthened the Immortal parts thereof with mortal out-works, as it was for the present impregnable. Said the Emperess, If there be such an Infinite number of Worlds, I am sure, not onely my friend, the Duchess, but any other might obtain one. Yes, answered the Spirits, if those Worlds were uninhabited; but they are as populous as this, your Majesty governs. Why, said the Emperess, it is not impossible to conquer a World. No, answered the Spirits, but, for the most part, Conquerers seldom enjoy their conquest, for they being more feared then loved, most commonly come to an untimely end. If you will but direct me, said the Duchess to the Spirits, which World is easiest to be conquered, her Majesty will assist me with means, and I will trust to Fate and Fortune; for I had rather die in the adventure of noble atchievements, then live in obscure and sluggish security; since by the one, I may live in a glorious Fame, and by the other I am buried in oblivion. The Spirits answered, That the lives of Fame were like other lives; for some lasted long, and some died soon. 'Tis true, said the Duchess, but yet the shortest-lived Fame lasts longer then the longest life of Man. But, replied the Spirits, if occasion does not serve you, you must content your self to live without such atchievements that may gain you a Fame: But we wonder, proceeded the Spirits, that you desire to be Emperess of a Terrestrial World, when as you can create your self a Celestial World if you please. What, said the Emperess, can any Mortal be a Creator? Yes, answered the Spirits; for every humane Creature can create an Immaterial World fully inhabited by immaterial Creatures, and populous of immaterial subjects, such as we are, and all this within the compass of the head or scull;[2] nay, not onely so, but

---

1 Lucian of Samosata: second-century Greek satirist; Jan van Helmont (1579-1644): Flemish scientist whose mystical philosophy was incorporated into his medical and chemical investigations.
2 skull

he may create a World of what fashion and Government he will, and give the Creatures thereof such motions, figures, forms, colours, perceptions, &c. as he pleases, and make Whirl-pools, Lights, Pressures and Reactions, &c. as he thinks best; nay, he may make a World full of Veins, Muscles, and Nerves, and all these to move by one jolt or stroke: also he may alter that world as often as he pleases, or change it from a natural world, to an artificial; he may make a world of Ideas, a world of Atomes, a world of Lights, or whatsoever his fancy leads him to. And since it is in your power to create such a world, What need you to venture life, reputation and tranquility, to conquer a gross material world? For you can enjoy no more of a material world then a particular Creature is able to enjoy, which is but a small part, considering the compass of such a world; and you may plainly observe it by your friend the Emperess here, which although she possesses a whole world, yet enjoys she but a part thereof; neither is she so much acquainted with it, that she knows all the places, Countries and Dominions she Governs. The truth is, a Soveraign Monarch has the general trouble; but the Subjects enjoy all the delights and pleasures in parts; for it is impossible, that a Kingdom, nay, a County should be injoyed by one person at once, except he take the pains to travel into every part, and endure the inconveniencies of going from one place to another; wherefore, since glory, delight and pleasure lives but in other mens opinions, and can neither add tranquility to your mind, nor give ease to your body, why should you desire to be Emperess of a material world, and be troubled with the cares that attend Government? when as by creating a world within your self, you may enjoy all both in whole and in parts, without controle or opposition, and may make what world you please, and alter it when you please, and enjoy as much pleasure and delight as a world can afford you? You have converted me, said the Duchess to the Spirits, from my ambitious desire; wherefore I'le take your advice, reject and despise all the worlds without me, and create a world of my own. The Emperess said, If I do make such a world, then I shall be Mistress of two worlds, one within, and the other without me. That your Majesty may, said the Spirits; and so left these two Ladies to create two worlds within themselves: who did also part from each other, until such time as they had brought their worlds to perfection. The Duchess of *Newcastle* was most earnest and industrious to make her world, because she had none at present; and first she resolved to frame it according to the opinion of *Thales*,[1] but she found her self so much troubled with Dæmons, that they would not suffer her to take her own will, but forced her to obey their orders and commands; which she being unwilling to do, left off from making a world that way, and began to frame one according to *Pythagoras's*[2] Doctrine; but in the Creation thereof, she was so puzled with numbers, how to order and compose the several parts, that she having no skill in Arithmetick, was forced also to desist from the making of that world. Then she intended to create a world according to the opinion of *Plato*;[3] but she found more trouble and difficulty in that, then in the two former; for the numerous Ideas having no other motion but what was derived from her mind, whence they did flow and issue out, made it a far harder business to her, to impart motion to them, then Puppit-players have in giving motion to every several Puppit; in so much, that her patience was not able to endure the trouble which those Ideas caused her; wherefore she annihilated also that world, and was resolved to make one according to the Opinion of *Epicurus*;[4] which she had no sooner begun, but the infinite Atomes made such a mist, that it quite blinded the perception of her mind; neither was she able to make a *Vacuum* as a receptacle for those Atomes, or a place which they might retire into; so that partly for the want of it, and of a good order and method, the confusion of those Atomes produced such strange and monstrous figures, as did more affright then delight her, and caused such a Chaos in her mind, as had almost dissolved it. At last, having with much ado cleansed and cleared her mind of these dusty and misty particles, she endeavoured to create a World according to *Aristotle's* Opinion; but remembring that her mind, as most of the Learned hold it, was Immaterial, and that according to *Aristotle's* Principle, out of Nothing, Nothing could be made;[5] she was forced also to desist from that

---

1   Thales of Miletus (c. 625- c. 545 BCE), Greek natural philosopher, who taught that water was the source of all things.

2   Pythagoras of Samos (fl. c. 531- c. 496 BCE), Greek mathematician and philosopher, founder of a religion that interpreted the world through numbers and their relationships

3   a world composed of abstract ideas rather than material objects

4   Epicurus of Samos (341-270 BCE), Greek atomistic philosopher

5   a classical dictum often quoted satirically by early modern writers; see for example *King Lear*, I.i.90.

work, and then she fully resolved, not to take any more patterns from the Ancient Philosophers, but to follow the Opinions of the Moderns; and to that end, she endeavoured to make a World according to *Des Cartes* Opinion;[1] but when she had made the Æthereal Globules, and set them a moving by a strong and lively imagination, her mind became so dizzie with their extraordinary swift turning round, that it almost put her into a swoon; for her thoughts, by their constant tottering, did so stagger, as if they had all been drunk: wherefore she dissolved that World, and began to make another, according to *Hobbs's* Opinion;[2] but when all the parts of this Imaginary World came to press and drive each other, they seemed like a company of Wolves that worry Sheep, or like so many Dogs that hunt after Hares; and when she found a reaction equal to those pressures, her mind was so squeesed together, that her thoughts could neither move forward nor backward, which caused such an horrible pain in her head, that although she had dissolved that World, yet she could not, without much difficulty, settle her mind, and free it from that pain which those pressures and reactions had caused in it.

At last, when the Duchess saw that no patterns would do her any good in the framing of her World; she was resolved to make a World of her own invention, and this World was composed of sensitive and rational self-moving Matter; indeed, it was composed onely of the rational, which is the subtilest and purest degree of Matter; for as the sensitive did move and act both to the perceptions and consistency of the body, so this degree of Matter at the same point of time (for though the degrees are mixt, yet the several parts may move several ways at one time) did move to the Creation of the Imaginary World; which World after it was made, appear'd so curious and full of variety, so well order'd and wisely govern'd, that it cannot possibly be expressed by words, nor the delight and pleasure which the Duchess took in making this world of her own.

In the mean time the Emperess was also making and dissolving several worlds in her own mind, and was so puzled, that she could not settle in any of them; wherefore she sent for the Duchess, who being

---

1 Descartes's theory of vortices, a supposed rotary movement of cosmic matter around a central axis

2 Thomas Hobbes's portrayal in *Leviathan* (1651) of mankind in a state of nature as a state of "war of everyone against everyone."

ready to wait on the Emperess, carried her beloved world along with her, and invited the Emperess's Soul to observe the frame, order and Government of it. Her Majesty was so ravished with the perception of it, that her soul desired to live in the Duchess's World; but the Duchess advised her to make such another World in her own mind; for, said she, your Majesties mind is full of rational corporeal motions, and the rational motions of my mind shall assist you by the help of sensitive expressions, with the best instructions they are able to give you.

The Emperess being thus perswaded by the Duchess to make an imaginary World of her own, followed her advice; and after she had quite finished it, and framed all kinds of Creatures proper and useful for it, strengthened it with good Laws, and beautified it with Arts and Sciences; having nothing else to do, unless she did dissolve her imaginary world, or made some alterations in the Blazing-world, she lived in, which yet she could hardly do, by reason it was so well ordered that it could not be mended; for it was governed without secret and deceiving Policy; neither was there any ambition, factions, malicious detractions, civil dissensions, or home-bred quarrels, divisions in Religion, forreign Wars, &c. but all the people lived in a peaceful society, united Tranquility, and Religious Conformity; she was desirous to see the world the Duchess came from, and observe therein the several soveraign Governments, Laws and Customs of several Nations. The Duchess used all the means she could, to divert her from that Journey, telling her, that the world she came from, was very much disturbed with factions, divisions and wars; but the Emperess would not be perswaded from her design; and lest the Emperour, or any of his subjects should know of her travel, and obstruct her design, she sent for some of the Spirits she had formerly conversed withal, and inquired whether none of them could supply the place of her soul in her body at such a time, when she was gone to travel into another World? They answered, Yes, they could; for not onely one, said they, but many Spirits may enter into your body, if you please. The Emperess replied, she desired but one Spirit to be Vice-Roy of her body in the absence of her Soul; but it must be an honest and ingenious Spirit; and if it was possible, a female Spirit. The Spirits told her, that there was no difference of Sexes amongst them; but, said they, we will chuse an honest and ingenious Spirit, and such a one as shall so resemble your soul, that neither the Emperour, nor any of his subjects, although the most Divine, shall know whether it be your own soul, or not: which the Emperess was very glad at, and after the Spirits were gone, asked the Duchess, how her body was supplied in the absence of her soul? who answered Her Majesty, That her body, in the absence of her soul, was governed by her sensitive and rational corporeal motions. Thus those two female souls travelled together as lightly as two thoughts into the Duchess her native World; and which is remarkable, in a moment viewed all the parts of it, and all the actions of all the Creatures therein, especially did the Emperess's soul take much notice of the several actions of humane Creatures in all the several Nations and parts of that World, and wonder'd that for all there were so many several Nations, Governments, Laws, Religions, Opinions, &c. they should all yet so generally agree in being Ambitious, Proud, Self-conceited, Vain, Prodigal, Deceitful, Envious, Malicious, Unjust, Revengeful, Irreligious, Factious, &c. She did also admire,[1] that not any particular State, Kingdom or Common-wealth, was contented with their own shares, but endeavoured to encroach upon their neighbours, and that their greatest glory was in Plunder and Slaughter, and yet their victories less then their expenses, and their losses more then their gains, but their being overcome in a manner their utter ruine. But that she wonder'd most at, was, that they should prize or value dirt more then mens lives, and vanity more then tranquillity; for the Emperor of a world, said she, injoys but a part, not the whole; so that his pleasure consists in the opinions of others. It is strange to me, answered the Duchess, that you should say thus, being your self, an Emperess of a World, and not onely of a world, but of a peaceable, quiet, and obedient world. 'Tis true, replied the Emperess, but although it is a peaceable and obedient world, yet the Government thereof is rather a trouble, then a pleasure; for order cannot be without industry, contrivance and direction; besides, the Magnificent state,[2] that great Princes keep or ought to keep, is troublesome. Then by your Majesties discourse, said the Duchess, I perceive that the greatest happiness in all Worlds consist in Moderation: No doubt of it, replied the Emperess; and after these two souls had visited all the several places,

---

1 wonder
2 pomp and ceremony

Congregations and Assemblies both in Religion and State, the several Courts of Judicature, and the like, in several Nations, the Emperess said, That of all the Monarchs of the several parts of that World, she had observed the Grand-Signior[1] was the greatest; for his word was a Law, and his power absolute. But the Duchess pray'd the Emperess to pardon her that she was of another mind; for, said she, he cannot alter *Mahomets* Laws and Religion; so that the Law and Church do govern the Emperor, and not the Emperor them. But, replied the Emperess, he has power in some particulars; as for example, to place and displace subjects in their particular Governments of Church and State, and having that, he has the Command both over Church and State, and none dares oppose him. 'Tis true, said the Duchess; but if it pleases your Majesty, we will go into that part of the world whence I came to wait on your Majesty, and there you shall see as powerful a Monarch as the Grand-Signior; for though his Dominions are not of so large extent, yet they are much stronger, his Laws are easie and safe, and he governs so justly and wisely, that his subjects are the happiest people of all the Nations or parts of that world. This Monarch, said the Emperess, I have a great mind to see: Then they both went, and in a short time arrived into his Dominions; but coming into the Metropolitan City, the Emperess's soul observed many Galants go into an house, and enquiring of the Duchess's soul, what house that was? She told her, It was one of the Theatres where Comedies and Tragedies were acted. The Emperess asked, Whether they were real? No, said the Duchess, They are feigned. Then the Emperess desired to enter into the Theatre, and when she had seen the Play that was acted, the Duchess asked her how she liked that Recreation? I like it very well, said the Emperess; but I observe, that the Actors make a better show then the Spectators, and the Scenes a better then the Actors, and the Musick and Dancing is more pleasant and acceptable then the Play it self; for I see, the Scenes stand for wit, the Dancing for humour, and the Musick is the Chorus. I am sorry, replied the Duchess, to hear your Majesty say so; for if the Wits of this part of the World should hear you, they would condemn you. What, said the Emperess, would they condemn me for preferring a natural face before a sign-post, or a natural humour before an artificial dance, or Musick before a true and profitable Relation? As for relation, replied the Duchess, our Poets

---

1   Sultan of Turkey

defie and condemn it into a Chimney-corner, fitter for old Womens Tales, then Theatres. Why, said the Emperess, do not your Poets actions comply with their judgments? for their Plays are composed of old stories, either of Greek or Roman, or some new-found World. The Duchess answered her Majesty, that it was true, that all or most of their Plays were taken out of old Stories, but yet they had new actions, which being joined to old stories, together with the addition of new Prologues, Scenes, Musick and Dancing, made new Plays.

After this, both the Souls went to the Court, where all the Royal Family was together, attended by the chief of the Nobles of their Dominions, which made a very magnificent show; and when the soul of the Emperess viewed the King and Queen, she seemed to be in amaze, which the Duchess's soul perceiving, asked the Emperess how she liked the King, the Queen, and all the Royal Race? She answered, that in all the Monarchs she had seen in that World, she had not found so much Majesty and affability mixt so exactly together, that none did overshadow or eclipse the other; and as for the Queen, she said, that Vertue sat Triumphant in her face, and Piety was dwelling in her heart, and that all the Royal Family seem'd to be endued with a Divine splendor: but when she had heard the King discourse, she believ'd, that *Mercury* and *Apollo* had been his Celestial instructors; and my dear Lord and Husband, added the Duchess, has been his Earthly Governour.[1] But after some short stay in the Court, the Duchess's soul grew very Melancholy; the Emperess asking the cause of her sadness? She told her, that she had an extreme desire to converse with the soul of her noble Lord and dear Husband, and that she was impatient of a longer stay. The Emperess desired the Duchess to have but patience so long, until the King, the Queen, and the Royal Family were retired, and then she would bear her company to her Lord and Husbands Soul, who at that time lived in the Country some 112 miles off; which she did: and thus these two souls went towards those parts of the Kingdom where the Duke of *Newcastle* was.

But one thing I forgot all this while, which is, That although thoughts are the natural language of souls, yet by reason souls cannot travel without Vehicles, they use such language as the nature and propriety of their Vehicles require, and the Vehicles of those two souls

---

1   For the Earl of Newcastle's stint as governor to Prince Charles (later Charles II) in 1638-1641, see Grant 60-61, and Mendelson, *Mental World*, 18.

Illustration 9: An engraving from William Cavendish's *La Méthode Nouvelle et Invention Extraordinaire de Dresser les Chevaux* ... (1658) depicts the Marquis of Newcastle on horseback, along with other human and non-human inhabitants of the park around his Welbeck estate in Nottinghamshire. The idealized harmony presented here resonates with Margaret Cavendish's idealized description, in *Blazing world,* of a peaceable estate in Sherwood Forest. (Courtesy the Bodleian Library, Oxford, Antiq. b. B. 1658.1 plate 38.)

being made of the purest and finest sort of air, and of a humane shape; this purity and fineness was the cause that they could neither be seen nor heard by any humane Creature; when as, had they been of some grosser sort of Air, the sound of that Airs language would have been as perceptible as the blowing of *Zephyrus*.

And now to return to my former Story; when the Emperess's and Duchess's Soul were travelling into *Nottingham*-shire, for that was the place where the Duke did reside; passing through the forrest of *Shere-wood*, the Emperess's soul was very much delighted with it, as being a dry, plain and woody place, very pleasant to travel in both in Winter and Summer; for it is neither much dirty, nor dusty at no time: at last they arrived at *Welbeck*,[1] a house where the Duke dwell'd, surrounded

---

1   For Welbeck and Bolsover, Newcastle's two northern residences, see Grant 57-9 and 180-82. Ben Jonson composed masques for Newcastle's entertainment of King Charles I at Welbeck (1633) and Bolsover (1634), *The King's Entertainment at Welbeck* and *Love's Welcome at Bolsover* (see Introduction).

Illustration 10: From William Cavendish's *La Méthode Nouvelle et Invention Extraordi-naire de Dresser les Chevaux ...* (1658), a book demonstrating Cavendish's expertise in the dressing and training of horses, and published while he was in exile. He is depicted here as a young man on his horse in front of his Bolsover Castle in Nottinghamshire, where he built an indoor riding school for manage, which still stands. (Courtesy the Bodleian Library, Oxford, Antiq. b. B. 1658.1 plate 32.)

all with Wood, so close and full, that the Emperess took great pleasure and delight therein, and told the Duchess she never had observed more wood in so little a compass in any part of the Kingdom she had passed through; The truth is, said she, there seems to be more wood on the Seas, she meaning the Ships, then on the Land. The Duchess told her, the reason was, that there had been a long Civil War in that Kingdom,[1] in which most of the best Timber-trees and Principal Palaces were ruined and destroyed; and my dear Lord and Husband, said she, has lost by it half his Woods, besides many Houses, Land, and moveable Goods; so that all the loss out of his particular Estate, did amount to above half a Million of Pounds.[2] I wish, said the Emperess, he had some of the Gold that is in the Blazing-world, to repair his losses. The Duchess most humbly thank'd her Imperial Majesty for

---

1   the English Civil War (1642-1660)
2   For Cavendish's calculations of her husband's financial losses during the Civil War, see Mendelson, *Mental World*, 49-50.

her kind wishes; but, said she, wishes will not repair his ruines: however, God has given my Noble Lord and Husband great Patience, by which he bears all his losses and misfortunes. At last, they enter'd into the Dukes House, an habitation not so magnificent, as useful; and when the Emperess saw it, Has the Duke, said she, no other house but this? Yes, answered the Duchess, some five miles from this place, he has a very fine Castle, called *Bolesover*.[1] That place then, said the Emperess, I desire to see. Alas! replied the Duchess, it is but a naked house, and uncloath'd of all Furniture. However, said the Emperess, I may see the manner of its structure and building. That you may, replied the Duchess: and as they were thus discoursing, the Duke came out of the House into the Court, to see his Horses of mannage;[2] whom when the Duchess's soul perceived, she was so overjoyed, that her aereal Vehicle became so splendorous, as if it had been enlightned by the Sun; by which we may perceive, that the passions of Souls or Spirits can alter their bodily Vehicles. Then these two Ladies Spirits went close to him, but he could not perceive them; and after the Emperess had observed the Art of Mannage, she was much pleased with it, and commended it as a noble pastime, and an exercise fit and proper for noble and heroick Persons: But when the Duke was gone into the house again, those two Souls followed him; where the Emperess observing, that he went to the exercise of the Sword, and was such an excellent and unparallell'd Master thereof, she was as much pleased with that exercise, as she was with the former: But the Duchess's soul being troubled, that her dear Lord and Husband used such a violent exercise before meat, for fear of overheating himself, without any consideration of the Emperess's soul, left her aereal Vehicle and entred into her Lord. The Emperess's soul perceiving this, did the like: And then the Duke had three Souls in one Body; and had there been but some such Souls more, the Duke would have been like the Grand-Signior in his Seraglio,[3] onely it would have been a Platonick Seraglio. But the Dukes soul being wise, honest, witty, complaisant and noble, afforded such delight and pleasure to the Emperess's soul

---

1   Bolsover

2   manage: the art of training a horse in its paces; Newcastle's lavishly illustrated instruction manual on the art of manage, *La Méthode Nouvelle et Invention Extraordinaire de dresser les Chevaux*, was printed in Antwerp in 1658 (see illustration p. 56, 220, 221)

3   harem

by her conversation, that these two souls became enamoured of each other; which the Duchess's soul perceiving, grew jealous at first, but then considering that no Adultery could be committed amongst Platonick Lovers, and that Platonism was Divine, as being derived from Divine *Plato*, cast forth of her mind that Idea of Jealousie. Then the Conversation of these three souls was so pleasant, that it cannot be expressed; for the Dukes soul entertained the Emperesses soul with Scenes, Songs, Musick, witty Discourses, pleasant Recreations, and all kinds of harmless sports; so that the time passed away faster then they expected. At last, a Spirit came and told the Emperess, that although neither the Emperour, nor any of his subjects knew that her soul was absent; yet the Emperours soul was so sad and melancholy, for want of his own beloved soul, that all the Imperial Court took notice of it. Wherefore he advised the Emperess's Soul to return into the Blazing-world, into her own body she left there; which both the Dukes and Duchess's soul was very sorry for, and wished, that if it had been possible, the Emperess's soul might have stayed a longer time with them; but seeing it could not be otherwise, they pacified themselves: But before the Emperess returned into the Blazing-world, the Duchess desired a favour of her, to wit, that she would be pleased to make an agreement between her Noble Lord, and Fortune. Why, said the Emperess, are they enemies? Yes, answered the Duchess, and they have been so ever since I have been his Wife; nay, I have heard my Lord say, that she hath crossed him in all things ever since he could remember. I am sorry for that, replied the Emperess, but I cannot discourse with Fortune without the help of an Immaterial Spirit, and that cannot be done in this World, for I have no Fly- nor Bird-men here, to send into the region of the Air, where, for the most part, their habitations are. The Duchess said, she would intreat her Lord to send an Attorney or Lawyer, to plead his cause. Fortune will bribe them, replied the Emperess, and so the Duke may chance to be cast;[1] Wherefore the best way will be for the Duke to chuse a friend on his side, and let Fortune chuse another, and try whether by this means it be possible to compose the difference. The Duchess said, They will never come to an agreement, unless there be a Judg or Umpire to decide the Case. A Judg, replied the Emperess, is easie to be had, but to get an Impartial

---

1   to be cast: to be defeated

Judg, is a thing so difficult, that I doubt we shall hardly find one; for there is none to be had neither in Nature, nor in Hell, but onely from Heaven, and how to get such a Divine and Celestial Judg, I cannot tell: Nevertheless, if you will go along with me into the Blazing-world, I'le try what may be done. 'Tis my duty, said the Duchess, to wait on your Majesty, and I shall most willingly do it, for I have no other interest to consider. Then the Duchess spake to the Duke concerning the difference between him and Fortune, and how it was her desire that they might be friends. The Duke answered, That for his part, he had always with great industry, sought her friendship, but as yet he could never obtain it, for she had always been his enemy: However, said he, I'le try, and send my two friends, *Prudence* and *Honesty*, to plead my cause. Then these two friends went with the Duchess and the Emperess into the Blazing-world; (for it is to be observed, that they are somewhat like Spirits, because they are immaterial, although their actions are corporeal:) and after their arrival there, when the Emperess had refreshed her self, and rejoiced with the Emperor, she sent her Fly-men for some of the Spirits, and desired their assistance, to compose the difference between *Fortune*, and the *Duke* of *Newcastle*. But they told her Majesty, That Fortune was so inconstant, that although she would perhaps promise to hear their cause pleaded, yet it was a thousand to one, but she would never have the patience to do it: Nevertheless, upon Her Majesties request, they tried their utmost, and at last prevailed with Fortune so far, that she chose *Folly*, and *Rashness*, for her Friends, but they could not agree in chusing a Judg; until at last, with much ado, they concluded, that *Truth* should hear, and decide the cause. Thus all being prepared, and the time appointed, both the Emperess's and Duchess's soul went to hear them plead; and when all the Immaterial company was met, *Fortune* standing upon a Golden-Globe, made this following Speech:

Noble Friends, We are met here to hear a Cause pleaded concerning the difference between the Duke of *Newcastle*, and my self; and though I am willing upon the perswasions of the Ambassadors of the Emperess, the Immaterial Spirits, to yield to it, yet it had been fit, the *Dukes* Soul should be present also, to speak for her self;[1] but since she is not here, I shall declare my self to his Wife, and his Friends, as also

---

1 souls were thought to be of the female gender

to my Friends, especially the Emperess, to whom I shall chiefly direct my Speech. First, I desire, your Imperial Majesty may know, that this *Duke* who complains or exclaims so much against me, hath been always my enemy; for he has preferred *Honesty* and *Prudence* before me, and slighted all my favours; nay, not onely thus, but he did fight against me, and preferred his Innocence before my Power. His friends *Honesty* and *Prudence*, said he most scornfully, are more to be regarded, then Inconstant *Fortune*, who is onely a friend to Fools and Knaves; for which neglect and scorn, whether I have not just reason to be his enemy, your Majesty may judg your self.

After Fortune had thus ended her Speech, the Duchess's Soul rose from her seat, and spake to the Immaterial Assembly in this manner:

Noble Friends, I think it fit, by your leave, to answer Lady Fortune in the behalf of my Noble Lord and Husband, since he is not here himself; and since you have heard her complaint concerning the choice my Lord made of his friends, and the neglect and disrespect he seemed to cast upon her; give me leave to answer that, first concerning the Choice of his Friends, He has proved himself a wise man in it; and as for the dis-respect and rudeness, her Ladiship accuses him of, I dare say, he is so much a Gentleman, that I am confident he would never slight, scorn or disrespect any of the Female Sex in all his life time; but was such a servant and Champion for them, that he ventured Life and Estate in their service; but being of an honest, as well as an honourable Nature, he could not trust Fortune with that which he preferred above his life, which was his Reputation, by reason Fortune did not side with those that were honest and honourable, but renounced them; and since he could not be of both sides, he chose to be of that which was agreeable both to his Conscience, Nature and Education; for which choice Fortune did not onely declare her self his open Enemy, but fought with him in several Battels; nay, many times, hand to hand; at last, she being a Powerful Princess, and as some believe, a Deity,[1] overcame him, and cast him into a Banishment, where she kept him in great misery, ruined his Estate, and took away from him most of his Friends; nay, even when she favoured many that were against her, she still frowned on him; all

---

1   Fortuna, the classical goddess of chance or luck and changeability

which he endured with the greatest patience, and with that respect to Lady Fortune, that he did never in the least endeavour to disoblige any of her Favourites, but was onely sorry that he, an honest man, could find no favour in her Court; and since he did never injure any of those she favoured, he neither was an enemy to her Ladiship, but gave her always that respect and worship which belonged to her power and dignity, and is still ready at any time honestly and prudently to serve her; he onely begs her Ladiship would be his friend for the future, as she hath been his enemy in times past.

As soon as the *Duchess's* Speech was ended, *Folly* and *Rashness* started up, and both spake so thick and fast at once, that not onely the Assembly, but themselves were not able to understand each other: At which Fortune was somewhat out of countenance, and commanded them either to speak singly, or be silent: But Prudence told her Ladiship, she should command them to speak wisely, as well as singly; otherwise, said she, it were best for them not to speak at all: Which Fortune resented very ill, and told Prudence, she was too bold; and then commanded Folly to declare what she would have made known: but her Speech was so foolish, mixt with such non-sence, that none knew what to make of it; besides, it was so tedious, that Fortune bid her to be silent, and commanded Rashness to speak for her, who began after this manner:

> *Great Fortune*; The Duchess of *Newcastle* has proved her self, according to report, a very Proud and Ambitious Lady, in presuming to answer you her own self, in this noble Assembly without your Command, in a Speech wherein she did not onely contradict you, but preferred Honesty and Prudence before you; saying, that her Lord was ready to serve you honestly and prudently; which presumption is beyond all pardon; and if you allow Honesty and Prudence to be above you, none will admire, worship or serve you; but you'l be forced to serve your self, and will be despised, neglected and scorned by all; and from a Deity, become a miserable, dirty, begging mortal in a Church-yard-Porch, or Noble-mans Gate:[1] Wherefore, to prevent such disasters, fling as many misfortunes and neglects on the Duke

---

1   Beggars routinely stationed themselves at these places.

and Duchess of *Newcastle*, and their two friends, as your power is able to do; otherwise Prudence and Honesty will be the chief and onely Moral Deities of Mortals.

Rashness having thus ended her Speech, *Prudence* rose and declared her self in this manner:

Beautiful *Truth, Great Fortune, and you the rest of my noble Friends*; I am come a great and long journey in the behalf of my dear Friend the *Duke* of *Newcastle*, not to make more wounds, but, if it be possible, to heal those that are made already. Neither do I presume to be a Deity; but my onely request is, that you would be pleased to accept of my offering, I being an humble and devout supplicant, and since no offering is more acceptable to the Gods, then the offering of Peace; in order to that, I desire to make an agreement between *Fortune*, and the *Duke* of *Newcastle*.

Thus she spake, and as she was going on, up started *Honesty* (for she has not always so much discretion as she ought to have) and interrupted *Prudence*.

I came not here, said she, to hear *Fortune* flattered, but to hear the Cause decided between *Fortune* and the *Duke*; neither came I hither to speak Rhetorically and Eloquently, but to propound the case plainly and truly; and I'le have you know, that the *Duke*, whose Cause we argue, was and is my Foster-son; For I *Honesty* bred him from his Childhood, and made a perpetual friendship betwixt him and Gratitude, Charity and Generosity; and put him to School to *Prudence*, who taught him Wisdom, and informed him in the Rules of Temperance, Patience, Justice, and the like; then I put him into the University of Honour, where he learned all honourable Qualities, Arts, and Sciences; afterward I sent him to travel through the World of Actions, and made Observation his Governour; and in those his travels, he contracted a friendship with Experience; all which, made him fit for Heavens Blessings, and Fortunes Favours: But she hating all those that have merit and desert, became his inveterate Enemy; doing him all the mischief she could, until the God of Justice opposed Fortunes

Malice, and pull'd him out of those ruines she had cast upon him: For this Gods Favours were the Dukes Champions; wherefore to be an Enemy to him, were to be an Enemy to the God of Justice: In short, the true cause of *Fortunes* Malice to this *Duke*, is, that he would never flatter her; for I *Honesty*, did command him not to do it, or else he would be forced to follow all her inconstant ways, and obey all her unjust commands, which would cause a great reproach to him: but, on the other side, *Prudence* advised him not to despise *Fortunes* favours, for that would be an obstruction and hinderance to his worth and merit; and He to obey both our advice and counsels, did neither flatter nor despise Her, but was always humble and respectful to her, so far as Honour, Honesty and Conscience would permit: all which I refer to *Truths* Judgment, and expect her final sentence.

Fortune hearing thus *Honesties* plain Speech, thought it very rude, and would not hearken to *Truths* Judgment, but went away in a Passion: At which, both the Emperess and Duchess were extreamly troubled, that their endeavours should have no better effect: but *Honesty* chid the Duchess, and said, she was to be punished for desiring so much Fortunes favours; for it appears, said she, that you mistrust the Gods blessings: At which the Duchess wept, answering *Honesty*, that she did neither mistrust the Gods blessings, nor rely upon *Fortunes* favours; but desired onely that her Lord might have no potent Enemies. The Emperess being much troubled to see her weep, told *Honesty* in anger, she wanted the discretion of *Prudence*; for though you are commendable, said she, yet you are apt to commit many indiscreet actions, unless *Prudence* be your guide. At which reproof *Prudence* smiled, and *Honesty* was somewhat out of countenance; but they soon became very good friends: and after the Duchess's soul had stayed some time with the Emperess in the Blazing-world, she begg'd leave of her to return to her Lord and Husband; which the Emperess granted her, upon condition she should come and visit her as often as conveniently she could, promising that she would do the same to the Duchess.

Thus the *Duchess's* soul, after she had taken her leave of the *Emperess*, as also of the *Spirits*, who with great civility, promised her, that they would endeavour in time to make a peace and agreement between *Fortune* and the *Duke*, returned with *Prudence* and *Honesty* into her own World: But when she was just upon her departure, the

Emperess sent to Her, and desired that she might yet have some little conference with her before she went; which the *Duchess* most willingly granted her Majesty, and when she came to wait on Her, the *Emperess* told the *Duchess*, that she being Her dear Platonick friend, of whose just and impartial judgment, she had always a very great esteem, could not forbear, before she went from her, to ask her advice concerning the Government of the *Blazing-world*; For, said she, although this World was very well and wisely order'd and governed at first, when I came to be Emperess thereof; yet the nature of Women, being much delighted with change and variety,[1] after I had received an absolute Power from the Emperour, did somewhat alter the Form of Government from what I found it; but now perceiving that the world is not so quiet as it was at first, I am much troubled at it; especially there are such continual contentions and divisions between the *Worm- Bear-* and *Fly*-men, the *Ape*-men, the *Satyrs*, the *Spider*-men, and all others of such sorts, that I fear they'l break out into an open Rebellion, and cause a great disorder and ruine of the Government; and therefore I desire your advice and assistance, how I may order it to the best advantage, that this World may be rendred peaceable, quiet and happy, as it was before. Whereupon the Duchess answered, That since she heard by her Imperial Majesty, how well and happily the World had been governed when she first came to be Emperess thereof, she would advise her Majesty to introduce the same form of Government again, which had been before; that is, to have but one Soveraign, one Religion, one Law, and one Language, so that all the World might be but as one united Family, without divisions; nay, like God, and his Blessed Saints and Angels: Otherwise, said she, it may in time prove as unhappy, nay, as miserable a World as that is from which I came, wherein are more Soveraigns then Worlds, and more pretended Governours then Governments, more Religions then Gods, and more Opinions in those Religions then Truths; more Laws then Rights, and more Bribes then Justices, more Policies then Necessities, and more Fears then Dangers; more Covetousness then Riches, more Ambitions then Merits, more Services then Rewards, more Languages then Wit, more Controversie then Knowledg, more Reports then noble Actions, and more Gifts by partiality, then according to

---

1   For early modern assumptions about the nature of womankind, see Mendelson and Crawford ch. 1.

merit; all which, said she, is a great misery, nay, a curse, which your blessed *Blazing-world* never knew, nor 'tis probable, will never know of, unless your Imperial Majesty alter the Government thereof from what it was when you began to govern it: And since your Majesty complains much of the factions of the *Bear- Fish- Fly- Ape-* and *Worm*-men, the *Satyrs*, *Spider-men* and the like, and of their perpetual disputes and quarrels, I would advise your Majesty to dissolve all their societies; for 'tis better to be without their intelligences, then to have an unquiet and disorderly Government. The truth is, said she, where-soever is Learning, there is most commonly also Controversie and Quarrelling; for there be always some that will know more, and be wiser then others; some think their arguments come nearer to truth, and are more rational then others; some are so wedded to their own opinions, that they'l never yield to Reason; and others, though they find their Opinions not firmly grounded upon Reason, yet for fear of receiving some disgrace by altering them, will nevertheless maintain them against all sense and reason, which must needs breed factions in their Schools, which at last break out into open Wars, and draw some-times an utter ruine upon a State or Government. The Emperess told the Duchess, that she would willingly follow her advice, but she thought it would be an eternal disgrace to her, to alter her own Decrees, Acts and Laws. To which the Duchess answered, That it was so far from a disgrace, as it would rather be for her Majesties eternal honour, to return from a worse to a better, and would express and declare Her to be more then ordinary wise and good; so wise, as to perceive her own errors, and so good, as not to persist in them, which few did; for which, said she, you will get a glorious fame in this World, and an Eternal glory hereafter; and I shall pray for it so long as I live. Upon which advice, the Emperess's Soul embraced and kiss'd the Duchess's soul with an immaterial kiss, and shed immaterial tears, that she was forced to part from her, finding her not a flattering Parasite, but a true friend; and, in truth, such was their Platonick Friendship, as these two loving Souls did often meet and rejoice in each others Conversation.

THE SECOND PART OF THE DESCRIPTION OF THE NEW BLAZING WORLD.

The Emperess having now ordered and setled her Government to the best advantage and quiet of her *Blazing-world*, lived and reigned most happily and blessedly, and received oftentimes visits from the Immaterial Spirits, who gave her Intelligence of all such things as she desired to know, and they were able to inform her of: One time they told her, how the World she came from, was embroiled in a great War,[1] and that most parts or Nations thereof made war against that Kingdom, which was her Native Country, where all her Friends and Relations did live, at which the Emperess was extreamly troubled; insomuch that the Emperor perceived her grief by her tears, and examining the cause thereof, she told him that she had received Intelligence from the Spirits, that that part of the World she came from, which was her native Country, was like to be destroyed by numerous Enemies that made war against it. The Emperor being very sensible of this ill news, especially of the Trouble it caused to the Emperess, endeavoured to comfort her as much as possibly he could, and told her, that she might have all the assistance which the *Blazing-world* was able to afford. She answered, That if there were any possibility of transporting Forces out of the Blazing-world, into the World she came from, she would not fear so much the ruine thereof: but, said she, there being no probability of effecting any such thing, I know not how to shew my readiness to serve my Native Country. The Emperor asked, Whether those Spirits that gave her Intelligence of this War, could not with all their Power and Forces assist her against those Enemies? She answered, That Spirits could not arm themselves, nor make any use of Artificial Arms or Weapons; for their Vehicles were Natural Bodies, not Artificial: Besides, said she, the violent and strong actions of War, will never agree with Immaterial Spirits; for Immaterial Spirits cannot fight, nor make Trenches, Fortifications, and the like. But, said the Emperor, their Vehicles can; especially if those Vehicles be mens Bodies, they may be serviceable in all the actions of War. Alas, replied the Emper-

---

1   This and following passages may have been influenced by Cavendish's awareness that in 1665-67 England was involved in the "Second Dutch War," rooted in naval, commercial, and colonial rivalry between the two countries; the Netherlands was joined by France in 1666, the year *The Blazing World* was first published.

ess, that will never do; for first, said she, it will be difficult to get so many dead Bodies for their Vehicles, as to make up a whole Army, much more to make many Armies to fight with so many several Nations; nay, if this could be, yet it is not possible to get so many dead and undissolved bodies in one Nation; and for transporting them out of other Nations, would be a thing of great difficulty and improbability: But put the case, said she, all these difficulties could be overcome, yet there is one obstruction or hinderance which can no ways be avoided; for although those dead and undissolved Bodies did all die in one minute of time, yet before they could Rendezvouze,[1] and be put into a posture of War, to make a great and formidable Army, they would stink and dissolve; and when they came to a fight, they would moulder into dust and ashes, and so leave the purer Immaterial Spirits naked: nay, were it also possible, that those dead bodies could be preserved from stinking and dissolving, yet the souls of such bodies would not suffer Immaterial Spirits to rule and order them, but they would enter and govern them themselves, as being the right owners thereof, which would produce a War between those Immaterial Souls, and the Immaterial Spirits in Material Bodies; all which would hinder them from doing any service in the actions of War, against the Enemies of my Native Countrey. You speak Reason, said the Emperor, and I wish with all my Soul I could advise any manner or way, that you might be able to assist it; but you having told me of your dear Platonick Friend the Duchess of *Newcastle*, and of her good and profitable Counsels, I would desire you to send for her Soul, and confer with her about this business.

The Emperess was very glad of this motion of the Emperor, and immediately sent for the Soul of the said Duchess, which in a minute waited on her Majesty. Then the Emperess declared to her the grievance and sadness of her mind, and how much she was troubled and afflicted at the News brought her by the Immaterial Spirits, desiring the Duchess, if possible, to assist her with the best counsels she could, that she might shew the greatness of her love and affection which she bore to her Native Countrey. Whereupon the Duchess promised her Majesty to do what lay in her power; and since it was a business of great Importance, she desired some time to consider of it; for, said she,

---

1 rendezvous: come together

Great Affairs require deep considerations; which the Emperess will-ingly allowed her. And after the Duchess had considered some little time, she desired the Emperess to send some of her *Syrenes* or Mear-men,[1] to see what passages they could find out of the Blazing-World, into the World she came from; for said she, if there be a passage for a Ship to come out of that World into this; then certainly there may also a Ship pass thorow the same passage out of this World into that. Hereupon the Mear- or Fish-men were sent out; who being many in number, employ'd all their industry, and did swim several ways; at last having found out the passage, they returned to the Emperess, and told her, That as their Blazing-World had but one Emperor, one Govern-ment, one Religion, and one Language, so there was but one Passage into that World, which was so little, that no Vessel bigger than a Pack-et-boat could go thorow; neither was that Passage always open, but sometimes quite frozen up. At which Relation both the Emperess and Duchess seemed somewhat troubled, fearing that this would perhaps be an hinderance or obstruction to their Design.

At last the Duchess desired the Emperess to send for her Ship-wrights, and all her Architects, which were Giants; who being called, the Duchess told them how some in her own World had been so ingenious, and contrived Ships that could swim under Water, and asked whether they could do the like? The Gyants answered, They had never heard of that Invention; nevertheless, they would try what might be done by Art, and spare no labour or industry to find it out. In the mean time, while both the Emperess and Duchess were in a serious Counsel, after many debates, the Duchess desired but a few Ships to transport some of the Bird- Worm- and Bear-men. Alas! said the Emperess, What can such sorts of Men do in the other World? especially so few? They will be soon destroyed, for a Musket will destroy numbers of Birds at one shot. The Duchess said, I desire your Majesty will have but a little patience, and rely upon my advice, and you shall not fail to save your own Native Country, and in a manner become Mistress of all that World you came from.[2] The Emperess, who loved the Duchess as her own Soul, did so; the Gyants returned soon after, and told her Majesty, that they had found out the Art

---

1   sirens or mermen, i.e. male mermaids
2   From this and other passages it appears that the Empress and the Duchess do not
    share the same "native country."

which the Duchess had mentioned, to make such Ships as could swim under Water; which the Emperess and Duchess were both very glad at, and when the Ships were made ready, the Duchess told the Emperess, that it was requisite that her Majesty should go her self in body as well as in Soul; but, I, said she, can onely wait on your Majesty after a Spiritual manner, that is, with my Soul. Your Soul, said the Emperess, shall live with my Soul, in my Body; for I shall onely desire your Counsel and Advice. Then said the Duchess, Your Majesty must command a great number of your Fish-men to wait on your Ships; for you know that your Ships are not made for Cannons, and therefore are no ways serviceable in War; for though by the help of your Engines they can drive on, and your Fish-men may by the help of Chains or Ropes, draw them which way they will, to make them go on, or flye back, yet not so as to fight: And though your Ships be of Gold, and cannot be shot thorow, but onely bruised and battered; yet the Enemy will assault and enter them, and take them as Prizes; wherefore your Fish-men must do you Service instead of Cannons. But how, said the Emperess, can the Fish-men do me service against an Enemy, without Canons and all sorts of Arms? That is the reason, answered the Duchess, that I would have numbers of Fish-men, for they shall destroy all your Enemies Ships, before they can come near you. The Emperess asked in what manner that could be? Thus, answered the Duchess: Your Majesty must send a number of Worm-men to the Burning-Mountains (for you have good store of them in the Blazing-World) which must get a great quantity of the Fire-stone, whose property, you know, is, that it burns so long as it is wet; and the Ships in the other World being all made of Wood, they may by that means set them all on fire; and if you can but destroy their Ships, and hinder their Navigation, you will be Mistress of all that World, by reason most parts thereof cannot live without Navigation. Besides, said she, the Fire-stone will serve you instead of light or torches; for you know, that the World you are going into, is dark at nights (especially if there be no Moon-shine, or if the Moon be overshadowed by Clouds) and not so full of Blazing-Stars as this World is, which make as great a light in the absence of the Sun, as the Sun doth when it is present; for that World hath but little blinking Stars, which make more shadows then light, and are onely able to draw up Vapours from the Earth, but not to rarefie or clarifie them, or to convert them into serene air.

This Advice of the Duchess was very much approved, and joyfully embraced by the Emperess, who forthwith sent her Worm-men to get a good quantity of the mentioned Fire-stone. She also commanded numbers of Fish-men to wait on her under water, and Bird-men to wait on her in the air; and Bear- and Worm-men to wait on her in Ships, according to the Duchess's advice; and indeed the Bear-men were as serviceable to her as the North-Star; but the Bird-men would often rest themselves upon the Decks of the Ships; neither would the Emperess, being of a sweet and noble Nature, suffer that they should tire or weary themselves by long flights; for though by Land they did often flye out of one Countrey into another, yet they did rest in some Woods, or on some Grounds, especially at night, when it was their sleeping time: And therefore the Emperess was forced to take a great many Ships along with her, both for transporting those several sorts of her loyal and serviceable Subjects, and to carry provisions for them: Besides, she was so wearied with the Petitions of several others of her Subjects who desired to wait on her Majesty, that she could not possibly deny them all; for some would rather chuse to be drowned, then not tender their duty to her.

Thus after all things were made fit and ready, the Emperess began her Journey, I cannot properly say, she set Sail, by reason in some Part, as in the passage between the two Worlds (which yet was but short) the Ships were drawn under water by the Fish-men with Golden Chains, so that they had no need of Sails there, nor of any other Arts, but onely to keep out water from entering into the Ships, and to give or make so much Air as would serve for breath or respiration, those Land Animals that were in the Ships; which the Giants had so Artificially contrived, that they which were therein found no inconveniency at all: And after they had passed the Icy Sea, the Golden Ships appeared above water, and so went on until they came near the Kingdom that was the Emperess's Native Countrey; where the Bear-men through their Telescopes discovered a great number of Ships which had beset all that Kingdom, well rigg'd and mann'd.

The Emperess before she came in sight of the Enemy, sent some of her Fish- and Bird-men to bring her Intelligence of their Fleet; and hearing of their number, their station and posture, she gave order that when it was Night, her Bird-men should carry in their beaks some of the mentioned Fire-stones, with the tops thereof wetted; and the Fish-men should carry them likewise, and hold them out of the

Water; for they were cut in the form of Torches or Candles, and being many thousands, made a terrible shew; for it appear'd as if all the Air and Sea had been of a flaming Fire; and all that were upon the Sea, or near it, did verily believe, the time of Judgment, or the Last Day was come, which made them all fall down, and Pray.

At the break of Day, the Emperess commanded those Lights to be put out, and then the Naval Forces of the Enemy perceived nothing but a Number of Ships without Sails, Guns, Arms, and other Instruments of War; which Ships seemed to swim of themselves, without any help or assistance: which sight put them into a great amaze; neither could they perceive that those Ships were of Gold, by reason the Emperess had caused them all to be coloured black, or with a dark colour; so that the natural colour of the Gold could not be perceived through the artificial colour of the paint, no not by the best Telescopes. All which put the Enemies Fleet into such a fright at night, and to such wonder in the morning, or at day time, that they knew not what to judg or make of them; for they knew neither what Ships they were, nor what Party they belonged to, insomuch that they had no power to stir.

In the mean while, the Emperess knowing the Colours of her own Country, sent a Letter to their General, and the rest of the chief Commanders, to let them know, that she was a great and powerful Princess, and came to assist them against their Enemies; wherefore she desired they should declare themselves, when they would have her help and assistance.

Hereupon a Councel was called, and the business debated; but there were so many cross and different Opinions, that they could not suddenly resolve what answer to send the Emperess; at which she grew angry, insomuch that she resolved to return into her Blazing-world, without giving any assistance to her Country-men: But the Duchess of *Newcastle* intreated her Majesty to abate her passion; for, said she, Great Councels are most commonly slow, because many men have many several Opinions: besides, every Councellor striving to be the wisest, makes long speeches, and raises many doubts, which cause retardments. If I had long speeched Councellours, replied the Emperess, I would hang them, by reason they give more Words, then Advice. The Duchess answered, that her Majesty should not be angry, but consider the differences of that and her Blazing-world; for, said she, they are not both alike; but there are grosser and duller under-standings in this, then in the Blazing-world.

At last a Messenger came out, who returned the Emperess thanks for her kind profer, but desired withal to know from whence she came, and how, and in what manner her assistance could be service-able to them? The Emperess answered, That she was not bound to tell them whence she came; but as for the manner of her assistance, I will appear, said she, to your Navy in a splendorous Light, surrounded with Fire. The Messenger asked at what time they should expect her coming? I'le be with you, answered the Emperess, about one of the Clock at night. With this report the Messenger returned; which made both the poor Counsellers and Sea-men much afraid; but yet they longed for the time to behold this strange sight.

The appointed hour being come, the Emperess appear'd with Gar-ments made of the Star-stone, and was born[1] or supported above the Water, upon the Fish-mens heads and backs, so that she seemed to walk upon the face of the Water, and the Bird- and Fish-men carried the Fire-stone, lighted both in the Air, and above the Waters.

Which sight, when her Country-men perceived at a distance, their hearts began to tremble; but coming something nearer, she left her Torches, and appeared onely in her Garments of Light, like an Angel, or some Deity, and all kneeled down before her, and worshipped her with all submission and reverence: But the Emperess would not come nearer then at such a distance where her voice might be generally heard, by reason she would not have that of her Accoustrements any thing else should be perceived, but the splendor thereof; and when she was come so near that her voice could be heard and understood by all, she made this following Speech:

> *Dear Countrymen,* for so you are, although you know me not; I being a Native of this Kingdom, and hearing that most part of this World had resolved to make War against it, and sought to destroy it, at least to weaken its Naval Force and Power; have made a Voyage out of another World, to lend you my assistance against your Enemies. I come not to make bargains with you, or to regard my own Interest, more then your safety; but I

---

1 borne

intend to make you the most powerful Nation of this World; and therefore I have chosen rather to quit my own Tranquility, Riches and Pleasure, then suffer you to be ruined and destroyed. All the return I desire, is but your Grateful acknowledgment, and to declare my Power, Love and Loyalty to my Native Country; for although I am now a great and absolute Princess and Emperess of a whole World, yet I acknowledg that once I was a Subject of this Kingdom, which is but a small part of this World; and therefore I will have you undoubtedly believe, that I shall destroy all your Enemies before this following Night, I mean those which trouble you by Sea; and if you have any by Land, assure your self I shall also give you my Assistance against them, and make you Triumph over all that seek your Ruine and Destruction.

Upon this Declaration of the Emperess, when both the General, and all the Commanders in their several Ships had return'd their humble and hearty Thanks to Her Majesty for so great a favour to them, she took her leave and departed to her own Ships. But, Good Lord! what several Opinions and Judgments did this produce in the minds of her Country-men; some said she was an Angel; others, she was a Sorceress; some believed her a Goddess; others said the Devil deluded them in the shape of a fine Lady.

The morning after, when the Navies were to fight, the Emperess appear'd upon the face of the Waters, dress'd in her Imperial Robes, which were all of Diamonds and Carbuncles; in one hand she held a Buckler, made of one intire Carbuncle, and in the other hand a Spear of one intire Diamond; on her head she had a Cap of Diamonds, and just upon the top of the Crown, was a Star made of the Star-stone, mentioned heretofore, and a Half-moon made of the same stone, was placed on her forehead; all her other Garments were of several sorts of precious Jewels; and having given her Fish-men directions how to destroy the Enemies of her Native Country, she proceeded to effect her design. The Fish-men were to carry the Fire-stones in cases of Diamonds (for the Diamonds in the Blazing-world are in splendor so far beyond the Diamonds of this World, as Peble-stones are to the best sort of this Worlds Diamonds) and to uncase or uncover those Fire-stones no sooner but when they were just under the Enemies Ships, or close at their sides, and then to wet them, and set their Ships on fire; which was no sooner done, but all the Enemies Fleet was of a Flaming-Fire; and coming to the place where the Powder[1] was, it streight blew them up; so that all the several Navies of the Enemies, were destroyed in a short time: which when her Country-men did see, they all cried out with one voice, that she was an Angel sent from God to deliver them out of the hands of their Enemies: Neither would she return into the Blazing-world, until she had forced all the rest of that World to submit to that same Nation.

In the mean time, the General of all their Naval Forces sent to their Soveraign to acquaint him with their miraculous Delivery and Conquest, and with the Emperess's design of making him the most powerful Monarch of all that World. After a short time, the Emperess sent her self to the Soveraign of that Nation to know in what she could be serviceable to him; who returning her many thanks, both for her assistance against his Enemies, and her kind profer to do him further service for the good and benefit of his Nations (for he was King over several Kingdoms) sent her word, that although she did partly destroy his Enemies by Sea, yet they were so powerful, that they did hinder the Trade and Traffick of his Dominions. To which the Emperess returned this answer, That she would burn and sink all those Ships that would not pay him Tribute; and forthwith sent to all the Neighbouring Nations, who had any Traffick by Sea, desiring them to pay Tribute to the King and Soveraign of that Nation where she was born; But they denied it with great scorn. Whereupon she immediately commanded her Fish-men to destroy all strangers Ships that traffick'd on the Seas; which they did according to the Emperess's Command; and when the neighbouring Nations and Kingdoms perceived her power, they were so discomposed in their affairs and designs, that they knew not what to do: At last they sent to the Emperess, and desired to treat with her, but could get no other conditions then to submit and pay Tribute to the said King and Soveraign of her Native Country, otherwise, she was resolved to ruine all their Trade and Traffick by burning their Ships. Long was this Treat,[2] but in

---

1   gunpowder
2   treat: parley

fine, they could obtain nothing, so that at last they were forced to submit; by which the King of the mentioned Nations became absolute Master of the Seas, and consequently of that World; by reason, as I mentioned heretofore, the several Nations of that World could not well live without Traffick and Commerce, by Sea, as well as by Land.

But after a short time, those Neighbouring Nations finding themselves so much inslaved, that they were hardly able to peep out of their own Dominions without a chargeable Tribute, they all agreed to join again their Forces against the King and Soveraign of the said Dominions; which when the Emperess receiv'd notice of, she sent out her Fish-men to destroy, as they had done before, the remainder of all their Naval Power, by which they were soon forced again to submit, except some Nations which could live without Forreign Traffick, and some whose Trade and Traffick was meerly by Land; these would no wayes be Tributary to the mentioned King. The Emperess sent them word, That in case they did not submit to him, she intended to fire all their Towns and Cities, and reduce them by force, to what they would not yield with a good will. But they rejected and scorned her Majesties Message, which provoked her anger so much, that she resolved to send her Bird- and Worm-men thither, with order to begin first with their smaller Towns, and set them on fire (for she was loath to make more spoil then she was forced to do) and if they remain'd still obstinate in their resolutions, to destroy also their greater Cities. The onely difficulty was, how to convey the Worm-men conveniently to those places; but they desired that her Majesty would but set them upon any part of the Earth of those Nations, and they could travel within the Earth as easily, and as nimbly as men upon the face of the Earth; which the Emperess did according to their desire.

But before both the Bird- and Worm-men began their Journey, the Emperess commanded the Bear-men to view through their Telescopes what Towns and Cities those were that would not submit; and having a full information thereof, she instructed the Bird- and Bear-men what Towns they should begin withall; in the mean while she sent to all the Princes and Soveraigns of those Nations, to let them know that she would give them a proof of her Power, and check their Obstinacies by burning some of their smaller Towns; and if they continued still in their Obstinate Resolutions, that she would convert their smaller Loss into a Total Ruine. She also commanded her Bird-men to make their flight at night, lest they be perceived. At last when both the Bird- and Worm-men came to the designed places, the Worm-men laid some Fire-stones under the Foundation of every House, and the Bird-men placed some at the tops of them, so that both by rain, and by some other moisture within the Earth, the stones could not fail of burning. The Bird-men in the mean time having learned some few words of their Language, told them, That the next time it did rain, their Towns would be all on fire; at which they were amaz'd to hear men speak in the air; but withall they laughed when they heard them say that rain should fire their Towns, knowing that the effect of Water was to quench, not produce fire.

At last a rain came, and upon a sudden all their Houses appeared of a flaming Fire, and the more Water there was poured on them, the more they did flame and burn; which struck such a Fright and Terror into all the Neighbouring Cities, Nations and Kingdoms, that for fear the like should happen to them, they and all the rest of the parts of that World granted the Emperess's desire, and submitted to the Monarch and Soveraign of her Native Country, the King of E S F I;[1] save one, which having seldom or never any rain, but onely dews, which would soon be spent in a great fire, slighted her Power: The Emperess being desirous to make it stoop, as well as the rest, knew that every year it was watered by a flowing Tide, which lasted some weeks; and although their Houses stood high from the ground, yet they were built upon Supporters which were fixt into the ground. Wherefore she commanded both her Bird- and Worm-men to lay some of the Fire-stones at the bottom of those Supporters, and when the Tide came in, all their Houses were of a Fire, which did so rarifie the Water, that the Tide was soon turn'd into Vapour, and this Vapour again into Air; which caused not onely a destruction of their Houses, but also a general barrenness over all their Countrey that year, and forced them to submit as well as the rest of the World had done.

Thus the Emperess did not onely save her Native Countrey, but made it the absolute Monarchy of all that World; and both the effects of her Power and her Beauty did kindle a great desire in all the greatest Princes to see her; who hearing that she was resolved to return into her own Blazing-World, they all entreated the favour, that they

---

1   Charles II, like his predecessors on the English throne, was styled King of England, Scotland, France, and Ireland.

might wait on her Majesty before she went. The Emperess sent word, That she should be glad to grant their Requests; but having no other place of reception for them, she desired that they would be pleased to come into the open Seas with their Ships, and make a Circle of a pretty large compass, and then her own Ships should meet them, and close up the Circle, and she would present her self to the view of all those that came to see her: Which Answer was joyfully received by all the mentioned Princes, who came, some sooner, and some later, each according to the distance of his Countrey, and the length of the voyage. And being all met in the form and manner aforesaid, the Emperess appeared upon the face of the Water in her Imperial Robes; in some part of her hair she had placed some of the Star-Stone, near her face, which added such a lustre and glory to it, that it caused a great admiration in all that were present, who believed her to be some Celestial Creature, or rather an uncreated[1] Goddess, and they all had a desire to worship her; for surely, said they, no mortal creature can have such a splendid and transcendent beauty, nor can any have so great a power as she has, to walk upon the Waters, and to destroy whatever she pleases, not onely whole Nations, but a whole World.

The Emperess expressed to her own Countreymen, who were also her Interpreters to the rest of the Princes that were present, that she would give them an entertainment at the darkest time of night; which being come, the Fire-Stones were lighted, which made both Air and Seas appear of a bright shining flame, insomuch that they put all Spectators into an extream fright, who verily believed, they should all be destroyed; which the Emperess perceiving, caused all the Lights of the Fire-Stones to be put out, and onely shewed her self in her Garments of Light: The Bird-men carried her upon their backs into the Air, and there she appear'd as glorious as the Sun. Then she was set down upon the Seas again, and presently there was heard the most melodious and sweetest Consort of Voices, as ever was heard out of the Seas, which was made by the Fish-men; this Consort was answered by another, made by the Bird-men in the Air, so that it seem'd as if Sea and Air had spoke and answered each other by way of Singing Dialogues, or after the manner of those Plays that are acted by singing Voices.

---

1 existent without being created

But when it was upon break of day, the Emperess ended her entertainment, and at full day light all the Princes perceived that she went into the Ship wherein the Prince and Monarch of her Native Country was, the King of E S F I with whom she had several Conferences; and having assured him of the readiness of her assistance whensoever he required it, telling him withal, that she wanted no Intelligence,[1] she went forth again upon the Waters, and being in the midst of the Circle made by those Ships that were present, she desired them to draw somewhat nearer, that they might hear her speak; which being done, she declared her self in this following manner:

Great, Heroick, and Famous Monarchs: I came hither to assist the King of E S F I against his Enemies, he being unjustly assaulted by many several Nations, which would fain take away his Hereditary Rights and Prerogatives of the Narrow Seas;[2] at which Unjustice Heaven was much displeased; and for the Injuries he received from his Enemies, rewarded him with an absolute Power, so that now he is become the Head-Monarch of all this World; which Power, though you may envy, yet you can no ways hinder him; for all those that endeavour to resist his Power, shall onely get loss for their labour, and no Victory for their profit. Wherefore my advice to you all is, to pay him Tribute justly and truly, that you may live Peaceably and Happily, and be rewarded with the Blessings of Heaven, which I wish you from my Soul.

After the Emperess had thus finished her Speech to the Princes of the several Nations of that World, she desired that their Ships might fall back, which being done, her own Fleet came into the Circle, without any visible assistance of Sails or Tide; and her self being entred into her own Ship, the whole Fleet sunk immediately into the bottom of the Seas, and left all the Spectators in a deep amazement; neither would she suffer any of her Ships to come above the Waters until she arrived into the Blazing-world.

In time of the Voyage, both the Emperess's and Duchess's Soul

---

1 wanted no intelligence: was well-informed
2 narrow seas: the channels separating Great Britain from the Continent and from Ireland

were very gay and merry, and sometimes they would converse very seriously with each other: amongst the rest of their discourses, the Duchess said, she wondered much at one thing, which was, that since her Majesty had found out a passage out of the Blazing-world into the World she came from, she did not inrich that part of the World where she was born, at least her own Family, when as yet she had enough to inrich the whole World. The Emperess's Soul answered, that she loved her Native Country and her own Family as well as any Creature could do, and that this was the reason why she would not inrich them; for said she, not onely particular Families or Nations, but all the World, their natures are such, that much Gold, and great store of Riches makes them mad, insomuch as they endeavour to destroy each other for Gold, or Riches sake. The reason thereof is, said the Duchess, that they have too little Gold and Riches, which makes them so eager to have it. No, replied the Emperess's Soul, their particular covetousness is beyond all the wealth of the richest World, and the more Riches they have, the more Covetous they are, for their Covetousness is Infinite; But, said she, I would there could a passage be found out of the Blazing-world into the World whence you came, and I would willingly give you as much riches as you desir'd. The Duchess's Soul gave her Majesty humble thanks for her great favour, and told her that she was not covetous, nor desir'd any more wealth then what her Lord and Husband had before the Civil Wars; Neither, said she, should I desire it for my own, but my Lord's Posterities sake. Well, said the Emperess, I'le command my Fish-men to use all their skill and industry to find out a passage into that World which your Lord and Husband is in. I do verily believe, answered the Duchess, that there will be no passage found into that World;[1] but if there were any, I should not Petition your Majesty for Gold and Jewels, but onely for the Elixir that grows in the midst of the Golden Sands, for to preserve Life and Health; but without a passage it is impossible to carry away any of it, for whatsoever is Material, cannot travel like Immaterial Beings such as Souls and Spirits are; Neither do Souls require any such thing that might revive them, or prolong their lives, by reason they are unalterable: for were Souls like Bodies, then my Soul might have had the benefit of that Natural Elixir that grows in your Blaz-

---

1 another passage suggesting that the Empress's and the Duchess's native countries were not the same (see above, p. 233)

ing-world. I wish earnestly, said the Emperess, that a passage might be found, and then both your Lord and your self should neither want Wealth, nor long Life; nay, I love you so well, that I would make you as great and Powerful a Monarchess as I am of the Blazing-world. The Duchess's Soul humbly thank'd her Majesty, and told her, that she acknowledged and esteemed her love beyond all things that are in Nature.

After this Discourse they had many other Conferences, which for brevities sake I'le forbear to rehearse. At last, after several questions which the Emperess's Soul asked the Duchess, she desired to know the reason why she did take such delight when she was joyned to her body, in being singular both in Accoustrements, Behaviour and Discourse?[1] The Duchess's Soul answered, she confessed that it was extravagant, and beyond what was usual and ordinary; but yet her ambition being such, that she would not be like others in any thing if it were possible; I endeavour, said she, to be as singular as I can; for it argues but a mean Nature to imitate others; and though I do not love to be imitated if I can possibly avoid it; yet rather then imitate others, I should chuse to be imitated by others; for my nature is such, that I had rather appear worse in singularity, then better in the Mode. If you were not a great Lady, replied the Emperess, you would never pass in the World for a wise Lady; for the World would say your singularities are Vanities.[2] The Duchess's Soul answered, she did not at all regard the censure of this or any other age concerning vanities; but, said she, neither this present, nor any of the future ages can or will truly say that I am not Vertuous and Chast; for I am confident, all that were or are acquainted with me, and all the Servants which ever I had, will or can upon their Oaths declare my actions no otherwise then Vertuous; and certainly there's none, even of the meanest Degree, which have not their Spies and Witnesses, much more those of the Nobler sort, which seldom or never are without attendants, so that their faults (if they have any) will easily be known, and as easily divulged: Wherefore happy are those Natures that are Honest, Virtuous and Noble, not only happy to themselves, but happy to their Families. But, said the

---

1 For Margaret Cavendish's autobiographical account of her love of singularity in dress see *A True Relation*, above, pp. 59-60.
2 For an example of contemporary opinion of Cavendish's dress and deportment, see Mary Evelyn's letter to Mr. Bohun, above, pp. 91-3.

Emperess, if you glory so much in your Honesty and Vertue, how comes it that you plead for Dishonest and Wicked persons in your Writings? The Duchess answered, it was onely to show her Wit, not her Nature.

At last the Emperess arrived into the Blazing World, and coming to her Imperial Palace, you may sooner imagine than expect that I should express the joy which the Emperor had at her safe return; for he loved her beyond his Soul; and there was no love lost, for the Emperess equal'd his Affection with no less love to him. After the time of rejoicing with each other, the Duchess's Soul begg'd leave to return to her Noble Lord; but the Emperor desir'd, That before she departed, she would see how he had employed his time in the Emperess's absence; for he had built Stables and Riding-Houses, and desired to have Horses of Manage, such as, according to the Emperess's Relation, the Duke of *Newcastle* had: The Emperor enquired of the Duchess, the Form and Structure of her Lord and Husbands Stables and Riding-House. The Duchess answer'd his Majesty, That they were but plain and ordinary; but said she, had my Lord Wealth, I am sure he would not spare it, in rendering his Buildings as Noble as could be made. Hereupon the Emperor shew'd the Duchess the Stables he had built, which were most stately and magnificent; among the rest there was one double Stable that held a hundred Horses on a side, the main Building was of Gold, lined with several sorts of precious Materials; the roof was Arched with Agats, the sides of the Walls were lined with Cornelian,[1] the Floor was paved with Amber, the Mangers were Mother of Pearl, the Pillars, as also the middle Isle or Walk of the Stables, were of Crystal; the Front and Gate was of Turquois, most neatly cut and carved. The riding-house was lined with Saphirs, Topases and the like; the Floor was all of Golden-sand, so finely sifted, that it was extreamly soft, and not in the least hurtful to the Horses feet, and the Door and Frontispiece was of Emeralds, curiously carved.

After the view of these Glorious and Magnificent Buildings, which the Duchess's Soul was much delighted withal, she resolved to take her leave; but the Emperor desired her to stay yet some short time more, for they both loved her company so well, that they were unwilling to have her depart so soon: Several Conferences and Dis-

---

1 a reddish variety of semi-transparent quartz

courses pass'd between them; amongst the rest the Emperor desir'd her advice how to set up a Theatre for Plays. The Duchess confessed her Ignorance in this Art, telling his Majesty that she knew nothing of erecting Theatres or Scenes, but what she had by an Immaterial Observation when she was with the Emperess's Soul in the chief City of *E*. Entering into one of their Theatres, whereof the Emperess could give as much account to His Majesty as her self. But both the Emperor and Emperess told the Duchess, That she could give directions how to make Plays. The Duchess answered, that she had as little skill to form a Play after the Mode, as she had to paint or make a Scene for shew. But you have made Playes, replied the Emperess:[1] Yes, answered the Duchess, I intended them for Playes; but the Wits of these present times condemned them as uncapable of being represented or acted, because they were not made up according to the Rules of Art;[2] though I dare say, that the Descriptions are as good as any they have writ. The Emperor ask'd, Whether the Property of Playes were not to describe the several humours, actions and fortunes of Mankind? 'Tis so, answered the Duchess: Why then, replied the Emperor, the natural Humours, Actions and Fortunes of Mankind, are not done by the Rules of Art: But said the Duchess, it is the Art and Method of our Wits to despise all Descriptions of Wit, Humour, Actions and Fortunes that are without such Artificial Rules. The Emperor ask'd, Are those good Playes that are made so Methodically and Artificially? The Duchess answer'd, They were Good according to the Judgment of the Age, or Mode of the Nation, but not according to her Judgment; for truly, said she, in my Opinion, their Playes will prove a Nursery of Whining Lovers, and not an Academy or School for Wise, Witty, Noble, and well-behaved men. But I, replied the Emperor, desire such a Theatre as may make wise Men; and will have such Descriptions as are Natural, not Artificial. If your Majesty be of that Opinion, said the Duchess's Soul, then my Playes may be acted in your Blazing-World, when they cannot be acted in the Blinking World of Wit; and the next time I come to visit your Majesty, I shall

---

1   *Playes* (1662), and *Plays Never Before Printed* (1668); for an example see *The Convent of Pleasure*, above, pp. 97-135.

2   the classical dramatic unities first formulated by Aristotle in his *Poetics*, and re-interpreted by neo-classical authors of the 1660s such as Dryden in his *Essay on Dramatic Poesie* (1668)

endeavour to order your Majesties Theatre, to present such Playes as my Wit is capable to make. Then the Emperess told the Duchess, That she loved a foolish farce added to a wise Play. The Duchess answered, That no World in Nature had fitter Creatures for it then the Blazing-World; for, said she, the Lowse-men, the Bird-men, the Spider- and Fox-men, the Ape-men and Satyrs appear in a Farce extraordinary pleasant.

Hereupon both the Emperor and the Emperess intreated the Duchess's Soul to stay so long with them, till she had ordered her Theatre, and made Playes and Verses fit for them; for they onely wanted that sort of Recreation; But the Duchess's Soul begg'd their Majesties to give her leave to go into her Native World; for she long'd to be with her dear Lord and Husband, promising, that after a short time she would return again. Which being granted, though with much difficulty, she took her leave with all Civility and respect, and so departed from their Majesties.

After the Duchess's return into her own body, she entertained her Lord (when he was pleased to hear such kind of Discourses) with Forreign Relations; but he was never displeased to hear of the Emperess's kind Commendations, and of the Characters she was pleased to give of him to the Emperor. Amongst other Relations she told him all what had past between the Emperess, and the several Monarchs of that World whither she went with the Emperess; and how she had subdued them to pay Tribute and Homage to the Monarch of that Nation or Kingdom to which she owed both her Birth and Education. She also related to her Lord what Magnificent Stables and Riding-Houses the Emperor had built, and what fine Horses were in the Blazing-World, of several shapes and sizes, and how exact their shapes were in each sort, and of many various Colours, and fine Marks, as if they had been painted by Art, with such Coats or Skins, that they had a far greater gloss and smoothness than Satin; and were there but a passage out of the Blazing-World into this, said she, you should not onely have some of those Horses, but such Materials, as the Emperor has, to build your Stables and Riding-houses withall; and so much Gold, that I should never repine at your Noble and Generous Gifts. The Duke smilingly answered her, That he was sorry there was no Passage between those two Worlds; but said he, I have alwayes found an Obstruction to my Good Fortunes.

One time the Duchess chanced to discourse with some of her

acquaintance, of the Emperess of the Blazing-world, who asked her what Pastimes and Recreations Her Majesty did most delight in? The Duchess answered, that she spent most of her time in the study of Natural Causes and Effects, which was her chief delight and pastime, and that she loved to discourse sometimes with the most Learned persons of that World; and to please the Emperor and his Nobles, who were all of the Royal Race, she went often abroad to take the air, but seldom in the day time, always at Night, if it might be called Night; for, said she, the Nights there are as light as Days, by reason of the numerous Blazing-stars, which are very splendorous, onely their Light is whiter then the Sun's Light; and as the Suns Light is hot, so their Light is cool, not so cool as our twinkling Star-light, nor is their Sun-light so hot as ours, but more temperate; And that part of the Blazing-world where the Emperess resides, is always clear, and never subject to any Storms, Tempests, Fogs or Mists, but has onely refreshing Dews that nourish the Earth; the Air of it is sweet and temperate, and, as I said before, as much light in the Suns absence, as in its presence, which makes that time we call Night, more pleasant there then the Day; and sometimes the Emperess goes abroad by Water in Barges, sometimes by Land in Chariots, and sometimes on Horseback; her Royal Chariots are very Glorious; the body is one intire green Dia-mond; the four small Pillars that bear up the Top-cover, are four white Diamonds, cut in the form thereof; the top or roof of the Chariot is one intire blew Diamond, and at the four corners are great sprigs of Rubies; the seat is made of Cloth of Gold, stuffed with Amber-greece[1] beaten small; the Chariot is drawn by Twelve Unicorns, whose Trappings are all Chains of Pearl; And as for her Barges, they are onely of Gold. Her Guard for State (for she needs none for secu-rity, there being no Rebels or Enemies) consists of Gyants, but they seldom wait on their Majesties abroad, because their extraordinary height and bigness does hinder their prospect. Her Entertainment when she is upon the Water, is the Musick of the Fish- and Bird-men, and by Land are Horse and Foot-matches; for the Emperess takes much delight in making Race-matches with the Emperor, and the Nobility; some Races are between the Fox- and Ape-men, which sometimes the Satyrs strive to outrun, and some are between the Spider-men and Lice-men. Also there are several Flight-matches,

---

1 ambergris: waxy substance used in perfumes

between the several sorts of Bird-men, and the several sorts of Fly-men; and Swimming-matches, between the several sorts of Fish-men. The Emperor, Emperess, and their Nobles, take also great delight to have Collations; for in the Blazing-world, there are most delicious Fruits of all sorts, and some such as in this World were never seen nor tasted; for there are most tempting sorts of Fruit: After their Collations are ended, they Dance; and if they be upon the Water, they dance upon the Water, there lying so many Fish-men close and thick together, as they can dance very evenly and easily upon their backs, and need not fear drowning. Their Musick, both Vocal and Instrumental, is according to their several places: Upon the Water it is of Water Instruments, as shells filled with Water, and so moved by Art, which is a very sweet and delightful harmony; and those Dances which they dance upon the Water, are, for the most part such as we in this World call Swimming Dances, where they do not lift up their feet high: In Lawns or upon Plains they have Wind-Instruments, but much better then those in our World; And when they dance in the Woods they have Horn-Instruments, which although they are a sort of Wind-Instruments, yet they are of another Fashion then the former; In their Houses they have such Instruments as are somewhat like our Viols, Violins, Theorboes,[1] Lutes, Citherins,[2] Gittars, Harpsichords, and the like, but yet so far beyond them, that the difference cannot well be exprest; and as their places of Dancing and their Musick is different, so is their manner or way of Dancing. In these, and the like Recreations, the Emperor, Emperess, and the Nobility pass their time.

THE EPILOGUE TO THE READER.

By this Poetical Description, you may perceive, that my ambition is not onely to be Emperess, but Authoress of a whole World; and that the Worlds I have made, both the *Blazing-* and the other *Philosophical* World, mentioned in the first part of this Description, are framed and composed of the most pure, that is, the rational parts of Matter, which are the parts of my Mind; which Creation was more easily and suddenly effected, then the Conquests of the two famous Monarchs of the World, *Alexander* and *Cæsar.* Neither have I made such distur-

---

1   theorbo: a large double-necked lute
2   cithern: a kind of guitar

bances, and caused so many dissolutions of particulars, otherwise named deaths, as they did; for I have destroyed but some few men in a little Boat, which died through the extremity of cold, and that by the hand of Justice, which was necessitated to punish their crime of stealing away a young and beauteous Lady. And in the formation of those Worlds, I take more delight and glory, then ever *Alexander* or *Cæsar* did in conquering this terrestrial world; and though I have made my *Blazing-world,* a Peaceable World, allowing it but one Religion, one Language, and one Government; yet could I make another World, as full of Factions, Divisions, and Wars, as this is of Peace and Tranquility; and the rational figures of my Mind might express as much courage to fight, as *Hector* and *Achilles* had; and be as wise as *Nestor,* as Eloquent as *Ulysses,* and as beautiful as *Helen.*[1] But I esteeming Peace before War, Wit before Policy, Honesty before Beauty; instead of the figures of *Alexander, Cæsar, Hector, Achilles, Nestor, Ulysses, Helen, &c.* chose rather the figure of Honest *Margaret Newcastle,* which now I would not change for all this terrestrial World; and if any should like the World I have made, and be willing to be my Subjects, they may imagine themselves such, and they are such; I mean, in their Minds, Fancies or Imaginations; but if they cannot endure to be subjects, they may create Worlds of their own, and Govern themselves as they please: But yet let them have a care, not to prove unjust Usurpers, and to rob me of mine; for concerning the *Philosophical* World, I am Emperess of it my self; and as for the *Blazing*-world, it having an Emperess already, who rules it with great wisdom and conduct, which Emperess is my dear Platonick Friend; I shall never prove so unjust, treacherous and unworthy to her, as to disturb her Government, much less to depose her from her Imperial Throne, for the sake of any other; but rather chuse to create another World for another Friend.

---

1   Hector, Achilles, Nestor, Ulysses, Helen: heroes of Homer's *Iliad* and *Odyssey*

2. SELECTIONS FROM
POEMS AND FANCIES (1653)

Poems and Fancies (1653), a collection of poems on a variety of
scientific and miscellaneous themes, was Margaret Cavendish's first
published work. The poems included here give some idea of the
scope of her early interest in theoretical speculations of the new science, and of her intense and imaginative empathy with the world of
nature.

OF MANY WORLDS *IN THIS* WORLD.

Just like unto a *Nest* of *Boxes* round,
Degrees of *sizes* within each *Boxe* are found.
So in this *World*, may many *Worlds* more be,
Thinner, and lesse, and lesse still by degree;
Although they are not subject to our *Sense*,
A *World* may be no bigger then *two-pence*.
Nature is curious, and such *worke* may make,
That our dull *Sense* can never finde, but scape.[1]
For Creatures, small as *Atomes*, may be there,
If every *Atome* a *Creatures Figure* beare.
If foure *Atomes* a *World* can make,[2] then see,
What severall *Worlds* might in an *Eare-ring* bee.
For *Millions* of these *Atomes* may bee in
The *Head* of one *small*, little, *single Pin*.
And if thus *small*, then *Ladies* well may weare
A *World* of *Worlds*, as *Pendents* in each *Eare*.

---

1   escape
2   *As I have before shewed* they *do, in my* Atomes. [M.C.] "The foure principall Figur'd
    Atomes make the foure Elements, as Square, Round, Long, and Sharpe," in *Poems
    and Fancies* (1653) 6-7

A WORLD *IN AN* EARE-RING.

An *Eare-ring round* may well a *Zodiacke* bee,
Where in a *Sun* goeth round, and we not see.
And *Planets seven*[1] about that *Sun* may move,
And *Hee* stand still, as *some wise men* would prove.
And *fixed Stars,* like *twinkling Diamonds*, plac'd
About this *Eare-ring*, which a *World* is vast.
That same which doth the *Eare-ring* hold, the *hole*,
Is that, which we do call the *Pole*.
There *nipping Frosts* may be, and *Winter* cold,
Yet never on the *Ladies Eare* take hold.
And *Lightnings, Thunder*, and great *Winds* may blow
Within this *Eare-ring*, yet the *Eare* not know.
There *Seas* may *ebb*, and *flow*, where *Fishes* swim,
And *Islands* be, where *Spices* grow therein.
There *Christall Rocks* hang dangling at each *Eare*,
And *Golden Mines* as *Jewels* may they weare.
There *Earth-quakes* be, which *Mountaines* vast downe fling,
And yet nere stir the *Ladies Eare*, nor *Ring*.
There *Meadowes* bee, and *Pastures fresh*, and *greene*,
And *Cattell* feed, and yet be never seene:
And *Gardens* fresh, and *Birds* which sweetly sing,
Although we heare them not in an *Eare-ring*.
There *Night*, and *Day*, and *Heat*, and *Cold*, and so
May *Life*, and *Death*, and *Young*, and *Old*, still grow.
Thus *Youth* may *spring*, and severall *Ages* dye,
Great *Plagues* may be, and no *Infections* nigh.
There *Cityes* bee, and stately *Houses* built,
Their inside *gaye*, and finely may be gilt.
There *Churches* bee, and *Priests* to teach therein,
And *Steeple* too, yet heare the *Bells* not ring.
From thence may pious *Teares* to *Heaven* run,
And yet the *Eare* not know which way they're gone.
There *Markets* bee, and things both bought, and sold,
Know not the price, nor how the *Markets* hold.

---

1 Neptune and Pluto had not yet been discovered.

There *Governours* do rule, and *Kings* do Reigne,
And *Battels* fought, where many may be slaine.
And all within the *Compasse* of this *Ring*,
And yet not tidings to the *Wearer* bring.
Within the *Ring* wise *Counsellors* may sit,
And yet the *Eare* not one wise word may get.
There may be *dancing* all Night at a *Ball*,
And yet the *Eare* be not disturb'd at all.
There *Rivals Duels* fight, where some are slaine;
There *Lovers mourne*, yet heare them not complaine.
And *Death* may dig a *Lovers Grave*, thus were
A *Lover* dead, in a faire *Ladies Eare*.
But when the *Ring* is broke, the *World* is done,
Then *Lovers* they into *Elysium* run.

THE SQUARING OF THE CIRCLE.[1]

Within the *Head* of *Man's* a *Circle Round*
Of *Honesty*, no *Ends* in it is found.
To *Square* this *Circle* many think it fit,
But *Sides* to take without *Ends*, hard is it.
Prudence and *Temperance*, as two *Lines* take;
With *Fortitude* and *Justice*, foure will make.
If th' *Line* of *Temperance* doth prove too short,
Then add a *Figure* of a *discreet Thought*;
Let *Wisedomes Point* draw up *Discretions Figure*,
That make two equall *Lines* joyn'd both together.
Betwixt the Line *Temperance*, and *Justice*, *Truth* must point,
Justice's Line draw downe to *Fortitude*, that *Corner joynt*;
Then *Fortitude* must draw in equall length,

---

1   The squaring of the circle was one of three famous construction problems of classical geometry, to be solved using only ruler and compass (the others were the tri-
section of an angle, and the doubling of a cube). These constructions were not
rigorously proved to be impossible until modern times; during the 1650s, the
philosopher Thomas Hobbes thought (mistakenly) he had found a solution for the
squaring of the circle. Cavendish learned of these and other mathematical problems
from her brother-in-law, Sir Charles Cavendish, a skilled mathematician who was
on friendly terms with leading mathematicians of seventeenth-century Europe.

To *Prudence Line, Temperance* must give the breadth.
And *Temperance* with *Justice Line* must run, yet stand
Betwixt *Prudence* and *Fortitude*, of either hand.
At every corner must a *Point* be layd,
Where every *Line* that meets, an *Angle's* made;
And when the *Points* too high, or low do fall,
Then must the *Lines* be stretch'd, to mak't even all.
And thus the *Circle Round* you'l find,
Is *Squar'd* with the *foure Virtues* of the *Mind*.

THE HUNTING OF THE HARE.

Betwixt two *Ridges* of *Plowd-land*, lay *Wat*,
Pressing his *Body* close to *Earth* lay squat.
His *Nose* upon his two *Fore-feet* close lies,
Glaring obliquely with his *great gray Eyes*.
His *Head* he alwaies sets against the *Wind*;
If turne his *Taile*, his *Haires* blow up behind:
Which *he* too cold will grow, but *he* is wise,
And keepes his *Coat* still downe, so warm *he* lies.
Thus resting all the *day*, till *Sun* doth set,
Then riseth up, his *Reliefe* for to get.
Walking about untill the *Sun* doth rise,
Then back returnes, downe in his *Forme he* lyes.
At last, *Poore Wat* was found, as *he* there lay,
By *Hunts-men*, with their *Dogs* which came that way.
Seeing, gets up, and fast begins to run,
Hoping some waies the *Cruell Dogs* to shun.
But they by *Nature* have so quick a *Sent*,[1]
That by their *Nose* they trace, what way *he* went.
And with their deep, wide *Mouths* set forth a *Cry*,
Which answer'd was by *Ecchoes* in the *Skie*.
Then *Wat* was struck with *Terrour*, and with *Feare*,
Thinkes every *Shadow* still the *Dogs* they were.
And running out some distance from the *noise*,

---

1   scent

To hide himselfe, his *Thoughts* he new imploies.
Under a *Clod* of *Earth* in *Sand-pit* wide,
Poore *Wat* sat close, hoping himselfe to hide.
There long he had not sat, but strait his *Eares*
The *Winding Hornes*, and crying *Dogs* he heares:
Starting with *Feare*, up leapes, then doth he run,
And with such speed, the *Ground* scarce treades upon.
Into a great thick *Wood he* strait way gets,
Where underneath a *broken Bough he* sits.
At every *Leafe* that with the *wind* did shake,
Did bring such *Terrour*, made his *Heart* to ake.
That *Place he* left, to *Champian*[1] *Plaines he* went,
Winding about, for to deceive their *Sent*.
And while they *snuffling* were, to find his *Track*,
Poore Wat, being weary, his swift pace did slack.
On his two *hinder legs* for ease did sit,
His *Fore-feet* rub'd his *Face* from *Dust*, and *Sweat*.
Licking his *Feet, he* wip'd his *Eares* so cleane,
That none could tell that *Wat* had hunted been.
But casting round about his *faire great Eyes*,
The *Hounds* in full *Careere he* neere him 'spies:
To *Wat* it was so terrible a *Sight*,
Feare gave him *Wings*, and made his *Body* light.
Though weary was before, by running long,
Yet now his *Breath* he never felt more strong.
Like those that *dying* are, think *Health* returnes,
When tis but a *faint Blast*, which *Life* out burnes.
For *Spirits* seek to guard the *Heart* about,
Striving with *Death*, but *Death* doth quench them out.
Thus they so fast came on, with such loud *Cries*,
That *he* no hopes hath left, nor *help* espies.
With that the *Winds* did pity *poore Wats* case,
And with their *Breath* the *Sent* blew from the *Place*.
Then every *Nose* is busily imployed,
And every *Nostrill* is set open, wide:
And every *Head* doth seek a severall way,

---

1 champaign: an expanse of open level country

To find what *Grasse*, or *Track*, the *Sent* on lay.
Thus quick Industry, that is not slack,
Is like to Witchery, brings lost things back.[1]
For though the *Wind* had tied the *Sent* up close,
A *Busie Dog* thrust in his *Snuffling Nose*:
And drew it out, with it did foremost run,
Then *Hornes* blew loud, for th'*rest* to follow on.
The *great slow-Hounds*, their throats did set a *Base*,
The *Fleet swift Hounds*, as *Tenours* next in place;
The little *Beagles* they a *Trebble* sing,
And through the *Aire* their *Voice* a round did ring?
Which made a *Consort*,[2] as they ran along;
If they but *words* could speak, might sing a *Song*,
The *Hornes* kept time, the *Hunters* shout for *Joy*,
And valiant seeme, *poore Wat* for to destroy:
Spurring their *Horses* to a full *Careere*,
Swim Rivers deep, leap Ditches without feare;
Indanger *Life*, and *Limbes*, so fast will ride,
Onely[3] to see how patiently *Wat* died.
For why, the *Dogs* so neere his *Heeles* did get,
That they their sharp *Teeth* in his *Breech*[4] did set.
Then tumbling downe, did fall with *weeping Eyes*,
Gives up his *Ghost*, and thus poore *Wat* he dies.
Men hooping loud, such *Acclamations* make,
As if the *Devill* they did *Prisoner* take.
When they do but a *shiftlesse*[5] *Creature* kill;
To hunt, there needs no *Valiant Souldiers* skill.
But *Man* doth think that *Exercise*, and *Toile*,
To keep their *Health*, is best, which makes most spoile.
Thinking that *Food*, and *Nourishment* so good,
And *Appetite*, that feeds on *Flesh*, and *Blood*.
When they do *Lions, Wolves, Beares, Tigers* see,

---

1 Witches or "wise women" were credited with the ability to locate and recover lost
   items by the use of magic.
2 a group of musicians making music together
3 only
4 hind-quarters
5 helpless

To kill poore *Sheep*, strait say, they cruell be.
But for themselves all *Creatures* think too few,
For *Luxury*,[1] wish *God* would make them new.
As if that *God* made *Creatures* for *Mans meat*,
To give them *Life*, and *Sense*, for *Man* to eat;
Or else for *Sport*, or *Recreations* sake,
Destroy those *Lifes* that *God* saw good to make:
Making their *Stomacks, Graves*, which full they fill
With *Murther'd Bodies*, that in sport they kill.
Yet *Man* doth think himselfe so gentle, mild,
When *he* of *Creatures* is most cruell wild.
And is so *Proud*, thinks onely he shall live,
That *God* a *God*-like *Nature* did him give.
And that all *Creatures* for his sake alone,
Was made for him, to *Tyrannize* upon.

A DIALOGUE *BETWEEN AN* OAKE, *AND A* MAN *CUTTING HIM DOWNE.*

Oake.

Why cut you off my *Bowes*, both large, and long,
That keepe you from the *heat*, and *scorching Sun*;
And did refresh your *fainting Limbs* from sweat?
From *thundring Raines I* keepe you free, from *Wet*;
When on my *Barke* your weary head would lay,
Where *quiet sleepe* did take all *Cares* away.
The whilst my *Leaves* a gentle noise did make,
And blew *coole Winds*, that you *fresh Aire* might take.
Besides, *I* did invite the *Birds* to sing,
That their sweet voice might you some pleasure bring.
Where every one did strive to do their best,
Oft chang'd their *Notes*, and strain'd their tender *Breast*.
In *Winter time*, my *Shoulders* broad did hold
Off *blustring Stormes*, that wounded with *sharpe Cold*.
And on my *Head* the *Flakes* of *Snow* did fall,

---

1   enjoyment

Whilst you under my *Bowes* sate free from all.
And will you thus requite my *Love, Good Will*,
To take away my *Life*, and *Body* kill?
For all my *Care*, and *Service I* have past,
Must *I* be cut, and laid on *Fire* at last?
And thus true *Love* you cruelly have *slaine*,
Invent alwaies to torture me with *paine*.
First you do peele my *Barke*, and flay my *Skinne*,
Hew downe my *Boughes*, so chops off every *Limb*.
With *Wedges* you do peirce my *Sides* to wound,
And with your *Hatchet* knock me to the ground.
I minc'd shall be in *Chips*, and *peeces* small,
And thus doth *Man* reward *good Deeds* withall.

Man.

Why grumblest thou, *old Oake*, when thou hast stood
This hundred yeares, as *King* of all the *Wood*.
Would you for ever live, and not resigne
Your *Place* to one that is of your owne *Line*?
Your *Acornes young*, when they grow big, and tall,
Long for your *Crowne*, and wish to see your fall;
Thinke every minute lost, whilst you do live,
And grumble at each *Office* you do give.
Ambition flieth high, and is above
All sorts of *Friend-ship* strong, or *Naturall Love*.
Besides, all *Subjects* they in *Change* delight,
When *Kings* grow *Old*, their *Government* they slight:
Although in *ease*, and *peace*, and *wealth* do live,
Yet all those *happy times* for *Change* will give.
Growes *discontent*, and *Factions* still do make;
What *Good* so ere *he* doth, as *Evill* take.
Were *he* as *wise*, as ever *Nature* made,
As *pious, good,* as ever *Heaven* sav'd:
Yet when *they* dye, such *Joy* is in their *Face*,
As if the *Devill* had gone from that place.
With *Shouts* of *Joy* they run a new to *Crowne*,
Although *next day* they strive to pull *him* downe.

Oake.

Why, said the *Oake,* because that *they* are mad,
Shall *I* rejoyce, for my owne *Death* be glad?
Because my *Subjects* all ingratefull are,
Shall *I* therefore my *health,* and *life* impaire.
Good Kings governe justly, as they ought,
Examines not their Humours, but their Fault.
For when their *Crimes* appeare, t'is *time to strike,*
Not to examine Thoughts how they do like.
If *Kings* are never *lov'd,* till they do dye,
Nor *wisht* to *live,* till in the *Grave* they lye:
Yet he that loves *himselfe* the lesse, because
He cannot get every mans *high applause*:
Shall by my *Judgment* be condemn'd to weare,
The *Asses Eares,* and *Burdens* for to beare.
But let me live the *Life* that *Nature* gave,
And not to please my *Subjects,* dig my *Grave.*

Man.

But here, *Poore Oake,* thou liv'st in *Ignorance,*
And never seek'st thy *Knowledge* to advance.
I'le cut the downe, 'cause *Knowledge* thou maist gaine,
Shalt be a *Ship,* to traffick on the *Maine*:[1]
There shalt thou *swim,* and cut the *Seas* in two,
And trample downe each *Wave,* as thou dost go.
Though they rise high, and big are sweld with *pride,*
Thou on their *Shoulders broad,* and *Back,* shalt ride:
Their *lofty Heads* shalt *bowe,* and make them *stoop,*
And on their *Necks* shalt set thy *steddy Foot*:
And on their *Breast* thy *stately Ship* shalt beare,
Till thy *Sharpe Keele* the *watry Wombe* doth teare.
Thus shalt thou round the *World,* new *Land* to find,
That from the rest is of *another kind.*

Oake.

O, said the *Oake, I* am contented well,

---

1   the high seas

Without that *Knowledge*, in my *Wood* to dwell.
For *I* had rather live, and simple be,
Then dangers run, some new strange *Sight* to see.
Perchance my *Ship* against a *Rock* may hit;
Then were *I* strait in sundry peeces split.
Besides, no rest, nor quiet *I* should have,
The *Winds* would tosse me on each *troubled Wave*.
The *Billowes rough* will beat on every side,
My *Breast* will *ake* to swim against the *Tide*.
And *greedy Merchants* may me over-fraight,
So should *I* drowned be with my owne weight.
Besides with *Sailes*, and *Ropes* my *Body* tye,
Just like a *Prisoner*, have no *Liberty*.
And being alwaies *wet*, shall take such *Colds*,
My *Ship* may get a *Pose*,[1] and leake through holes.
Which they to mend, will put me to great paine,
Besides, all *patch'd*, and *peec'd*, *I* shall remaine.
I care not for that *Wealth*, wherein the *paines*,
And *trouble*, is farre greater then the *Gaines*.
I am contented with what *Nature* gave,
I not Repine, but one *poore wish* would have,
Which is, that you my *aged Life* would save.

Man.

To build a *Stately House I'le* cut thee downe,
Wherein shall *Princes* live of great renowne.
There shalt *thou* live with the best *Companie*,
All their delight, and pastime *thou* shalt see.
Where *Playes*, and *Masques*, and *Beauties* bright will shine,
Thy *Wood* all oyl'd with Smoake of *Meat*, and *Wine*.
There thou shalt heare both *Men*, and *Women* sing,
Farre pleasanter then *Nightingals* in Spring.
Like to a *Ball*, their *Ecchoes* shall rebound
Against the *Wall*, yet can no *Voice* be found.

---

1 probably a printer's error for pox, a group of diseases characterized by pocks or
pustules, which are here interpreted as holes in the ship's sides

Oake.

Alas, what *Musick* shall *I* care to heare,
When on my *Shoulders I* such burthens beare?
Both *Brick,* and *Tiles,* upon my *Head* are laid,
Of this *Preferment I* am sore afraid.
And many times with *Nailes,* and *Hammers* strong,
They peirce my *Sides,* to hang their Pictures on.
My *Face* is smucht with Smoake of *Candle Lights,*
In danger to be burnt in *Winter Nights.*
No, let me here a poore *Old Oake* still grow;
I care not for these vaine *Delights* to know.
For *fruitlesse Promises I* do not care,
More *Honour* tis, my owne *green Leaves* to beare.
More *Honour* tis, to be in *Natures* dresse,
Then any *Shape,* that *Men* by *Art* expresse.
I am not like to *Man,* would Praises have,
And for *Opinion* make my selfe a *Slave.*

Man.

Why do you wish to live, and not to dye,
Since you no *Pleasure* have, but *Misery*?
For here you stand against the *scorching Sun*:
By's *Fiery Beames,* your *fresh green Leaves* become
Wither'd; with *Winter's* cold you quake, and shake:
Thus in no *time,* or *season,* rest can take.

Oake.

Yet *I* am happier, said the *Oake,* then *Man*;
With my condition *I* contented am.
He nothing loves, but what he cannot get,
And soon doth surfet[1] of one dish of meat:
Dislikes all Company, displeas'd alone,
Makes *Griefe* himselfe, if *Fortune* gives him none.
And as his *Mind* is restlesse, never pleas'd;
So is his *Body* sick, and oft diseas'd.
His *Gouts,* and *Paines,* do make him sigh, and cry,
Yet in the midst of *Paines* would live, not dye.

---

1   surfeit: to become disgusted or nauseated by an excess of something

Man.

    Alas, *poore Oake,* thou understandst, nor can
    Imagine halfe the misery of *Man.*
    All other *Creatures* onely in *Sense* joyne,
    But *Man* hath something more, which is *divine.*
    He hath a *Mind,* doth to the *Heavens* aspire,
    A *Curiosity* for to inquire:
    A *Wit* that nimble is, which runs about
    In every *Corner,* to seeke *Nature* out.
    For *She* doth hide her selfe, as fear'd to shew
    Man all *her workes,* least *he* too powerfull grow.
    Like to a *King,* his *Favourite* makes so great,
    That at the last, *he* feares his *Power* hee'll get.
    And what creates *desire* in *Mans Breast,*
    A *Nature* is *divine,* which seekes the best:
    And never can be satisfied, untill
    He, like a *God,* doth in *Perfection* dwell.
    If you, as *Man,* desire like *Gods* to bee,
    I'le spare your *Life,* and not cut downe your *Tree.*

3. FRANCIS BACON, *NEW ATLANTIS*
(1627)

Francis Bacon (1561–1626), statesman, philosopher, essayist, is best known as a pioneer theoretician of the scientific revolution. In *Advancement of Learning* (1605) and the *Novum Organum* [*New Organon*] (1620), Bacon developed a systematic method for the study of nature. Bacon's *New Atlantis* is included here as an example of a utopian society , which can be contrasted in interesting ways with Cavendish's *Blazing World*. In *New Atlantis*, Bacon envisions an island nation, known as Bensalem, that has developed laws, customs, and institutions that support the advancement of science and technology. Said to be the model for the Royal Society (founded in 1662), Salomon's House, the scientific institution described in *New Atlantis*, is charged with investigating "the knowledge of Causes, and secret motions of things; and the enlarging of the bounds of Human Empire, to the effecting of all things possible." *New Atlantis* was probably written in 1624, although it was published unfinished by William Rawley in 1627, after Bacon's death.

NEW ATLANTIS.

A Worke unfinished.
Written by the Right Honourable,
FRANCIS
Lord Verulam, Viscount St. Alban.

To the Reader

This *Fable* my *Lord* devised, to the end that Hee might exhibit therein, a *Modell* or *Description* of a *College*, instituted for the *Interpreting* of *Nature*, and the Producing of *Great* and *Marvellous Works* for the *Benefit* of *Men*; Under the Name of *Salomons House*, or the *College of the Six dayes Works*. And even so farre his *Lordship* hath proceeded, as to finish that Part. Certainly, the *Modell* is more Vast, and High, than can possibly be imitated in all things; Notwithstanding most Things therein are within Mens Power to effect. His *Lordship* thought also in this present *Fable*, to have composed a *Frame* of *Lawes*, or of the *best State* or *Mould* of a *Common-wealth*; but fore-seeing it would be a long Worke, his Desire of Collecting the *Naturall Historie* Diverted him, which He preferred many degrees before it.

This Worke of the *New Atlantis*, (as much as concerneth the *English Edition*) his Lordship designed for this Place; In regard it hath so neere Affinitie (in one Part of it) with the Preceding *Naturall Historie*.[1]

W: Rawley.[2]

NEW ATLANTIS.

Wee sailed from *Peru*, (where we had continued by the space of one whole yeare,) for *China* and *Japan*, by the South Sea; taking with us Victuals for twelve Moneths; And had good Winds from the East, though soft and weake, for five Moneths space, and more. But then the Wind came about, and setled in the West for many dayes, so as we could make little or no way, and were sometimes in purpose to turne back. But then again there arose Strong and Great Winds from the South, with a Point East; which carried us up, (for all that we could doe) towards the North: By which time our Victualls failed us, though we had made good spare[3] of them. So that finding our selves, in the Midst of the greatest Wildernesse of Waters in the World, without Victuall, wee gave our selves for lost Men, and prepared for Death. Yet wee did lift up our Hearts and Voices to GOD above, who *sheweth his Wonders in the Deepe*;[4] Beseeching him of his Mercie, that as in the *Beginning* He discovered[5] the *Face* of the *Deepe*, and brought forth *Dry-Land*;[6] So he would now discover Land to us, that wee mought not perish. And it came to passe, that the next Day about Evening, wee saw within a Kenning[7] before us, towards the North, as it were

---

1   *New Atlantis* was placed at the end of *Sylva Sylvarum*.

2   William Rawley (1588-1667) was Bacon's chaplain and his first biographer.

3   good spare: a generous quantity

4   Psalms 107:24

5   uncovered, revealed

6   Genesis 1:9

7   range of ordinary vision, especially at sea; a marine measure of about 20 to 21 miles

thicke Clouds, which did put us in some hope of Land; Knowing how that part of the South Sea was utterly unknowne; And might have Islands, or Continents, that hitherto were not come to light. Wherefore wee bent our Course, thither, where we saw the Appearance of Land, all that night; And in the Dawning of the next Day, wee might plainly discerne that it was a Land; Flat to our sight, and full of Boscage;[1] which made it shew the more Dark. And after an Houre and an halfes Sayling, we entred into a good *Haven*, being the Port of a faire *Citie*; Not great indeed, but well built, and that gave a pleasant view from the Sea: And we thinking everie Minute long, till wee were on Land, came close to the Shore, and offered to land. But straight-wayes we saw divers of the People, with Bastons[2] in their Hands, (as it were) forbidding us to land; Yet without any Cries or Fierceness, but onely[3] as warning us off, by Signes that they made. Whereupon being not a little discomforted, wee were advising with our selves, what we should doe. During which time, there made forth to us a small Boat, with about eight Persons in it; whereof One of them had in his Hand a Tipstaffe of a yellow Cane, tipped at both ends with Blew, who came aboord our Shipp, without any shew of Distrust at all. And when hee saw one of our Number, present himselfe somewhat afore the rest, hee drew forth a little Scroule of Parchment, (somewhat yellower than our Parchment, and shining like the Leaves of Writing Tables, but otherwise soft and flexible,) and delivered it to our foremost Man. In which Scroule were written in ancient *Hebrew*, and in ancient *Greeke*, and in good *Latine* of the Schoole,[4] and in *Spanish*, these words; *Land yee not, none of you; And provide to be gone, from this Coast, within sixteen dayes, except you have further time given you. Meanewhile, if you want Fresh Water, or Victuall, or help for your Sick, or that your Ship needeth repaire, write downe your wants, and you shall have that, which belongeth to Mercie.* This Scroule was Signed with a Stamp of Cherubins Wings, not spred, but hanging downwards; And by them a *Crosse.* This being delivered, the *Officer* returned, and left onely a Servant with us to receive our Answer. Consulting hereupon amongst our Selves, we were much perplexed. The Deniall of Landing, &

1   woody undergrowth
2   batons: cudgels, clubs
3   only
4   Latin of the School: medieval or scholastic Latin

Hastie Warning us away, troubled us much; On the other side, to finde that the People had Languages, and were so full of Humanitie, did comfort us not a little. And above all, the Signe of the *Crosse* to that Instrument, was to us a great Rejoycing, and as it were a certaine Presage of Good. Our Answer was in the *Spanish* Tongue; *That for our Ship, it was well; For wee had rather mett with Calmes, and contrarie winds, than any Tempests. For our Sicke, they were many, and in verie ill Case; so that if they were not permitted to Land, they ran in danger of their Lives.* Our other Wants we set downe in particular, adding; *That we had some little store of Merchandize, which if it pleased them to deale for, it might supply our Wants, without being chargeable unto them.* Wee offered some Reward in Pistolets[1] unto the Servant, and a peece of crimson Velvett to be presented to the *Officer.* But the Servant tooke them not, nor would scarce look upon them; And so left us, and went back in another little Boat, which was sent for him.

About three Houres after wee had dispatched our Answer, there came towards us, a Person (as it seemed) of Place.[2] He had on him a Gowne with wide Sleeves, of a kinde of Water Chamolett,[3] of an excellent Azure Colour, farre more glossie than ours: His under Apparell was Greene; And so was his Hatt, being in the forme of a Turban, daintily made, and not so huge as the *Turkish* Turbans; And the Locks of his Haire came down below the Brimms of it. A Reverend Man was hee to behold. Hee came in a Boat, gilt in some part of it, with foure Persons more onely in that Boat; And was followed by another Boat, wherein were some Twentie. When hee was come within a Flight-shott[4] of our Shipp, Signes were made to us, that we should send forth some to meet him upon the Water; which wee presently did in our Shipp-Boat, sending the principall Man amongst us save one, and foure of our Number with him. When wee were come within six yards of their Boat, they called to us to stay, and not to approach further; which we did. And thereupon the Man, whom I before described, stood up, and with a loud voice, in *Spanish*, asked; *Are yee Christians?* Wee answered; *Wee were;* fearing the lesse, because of the *Crosse* we had seen in the Subscription. At which Answer the

---

1   Spanish gold coins
2   of high status
3   water camlet: a beautiful expensive fabric (originally of camel hair, later of silk or wool or blend) with a wavy or watery surface
4   distance to which a flight arrow is shot

said Person lift up his Right Hand towards Heaven, and drew it softly to his Mouth, (which is the Gesture they use when they thanke GOD;) And then said: *If yee will sweare, (all of you,) by the Merits of the* SAVIOUR, *that yee are no Pirates; Nor have shed bloud, lawfully, nor unlawfully, within fortie dayes past; you may have License to come on Land.* Wee said, *Wee were all ready to take that Oath.* Whereupon one of those that were with him, being (as it seemed) a *Notarie*, made an *Entrie* of this Act. Which done, another of the Attendants of the Great Person, which was with him in the same Boat, after his Lord had spoken a little to him, said aloud; *My Lord would have you know, that it is not of Pride, or Greatnesse, that hee commeth not aboord your Shipp; But for that, in your Answer, you declare, that you have many Sicke amongst you, hee was warned by the Conservatour of* Health, *of the* Citie, *that hee should keepe a distance.* Wee bowed our selves towards him, and answered; *Wee were his humble Servants; And accounted for great Honour, and singular Humanitie towards us, that which was already done; But hoped well, that the Nature of the Sicknesse, of our Men, was not infectious.* So hee returned; And a while after came the Notarie to us aboord our Ship; Holding in his hand a Fruit of that Countrey, like an Orenge, but of colour between Orenge-tawney and Scarlet; which cast a most excellent Odour. He used it (as it seemeth) for a Preservative against Infection. Hee gave us our Oath; *By the name of Jesus, and his Merits:* And after told us, that the next day, by six of the Clocke, in the Morning, we should be sent to, and brought to the *Strangers House*, (so he called it,) where we should be accommodated of things, both for our Whole, and for our Sicke. So he left us; And when wee offered him some Pistoletts, hee smiling said; *He must not be twice paid, for one Labour*: Meaning (as I take it) that he had Salarie sufficient of the *State* for his Service. For (as I after learned) they call an Officer, that taketh Rewards, *Twice-paid*.

The next Morning earely, there came to us the same *Officer*, that came to us at first with his Cane, and told us; *Hee came to conduct us to the* Strangers House; *And that hee had prevented*[1] *the Houre, because wee might have the whole day before us, for our Businesse.* For (said hee) *If you will follow mine Advice, there shall first goe with mee some few of you, and see the place, and how it may be made convenient for you; And then you may send for your Sicke, and the rest of your Number, which yee will bring on*

---

1 anticipated

Land. Wee thanked him, and said; *That this Care, which he tooke of desolate Strangers, GOD would reward.* And so six of us went on Land with him: And when wee were on Land, hee went before us, and turned to us, and said; *Hee was but our Servant, and our Guide.* Hee ledd us thorow three faire Streets; And all the way wee went, there were gathered some People on both sides, standing in a Row; But in so civill a fashion, as if it had beene, not to wonder at us, but to welcome us: And divers of them, as wee passed by them, put their Armes a little abroad; which is their Gesture, when they bid any welcome. The *Strangers House* is a faire and spacious House, built of Brick, of somewhat a blewer Colour than our Brick; And with handsome windowes, some of Glasse, some of a kinde of Cambrick oyl'd. Hee brought us first into a faire Parlour above staires, and then asked us; *What Number of Persons we were? And how many sicke?* We answered, *Wee were in all, (sicke and whole,) one and fiftie Persons, whereof our sicke were seventeene.* He desired us to have patience a little, and to stay till hee came backe to us; which was about an Houre after; And then hee led us to see the Chambers, which were provided for us, being in number nineteene. They having cast it (as it seemeth) that foure of those Chambers, which were better than the rest, might receive foure of the principall Men of our Company; And lodge them alone by themselves; And the other 15 Chambers were to lodge us two and two together. The Chambers were handsome and cheerefull Chambers, and furnished civilly. Then hee ledd us to a long Gallerie, like a Dorture,[1] where hee shewed us all along the one side (for the other side was but Wall and Window,) seventeene Cells, verie neat ones, having partitions of Cedar wood. Which Gallerie, and Cells, being in all fortie, (many more than we needed,) were instituted as an Infirmarie for sicke Persons. And hee told us withall, that as any our Sick waxed well, hee might be removed from his Cell, to a Chamber: For which purpose, there were set forth ten spare Chambers, besides the Number wee spake of before. This done, hee brought us back to the Parlour, and lifting up his Cane a little, (as they doe when they give any Charge or Command) said to us; *Yee are to know, that the Custome of the Land requireth, that after this day, and to morrow, (which wee give you for removing of your People from your Ship,) you are to keep within dores for three daies.*

---

1   dormitory

But let it not trouble you, nor doe not think your selves restrained, but rather left to your Rest and Ease. You shall want nothing, and there are six of our People appointed to attend you, for any Businesse you may have abroad. Wee gave him thankes, with all Affection and Respect, and said; GOD *surely is manifested in this Land.* Wee offered him also twentie Pistoletts; But hee smiled, and onely said; *What? twice paid!* And so he left us. Soone after our Dinner was served in; Which was right good Viands, both for Bread, and Meat: Better than any *Collegiate* Diett, that I have knowne in *Europe.* We had also Drinke of three sorts, all wholesome and good; Wine of the Grape; A Drinke of Graine, such as is with us our Ale, but more cleare: And a kinde of Sider[1] made of a Fruit of that Countrey; A wonderfull pleasing & Refreshing Drink. Besides, there were brought in to us, great store of those Scarlett Orenges, for our Sick; which (they said) were an assured Remedy for sicknes taken at Sea. There was given us also, a Box of small gray, or whitish Pills, which they wished our Sicke should take, one of the Pills, everie night before sleepe; which (they said) would hasten their Recoverie. The next day, after that our Trouble of Carriage, and Removing of our Men, and Goods, out of our Shipp, was somewhat setled and quiett, I thought good to call our Company together, and when they were assembled, said unto them; *My deare Friends; Let us know our selves, and how it standeth with us. Wee are Men cast on Land, as* Jonas *was, out of the* Whales Belly, *when wee were as buried in the Deepe: And now wee are on Land, wee are but betweene Death and Life; For we are beyond, both the Old World, and the New; And whether ever wee shall see* Europe, GOD *onely knoweth. It is a kinde of Miracle hath brought us hither: And it must bee little lesse, that shall bring us hence. Therefore in regard of our Deliverance past, and our danger present, and to come, let us looke up to* GOD, *and everie man reforme his owne wayes. Besides we are come here amongst a* Christian People, *full of Pietie and Humanitie: Let us not bring that Confusion of face upon our selves, as to shew our vices, or unworthinesse before them. Yet there is more. For they have by Commandement, (though in forme of Courtesie) Cloistered us within these Walls, for three dayes: Who knoweth, whether it be not, to take some taste of our manners and conditions? And if they finde them bad, to banish us straight-wayes; If good, to give us further time. For these Men, that they have given us for Attendance, may withall have an eye upon*

---

1   cider

us. Therefore for G O D S *love, and as we love the weale of our Soules and Bodies, let us so behave our selves, as wee may be at peace with* G O D, *and may finde grace in the Eyes of this People.* Our Company with one voyce thanked mee for my good Admonition, and promised me to live soberly and civilly, and without giving any the least occasion of Offence. So wee spent our three dayes joyfully, and without care, in expectation what would be done with us, when they were expired. During which time, wee had everie houre joy of the Amendment of our Sicke; who thought themselves cast into some Divine *Poole* of *Healing;* They mended so kindly,[1] and so fast.

The Morrow after our three dayes were past, there came to us a new Man, that wee had not seene before, cloathed in Blew as the former was, save that his Turban was white, with a small red Crosse on the Topp. He had also a Tippet[2] of fine Linnen. At his Comming in, hee did bend to us a little, and put his Armes abroad. Wee of our parts saluted him in a verie lowly and submissive manner; As looking that from him, wee should receive Sentence of Life, or Death. He desired to speake with some few of us: Whereupon six of us onely stayed, and the rest avoyded the Roome. Hee said; *I am by Office Governour of this House of Strangers, and by Vocation I am a* Christian Priest; *And therefore am come to you, to offer you my service, both as Strangers, and chiefly as* Christians. *Some things I may tell you, which I thinke you will not bee unwilling to heare. The State hath given you Licence to stay on Land, for the space of six weekes: And let it not trouble you, if your occasions aske further time, for the Law in this point is not precise; And I doe not doubt, but my selfe shall be able, to obtaine for you, such further time, as may be convenient. Yee shall also understand, that the* Strangers House, *is at this time Rich, and much aforehand; For it hath laid up Revenue these* 37. *yeares; For so long it is, since any Stranger arrived in this part. And therefore take yee no care; The* State *will defray you all the time you stay: Neither shall you stay one day the lesse for that. As for any Merchandize yee have brought, yee shall be well used, and have your returne, either in Merchandize, or in Gold and Silver: For to us it is all one. And if you have any other Request to make, hide it not. For yee shall finde, wee will not make your Countenance to fall, by the Answer yee shall receive. Only this I must tell you, that none of you must goe*

---

1 naturally, properly
2 cape

above a Karan, (that is with them a Mile and an halfe) *from the walls of the Citie, without especiall leave.* Wee answered, after wee had looked a while one upon another, admiring this gracious and parent-like usage; *That wee could not tell what to say: For wee wanted words to expresse our Thanks; And his Noble free Offers left us nothing to aske. It seemed to us, that wee had before us a picture of our* Salvation *in* Heaven; *For wee that were a while since in the Jawes of Death, were now brought into a place, where wee found nothing but Consolations. For the Commandement laid upon us, we would not faile to obey it, though it was impossible, but our Hearts should be enflamed to tread further upon this Happie and Holy Ground.* Wee added; *That our Tongues should first cleave to the Roofes of our Mouths, ere we should forget, either his Reverend Person, or this whole Nation, in our Prayers.* Wee also most humbly besought him, to accept of us as his true servants, by as just a Right, as ever Men on earth were bounden; laying and presenting, both our Persons, and all wee had, at his feet. Hee said; *Hee was a Priest, and looked for a Priests reward; which was our Brotherly love, and the Good of our Soules and Bodies.* So hee went from us, not without teares of Tendernesse in his Eyes; And left us also confused with Joy and Kindnesse, saying amongst our selves; *That wee were come into a Land of Angells, which did appeare to us daily, and prevent us with Comforts, which we thought not of, much lesse expected.*

The next day about 10. of the Clocke, the Governour came to us againe, and after Salutations. said familiarly; *That hee was come to visit us;* And called for a Chaire, and satt him downe; And wee being some 10. of us, (the rest were of the meaner Sort; or else gone abroad;) sate downe with him. And when wee were sett, hee began thus. *Wee of this Island of Bensalem* (for so they call it in their Language) *have this; That by means of our solitarie Situation; and of the Lawes of Secrecie, which wee have for our Travellers; and our rare Admission of Strangers; we know well most part of the Habitable World, and are our selves unknowne. Therefore because hee that knoweth least, is fittest to aske Questions, it is more Reason, for the Entertainment of the time, that yee aske me Questions, than that I aske you.* We answered; *That wee humbly thanked him, that he would give us leave so to doe: And that wee conceived by the taste wee had already, that there was no worldly thing on Earth, more worthy to be knowne, than the State of that happie Land. But above all* (wee said) *since that wee were mett from the severall Ends of the World; and hoped assuredly, that wee should meet one day in the* Kingdome *of* Heaven *(for that wee were both parts* Christians) *wee desired to know (in respect that Land was so remote, and so divid-*

ed by vast and unknowne Seas, from the Land, where our SAVIOUR walked on Earth) who was the Apostle of that Nation, and how it was converted to the Faith ? It appeared in his face, that hee tooke great Contentment in this our Question: Hee said; *Yee knit my Heart to you, by asking this Question in the first place; For it sheweth that you First seeke the King-dome of Heaven; And I shall gladly, and briefly, satisfie your demand.*

About twenty Yeares after the Ascension of our SAVIOUR, *it came to passe, that there was seene by the People of* Renfusa, *(a Citie upon the Easterne Coast of our Island,) within Night, (the Night was Cloudie, and Calme,) as it might be some mile into the Sea, a great Pillar of Light; Not sharp, but in forme of a Columne, or Cylinder, rising from the Sea, a great way up towards Heaven; and on the topp of it was seene a large Crosse of Light, more bright and resplendent than the Bodie of the Pillar. Upon which so strange a Specta-cle, the People of the Citie gathered apace together upon the Sands, to wonder; And so after put themselves into a number of small Boats, to goe neerer to this Marvellous sight. But when the Boats were come within (about) 60. yeards of the Pillar, they found themselves all bound, and could goe no further; yet so as they might move to goe about, but might not approach neerer: So as the Boats stood all as in a Theater, beholding this Light, as an Heavenly Signe. It so fell out, that there was in one of the Boats, one of our Wise Men, of the Societie of* Salomons House; *which* House, *or* College *(my good Brethren) is the verie Eye of this Kingdome; Who having a while attentively and devoutly viewed, and contemplated this Pillar, and Crosse, fell downe upon his face; And then raised himselfe upon his knees, and lifting up his Hands to Heaven, made his prayers in this manner.*

Lord GOD *of Heaven and Earth; thou hast vouchsafed of thy Grace, to those of our Order, to know thy Works of Creation, and the Secretts of them; And to discerne (as farre as appertaineth to the Generations of Men) Between Divine Miracles, Works of Nature, Works of Art, and Impostures and Illusions of all sorts. I doe here acknowledge and testifie before this people, that the Thing which we now see before our eyes, is thy* Finger, *and a true* Miracle. *And for-as-much as we learne in our Books, that thou never Workest Miracles, but to a Divine and Excellent End, (for the Lawes of Nature are thine owne Lawes, and thou exceedest them not but upon great cause) wee most humbly beseech thee, to prosper this great Signe; And to give us the Interpretation and use of it in Mercie; Which thou doest in some part secretly promise, by sending it unto us.*

When hee had made his Prayer, hee presently found the Boat he was in, moveable, and unbound; whereas all the rest remained still fast; And taking that for an assurance of Leave to approach, hee caused the Boat to be softly, and with silence, rowed towards the Pillar. But ere hee came neere it; the Pillar and Crosse of Light brake up, and cast it selfe abroad, as it were, into a Firmament of many Starres; which also vanished soone after, and there was nothing left to be seene, but a small Arke, or Chest of Cedar, drie, and not wett at all with water, though it swam. And in the Fore-end of it, which was towards him, grew a small greene Branch of Palme; And when the wise Man had taken it, with all reverence, into his Boat, it opened of it selfe, and there were found in it, a Booke, and a Letter; Both written in fine Parchment, and wrapped in Sindons[1] of Linnen. The Booke contained all the Canonicall Bookes of the Old and New Testament, according as you have them; (For wee know well what the Churches with you receive;) And the Apocalypse it selfe; And some other Bookes of the New Testament, which were not at that time written, were neverthelesse in the Booke. And for the Letter, it was in these words.

I Bartholomew,[2] a Servant of the Highest, and Apostle of JESUS CHRIST, was warned by an Angell, that appeared to me, in a vision of Glorie, that I should commit this Arke to the flouds of the Sea. Therefore, I doe testifie amd declare, unto that People, where GOD shall ordaine this Arke to come to Land, that in the same day, is come unto them Salvation and Peace, and Good Will, from the Father, and from the LORD JESUS.

There was also in both these writings, as well the Booke, as the Letter, wrought a great Miracle, Conforme to that of the Apostles, in the Originall Gift of Tongues. For there being at that time, in this Land, Hebrewes, Persians, and Indians, besides the Natives, everie one read upon the Booke, and Letter, as if they had beene written in his owne Language. And thus was this Land saved from Infidelitie, (as the Remaine of the Old World was from Water) by an Arke, through the Apostolicall and Miraculous Evangelisme of Saint Bartholomew. And here hee paused, and a Messenger came, and called him from us. So this was all that passed in that Conference.

The next Day, the same Governour came againe to us, immediate-

---

1 fine fabric wrappings

2 The popular tradition about this lesser known apostle not only records Bartholomew's voyages to foreign parts, including India, to preach the gospel, but also contains legends about journeys attributed to his relics.

ly after Dinner, and excused himselfe, saying; *That the Day before, hee was called from us, somewhat abruptly, but now he would make us amends, and spend time with us; if wee held his Company, and Conference agreeable.* Wee answered; *That wee held it so agreeable and pleasing to us, as wee forgot both Dangers past, and Feares to come, for the time wee heard him speake; And that wee thought, an Houre spent with him, was worth Yeares of our former life.* Hee bowed himselfe a little to us, and after we were set againe, he said; *Well, the Questions are on your part.* One of our Number said, after a little Pause; *That there was a Matter, wee were no lesse desirous to know, than fearefull to aske, lest wee might presume too farre. But encouraged by his rare Humanitie towards us, (that could scarce thinke our selves Strangers, being his vowed and professed Servants,) we would take the Hardines to propound it: Humbly beseeching him, if he thought it not fit to bee answered, that he would pardon it, though he rejected it.* Wee said; *Wee well observed those his words, which he formerly spake, that this happie Island, where we now stood, was knowne to few, and yet knew most of the Nations of the World; which we found to be true, considering they had the Languages of* Europe, *and knew much of our State and Businesse; And yet we in* Europe, *(notwithstanding all the remote Discoveries, and Navigations of this last Age) never heard any of the least Inkling or Glimse of this Island. This we found wonderfull strange; For that all Nations have Enterknowledge[1] one of another, either by Voyage into Forraigne Parts, or by Strangers that come to them: And though the Travailer into a Forreine Countrey, doth commonly know more by the Eye, than he that stayeth at home can by relation of the Travailer; Yet both wayes suffice to make a mutuall Knowledge, in some degree, on both parts. But for this Island, wee never heard tell of any Shipp of theirs, that had beene seene to arrive upon any shore of* Europe; *No, nor of either the* East *or* West Indies, *nor yet of any Shipp of any other part of the World, that had made returne from them. And yet the Marvell rested not in this; For the Situation of it (as his Lordship said,) in the secret Conclave[2] of such a vast Sea mought[3] cause it. But then, that they should have Knowledge of the Languages, Bookes, Affaires, of those that lye such a distance from them, it was a thing wee could not tell what to make of; For that it seemed to us a condition and Proprietie of Divine Powers and Beings, to be hidden and*

---

1   interknowledge: mutual or reciprocal knowledge

2   space or room that can be locked up, used here figuratively; from Latin con (with) and *clavis* (key)

3   might

unseene to others, and yet to have others open, and as in a light to them. At this speech the Governour gave a gracious smile, and sayd; *That wee did well to aske pardon for this Question wee now asked; For that it imported, as if we thought this Land, a Land of Magicians, that sent forth Spirits of the Ayre into all parts, to bring them Newes and Intelligence of other Countries.* It was answered by us all, in all possible humblenesse, but yet with a Countenance taking knowledge, that we knew he spake it but merrily; *That wee were apt enough to thinke, there was somewhat supernaturall in this Island; but yet rather as Angelicall, than Magicall. But to let his Lordship know truely, what it was, that made us tender and doubtfull to aske this Question, it was not any such conceit, but because we [re]membred, he had given a Touch in his former Speech, that this Land had Lawes of Secrecy touching Strangers.* To this he said; *You remember it aright: And therefore in that I shall say to you, I must reserve some particulars, which it is not lawfull for me to reveale, but there will be enough left, to give you satisfaction.*

You shall understand (that which perhaps you will scarce think credible) that about three thousand Yeares agoe, or somewhat more, the Navigation of the World (specially for remote Voyages) was greater than at this Day. Doe not thinke with your selves, that I know not how much it is encreased with you, within these sixscore Yeares: I know it well; And yet I say, greater then, than now: Whether it was, that the Example of the Ark, *that saved the Remnant of Men, from the* universall Deluge, *gave Men confidence to adventure upon the Waters; Or what it was; but such is the Truth. The* Phoeniceans, *and specially the* Tyrians, *had great Fleetes. So had the* Carthaginians *their Colony, which is yet further West. Toward the East the Shipping of* Egypt, *and of* Palestina *was likewise great.* China *also, and the great* Atlantis *(that you call* America) *which have now but Junks. and Cano's,[1] abounded then in tall Ships. This Island, (as appeareth by faithfull Registers of those times) had then fifteene hundred strong Ships, of great content. Of all this, there is with you sparing Memory, or none; But we have large Knowledge thereof.*

At that time, this Land was knowne and frequented by the Shipps and Vessells of all the Nations before named. And (as it commeth to passe) they had many times Men of other Countries, that were no Saylers, that came with them; as Persians, Chaldeans, Arabians; *So as almost all Nations of Might and Fame resorted hither; Of whom we have some Stirps,[2] and little Tribes*

---

1 canoes

2 descendents

with us, at this day. And for our owne Shippes, they went sundry Voyages; as well to your Streights, which you call the Pillars of Hercules,[1] As to other parts in the Atlantique and Mediterrane Seas; As to Paguin,[2] (which is the same with Cambaline) and Quinzy,[3] upon the Orientall Seas, as farre as to the Borders of the East Tartary.[4]

At the same time, and an Age after, or more, the Inhabitants of the great Atlantis did flourish. For though the Narration and Description, which is made by a great Man[5] with you, that the Descendents of Neptune planted there; and of the Magnificent Temple, Palace, City, & Hill; And the manifold streames of goodly Navigable Rivers, (which as so many Chaines environed the same Site, and Temple;) And the severall Degrees of Ascent, whereby Men did climb up to the same, as if it had bin a Scala Caeli,[6] be all Poeticall and Fabulous: Yet so much is true, that the said Country of Atlantis; As well that of Peru then called Coya, as that of Mexico then named Tyrambel, were mighty and proud Kingdomes, in Armes, Shipping, & Riches: So Mighty, as at one time, (or at least within the space of ten yeares,) they both made two great Expeditions; They of Tirambel through the Atlantique to the Mediterrane Sea; and they of Coya through the South Sea upon this our Island: And for the former of these, which was into Europe, the same Author amongst you, (as it seemeth,) had some relation from the Egyptian Priest, whom he citeth. For assuredly such a thing there was. But whether it were the Ancient Athenians, that had the glory of the Repulse, and Resistance of those Forces, I can say nothing: But certaine it is, there never came backe, either Ship, or Man, from that Voyage. Neither had the other Voyage of those of Coya upon us, had better fortune, if they had not met with Enemies of greater clemency. For the King of this Island, (by name Altabin,) a wise Man, and a great Warrier; Knowing well both his owne strength, and that of his Enemies; handled the matter so, as he cut off their Land-Forces, from their Ships; and entoyled[7] both their Navy, and their Campe, with a greater Power than theirs, both by Sea and Land: And compelled them to render themselves without

---

1   rocky columns framing the Straits of Gilbraltar
2   Peking [Beijing]
3   Marco Polo makes reference to Quinsey or Kin-sai [Hangzhou], the Celestial City.
4   Tartary, the country of the Tartars, extending east from central Asia to the Caspian Sea
5   Plato, who relates the myth of Atlantis in his dialogues *Timaeus* (*Tim.* 24-25) and *Critias* (*passim*.)
6   ladder of heaven
7   brought into toils or snares; entrapped

striking stroke: And after they were at his Mercy, contenting himselfe onely with their Oath, that they should no more beare Armes against him, dismissed them all in safetie. But the Divine Revenge *overtooke not long after those proud Enterprises. For within lesse than the space of one Hundred Yeares, the* Great Atlantis *was utterly lost and destroyed: Not by a great Earthquake, as your* Man *saith; (For that whole Tract is little subject to Earthquakes;) But by a particular Deluge or Inundation; Those Countries having, at this Day, far greater Rivers, and far higher Mountaines, to powre downe Waters, than any part of the Old World. But it is true, that the same Inundation was not deepe; Not past fortie foot, in most places, from the Ground; So that, although it destroyed Man and Beast generally, yet some few wild Inhabitants of the Wood escaped. Birds also were saved by flying to the high Trees and Woods. For as for Men, although they had Buildings in many places, higher than the Depth of the Water; Yet that Inundation, though it were shallow, had a long Continuance; whereby they of the Vale, that were not drowned, perished for want of Food, and other things necessary. So as marvaile you not at the thinne Population of* America, *nor at the Rudenesse and Ignorance of the People; For you must account your Inhabitants of* America *as a young People; Younger a thousand yeares, at the least, than the rest of the World: For that there was so much time, betweene the* Universall Floud, *and their* Particular Inundation. *For the poore Remnant of Humane Seed, which remained in their Mountaines, Peopled the Countrey againe slowly, by little and little; And being simple and savage People, (Not like* Noah *and his* Sonnes, *which was the chiefe Family of the Earth) they were not able to leave Letters, Arts, and Civilitie, to their Posteritie; And having likewise in their Mountanous Habitations beene used, (in respect of the Extreme Cold of those* Regions,) *to cloath themselves with the Skinnes of Tygers, Beares, and great Hairy Goates, that they have in those Parts; When after they came downe into the Valley, and found the intolerable Heats which are there, and knew no meanes of lighter Apparell; they were forced to beginne the Custome of Going Naked, which continueth at this day. Onely they take great pride and delight, in the Feathers of Birds; And this also they tooke from those their Ancestours of the Mountaines, who were invited unto it, by the infinite Flights of Birds, that came up to the high Grounds, while the Waters stood below. So you see, by this maine Accident of Time, wee lost our Traffique with the* Americans, *with whom, of all others, in regard they lay nearest to us, wee had most Commerce. As for the other Parts of the World, it is most manifest, that in the Ages following, (whether it were in respect of Warres, or by a naturall Revolution of Time,)*

Navigation did every where greatly decay; And specially, farre Voyages, (the rather by the use of Gallies, and such Vessells, as could hardly brooke the Ocean,) were altogether left and omitted. So then, that part of Entercourse,[1] which could be from other Nations, to Sayle to us, you see how it hath long since ceased; Except it were by some rare Accident, as this of yours. But now of the Cessation of that other Part of Entercourse, which mought[2] be by our Sayling to other Nations, I must yeeld you some other Cause. For I cannot say, (if I shall say truely,) but our Shipping, for Number, Strength, Mariners, Pylots, and all things that appertaine to Navigation, is as great as ever; And therefore why we should sit at home, I shall now give you an account by it selfe; And it will draw nearer, to give you satisfaction, to your principall Question.

There raigned in this Island; about 1900. yeares agoe, a King, whose memory of all others we most adore; Not Superstitiously, but as a Divine Instrument, though a Mortall Man: his Name was Salomona: And we esteeme him as the Law-giver of our Nation. This King had a large heart, inscrutable for good; And was wholly bent to make his Kingdome and People Happie. He therefore taking into Consideration, how sufficient and substantive this Land was, to Maintain it selfe, without any ayd (at all) of the Forrainer; Being 5600. Miles in circuit, and of rare Fertilitie of Soyle, in the greatest part thereof; And finding also the Shipping of this Country mought be plentifully set on worke, both by Fishing, and by Transportations from Port to Port, and likewise by Sayling unto some small Islands that are not farre from us, and are under the Crowne and Lawes of this State; And recalling into his Memory, the happy and flourishing Estate, wherein this Land then was; So as it mought be a thousand wayes altered to the worse, but scarce any one way to the better; thought nothing wanted to his Noble and Heroicall Intentions, but onely (as farre as Humane foresight mought reach) to give perpetuitie to that, which was in his time so happily established. Therefore amongst his other Fundamentall Lawes of this Kingdome, he did ordaine the Interdicts and Prohibitions, which wee have touching Entrance of Strangers; which at that time (though it was after the Calamitie of America) was frequent; Doubting Novelties, and Commixture of Manners. It is true, the like Law, against the Admission of Strangers without License, is an Ancient Law, in the Kingdome of China, and yet continued in use. But there it is a poore Thing; And hath made them a curious, ignorant, fearefull, foolish Nation. But

---

1   intercourse
2   might

our Law-giver *made his Law of another temper. For first, hee hath preserved all points of Humanitie, in taking Order, and making Provision for the Reliefe of Strangers distressed; whereof you have tasted.* At which Speech (as reason was) wee all rose up, and bowed our selves. Hee went on. *That* King *also still desiring to joyne Humanitie and Policie together; And thinking it against Humanitie, to detaine Strangers here against their wills; And against Policy, that they should returne, and discover their Knowledge of this Estate, he tooke this Course: He did ordaine, that of the Strangers, that should be permitted to Land, as many (at all times) mought depart as would; But as many as would stay, should have very good Conditions, and Meanes to live, from the* State. *Wherein hee saw so farre, that now in so many Ages since the Prohibition, wee have memory not of one Ship that ever returned, and but of thirteene Persons onely, at severall times, that chose to returne in our Bottomes. What those few that returned may have reported abroad I know not. But you must thinke, Whatsoever they have said, could bee taken where they came, but for a Dreame. Now for our Travelling from hence into Parts abroad, our* Law-giver *thought fit altogether to restraine it. So is it not in* China. *For the* Chineses *sayle where they will, or can; which sheweth, that their Law of Keeping out Strangers, is a Law of Pusillanimitie, and feare. But this restraint of ours, hath one onely Exception, which is admirable; Preserving the good which commeth by communicating with Strangers, and avoyding the Hurt; And I will now open it to you. And here I shall seeme a little to digresse, but you will by and by finde it pertinent. Yee shall understand, (my deare Friends,) that amongst the Excellent Acts of that* King, *one above all hath the preheminence. It was the Erection, and Institution of an* Order, *or* Societie, *which we call* Salomons House; *The Noblest Foundation, (as wee thinke,) that ever was upon the Earth; And the Lanthorne of this Kingdome. It is dedicated to the Study of the* Works, *and* Creatures *of God. Some thinke it beareth the Founders Name a little corrupted, as if it should be* Solamona's *House. But the Records write it, as it is spoken. So as I take it to be denominate of the* King *of the* Hebrewes, *which is famous with you, and no Stranger to us; For wee have some Parts of his Works, which with you are lost; Namely that* Naturall History, *which hee wrote of all* Plants, *from the* Cedar *of Libanus,[1] to the* Mosse *that groweth out of the Wall; And of all* things that have Life and Motion. *This maketh me thinke, that our* King *finding himselfe to Symbolize, in many things, with that* King *of the* Hebrewes *(which lived*

---

1   cedar of Lebanon

*many yeares before him) honoured him with the Title of this Foundation. And
I am the rather induced to be of this Opinion, for that I finde in ancient
Records, this* Order or Societie *is sometimes called* Salomons House; *And
sometimes the* Colledge of the Six Dayes Workes; *whereby I am satisfied,
That our Excellent* King *had learned from the* Hebrewes, *That* God *had
created the World, and all that therein is, within six Dayes; And therefore hee
instituting that* House, *for the finding out of the true Nature of all Things,
(whereby* God *mought have the more Glory in the Workemanship of them,
and Men the more fruit in the Use of them,) did give it also that second
Name. But now to come to our present purpose. When the* King *had forbidden, to all his People, Navigation into any Part, that was not under his
Crowne, he made neverthelesse this Ordinance; That every twelve years there
should be set forth, out of this* Kingdome, *two Shippes, appointed to severall
Voyages; That in either of these Shippes, there should be a Mission of three of
the* Fellowes, or Brethren of Salomons House; *whose Errand was onely to
give us Knowledge of the Affaires and State of those Countries, to which they
were designed; And especially of the Sciences, Arts, Manufactures, and Inventions of all the World; And withall to bring unto us, Bookes, Instruments, and
Patternes, in every kinde: That the Ships, after they had landed the* Brethren,
should returne; And that the Brethren *should stay abroad till the new Mission. These Ships are not otherwise fraught, than with Store of Victualls, and
good Quantitie of Treasure to remaine with the* Brethren, *for the buying of
such Things, and rewarding of such Persons, as they should thinke fit. Now for
me to tell you, how the Vulgar sort of Marriners are contained from being discovered at Land; And how they that must be put on shore for any time, colour
themselves under the Names of other Nations; And to what places these Voyages have beene designed; And what places of* Rendez-Vous *are appointed
for the new Missions; And the like Circumstances of the Practique;[1] I may not
doe it; Neither is it much to your desire. But thus you see, wee maintaine a
Trade, not for Gold, Silver, or Jewels; Nor for Silkes; Nor for Spices; Nor any
other Commoditie of Matter; But onely for* Gods *first Creature, which was*
Light: *To have* Light *(I say) of the Growth of all Parts of the World.* And
when he had said this, he was silent; And so were we all. For indeed
wee were all astonished, to heare so strange things so probably told.
And he perceiving, that we were willing to say somewhat, but had it
not ready, in great Courtesie tooke us off, and descended to aske us

---

1   practice

Questions of our Voyage and Fortunes, and in the end concluded, that wee mought doe well, to thinke with our selves, what Time of stay wee would demand of the State; And bad[e] us not to scant our selves; For he would procure such Time as wee desired. Whereupon wee all rose up, and presented our selves to kisse the skirt of his Tippet;[1] But hee would not suffer us; And so tooke his leave. But when it came once amongst our People, that the State used to offer Conditions to Strangers that would stay, wee had Worke enough to get any of our Men to looke to our Shipp; And to keepe them from going presently to the Governour, to crave Conditions. But with much adoe we refrained[2] them, till we mought agree what Course to take.

We took our selves now for free men, seeing there was no danger of our utter Perdition; And lived most joyfully, going abroad, and seeing what was to be seen, in the Citie, and places adjacent, within our *Tedder;*[3] And obtaining Acquaintance with many of the Citie, not of the meanest Qualitie; At whose hands we found such Humanitie, and such a Freedome and desire, to take Strangers, as it were, into their Bosome, as was enough to make us forget all that was deare to us, in our owne Countries; And continually wee mett with many things, right worthy of Observation, & Relation: As indeed, if there be a Mirrour in the World, worthy to hold Mens Eyes, it is that Countrey. One day there were two of our Company bidden to a *Feast* of the *Family,* as they call it. A most Naturall, Pious, and Reverend Custome it is, shewing that Nation to be compounded of all Goodnes. This is the manner of it. It is granted to any Man, that shall live to see thirtie Persons, descended of his Body, alive together, and all above 3. yeares old, to make this *Feast,* which is done at the Cost of the State. The *Father* of the *Family,* whom they call the *Tirsan,* two dayes before the *Feast,* taketh to him three of such Friends as he liketh to chuse; And is assisted also by the Governour of the Citie, or Place, where the *Feast* is celebrated; And all the *Persons* of the *Family,* of both Sexes, are summoned to attend him. These two dayes the *Tirsan* sitteth in Consultation, concerning the good Estate of the *Family.* There, if there be any Discord or suits between any of the Family, they are compounded[4]

---

1 a polite gesture of leave-taking by a social inferior, signifying humility or abasement
2 restrained
3 tether
4 composed

and appeased. There, if any of the Family be Distressed or Decayed, order is taken for their Releefe, and competent meanes to live. There, if any be subject to vice, or take ill Courses, they are reproved and Censured. So likewise, Direction is given touching Marriages, and the Courses of life, which any of them should take, with divers other the like Orders and Advices. The Governour assisteth, to the end, to put in Execution. by his Publike Authoritie, the Decrees and Orders of the Tirsan, if they should be disobeyed; Though that seldome needeth; Such Reverence and Obedience they give, to the Order of Nature. The Tirsan doth also then, ever chuse one Man from amongst his Sonnes, to live in House with him: Who is called, ever after, the Sonne of the Vine. The Reason will hereafter appeare. On the Feast day, the Father or Tirsan commeth forth after Divine Service, into a large Roome, where the Feast is celebrated; Which Roome hath an Half-Pace[1] at the upper end. Against the wall, in the middle of the Half-pace, is a Chaire placed for him, with a Table and Carpet before it. Over the Chaire is a State,[2] made Round or Ovall, and it is of Ivie; an Ivie somewhat whiter than ours, like the Leafe of a Silver Aspe,[3] but more shining; For it is greene all Winter. And the State is curiously wrought with Silver and Silke of divers Colours, broyding[4] or bind-ing in the Ivie; And is ever of the worke, of some of the Daughters of the Family; And vailed over at the Topp, with a fine Nett of Silke and Silver. But the substance of it, is true Ivie; whereof, after it is taken downe, the Friends of the Family, are desirous to have some Leafe or Sprigg to keepe. The Tirsan commeth forth with all his Generation or Linage, the Males before him, and the Females following him; And if there be a Mother, from whose Body the whole Linage is descended, there is a Traverse[5] placed in a Loft above, on the right hand of the Chaire, with a privie Doore, and a carved Window of Glasse, leaded with Gold and blew; Where shee sitteth, but is not seene; When the Tirsan is come forth, hee sitteth downe in the Chaire; And all the Linage place themselves against the wall, both at his backe, and upon the Returne of the Half-pace, in Order of their yeares, without

---

1 low platform, part of the floor raised a half-step
2 canopy
3 aspen
4 ornamenting with needlework, embroidering
5 small compartment enclosed or shut off by a curtain or screen

difference of Sex, and stand upon their Feet. When hee is sett, the Roome being alwayes full of Company, but well kept and without Disorder, after some pause, there commeth in from the lower end of the Roome, a *Taratan*, (which is as much as an *Herald;*) And on either side of him two *young Lads;* Whereof one carrieth a Scrowle of their shining yellow Parchment; And the other a Cluster of Grapes of Gold, with a long Foot or Stalke. The *Herald*, and *Children*, are cloathed with Mantles of Sea-water greene Sattin; But the *Heralds* Mantle is streamed with Gold, and hath a Traine. Then the *Herald* with three Curtesies, or rather Inclinations, commeth up as farre as the Half-pace; And there first taketh into his Hand the Scrowle. This Scrowle is the *Kings Charter*, containing Gift of Revenue, and many Privileges, Exemptions, and Points of Honour, granted to the *Father* of the *Family;* And is ever stiled and directed; *To such an One, Our well-beloved Friend and Creditour:* Which is a Title proper onely to this Case. For they say, the King is Debtor to no Man, but for Propagation of his Subjects, The Seale set to the *Kings Charter*, is the Kings Image, Imbossed or moulded in Gold; And though such *Charters* be expidited of Course, and as of Right, yet they are varied by discretion, according to the Number and Dignitie of the *Family*. This *Charter* the *Herald* readeth aloud; And while it is read, the *Father* or *Tirsan*, standeth up, supported by two of his Sonnes, such as hee chooseth. Then the *Herald* mounteth the Half-Pace, and delivereth the *Charter* into his Hand; And with that there is an Acclamation, by all that are present, in their Language, which is thus much; *Happie are the people of Bensalem*. Then the *Herald* taketh into his Hand from the other Child, the Cluster of Grapes, which is of Gold; Both the Stalke, and the Grapes. But the Grapes are daintily enamelled; And if the Males of the *Family* be the greater number, the Grapes are enamelled Purple, with a little Sunne sett on the Topp; If the Females, then they are enamelled into a greenish yellow, with a Cressant on the Topp.[1] The Grapes are in number as many as there are Descendents of the *Family*. This Golden Cluster, the *Herald* delivereth also to the *Tirsan;* Who presently delivereth it over, to that Sonne, that hee had formerly chosen, to be in House with him; Who beareth it before his *Father*, as an Ensigne of Honour, when hee goeth in publike ever after; And is

---

1   For the gender symbolism of sun and moon, see Mendelson and Crawford, *Women in Early Modern England*, p.72.

thereupon called *the Sonne of the Vine*. After this Ceremonie ended, the *Father* or *Tirsan* retireth; And after some time commeth forth againe to Dinner, where hee sitteth alone under the State, as before; And none of his Descendants sit with him, of what Degree or Dignitie soever, except hee hap to be of *Salomons House*. Hee is served onely by his owne Children, such as are Male, who performe unto him all service of the Table upon the knee; And the Women only stand about him, leaning against the wall. The Roome below the Half-pace, hath Tables on the sides for the Ghests that are bidden; Who are served with great and comely Order; And towards the end of Dinner (which in the greatest Feasts with them, lasteth never above an Houre and an halfe) there is an *Hymne* sung, varied according to the Invention of him that composeth it; (for they have excellent Poesie;) But the Subject of it is, (alwayes,) the praises of *Adam*, and *Noah*, and *Abraham*; Whereof the former two Peopled the World, and the last was the *Father* of the *Faithfull*: Concluding ever with a Thanksgiving for the *Nativitie* of our *Saviour*, in whose Birth, the Births of all are onely Blessed. Dinner being done, the *Tirsan* retireth againe; And having withdrawne himselfe alone into a place; where hee maketh some private Prayers, hee commeth forth the third time, to give the Blessing; with all his Descendants, who stand about him, as at the first. Then hee calleth them forth by one and by one, by name, as hee pleaseth, though seldome the Order of Age be inverted. The person that is called, (the Table being before removed,) kneeleth downe before the Chaire, and the *Father* layeth his Hand, upon his Head, or her Head, and giveth the Blessing in these Words; *Sonne of Bensalem, (or Daughter of Bensalem,) thy Father saith it; The Man by whom thou hast Breath and Life speaketh the word; The Blessing of the Everlasting Father, the Prince of Peace, and the Holy Dove, be upon thee, and make the dayes of thy Pilgrimage, good, and many.* This hee saith to everie of them; And that done, if there be any of his Sonnes, of eminent Meritt and Vertue, (so they be not above two,) hee calleth for them againe; And saith, laying his Arme over their shoulders, they standing; *Sonnes, it is well yee are borne, give God the praise, and persevere to the end.* And withall delivereth to either of them a Jewell, made in the Figure of an Eare of Wheat, which they ever after weare in the front of their Turban, or Hat. This done, they fall to Musicke and dances, And other Recreations, after their manner, for the rest of the day. This is the full order of that *Feast*.

By that time, six or seven Dayes were spent, I was fallen into straight Acquaintance, with a *Merchant* of that *Citie*, whose Name was *Joabin*; Hee was a *Jew* and *Circumcised*: For they have some few Stirps of *Jewes*, yet remaining amongst them, whom they leave to their owne Religion. Which they may the better doe, because they are of a farre differing Disposition from the *Jewes* in other Parts. For whereas they hate the *Name* of CHRIST; And have a secret inbred Rancour against the People amongst whom they live; These (contrariwise) give unto our SAVIOUR many high Attributes, and love the *Nation of Bensalem*, extremely. Surely this Man, of whom I speake, would ever acknowledge, that CHRIST was borne of a *Virgin*; And that hee was more than a Man; And hee would tell how GOD made him Ruler of the *Seraphims*, which guard his Throane; And they call him also the *Milken Way*, and the *Eliah* of the *Messiah*; And many other High Names; which though they be inferiour to his Divine Majestie, Yet they are farre from the Language of other *Jewes*. And for the Countrey of *Bensalem*, this Man would make no end of commending it; Being desirous by Tradition amongst the *Jewes* there, to have it beleeved, that the People thereof, were of the Generations of *Abraham*, by another Sonne, whom they call *Nachoran*; And that *Moses* by a secret *Cabala*[1] ordained the Lawes of *Bensalem*, which they now use; And that when the *Messiah* should come, and sit in his Throne at *Hierusalem*, the King of *Bensalem*, should [sit] at his feet, whereas other Kings should keepe a great distance. But yet setting aside these *Jewish* Dreames, the Man was a wise Man, and learned, and of great Policie, and excellently seene in the Lawes and Customes of that Nation. Amongst other Discourses, one day, I told him, I was much affected with the Relation I had, from some of the Company, of their Custome, in holding the *Feast* of the *Family*; For that (mee thought) I had never heard of a Solemnitie, wherein Nature did so much preside. And because Propagation of Families, proceedeth from the Nuptiall Copulation, I desired to know of him, what Lawes and Customes they had concerning Marriage; And whether they kept Marriage well; And whether they were tyed to one Wife; For that where Population is so much affected,[2] and such as with them it seemed to be, there is

---

1   an unwritten or unrecorded tradition
2   where an increase in population is desired

commonly Permission of *Pluralitie of Wives*. To this he said; *You have Reason for to commend that excellent Institution of the* Feast *of the* Family. *And indeed wee have Experience, that those Families, that are partakers of the Blessing of that Feast, doe flourish and prosper ever after, in an extraordinarie manner. But heare me now, and I will tell you what I know. You shall understand, that there is not under the Heavens, so chaste a Nation, as this of Bensalem; Nor so free from all Pollution, or foulenesse. It is the Virgin of the World. I remember I have read in one of your* Europæan *Bookes, of an holy Hermit amongst you, that desired to see the* Spirit *of* Fornication, *and there appeared to him, a little foule ugly* Æthiope. *But if hee had desired to see the* Spirit *of* Chastitie *of* Bensalem, *it would have appeared to him, in the likenesse of a faire beautifull* Cherubin. *For there is nothing, amongst Mortall Men, more faire and admirable, than the Chaste Mindes of this People. Know therefore, that with them there are no Stewes,*[1] *no dissolute Houses, no Curtisans, nor any thing of that kinde. Nay they wonder (with detestation) at you in* Europe, *which permit such things. They say yee have put Marriage out of office: For Marriage is ordained a Remedy for unlawfull Concupiscence; And Naturall Concupiscence seemeth as a spurr to Marriage. But when Men have at hand a Remedy, more agreeable to their corrupt will, Marriage is almost expulsed. And therefore there are with you seene infinite Men, that marrie not, but chuse rather a libertine and impure single Life, than to be yoaked in Marriage; And many that doe marrie, marrie late, when the Prime and Strength of their Yeares is past. And when they doe marrie, what is Marriage to them, but a verie Bargaine; Wherein is sought Alliance, or Portion, or Reputation, with some desire (almost indifferent) of Issue; And not the faithfull Nuptiall Union of Man and Wife, that was first instituted. Neither is it possible, that those that have cast away so basely, so much of their Strength, should greatly esteeme Children, (being of the same Matter,) as Chaste Men doe. So likewise during Marriage is the Case much amended, as it ought to be if those things were tolerated onely for necessitie? No, but they remaine still as a verie Affront to Marriage. The Haunting of those dissolute places, or resort to Curtizans, are no more punished in Married Men, than in Batchelors. And the depraved Custome of change, and the Delight in Meretricious Embracements, (where sinne is turned into Art,) maketh Marriage a dull thing, and a kinde of Imposition, or Tax. They heare you defend these things, as done to avoid greater Evils; As Advoutries,*[2] *Deflouring of Virgins, Unnaturall lust, and the*

---

1   brothels

2   adulteries (obsolete form)

like. But they say, this is a preposterous Wisdome; And they call it Lot's offer, *who to save his Guests from abusing, Offered his Daughters* [Gen. 19:8]: *Nay they say further, That there is little gained in this; For that the same Vices and Appetites, doe still remaine and abound; Unlawfull Lust being like a Furnace, that if you stopp the Flames altogether, it will quench; But if you give it any vent, it will rage. As for Masculine Love, they have no touch of it; And yet there are not, so faithfull and inviolate Friendshipps, in the world againe, as are there: And to speake generally, (as I said before,) I have not read of any such Chastitie, in any People, as theirs: And their usuall saying is,* That whosoever is unchaste cannot reverence himselfe: *And they say;* That the Reverence of a Mans selfe, is, next Religion, the chiefest Bridle of all Vice. And when hee had said this, the good *Jew* paused a little; Whereupon, I farre more willing to hear him speake on, than to speake my selfe; yet thinking it decent, that upon his pause of Speech, I should not be altogether silent, said onely this; *That I would say to him, as the* Widow *of* Sarepta *said to* Elias; *that hee was come to bring to Memorie our Sinnes* [Kings 17:8-24]; *And that I confesse the* Righteousnesse *of* Bensalem, *was grater than the* Righteousnesse *of* Europe. At which speech hee bowed his Head, and went on in this manner. *They have also many wise and excellent Lawes touching* Marriage. *They allow no* Polygamie. *They have ordained that none doe intermarrie or contract, untill a Moneth be past from their first Inter-view.* Marriage *without consent of Parents they doe not make voyd, but they mulct it in the Inheritours: For the Children of such* Marriages, *are not admitted to inherit, above a third Part of their Parents Inheritance. I have read in a* Booke *of one of your* Men, *of a* Faigned Common-wealth,[1] *where the Married Couple are permitted, before they Contract, to see one another Naked. This they dislike: For they thinke it a Scorne, to give a Refusall after so Familiar Knowledge: But because of many hidden Defects in Men and Womens Bodies, they have a more civill Way: For they have neare everie Towne, a Couple of* Pooles, *(which they call* Adam *and* Eves Pooles,) *where it is permitted to one of the Friends of the Man, and another of the Friends of the Woman, to see them severally bathe Naked.*

And as wee were thus in Conference, there came one that seemed to be a Messenger, in a rich Huke,[2] that spake with the *Jew:* Whereupon hee turned to mee, and said; *You will pardon mee, for I am com-*

---

1 Sir Thomas More's *Utopia* (1516)
2 cape or mantle with hood

manded away in haste. The next Morning hee came to mee againe, joy-full as it seemed, and said; *There is word come to the Governour of the Citie, that one of the* Fathers *of* Salomons House, *will be here this day Seven-night: Wee have seene none of them this Dozen Yeares. His Comming is in State; But the Cause of his comming is secret. I will provide you, and your Fellowes, of a good Standing, to see his Entry.* I thanked him, and told him; *I was most glad of the Newes.* The Day being come he made his Entry. He was a *Man* of Middle Stature, and Age, comely of Person, and had an Aspect as if hee pittied Men. He was cloathed in a Roabe of fine blacke Cloth, with wide Sleeves, and a Cape. His under Gar-ment was of excellent white Linnen, downe to the Foot, girt with a Girdle of the same; And a Sindon or Tippett of the same about his Necke. He had Gloves, that were curious, and sett with Stone; And Shoes of Peach-coloured Velvet. His Neck was bare to the Shoulders. His Hatt was like a Helmet, or *Spanish Montera*; And his Locks curled below it decently: They were of Colour browne. His Beard was cutt round, and of the same colour with his Haire, somewhat lighter. He was carried in a rich Chariott, without wheeles, Litter-wise; With two Horses at either end, richly trapped in blew Velvet Embroydered; and two Footmen on each side in the like Attire. The Chariot was all of Cedar, gilt, and adorned with Chrystall; Save that the Fore-end had Pannels of Sapphires, set in Borders of Gold; And the Hinder-end the like of Emerauds of the *Peru* Colour. There was also a Sunn of Gold, Radiant, upon the Topp, in the Midst; And on the Top before, a small *Cherub* of Gold, with Wings displayed. The Chariott was covered with Cloth of Gold tissued upon Blew. He had before him fifty Atten-dants, young Men all, in white *Satten* loose Coates to the Mid Legg; And Stockins of white Silk; And Shoes of blew Velvet; And Hatts of blew Velvett; with fine Plumes of diverse Colours, sett round like Hat-bands. Next before the Chariott, went two Men, bare-headed, in Linnen Garments downe to the Foot, girt, and Shoes of blew Velvett; Who carried, the one a Crosier, the other a Pastorall Staffe like a Sheep-hooke: Neither of them of Mettall, but the Crosier of Balme-wood, the Pastorall Staffe of Cedar. Horse-Men he had none, neither before, nor behinde his Chariott: As it seemeth to avoyd all Tumult and Trouble. Behinde his Chariot, went all the Officers and Princi-palls of the Companies of the Cittie. He sate alone, upon Cushions, of a kinde of excellent Plush, blew; And under his Foote curious Car-petts of Silk of divers Colours, like the Persian, but farre finer. He held up his bare Hand, as he went, as blessing the People, but in Silence. The Street was wonderfully well kept; So that there was never any Army had their Men stand in better Battell-Array, than the People stood. The Windowes likewise were not crouded, but every one stood in them, as if they had beene placed. When the shew was past, the *Jew* said to me; *I shall not be able to attend you as I would, in regard of some charge the Citie hath lay'd upon me, for the Entertaining of this Great Person.* Three dayes after the *Jew* came to mee againe, and said; *Yee are happie men; for the* Father *of* Salomons House *taketh knowledge of your Being here, and commanded me to tell you, that he will admit all your Company to his presence, and have private Conference with one of you, that yee shall choose: And for this hath appointed the next day after to Morrow. And because he meaneth to give you his Blessing, he hath appointed it in the Forenoone.* We came at our Day, and Houre, and I was chosen by my Fellowes for the private Accesse. We found him in a faire Chamber, richly hanged, and carpeted under Foote, without any Degrees to the State. He was sett upon a Low Throne richly adorned, and a rich Cloth of State over his Head, of blew Sattin Embroydered. He was alone, save that he had two Pages of Honour, on either Hand one, finely attired in White. His Under Garments were the like that we saw him weare in the Chariott; but in stead of his Gowne, he had on him a Mantle with a Cape, of the same fine Blacke, fastned about him. When wee came in, as wee were taught, we bowed Low at our first Entrance; And when wee were come neare his Chaire, he stood up, holding forth his Hand ungloved, and in Posture of Blessing; And we every one of us stooped downe, and kissed the Hemme of his Tippett. That done, the rest departed, and I remained. Then hee warned the Pages forth of the Roome, and caused me to sit downe beside him, and spake to me thus in the *Spanish Tongue*:

GOD *blesse thee, my Sonne; I will give thee the greatest Jewell I have: For I will impart unto thee, for the love of* GOD *and Men, a Relation of the true State of* Salomons House. Sonne, *to make you know the true State of* Salomons House, *I will keepe this order. First I will set forth unto you the* End *of our* Foundation. *Secondly, the* Preparations *and* Instruments *wee have for our* Workes. *Thirdly, the* severall Employments *and* Functions *whereto our* Fellowes *are assigned. And fourthly, the* Ordinances *and* Rites *which* wee observe.

The End *of our* Foundation *is the* Knowledge *of* Causes, *and* Secret Motions *of Things; And the* Enlarging *of the bounds of* Humane Empire, *to the Effecting of all Things possible.*

The Preparations *and* Instruments *are these. We have large and deepe* Caves *of severall Depths: The deepest are sunke 600.* Fathome: *And some of them are digged and made under great Hills and Mountaines: So that if you reckon together the Depth of the Hill, and the Depth of the* Cave, *they are (some of them) above three Miles deepe. For we finde, that the Depth of a Hill, and the Depth of a Cave from the Flat, is the same Thing; Both remote alike, from the Sunne and Heavens Beames, and from the Open Aire. These* Caves *we call the* Lower Region; *And wee use them for all* Coagulations, Indurations, Refrigerations, *and* Conservations *of* Bodies. *We use them likewise for the* Imitation *of* Naturall Mines: *And the* Producing *also of* New Artificiall Mettalls, *by* Compositions *and* Materials *which we use, and lay there for many yeares. We use them also sometimes, (which may seeme strange,) for* Curing *of some* Diseases *and for* Prolongation *of* Life, *in some* Hermits *that choose to live there, well accommodated of all things necessarie, and indeed live very long; By whom also wee learne many things.*

We have Burialls *in severall* Earths, *where we put diverse* Cements, *as the* Chineses *doe their* Porcellane. *But we have them in greater Varietie, and some of them more fine. We have also great varietie of* Composts, *and* Soiles, *for the Making of the* Earth *Fruitfull.*

We have High Towers; *The Highest about halfe a Mile in Height; And some of them likewise set upon High* Mountaines: *So that the vantage of the Hill with the* Tower, *is in the highest of them three Miles at least. And these Places wee call the* Upper Region; *Accounting the Aire between the High Places, and the Lowe, as a* Middle Region. *Wee use these* Towers, *according to their severall Heights, and Situations, for* Insolation,[1] Refrigeration, Conservation; *And for the* View *of divers* Meteors; *As* Windes, Raine, Snow, Haile; *And some of the* Fiery Meteors *also. And upon them, in some Places, are Dwellings of* Hermits, *whom we visit sometimes, and instruct what to observe.*

We have great Lakes, *both* Salt, *and* Fresh; *whereof we have use for the* Fish, *and* Fowle. *We use them also for* Burialls *of some* Naturall Bodies: *For we finde a Difference in Things buried in* Earth, *or in* Aire *below the*

---

1 exposure to the sun

Earth, *and things buried in* Water. *We have also* Pooles, *of which some doe straine* Fresh Water *out of* Salt; *And others by Art doe turn* Fresh Water *into* Salt. *We have also some* Rocks *in the Midst of the* Sea; *And some* Bayes *upon the* Shore *for some* Works, *wherein is required the* Aire *and* Vapour *of the* Sea. *We have likewise* Violent Streames *and* Cataracts, *which serve us for many* Motions: *And likewise* Engines *for* Multiplying *and* Enforcing *of* Windes, *to set also on going diverse* Motions.

We have also a Number of Artificiall Wels, *and* Fountaines, *made in Imitation of the* Naturall Sources *and* Baths; *As tincted upon* Vitrioll, Sulphur, Steele, Brasse, Lead, Nitre, *and other* Mineralls. *And againe we have little* Wells *for* Infusions *of many* Things, *where the* Waters *take the Vertue quicker and better, than in* Vessells *or* Basins. *And amongst them we have a* Water, *which we call* Water *of* Paradise, *being, by that we doe to it, made very* Soveraigne *for* Health, *and* Prolongation *of* Life.

We have also Great *and* Spacious Houses, *where we imitate and demon-strate* Meteors; *As* Snow, Haile, Raine, *some* Artificiall Raines *of* Bodies, *and not of* Water, Thunders, Lightnings; *Also* Generations *of* Bodies *in* Aire; *As* Froggs, Flies, *and diverse* Others.

We have also certaine Chambers, *which we call* Chambers of Health, *where we qualifie the* Aire *as we thinke good and proper for the* Cure *of diverse* Diseases, & Preservation *of* Health.

Wee have also faire and large Baths, *of severall* Mixtures, *for the* Cure *of* Diseases, *and the* Restoring *of* Mans Body *from* Arefaction:[1] *And Oth-ers for the* Confirming *of it in* Strength *of* Sinnewes, Vitall Parts, *and the very* Juyce *and* Substance *of the* Body.

We have also large and various Orchards, *and* Gardens; *Wherein we doe not so much respect* Beautie, *as* Varietie *of* Ground *and* Soyle, *proper for diverse* Trees, *and* Herbs: *And some very spatious, where* Trees, *and* Berries *are set, wherof we make diverse* Kinds *of* Drinks, *besides the* Vineyards. *In these wee practise likewise all* Conclusions[2] *of* Grafting, *and* Inoculating, *as well of* Wild-Trees, *as* Fruit-Trees, *which produceth many* Effects. *And we make (by* Art) *in the same* Orchards, *and* Gardens, Trees *and* Flowers, *to come earlier, or later, than their* Seasons; *And to come up and beare more speedily than by their* Naturall Course *they doe.* Wee *make them also by* Art *greater much than their* Nature; *And their* Fruit *greater, and sweeter, and of*

---

1   process of drying
2   we try experiments and come to conclusions about grafting

differing Taste, Smell, Colour, *and* Figure, *from their* Nature. *And many of them wee so Order as they become of* Medicinall Use.

We have also Meanes to make diverse Plants, *rise by* Mixtures *of* Earths *without* Seeds; *And likewise to make diverse New* Plants, *differing from the Vulgar;*[1] *and to make one* Tree *or* Plant *turne into another.*

Wee have also Parks, *and* Enclosures *of all Sorts, of* Beasts, *and* Birds; *which we use not onely for View or Rareness, but likewise for* Dissections, *and* Trialls;[2] *that therby we may take light, what may be wrought upon the* Body *of* Man. *Wherin we find many strange Effects; As* Continuing Life *in them though divers* Parts, *which you account* Vitall, *be perished, and taken forth;* Resussitating *of some that seeme* Dead *in* Appearance; *And the like. We try also all* Poysons, *and other* Medicines *upon them, as well of* Chyrurgery, *as* Physicke.[3] *By Art likewise, we make them* Greater, *or* Taller, *than their* Kinde *is; And contrary-wise* Dwarfe *them and stay their* Growth: *Wee make them more* Fruitfull, *and* Bearing *than their* Kind *is; And contrary-wise* Barren *and not* Generative. *Also we make them differ in* Colour, Shape, Activity, *many wayes. Wee finde Meanes to make* Com-mixtures *and* Copulations *of diverse* Kinds; *which have produced many* New Kinds, *and them not* Barren, *as the generall Opinion is. Wee make a Number of* Kinds, *of* Serpents, Wormes, Flies, Fishes, *of* Putrefaction; *Whereof some are advanced (in effect) to be* Perfect Creatures, *like* Beasts, *or* Birds, *And have* Sexes, *and doe* Propagate. *Neither doe we this by* Chance, *but wee know beforehand, of what* Matter *and* Commixture, *what* Kinde *of those* Creatures *will arise.*

Wee have also Particular Pooles, *where wee make* Trialls *upon* Fishes, *as we have said before of* Beasts, *and* Birds.

Wee have also Places *for* Breed *and* Generation *of those* Kindes *of* Wormes, *and* Flies, *which are of* Speciall Use; *Such as are with you your* Silk-wormes, *and* Bees.

I will not hold you long with recounting of our Brew-Houses, Bake-Houses, *and* Kitchins, *where are made diverse* Drinkes, Breads, *and* Meats, *Rare, and of speciall Effects.* Wines *we have of* Grapes; *And* Drinkes *of other* Juyce, *of* Fruits, *of* Graines, *and of* Roots; *And of* Mix-tures *with* Honey, Sugar, Manna, *and* Fruits dryed, *and* decocted: *Also of the* Teares *or* Woundings, *of* Trees; *And of the* Pulp *of* Canes. *And these*

---

1 the common or ordinary species

2 experiments

3 surgery and medicine

Drinkes *are of severall* Ages, *some to the* Age *or* Last *of forty yeares. We have* Drinkes *also brewed with severall* Herbs, *and* Roots, & Spices; *Yea with severall* Fleshes, *and* White-Meates; *Whereof some of the* Drinkes *are such, as they are in effect* Meat *and* Drinke *both: So that diverse, especially in* Age, *doe desire to live with them, with litle or no* Meat, *or* Bread. *And above all wee strive to have* Drinkes *of* Extreame Thin Parts, *to insinuate into the* Body, *and yet without all* Biting, Sharpnesse, *or* Fretting; *Insomuch as some of them, put upon the back of your* Hand, *will, with a little stay, passe through to the* Palme, *and yet taste* Mild *to the* Mouth. *We have also* Waters, *which we ripen in that fashion, as they become* Nourishing; *So that they are indeed excellent* Drinke; *And many will use no other.* Breads *wee have of severall* Graines, Roots, *and* Kernels; *Yea and some of* Flesh, *and* Fish, Dryed; *With diverse kindes of* Leavenings, *and* Seasonings: *So that some doe extreamely move* Appetites; *Some doe* Nourish *so, as diverse doe live of them, without any other* Meate; *Who live very long. So for* Meates, *we have some of them so* beaten, *and made* tender, & mortified, *yet without all* Corrupting, *as a* Weake Heate *of the* Stomach *will turne them into good* Chylus;[1] *As well as a* Strong Heat *would* Meat *otherwise prepared. We have some* Meats *also, and* Breads, *and* Drinks, *which taken by* Men, *enable them to* Fast *long after; And some other, that used make the very* Flesh *of* Mens Bodies, *sensibly, more* Hard & Tough; *And their* Strength *farre greater, than otherwise it would be.*

Wee have Dispensatories, *or* Shops *of* Medicines. *Wherein you may easily thinke, if wee have such* Variety *of* Plants, *and* Living Creatures, *more than you have in* Europe, *(for wee know what you have,) the* Simples,[2] Drugges, *and* Ingredients *of* Medicines, *must likewise be in so much the greater* Varietie. *Wee have them likewise of diverse* Ages, *and long* Fermentations. *And for their* Preparations, *wee have not onely all* Manner *of* Exquisite Distillations, *and* Separations, *and especially by* Gentle Heates, *and* Percolations *through diverse* Strainers, *yea and* Substances; *But also* Exact Formes *of* Composition, *whereby they incorporate almost, as they were* Naturall Simples.

We have also diverse Mechanicall Arts, *which you have not; And* Stuffes *made by them; As* Papers, Linnen, Silks, Tissues; *dainty* Workes *of* Feathers *of wonderfull Lustre; excellent* Dies, *and many others: And* Shops like-

---

1   chyle: digested food
2   medicinal herbs

wise, as well for such as are not brought into Vulgar use amongst us, as for those that are. For you must know, that of the Things before recited, many of them are growne into use throughout the Kingdome; But yet, if they did flow from our Invention, *we have of them also for* Patternes *and* Principalls.

We have also Fournaces *of great* Diversities, *and that keep great* Diversitie *of* Heats: Fierce *and* Quicke; Strong *and* Constant; Soft *and* Milde; Blowne, Quiet, Dry, Moist; *And the like. But above all wee have* Heats, *in Imitation of the* Sunnes *and* Heavenly Bodies Heats, *that passe diverse* Inequalities, *and (as it were)* Orbs, Progresses, *and* Returnes, *whereby we produce admirable effects. Besides wee have* Heats *of* Dungs; *and of* Bellies *and* Mawes *of* Living Creatures, *and of their* Blouds, *and* Bodies; *and of* Hayes *and* Herbs *layd up moist; of* Lime *unquenched; and such like.* Instruments *also which generate* Heat *onely by* Motion. *And further,* Places *for Strong* Insolations; *And againe,* Places *under the* Earth, *which by* Nature, *or* Art, *yeeld* Heat. *These diverse* Heats *we use, As the* Nature *of the* Operation, *which wee intend, requireth.*

We have also Perspective-Houses, *where we make* Demonstrations *of all* Lights, & Radiations: *And of all* Colours: *And out of* Things uncoloured *and* Transparent, *we can represent unto you all severall* Colours; *Not in* Raine-Bowes, *as it is in* Gemms, *and* Prismes,) *but of themselves Single. We represent also all* Multiplications *of* Light, *which we carry to great* Distance, *and make so* Sharp, *as to discerne small* Points *and* Lines. *Also all* Colourations *of* Light; *All* Delutions *and* Deceits *of the* Sight, *in* Figures, Magnitudes, Motions, Colours: *All* Demonstrations *of* Shadows. *We finde also diverse Means yet unknown to you, of* Producing *of* Light, *originally, from diverse* Bodies. *Wee procure meanes of Seeing* Objects a-far off; *As in the* Heaven, & Remote Places: *And represent* Things Neare *as* A-far off; *And* Things A-far off *as* Neare; *Making* Faigned Distances. *We have also* Helps *for the* Sight, *far above* Spectacles & Glasses *in use. We have also* Glasses *and* Meanes, *to see* Small *and* Minute Bodies, *perfectly and distinctly; As the* Shapes *and* Colours *of* Small Flies & Worms, Graines & Flawes *in* Gems *which cannot otherwise be seen,* Observations *in* Urine *and* Bloud, *not otherwise to be seene. We make* Artificiall Raine-Bowes, Halo's, & Circles *about* Light. *We represent also all manner of* Reflexions, Refractions, & Multiplications *of* Visuall Beames *of* Objects.

We have also Precious Stones *of all kinds, many of them of great Beauty, and to you unknowne:* Crystalls *likewise; And* Glasses *of diverse kinds;*

And amongst them some of Mettals Vitrificated, *and other* Materialls, *besides those of which you make* Glasse. *Also a Number of* Fossiles, *and* Imperfect Minerals, *which you have not. Likewise* Loadstones *of Prodigious Vertue: And other rare* Stones, *both* Naturall, & Artificiall. *We have also* Sound-Houses, *where we practise and demonstrate all* Sounds, & *their* Generation. *We have* Harmonies *which you have not, of* Quarter-Sounds,[1] *and lesser* Slides *of* Sounds. *Diverse* Instruments *of* Musick *likewise to you unknowne, some* Sweeter *than any you have; Together with* Bells *and* Rings *that are dainty and sweet. Wee represent* Small Sounds *as* Great *and* Deepe; *Likewise* Great Sounds, Extenuate *and* Sharpe; *We make diverse* Tremblings *and* Warblings *of* Sounds, *which in their* Originall *are* Entire. *We represent and imitate all* Articulate Sounds & Letters, *and the* Voices *and* Notes *of* Beasts *and* Birds. *We have certain* Helps, *which set to the* Eare *doe further the* Hearing *greatly. We have also diverse* Strange *and* Artificiall Eccho's, Reflecting *the* Voice *many times, and as it were* Tossing *it: And some that give back the* Voice Lowder *than it came, some* Shriller, *and some* Deeper; *Yea some rendering the* Voice, Differing *in the* Letters *or* Articulate Sound, *from that they receive. Wee have also meanes to convey* Sounds *in* Trunks *and* Pipes, *in strange* Lines, *and* Distances.

We have also Perfume-Houses; *wherewith we joyne also* Practices *of* Taste. *Wee* Multiply Smells, *which may seeme strange. We* Imitate Smells, *making all* Smells *to breath out of other* Mixtures *than those that give them. Wee make diverse* Imitations *of* Tast *likewise, so that they will deceive any* Mans Taste. *And in this* House *we containe also a* Confiture-House, *where wee make all* Sweet-Meats,[2] Dry *and* Moist; *And diverse pleasant* Wines, Milks, Broaths, *and* Sallets,[3] *farre in greater varietie, than you have.*

We have also Engine-Houses, *where are prepared* Engines *and* Instruments *for all* Sorts *of* Motions. *There we imitate and practise to make* Swifter Motions, *than any you have, either out of your* Musketts, *or any* Engine *that you have: And to* Make *them, and* Multiply *them more* Easily, *and with* small Force, *by* Wheeles, *and other* Meanes: *And to make them* Stronger, *and more* Violent, *than yours are; Exceeding your greatest* Cannons, *and* Basilisks. *We represent also* Ordnance *and* Instruments *of* Warre, *and* Engines *of all* Kindes: *And likewise New* Mixtures *and* Compositions *of* Gun-powder, Wild-Fires *burning in* Water, *and* Unquench-

---

1 quarter-tones
2 candies or candied fruits
3 salads

able. *Also* Fire-workes *of all* Varietie, *both for* Pleasure, *and* Use. *Wee imi-tate also* Flights *of* Birds; *We have some* Degrees *of* Flying *in the* Aire. *We have* Ships *and* Boats *for* Going under Water, *and* Brooking of Seas; *Also* Swimming-Girdles *and* Supporters. *We have diverse curious* Clocks; *And other like* Motions *of* Returne: *And some* Perpetuall Motions. *Wee imitate also* Motions *of* Living Creatures, *by* Images, *of* Men, Beasts, Birds, Fishes, *and* Serpents. *Wee have also a great Number of other various* Motions, *strange for* Equalitie, Fineness, *and* Subtiltie.

We have also a Mathematicall House, *where are represented all* Instruments, *as well of* Geometry, *as* Astronomy, *exquisitely made.*

Wee have also Houses of Deceits of the Senses; *where wee represent all manner of* Feats *of* Jugling, False Apparitions, Impostures, *and* Illusions; *And their* Fallac[i]es. *And surely you will easily beleeve that we, that have so many* Things *truely* Naturall, *which induce* Admiration, *could in a* World *of* Particulars deceive *the* Senses, *if we would disguise those* Things, *and labour to make them seeme more* Miraculous. *But wee doe hate all* Impostures, *and* Lies: *Insomuch as we have severely forbidden it to all our* Fellowes, *under paine of Ignominy and Fines, that they doe not shew any* Naturall Worke *or* Thing, Adorned *or* Swelling; *but onely* Pure *as it is, and without all* Affectation *of* Strangenesse.

These are (my Sonne) the Riches of Salomons House.

For the severall Employments *and* Offices *of our* Fellowes; *We have Twelve that* Sayle *into* Forraine Countries, *under the* Names *of other* Nations, *(for our owne wee conceal;) Who bring us the* Bookes, *and* Abstracts, *and* Patternes *of* Experiments *of all other* Parts. *These wee call* Merchants *of* Light.

Wee have Three that Collect *the* Experiments *which are in all* Bookes. *These wee call* Depredatours.

Wee have Three that Collect *the* Experiments *of all* Mechanicall Arts; *And also of* Liberall Sciences; *And also of* Practises *which are not* Brought into Arts. *These we call* Mystery-Men.

We have Three that try New Experiments, *such as themselves thinke good. These wee call* Pioners *or* Miners.

We have Three that Draw *the* Experiments *of the* Former Foure[1] *into* Titles, *and* Tables, *to give the better light, for the drawing of* Observations

---

1   the four aforementioned groups

and Axiomes *out of them. These we call* Compilers.

We have Three that bend themselves, Looking *into the* Experiments *of their* Fellowes, *and cast about how to draw out of them* Things *of* Use, *and* Practice *for* Mans life, *and* Knowledge, *as well for* Workes, *as for* Plaine Demonstration *of* Causes, Meanes *of* Naturall Divinations, *and the easie and cleare* Discovery, *of the* Vertues *and* Parts *of* Bodies. *These wee call* Dowry-men *or* Benefactours.

Then after diverse Meetings *and* Consults *of our whole* Number, *to consider of the former* Labours & Collections, *we have Three that take care, out of them, to* Direct New Experiments, *of a Higher* Light, *more* Penetrating *into* Nature *than the* Former. *These we call* Lamps.

We have Three others that doe Execute *the* Experiments *so* Directed, *and* Report *them. These we call* Inoculatours.

Lastly, we have Three that raise the former Discoveries *by* Experiments, *into* Greater Observations, Axiomes, *and* Aphorismes. *These we call* Interpreters *of* Nature.

Wee have also, as you must thinke, Novices *and* Apprentices, *that the Succession of the former Employed Men doe not faile; Besides, a great Number of* Servants *and* Attendants, Men *and* Women. *And this we doe also: Wee have* Consultations, *which of the* Inventions *and* Experiences, *which wee have discovered, shall be Published, and which not: And take all an* Oath *of* Secrecy, *for the Concealing of those which wee thinke fit to keepe Secret: Though some of those we doe reveale sometimes to the* State, *and some not.*

For our Ordinances *and* Rites: *Wee have two very* Long, *and* Faire Galleries: *In one of these wee place* Patterns *and* Samples *of all manner of the more* Rare *and* Excellent Inventions: *In the other wee place the* Statua's *of all* Principall Inventours. *There wee have the* Statua *of your* Columbus, *that discovered the* West-Indies: *Also the* Inventour *of* Shipps: *Your* Monke *that was the* Inventour *of* Ordnance, *and of* Gunpowder:[1] *The* Inventour *of* Musick: *The* Inventour *of* Letters: *The* Inventour *of* Printing: *The* Inventour *of* Observations *of* Astronomy: *The* Inventour *of* Works *in* Mettall: *The* Inventour *of* Glasse: *The* Inventour *of* Silke *of the* Worme: *The* Inventour *of* Wine: *The* Inventour *of* Corne *and* Bread: *The* Inventour *of* Sugars: *And all these, by more certaine Tradition, than you have. Then have we diverse* Inventours *of our* Own, *of* Excellent

---

1 Friar Roger Bacon (c. 1214–c. 1292), English scientist and philosopher

Workes; *Which since you have not seene, it were too long to make* Descriptions *of them; And besides, in the right Understanding of those* Descriptions, *you might easily erre. For upon every* Invention *of Valew, wee erect a* Statua *to the* Inventour, *and give him a Liberall and Honourable* Reward. *These* Statua's *are, some of* Brasse; *some of* Marble *and* Touch-stone; *some of* Cedar *and other speciall* Woods *guilt*[1] *and adorned; some of* Iron; *some of* Silver; *some of* Gold.

Wee have certaine Hymnes *and* Services, *which we say daily, of* Laud & Thanks *to* God, *for his Marvellous* Works: *And* Formes *of* Prayers, *imploring his* Aide *and* Blessing, *for the* Illumination *of our* Labours, *and the* Turning *of them into* Good *and* Holy Uses.

Lastly, we have Circuits *or* Visits, *of diverse* Principall Cities *of the* Kingdome; *where, as it commeth to passe, we doe publish such New* Profitable Inventions, *as we thinke good. And wee doe also declare* Naturall Divinations[2] *of* Diseases, Plagues, Swarmes *of* Hurtful Creatures, Scarcitie, Tempests, Earth-quakes, Great Inundations, Comets, Temperature *of the* Yeare, *and diverse other Things; And we give* Counsell *thereupon, what the* People *shall doe, for the* Prevention *and* Remedy *of them.*

And when Hee had sayd this, Hee stood up: And I, as I had beene taught, kneeled downe, and He layd his Right Hand upon my Head, and said; GOD *blesse thee, my* Sonne; *And* GOD *blesse this Relation, which I have made. I give thee leave to Publish it, for the Good of other Nations; For wee here are in* GODS Bosome, *a Land unknowne.* And so hee left me; Having assigned a Valew of about two Thousand Duckets, for a Bountie to mee and my Fellowes. For they give great Largesses, where they come, upon all occasions.

The rest was not Perfected.

MAGNALIA NATURAE,
PRAECIPUE QUOAD USUS HUMANOS.

The Prolongation *of* Life.
The Restitution *of* Youth *in some* Degree.
The Retardation *of* Age.

---

1 gilt
2 forecasts

The Curing *of* Diseases *counted* Incurable.

The Mitigation *of* Paine.

More Easie *and lesse* Loathsome Purgings.

The Increasing *of* Strength *and* Activitie.

The Increasing *of* Ability *to suffer* Torture *or* Paine.

The Altering *of* Complexions: *And* Fatnesse, *and* Leannesse.

The Altering *of* Statures.

The Altering *of* Features.

The Increasing *and* Exalting *of the* Intellectuall Parts.

Versions *of* Bodies *into other* Bodies.

Making *of* New Species.

Transplanting *of one* Species *into another.*

Instruments *of* Destruction, *as of* Warre, *and* Poyson.

Exhilaration *of the* Spirits, *and* Putting *them in good* Disposition.

Force *of the* Imagination, *either upon another* Body, *or upon the* Body *it selfe.*

Acceleration *of* Time *in* Maturations.

Acceleration *of* Time *in* Clarifications.

Acceleration *of* Putrefaction.

Acceleration *of* Decoction.

Acceleration *of* Germination.

Making Rich Composts *for the* Earth.

Impressions *of the* Aire, *and* Raising *of* Tempests.

Great Alteration; *As in* Induration, Emollition, &c.

Turning Crude *and* Watry Substances *into* Oyly *and* Unctuous Substances.

Drawing of New Foods *out of* Substances *not now in* Use.

Making New Threds *for* Apparell; *And* New Stuffes; *Such as are* Paper,
Glasse, &c.

Naturall Divinations.

Deceptions *of the* Senses.

Greater Pleasures *of the* Senses

Artificiall Mineralls *and* Cements.

FINIS

4. SELECTIONS FROM *LETTERS AND POEMS IN HONOUR OF...MARGARET, DUCHESS OF NEWCASTLE* (1676)

This compilation of letters and poems addressed to Margaret Cavendish during her lifetime was published posthumously by her husband as a memorial volume, appearing in 1676, the year of the Duke's own death. It includes not only the usual quota of complimentary acknowledgments from recipients of her patronage, but also suggestive evidence of some lively intellectual exchanges between Cavendish and well-known scientists such as Christiaan Huygens, as they debated the scientific issues and enigmas of the day.

[From Joseph Glanvill]

Madam,

I am very sorry that my unhappy Fate hath necessitated an unbecoming Slowness in acknowledging a Favour, that requires all possibilities of Gratitude, and exceeds them. But yet, had I nothing else to say in excuse of my no earlier return to the last Noble effects of your Graces[1] goodness, it were sufficient; That my sence of that mighty Honour was too big for my Pen; and when I began to speak my resentments[2] of it, I found my self as unable to express them, as to deserve their occasion. But yet, Madam, this is not all the reason, for I was from home when your Grace's Present came, and have been so almost ever since; otherwise I had not added to my want of merit on other accounts, that also of appearing insensible, and defective in endeavours of acknowledgment; I must say endeavours, for my Gratitude can rise no higher. Since my receipt of your Grace's ingenious Works, I have, as my occasions would permit, cast my Eyes again into them, and I am sorry they cannot dwell there, where I find so pleasing, and so instructive an entertainment. And though I must crave your Pardon for dissenting from your Grace's Opinion in some things, I admire the quickness, and vigor of your Conceptions, in all: In which your Grace hath this peculiar among Authors that they are,

---

1   Dukes and Duchesses were addressed as "your grace."
2   deep appreciation

in the strictest sense, your own, your Grace being indebted to nothing for them, but your own happy Wit, and Genius; a thing so uncommon even among the most celebrated Writers of our Sex, that it ought to be acknowledged with wonder in yours. And really, Madam, your Grace hath set us a patern, that we ought to admire, but cannot imitate. And whereas you are pleased sometimes to mention your being no Scholar, as an excuse of defects, your modesty supposeth; By that acknowledgment you shew our imperfections that pretend we are so, rather than discover any of your own.[1]

As for the last Trifle I was bold to present to your Graces Eye, it is much indebted to the obliging reception you were pleased to afford it; and the re[2] is nothing that sets such a lustre on your Graces great Wit, and Intellectual Perfections, as that sweet candor of your Spirit that renders you so accessible, even to your meanest admirers. Whereas your Grace is pleased to object against some part of the design of my Discourse, that it sets the perfection of the sense higher than that of Ratiocination; I humbly desire that your Grace would consider, that there are two sorts of Reasoning, *viz.* Those that the Mind advanceth from its own imbred *Idæa's* and native Store, such are all Metaphysical Contemplations. And those natural researches which are raised from experiment, and the objects of sense. The former are indeed most perfect when they are most abstracted from the grosness of things sensible, but the others are then most compleat when they are most accomodated to them; and when they are not, they are Aery, and Phantastick. Now what I have said about those matters is to tie down the mind in Physical things, to consider Nature as it is, to lay a Foundation in sensible collections,[3] and from thence to proceed to general Propositions, and Discourses. So that my aim is, that we may arise according to the order of nature by degrees from the exercise of our Senses, to that of our Reasons; which indeed is most noble and most perfect when it concludes aright, but not so when 'tis mistaken: And that it may so conclude and arrive to that perfection, it must begin in sense: And the more experiments our reasons have to work on, by so much they are the more likely to be certain in their conclu-

---

1 I.e., by modestly declaring you are not a scholar so as to excuse your own imagined faults, you reveal the shortcomings of those of us who profess to be real scholars.

2 *re* (Latin *res*): thing or matter

3 sensory data

sions, and consequently more perfect in their actings. But Madam, I doubt I begin to be tedious, and therefore, at present dare add no more, but that I am,

Illustrious Madam,
Your Grace's most Humble and most devoted Servant,
Jos. Glanvill.[1]

[From Walter Charleton]

To the Incomparable Princess, Margaret, Dutchess of New-castle.
Madam,

Among many other things, by which your Grace is pleased to distinguish your self from other Writers, this seems to be not the least remarkable; that whereas they imploy only their wit, labour, and time, in composing Books, You bestow also great summs of Money in Printing Yours: and not content to enrich our Heads alone, with your rare Notions, you go higher, and adorn our Libraries, with your elegant Volumes. To that general Charity, which disposeth you to benefit all Mankind, you have added a singular Bounty, whereby you oblige particular Persons: and out of a Nobleness peculiar to your Nature, you cause your Munificence to Rival your Industry.

This, *Madam,* among many other your Excellencies, Gratitude commands me to acknowledge; Your Grace having been pleased to number me among those, whom you vouchsafed to honour with such extraordinary Presents. For which I know not how to shew my self duely thankful, otherwise than by celebrating your Generosity, and returning you some account of the good effects they wrought in me, while I perused them. Which considering the Noble End for which you wrote them, and my inability to make you a more proportionate retribution; will not, I hope, be unacceptable to you. To this purpose, therefore, I am bold to send your Grace this rude[2] Paper. Which yet I design, not as a Panegyric of your worth (for what affects us with admiration, strikes us also with dumbness: and Stars are best discerned by their own lustre) but as a short Scheme of my own grateful Sentiments. And if I be not so happy, to deliver them in

---

1 Joseph Glanvill (1636-80), an original Fellow of the Royal Society, author of *Philosophical Considerations touching Witches and Witchcraft* (1666)

2 unpolished

Language agreeable to the dignity of the Subject, I humbly beseech you to consider, that such occasions offer themselves very rarely; and that nothing is more difficult, than to make the Pen observe *Decorum*, where Reason is put into disorder; Justice, *Madam*, requires you should pardon the effects of that astonishment, whereof your Wonders are the cause.

They tell us, that the End of all Books is either profit, or pleasure: but I think that distinction (as many other in the Schools)[1] might well be spared: because, in truth, profit supposeth pleasure; and pleasure is the greatest profit; nor am I ashamed to profess, that in all my reading I have no other aim but pleasure. It will not then, I hope, *Madam*, be thought derogatory to the Profitableness of your Grace's Books, If I acknowledge my self to have received very great pleasure in reading them. And this pleasure was so charming, it so far transported me, as often to make me wish, you might never entertain a resolution of causing your works to be Translated into any other Language: that so all Ingenious Forreigners, invited by the Fame of your most delightful Writings, might be brought to do Honour to the *English* Tongue, by learning it on purpose to understand them. For I am zealous for the Reputation of my native Language, and of so communicative a temper, as to desire all men should participate of what I find delectable. Besides, I could not but remember, that I had known a great Man of our Nation, who studied *Italian*, only to acquaint himself with the Mathematiques of *Galileo*, in his *Del Movimento*, and *Saggiatore*; and *Spanish*, meerly out of love to the Incomparable History of *Don Quixot*:[2] and was thereupon the more apt to promise my self that your Grace's Works, no less admirable in their kind, than either of those, would have the like influence upon some of the *Bons Esprits* beyond Sea.[3] But this, *Madam*, was only my Wish: it is not now my Counsel. Should I here particularly recount to you, what the things were, that raised this so great delight in me, I should both offend by prolixity, and tacitly cast disparagement upon the rest. For,

---

1   the academic establishment, especially those who maintained Aristotelian or medieval scholastic traditions

2   Galileo Galilei (1564-1642): Italian physicist and astronomer; Miguel de Cervantes (1547-1616): Spanish author of *El Ingenioso Hidalgo Don Quixote de la Mancha* (1603)

3   European intellectuals

Pauperis est, numerare Pecus,
He is but poor, who can account his Wealth:

And what the witty *Roman Stoic* said of the excellent sayings of *Zeno,* *Cleanthes, Chrysippus* and other Princes of that Sect,[1] may be conveniently accommodated to the delightful Remarks every where occuring in your Books, *viz.* That *no choice can be made, where all things are equally Eminent.* However, because there is no satisfaction in Generals,[2] and that Order is necessary to plainness: give me leave to divide my Text into three parts, your *Natural Philosophy,*[3] your *Morals,*[4] and your *Poetry.*

For your NATURAL *Philosophy;* it is ingenious and free, and may be, for ought I know, Excellent: but give me leave, *Madam,* to confess, I have not yet been so happy, as to discover much therein that's *Apodictical,*[5] or wherein I think my self much obliged to acquiesce. But, that may be the fault of my own dull Brain: and Oracles have been after found true, that were at first Dark and *Enigmatical.* Again I am somewhat slow of belief also; a continual seeker: as conceiving, I have too much cause to be of *Seneca's*[6] opinion, that *Men may, indeed enquire and determine what is most probable, but God alone knows what's true, in the things of Nature.* Nor am I single in this Sceptical Judgement: The ROYAL SOCIETY[7] it self (the Tribunal of Philosophical Doctrines) is of a constitution exceedingly strict and rigid in the examination of Theories concerning Nature; no respecter of Persons or Authorities, where Verity is concerned; seldom, or never yielding assent without full conviction: and that's the Reason why it made choice of these three Words for its Motto, *Nullius in verba.*[8]

---

1 the Stoic school of philosophy; Zeno of Citium (335-263 BCE): Greek philosopher, founder of the Stoic school; Cleanthes (331-232 BCE): Greek Stoic philosopher, disciple of Zeno of Citium; Chrysippus (280-207 BCE): successor to Cleanthes as head of the Greek Stoic school
2 generalities
3 natural philosophy: the seventeenth-century term for science
4 ethics or moral philosophy
5 apodictic: demonstrated or established incontrovertibly
6 Lucius Annaeus Seneca (c. 4 BCE-65 CE), Roman politician and Stoic philosopher
7 Royal Society, founded in 1660, incorporated by Charles II in 1662 as the Royal Society of London for Improving Natural Knowledge, committed to the advancement of science
8 *nullius in verba*: nothing in (mere) words

This *Madam*, can be no discredit to your Philosophy in particular, because common to all others: and he is a bold Man, who dares to exempt the *Physics* of *Aristotle* himself, or of *Democritus*, or *Epicurus*, or *Des Cartes*, or Mr. *Hobbs*,[1] or any other hitherto known. For my part, Seriously, I should be loath to affirm, that they are any other but ingenious Comments of Mens Wits upon the dark and inexplicable Text of the World; plausible Conjectures at best; and no less different, perhaps, from the true History of Nature, than Romances are from the true actions of *Heroes*. Nor will I adventure to determine, which of the two, *Aristotle* or your Grace, hath given us the best definition of the Humane[2] Soul: He, when he calls it *Entelechia*;[3] or you when you say, it is a *Supernatural something, &c*. So difficult is it to make a judgement of what seems incomprehensible.

Nor are you to be discouraged, *Madam*, If your Philosophy have not the fate to be publickly read in all Universities of *Europe*, as your Grace, doubtless out of a most Heroic ambition to benefit Mankind, desires it should. For, while Men are Men, there will be different Interests, and consequently different Opinions: nor is the multitude of Followers a certain sign of the Soundness, but of the Gainfulness of any Doctrine. If, therefore, the World, which is obstinate (you know) and governed by prejudice, will not be induced to esteem, what you think useful; the blame lyes not at your Door, and you ought to consolate[4] your self with this reflexion; that you have sufficiently testified your good intentions, and done more than your Duty, in publishing your Conceptions. Besides, the *Virtuosi*[5] of our *English* Universities have, of late years, proclaimed open War against the tyranny of Dogmatizing in any Art or Science: and as for those of the *Roman Religion*; there is, I fear me, but little hope, of making them your Proselites.[6] Because those canting Polititians, called *School-men*, having made a

---

1 Democritus of Abdera (c. 460- c. 370 BCE): Greek philosopher, proponent of atomistic theory; Epicurus of Samos (341-270 BCE): Greek atomistic philosopher; René Descartes (1596-1650): French mathematician and philosopher; Thomas Hobbes (1588-1679): English philosopher

2 human

3 *entelechia*: in Aristotle's use, the condition in which a potentiality has become an actuality; the soul as opposed to the body

4 console

5 virtuoso: in seventeenth-century usage, a learned amateur of the arts and especially the sciences

6 Roman religion: Roman Catholicism; proselyte: a convert or follower

new and party-colour'd Vest for the Church, of a kind of Drugget, consisting of the Thrums of *Peripatetic* Philosophy, cunningly interwoven among the Golden threads of the Christian Faith; and prevailed, upon Princes to make it Piacular for any Scholar to appear with his Judgement clad in any other Livery:[1] it is not very unlikely, the Professors there will soon be brought to offend their Superiors, by laying aside the defence of *Aristotle's* Maxims, to assume the Patronage of New. So that in my silly conceipt, as the Cabbage is observed to starve the Vine, if set too near: so the Philosophy of *Thomas Aquinas*[2] and others of the same mystical Tribe, will hinder the growth of yours, in the same Ground.

For your MORAL Philosophy (for so I take liberty to call your occasional Reflections upon the Actions, Manners, and Fortunes of Men) Your Grace has not, indeed tied up your Pen to the laborious rules of Method, or the formality of a new Systeme in *Ethics*: but (what is as well) you have opportunely, and under various heads, dispersed many useful remarks, concerning Prudence, as well Civil, as Domestic, in most of your Writings. And this, it may be presumed, you were pleased to do, not for want of Skill to reduce your rules of life into the order of dependence and connexion; but with design, to shew your plenty, and surprize your Readers with good counsel even where they least expect it. You chose rather to regale us with delicate Fictions, under the veil whereof wholesom instructions are neatly contrived, than to embarass and tire us with the observation of a long train of Precepts, which are never so effectual, as when naturally flowing from agreeable Instances and Examples: Your very interludes contain adviso's, and your digressions are seasonably instructive: like

---

1   schoolmen: scholastic or Aristotelian philosophers; party-colour'd: multicoloured; drugget: material made half of wool and half of linen or silk, used for wearing apparel; thrums: ends of unwoven threads left on the loom when the web is cut off; Peripatetic school of philosophy: adherents of Aristotle's school, the *Peripatos*; piacular: sinful or wicked; livery: a distinctive badge or suit worn by servants or retainers; Charleton asserts here that the Catholic Church has used its political influence to force continental scholars to maintain traditional Aristotelian doctrines rather than adopt new scientific principles, hence they are unlikely to be receptive to Cavendish's theories

2   conceipt: conceit or opinion; Thomas Aquinas (c. 1225-74): medieval Italian philosopher and theologian, whose *Summa Theologica* aimed at reconciling Christian theology with Aristotelian philosophy

wise Husbandmen, you plant Fruit-Trees in your Hedge-rows, and set Strawberries and Rasberries among your Roses and Lillies. This, *Madam*, is a piece of no small art, though not obvious to common Eyes: and if any dislike the course you have taken in thus scattering and disguising your *Morals*; I would have him asked this Question, Whether or no it be folly for a man to refuse to gather Oranges and Citrons, only because the trees that offer them, are not ranged in the Order of *Cyrus's Quincunx?*[1] or whether a Nosegay be less fragrant, because pluck'd from Flowers growing dispersedly? To all who have read your *Comical Tales*, with the same purity of Mind, with which you wrote them, and are withal qualified to search into the Mythology of all your imaginary *Dialogues*: to all such, I say, it is evident, that you have drawn the Images of all the *Virtues*, on one hand, and their opposite *Vices*, on the other, so much to the life; that men, beholding them, must be, by grateful violence,[2] compelled to love the Pulchritude of those, and abhor the deformity of these.[3] Now, this, *Madam*, you could not have done had you not first had the *Ideas* of all Virtues within your self: it being absolutely necessary for a Painter, first to conceive the form or similitude of the thing he intends to represent, in his own Imagination; and then to make the resemblance according to that form. So that in strictness of truth, those Pictures we call *Originals*, are but Copies, yea Copies of Copies:[4] as being first drawn from the life in the Phantasy, and after pourtrai'd upon Tables.[5] Besides this, your Grace is further happy, in that the *Morals* of your *Pen* are clearly exemplified in those of your *Life*; in which I have never heard any thing blamed, any thing disputed, unless whether it hath been more *Innocent*, or more *Obliging*. In fine, the Documents of both your *Pen* and *Life* seem to be so good, that whoever is able to moderate his Passions, and regulate his Actions by them, needs not to seek further after *Happiness*: nor need I fear to pronounce him arrived at such perfec-

---

1   quincunx: an arrangement for planting or growing trees, with a tree placed at each of four corners, and one in the centre

2   agreeable force

3   love the pulchritude of those, i.e., the beauty of the virtues; abhor the deformity of these, i.e. of their opposite vices

4   Charleton here echoes Plato's denigration of the visual arts as the "copies of copies."

5   tables: boards or other flat surfaces on which a picture is painted

tion, that it will not be easy for him to be brought to do ill, either out of *Weakness*, or out of *Design*.

For your *POETRY*; therein your Grace hath more than a single advantage above others.

First, Your Vein appears equally facile, equally free, and copious upon all occasions, in all sorts of arguments.[1] The Buskin and the Sock[2] are equally fit for your Muses Legs. Your Phansy is too generous to be restrained: Your Invention too nimble to be fettered. Hence it is, that you do not always confine your Sense to Verse; nor your Verses to Rhythme; nor your Rhythme to the quantity and sounds of Sillables. Your Descriptions, Expressions, Similies, Allegories, Metaphors, Epithets, Numbers, all flow in upon you of their own accord, and in full Tides: and Verses stand ready minted in the Treasury of your Brain, as Tears in some Womens Eyes, waiting to be called forth. So that in you is verified the Doctrine of *Plato*, in his *Dialogue* intitled *Io*; that *Poesy* is not a faculty proceeding from judgement, or acquired by labour and industry; but a certain divine Fury, or *Enthusiasm*, which scorning the controle of Reason, transports the Spirit in Raptures, as *Jove's* Eagle did *Ganymed*,[3] or as Witches are said to be wafted above the Clouds on the wings of their Familiars. Which is, perhaps, the ground of that old saying, *nemo fit Poeta*, no Poet is made, but born so: as the rage and liberty of a Poetic Genius gave occasion to paint *Pegasus* with Wings, in a flying posture, and without a Bridle.[4]

Secondly, In your whole *Oglio* of Poems,[5] I find nothing which is not intirely *Your own*. Like good Housewifes in the Countrey, you, make a Feast wholly of your own provisions: yea, even the Dressing, Sawces, and Garniture of the Dishes are *Your own*. And were *Perilius Faustinus* revived (he, who out of envy to the Glory of *Virgil*, made

---

1   arguments: themes or subjects

2   buskin: the high boot worn in Athenian tragedy, opposed to the sock or low shoe worn in ancient Greek comedy

3   Ganymede: according to Greek mythology, a young Trojan prince who was carried off by an eagle to become Zeus's cupbearer

4   Pegasus: the winged horse who in striking his foot on the rock at Mount Helicon brought about the flow of the Hippocrene, a mythical spring believed to be the inspiration of poets; Charleton here implies that true poets, like Pegasus, are unbridled by artificial rules

5   olio: a Portuguese stew made with a variety of ingredients, hence a miscellany, such as Cavendish's *The Worlds Olio* (1655)

and published a large Catalogue of his Thefts from *Homer* and *Hesiod*) he could hardly discover so much as a single Verse borrowed, by you, from any Poet, antient or modern. So circumspect you are to avoid being thought a Plagiary, that you walk not in beaten Paths, but decline even the rules and methods of your Predecessors, and scorn Imitation, as a kind of Theft. A commendation, *Madam*, due to very few, perhaps to none besides your self. As your Grace, therefore, owes all your Poesy to the inspiration of your own happy Genius alone; so we owe all the Pleasure we are sensible of in reading your Poems, to you alone. I may have many rivals in these my thankful acknowledgements, you can have no Competitor in the Glory of their occasions.

This double Felicity is augmented by the accession of two others, no less worthy admiration. *One* is, that as you have made your self an *Original*, so are you likewise secure from being *Copied*. You have indeed, given the world an illustrious Example; but you have given what it cannot take, the Example being of that height, that it is hardly attainable. You provoke our Emulation, and at the same time cast us into despair. Your Poetical Fancies rather brave, than instruct our capacities: and by setting before our Eyes things inimitable, you vex our ambition, and oblige us to an unprofitable trouble.

Another is, that you exceed all of your delicate Sex, not only in this age, but in all ages past. It would puzle the best Historian to find your Parallel among the most famous Women: and in the Monuments of the *Roman* greatness, even while that Glorious Nation held the Empire as well of Virtue and Wit, as that of the World, I cannot meet with an *Heroine*, to whom I dare to compare you. There are, I confess, who tell us of a Noble *Roman* Lady, one *Sulpitia*, who composed a History of *Domitian's* times, in Hexametre Verses, and wrote many Elegant Poems besides;[1] and who hath been highly celebrated by *Martial, Tibullus, Sidonius Apollinaris*, and of late by *Scaliger*

---

1   Charleton appears to have conflated two Roman poets named Sulpicia. Sulpicia the wife of Calenus was praised for her poetry by the Roman poet Martial; a satire on Domitian's reign was also attributed to her. Sulpicia the daughter of Servius Sulpicius Rufus (a friend of Cicero and Tibullus) wrote six short elegies about her love for a young man named Cerinthus. See S. B. Pomeroy, *Goddesses, Whores, Wives, and Slaves* (London: Robert Hale & Co., 1975), pp. 172–4.

also,[1] as an eminent Pattern both of a Chast and Immaculate Life, and of a neat Poetical Wit: and once I had some thoughts of drawing a Parallel betwixt that Lady and your Grace. But, upon a second examination of the particular Remarks, wherein I had fansied the resemblance chiefly to consist; and a more serious review of the Story of her Life, and the remains of her Pen, (extant among the *Fragments* of *Latine Poets*, and usually annexed to *Petronius Arbiter*)[2] I perceived, I could not proceed in that resolution, without disadvantage on your part, by a conference so unequal; and thereupon resumed my former cogitation, that your Grace's Statue ought to be placed alone, and at the upper end, in the *Gallery of Heroic Women*, and upon a Pedestal more advanced than the rest. We read not that Nature hath been so Prodigal of her choicest Largesses, as to produce two *Cicero*'s, or two *Virgil*'s, or two *Ben Johnson*'s: why, then, should we seek after your Equal? It was their glory to be single[3]: and it must be yours, to have no Peer, for ought we know, you are the *First* great Lady, that ever Wrote so much and so much of your own: and, for ought we can divine, you will also be the *Last*.

These, *Madam*, are a few of those swarms of thoughts that crowded into my unquiet Head, when I proposed to my self to express some part at least of the great Honour and Reverence I owe your Grace. If I have so far obeyed the impulse of my Gratitude and Devotion, as to put them into Words, and offer them to your knowledge; it was not, I assure you, out of a vain conceipt, that they were answerable either to your vast Merits, or to my Obligations; but meerly upon Confidence, you would descend to exercise your Goodness and Candor, in receiving them as a simple recognition of both. And if I have suppressed the rest; it was out of good Manners, and a due fear of farther offending your Patience. I am not ignorant, *Madam*, that our Prayers to God, and our Addresses to Princes ought to be short. Resigning you, therefore, to the conversation of your own more

---

1 Martial (c. 40- c. 104 CE): Roman poet, celebrated for his epigrams; Tibullus (48?-19 BCE): Roman elegiac poet; Sidonius Apollinaris (c. 430- c. 479 CE): Gallo-Roman bishop, author of panagyric verse; Joseph Justus Scaliger (1540-1609): acclaimed Renaissance classical scholar and textual editor

2 Petronius Arbiter (died 65 CE): Roman author of the fragmentary novel *The Satyricon*; his story *The Matron of Ephesus* inspired Charleton's *Ephesian Matron* (1639)

3 unique

ingenious and useful thoughts, and to the Tranquill Fruition of those intellectual pleasures, that continually spring up in you from the Virtues of your Life, and the Fame of your Writings; I most humbly beg your favourable Interpretation of what I have here weakly said, and with all Submission imaginable, cast my self at your Feet, as becomes

Your Graces, Just Honourer, and most Intirely Devoted Servant,
Walter Charleton.[1]
From my House in Covent-Garden
May 7. 1667.

[From Christiaan Huygens]
Madam,

I had the Honour to hear so good Solutions given by your Excellency upon divers Questions moved in a whole Afternoon, you was pleased to bestow upon my unworthy Conversation, that I am turning to School with all speed, humbly beseeching your Excellence may be so bountiful towards my Ignorance, as to Instruct me about the Natural Reason of those Wonderful Glasses, which, as I told you, *Madam,* will fly into Powder, if one breaks but the least top of their tails: whereas without that way they are hardly to be broken by any weight or strength.[2] The King of *France* is, as yet unresolved in the Question, notwithstanding he hath been curious to move it to an Assembly of the best Philosophers of *Paris,* the *Microcosme* of his Kingdom. Your Excellence hath no cause to apprehend[3] the cracking blow of these little innoxious Gunns. If you did, *Madam,* a Servant may hold them close in his Fist, and your self can break the little end of their Tail without the least danger. But, as I was bold to tell your Excellence, I should be loath to believe any Female Fear should reign amongst so much over-masculine Wisdom, as the World doth admire in you. I pray God to bless your Excellence with a dayly increase of it, and your worthy self to grant, that among those Admirers, I may

---

1   Walter Charleton (1619-1707), physician to Charles I and Charles II, Royal Society fellow, and writer on medical and philosophical topics
2   glass drops known as "Rupert's drops," formed by dropping molten glass into water; the stresses set up by their rapid cooling caused them to explode when their glass tails were broken off (see Grant 194-5)
3   fear

strive to deserve, by way of my humble Service, the Honour to be accounted,

Madam,

Your Excellencies most Humble and most Obedient Servant

Huygens de Zulichem.[1]

Hague, March 12. 1657.

I have made bold to joyn unto these a couple of poor Epigrams *I did meditate in my Journey hither, where your Excellencies Noble Tales were my best entertainment. I hope Madam, you will perceive the intention of them, through the Mist of a Language I do but harp[2] and ghess at.*

---

1 Christiaan Huygens (1629-95), renowned Dutch mathematician and physicist
2 harp: to guess

5. APHRA BEHN, PREFACE TO HER TRANSLATION OF FONTENELLE'S *ENTRETIENS SUR LA PLURALITÉ DES MONDES* (1688)

Aphra Behn (c. 1649?-89) was a popular and prolific playwright and novelist, the author of twenty-two works for the stage, as well as a substantial *oeuvre* of poetry, novels, short stories and translations both of fiction and non-fiction.[1] Her translation of Fontenelle's *Entretiens sur la pluralité des mondes*, entitled *A Discovery of New Worlds* (1688), was one of several English versions that appeared soon after the original French publication of Fontenelle's very popular text. Well acquainted with an immense range of English and continental literature, Behn reveals a knowledgable familiarity with the scholarship and controversies of the new science in her introductory preface.

THE TRANSLATOR'S PREFACE.

The General Applause this little Book of the Plurality of Worlds has met with, both in *France* and *England* in the Original,[2] made me attempt to translate it into English. The Reputation of the Author, (who is the same, who writ the Dialogues of the Dead)[3] the Novelty of the Subject in vulgar Languages, and the Authors introducing a Woman as one of the speakers in these five Discourses, were further Motives for me to undertake this little work; for I thought an *English* Woman might adventure to translate any thing, a *French* Woman may be supposed to have spoken: But when I had made a Tryal, I found the Task not so easie as I believed at first: Therefore, before I say any thing, either of the Design of the Author, or of the Book it self, give me leave to say something of Translation of Prose in general: As for Translation of Verse, nothing can be added to that Incomparable Essay of the late Earl of *Roscommon*,[4] the nearer the Idioms or turn of the

---

1   For biographical details see Mendelson, *Mental World*, 116-92.
2   *Entretiens sur la pluralité des mondes* (1686), by Bernard le Bovier Fontenelle (1667-1757), French scientific popularizer
3   *Dialogues des morts* (1683)
4   Wentworth Dillon, fourth Earl of Roscommon (?1633-85), author of an *Essay on Translated Verse* (1684)

Phrase of two Languages agree, 'tis the easier to translate one into the other. The *Italian, Spanish* and *French*, are all three at best Corruptions of the *Latin*, with the mixture of *Gothick, Arabick* and *Gaulish* Words. The *Italian*, as it is nearest the *Latin*, is also nearest the *English*: For its mixture being composed of Latin, and the Language of the *Goths, Vandals*, and other *Northern* Nations, who over-ran the *Roman* Empire, and conquer'd its Language with its Provinces, most of these Northern Nations spoke the *Teutonick* or Dialects of it, of which the *English* is one also; and that's the Reason, that the *English* and *Italian* learn the Language of one another sooner than any other; because not only the Phrase, but the Accent of both do very much agree, the *Spanish* is next of kin to the *English*, for almost the same Reason: Because the *Goths* and *Vandals* having over-run *Africk*, and kept Possession of it for some hundred of Years, where mixing with the *Moors*, no doubt, gave them a great Tincture of their Tongue. These *Moors* afterwards invaded and conquered *Spain*; besides *Spain* was before that also invaded and conquered by the *Goths*, who possessed it long after the time of the two Sons of *Theodosius* the Great, *Arcadus* and *Honorius*. The *French*, as it is most remote from the *Latin*, so the Phrase and Accent differ most from the *English*: It may be, it is more agreeable with the *Welsh*, which is near a-kin to the *Basbritton* and *Biscagne*[1] Languages, which is derived from the old *Celtick* Tongue, the first that was spoken amongst the Ancient *Gauls,* who descended from the *Celts.*

The *French* therefore is of all the hardest to translate into *English*. For Proof of this, there are other Reasons also. And first, the nearer the Genious and Humour of two Nations agree, the Idioms of their Speech are the nearer; and every Body knows there is more Affinity between the *English* and *Italian* People, than the *English* and the *French*, as to their Humours; and for that Reason, and for what I have said before, it is very difficult to translate *Spanish* into *French*; and I believe hardly possible to translate *French* into *Dutch*. The second Reason is, the *Italian* Language is the same now it was some hundred of Years ago, so is the *Spanish*, not only as to the Phrase, but even as to the Words and Orthography; whereas the *French* Language has suffered more Changes this hundred Years past, since *Francis* the first,

---

1   Basque

than the Fashions of their Cloths and Ribbons, in Phrase, Words and Orthography. So that I am confident a *French* Man a hundred Years hence will no more understand an old Edition of *Froisard's* History, than he will understand *Arabick*. I confess the *French* Arms, Money and Intrigues have made their Language very universal of late, for this they are to be commended: It is an Accident, which they owe to the greatness of their King and their own Industry; and it may fall out hereafter to be otherwise. A third Reason is as I said before, that the *French* being a Corruption of the *Latin*, *French* Authors take a liberty to borrow whatever Word they want from the *Latin*, without farther Ceremony, especially when they treat of Sciences. This the *English* do not do, but at second hand from the *French*. It is Modish to Ape the *French* in every thing: Therefore, we not only naturalize their words, but words they steal from other Languages. I wish in this and several other things, we had a little more of the *Italian* and *Spanish* Humour, and did not chop and change our Language, as we do our Cloths, at the Pleasure of every *French* Tailor.

In translating *French* into *English,* most People are very cautious and unwilling to print a *French* Word at first out of a new Book, till Use has rendered it more familiar to us; and therefore it runs a little rough in *English*, to express one *French* Word, by two or three of ours; and thus much, as to the Ease and Difficulty of translating these Languages in general: But, as to the *French* in particular, it has as many Advantages of the *English*, as to the Sound, as ours has of the *French*, as to the Signification; which is another Argument of the different Genius of the two Nations. Almost all the Relatives, Articles, and Pronouns in the *French* Language, end in Vowels, and are written with two or three Letters. Many of their words begin with Vowels; so, that when a word after a Relative, Pronoun or Article, ends with a Vowel, and begins with another, they admit of their beloved Figure *Apostrophe*, and cut off the first Vowel. This they do to shun an ill sound; and they are so musical as to that, that they will go against all the Rules of Sense and Grammar, rather than fail; as for Example, speaking of a Man's Wife they say, *son Epouse*; whereas in Grammar, it ought to be *sa Epouse*; but this would throw a *French*-Man into a Fit of a Fever, to hear one say, by way of Apostrophe *S'Epouse*, as this makes their Language to run smoother, so by this they express several Words very shortly, as *qu'entend je,* in *English,* what do I hear? In this Example, three words have the Sound but of one, for Sound prevails with them in the beginning, middle and end. Secondly, their words generally end in Vowels, or if they do not, they do not pronounce the Consonant, for the most part, unless there be two together, or that the next word begins with a Vowel. Thirdly, by the help of their Relatives, they can shortly, and with ease resume a long Preceeding Sentence, in two or three short words; these are the Advantages of the *French* Tongue, all which they borrow from the *Latin*. But as the *French* do not value a plain Suit without a Garniture, they are not satisfied with the Advantages they have, but confound their own Language with needless Repetitions and Tautologies; and by a certain Rhetorical Figure, peculiar to themselves, imply twenty Lines, to express what an *English* Man would say, with more Ease and Sense in five; and this is the great Misfortune of translating *French* into *English*: If one endeavours to make it *English* Standard, it is no Translation. If one follows their Flourishes and Embroideries, it is worse than *French* Tinsel. But these defects are only comparatively, in respect of *English*: And I do not say this so much, to condemn the *French*, as to praise our own Mother-Tongue, for what we think a Deformity, they may think a Perfection; as the *Negroes* of *Guinney* think us as ugly, as we think them: But to return to my present Translation.

I have endeavoured to give you the true meaning of the Author, and have kept as near his Words as was possible; I was necessitated to add a little in some places, otherwise the Book could not have been understood. I have used all along the *Latin* Word *Axis*, which is *Axle-tree* in *English*, which I did not think so proper a Word in a Treatise of this nature; but 'tis what is generally understood by every Body. There is another Word in the two last *Nights*, which was very uneasie to me, and the more so for that it was so often repeated, which is *Tourbillion*, which signifies commonly a *Whirl-wind*; but Monsieur *Des Chartes*[1] understands it in a more general sense, and I call it a *Whirling*; the Author hath given a very good Definition of it, and I need say no more, but that I retain the Word unwillingly, in regard of what I have said in the beginning of this Preface.

I know a Character of the Book will be expected from me, and I am obliged to give it to satisfie my self for being at the pains to trans-

---

1 René Descartes (1596-1650), French mathematician and scientist

DISCOURSE OF THE PLURALITY OF WORLDS

Illustration 11: The frontispiece from John Glanvill's 1702 translation of Fontenelle's *Entretiens sur la pluralité des mondes* (1686), a book that uses a gendered dialogue to popularise science. A learned gentleman and a charming lady walk in a garden while he explains the Copernican system and she makes witty remarks. In her translation of Fontenelle's work, *A Discovery of New Worlds* (1688), Aphra Behn objects to Fontenelle's making the Lady Marquese "say a great many very silly things" (see below, p. 319). (Courtesy Special Collections, Mills Memorial Library, McMaster University.)

late it, but I wish with all my heart I could forbear it; for I have that Value for the ingenious *French* Author, that I am sorry I must write what some may understand to be a Satyr against him. The Design of the Author is to treat of this part of Natural Philosophy in a more familiar Way than any other hath done, and to make every body understand him: For this End, he introduceth a Woman of Quality as one of the Speakers in these five Discourses, whom he feigns never to have heard of any such thing as Philosophy before. How well he hath performed his Undertaking you will best judge when you have perused the Book: But if you would know before-hand my Thoughts, I must tell you freely, he hath failed in his Design; for endeavouring to render this part of Natural Philosophy familiar, he hath turned it into Ridicule; he hath pushed his wild Notion of the *Plurality of Worlds* to that heighth of Extravagancy, that he most certainly will confound those Readers, who have not Judgment and Wit to distinguish between what is truly solid (or, at least, probable) and what is trifling and airy: and there is no less Skill and Understanding required in this, than in comprehending the whole Subject he treats of. And for his Lady *Marquiese*, he makes her say a great many very silly things, tho' sometimes she makes Observations so learned, that the greatest Philosophers in *Europe* could make no better. His way of Arguing is extreamly fine, and his Examples and Comparisons are for the most part extraordinary, just, natural, and lofty, if he had not concluded with that of a *Rose*, which is very irregular. The whole Book is very unequal; the first, fourth, and the beginning of the fifth Discourses are incomparably the best. He ascribes all to Nature, and says not a Word of God Almighty, from the Beginning to the End; so that one would almost take him to be a *Pagan*. He endeavours chiefly two things; one is, that there are thousands of Worlds inhabited by Animals, besides our Earth, and hath urged this Fancy too far: I shall not presume to defend his Opinion, but one may make a very good use of many things he hath expressed very finely, in endeavouring to assist his wild Fancy; for he gives a magnificent *Idea* of the vastness of the Universe, and of the almighty and infinite Power of the Creator, to be comprehended by the meanest Capacity. This he proves judiciously, by the Appearances and Distances of the Planets and fixed Stars; and if he had let alone his learned Men, Philosophical Transactions, and Telescopes in the Planet *Jupiter*, and his Inhabitants not only there, but in all the fixed Stars, and even in the *Milky Way*, and only stuck to the greatness of the Universe, he had deserved much more Praise.

The other thing he endeavours to defend and assert, is, the System of *Copernicus*. As to this, I cannot but take his part as far as a Woman's Reasoning can go. I shall not venture upon the Astronomical part, but leave that to the Mathematicians; but because I know, that when this Opinion of *Copernicus* (as to the Motion of the Earth, and the Sun's being fixed in the Centre of the Universe, without any other Motion, but upon his own Axis) was first heard of in the World, those who neither understood the old System of *Ptolemy*,[1] nor the new one of *Copernicus*, said, That this new Opinion was expresly contrary to the holy Scriptures, and therefore not to be embraced; nay, it was condemned as Heretical upon the same Account: After it had been examined by the best Mathematicians in *Europe*, and that they found it answered all the *Phænomena*'s and Motions of the Spheres and Stars better than the System of *Ptolemy*; that it was plainer, and not so perplexing and confused as the old Opinion; several of these learned Men therefore embraced this; but those that held out, when they saw all Arguments against *Copernicus* would not do, they had recourse to what I said before, that this System was expresly against the holy Scriptures. Amongst this Number is the learned Father *Tacquit*,[2] a Jesuite; who, I am told, has writ a large Course of Mathematicks, and particularly, of Astronomy, which is deservedly much esteemed. In the end of this Treatise, he cites several Texts of Scripture; and particularly, the 19th. *Psalm, And the Sun standing still at the Command of* Joshua. If I can make it appear, that this Text of Scripture is, at least, as much for *Copernicus* as *Ptolemy*, I hope it will not be unacceptable to my Readers: Therefore, with all due Reverence and Respect to the Word of God, I hope I may be allowed to say, that the design of the Bible was not to instruct Mankind in Astronomy, Geometry, or Chronology, but in the Law of God, to lead us to Eternal Life; and the Spirit of God has been so condescending to our Weakness, that through the whole Bible, when any thing of that kind is mentioned, the Expressions are always turned to fit our Capacities, and to fit the common Accep-

---

1   The Ptolemaic model placed the unmoving earth at the centre of the universe, with the sun and all other heavenly bodies rotating around it.

2   Father André Tacquet (1612-60), Jesuit priest and mathematical writer

tance, or Appearances of things to the Vulgar.[1] As to Astronomy, I shall reserve that to the last, and shall begin with Geometry; and though I could give many Instances of all three, yet I shall give but one or two at most. The Measure and Dimensions of *Solomon's* Molten Brass Sea in 1 *King.* 7.23. the Words are these, *And he made a molten Sea, ten Cubits from one brim to the other, it was round all about, and his heighth was five Cubits, and a Line of thirty Cubits did compass it round about:* That is to say, the Diameter of this Vessel was a Third of its Circumference: This is indeed commonly understood to be so, but is far from a Geometrical Exactness, and will not hold to a Mathematical Demonstration, as to the just Proportion between the Diameter and Circumference of a Circle. In the next place, as to Chronology, I could give many Instances out of the Bible, but shall only name two that are very apparent, and easie to be understood by the meanest Capacity. See 1 *King.* 6.1. the Words are these, *And it came to pass, in the four hundred and fourscorth Year after the Children of Israel were come out of the Land of Egypt, in the fourth Year of Solomon's Reign over Israel, in the Month Zif, which is the second Month, he began to build the House of the Lord.* Compare this Text, and number of Years with *Act.* 13.17, 18, 19, 20, 21, 22. which is the beginning of St. *Paul's* Sermon to the Jews of *Antioch*, and the number of Years therein contained: The Words are these,

Ver. 17. *The God of this People of Israel chose our Fathers, and exalted the People when they dwelt as Strangers in the Land of Egypt, and with an high Hand brought he them out of it.*

Ver. 18. *And about the time of forty Years suffered he their Manners in the Wilderness.*

Ver. 19. *And when he had destroyed seven Nations in the Land of Canaan, he divided their Land to them by Lot.*

Ver. 20. *And after that, he gave unto them Judges, about the space of four hundred and fifty Years, until Samuel the Prophet.*

Ver. 21. *And afterwards they desired a King, and God gave them Saul, the Son of Kish, a Man of the Tribe of Benjamin, for the space of forty Years.*

Ver. 22. *And when he had removed him, he raised up unto them David to be their King.*

King *David* the Prophet reigned seven Years in *Hebron*, and thirty

---

1   ordinary or uneducated people

three Years in *Jerusalem*; and for this see 1 *King*. 2.11. To this you must add the first three Years of his Son *Solomon*, according to the Text I have cited, in 1 *King*. 6.1. Put all these Numbers together, which are contained in St. *Paul's* Sermon at *Antioch*, with the Reign of King *David*, the first three Years of *Solomon*, and seven Years of *Joshua's* Government, before the Land was divided by Lot, which is expresly set down in *Act*.13.19. the number of the Years will run thus: Forty Years in the Wilderness, the seven Years of *Joshua*, before the dividing the Land by Lot; from thence, till *Samuel*, four hundred and fifty Years; forty Years for the Reign of *Saul*, forty Years for the Reign of *David*, and the first three Years of *Solomon*; all these Numbers added together, make five hundred and eighty Years; which Computation differs an hundred Years from that in 1 *King*. 6.1. which is but four hundred and eighty. It is not my present Business to reconcile this difference; but I can easily do it; if any Body think it worth their Pains to quarrel with my Boldness, I am able to defend my self.

The second Instance is, as to the Reign of King *Solomon*; for this, see 1 *King*. 11.42. where it is said, he reigned but forty Years over *Israel*. *Josephus*[1] says expresly, in the third Chapter of his eighth Book of Antiquities, that King *Solomon* reigned eighty Years, and died at the Age of ninety four. I would not presume to name this famous Historian in contradiction to the Holy Scriptures, if it were not easie to prove by the Scriptures, that *Solomon* reigned almost twice forty Years. The *Greek* Version of the Bible, called commonly the *Septuagint*[2] or *seventy two Interpreters* has it most expresly in 3 *King*.2. But the first Book of Kings according to our Translation in *English*, says, that *Solomon sat upon the Throne of his Father David, when he was twelve Years of Age*. But for Confirmation, be pleas'd to see 1 Chr. 22.5. and 29.1. where it is said, that *Solomon was but young and tender for so great a work, as the building of the Temple*. Rehoboam the Son of Solomon was forty one Years old, when he began to reign, see 1 *King*.14.21. How was it possible then that *Solomon* could beget a Son, when he was but a Child himself, or of eleven Years of Age according to the *Septuagint?* This Difficulty did strangely surprise a Primitive Bishop, by Name, *Vitalis*,

---

1 Flavius Josephus (c. 37- c. 100 CE), Jewish historian, author of the *Jewish War* and *Antiquities of the Jews* (c. 94).

2 Septuagint: Greek translation of the Hebrew Bible, compiled circa second century BCE. In what follows Behn compares the Septuagint and the Hebrew Bible.

who proposed this Doubt to St. *Jerome*,[1] who was strangely put to it to return an Answer; and the Learned Holy Father is forc'd at last to say, *that the Letter of the Scripture does often kill, but the Spirit enlivens.* The Difficulty is still greater than what *Vitalis* proposed to St. *Jerome* in his Epistle. *Rehoboam* was the Son of *Naamah* an *Ammonitish*, stranger Woman, as you may see in 1 *King*.14.31. Now it is clear, that *Solomon* did not abandon the Law of God, nor give himself to strange Women till the end of his Reign, see 1 *King*.9. where he had so many strange Wives and Concubines, besides his lawful Queen, the King of *Ægypt's* Daughter; and I hope this will convince any rational Man, that the Scripture names only the first forty Years of the Reign of King *Solomon,* which was the time, wherein he did what was Right in the Sight of the Lord; which I think is Demonstration, that the Holy Scripture was not designed, to teach Mankind Geometry, or instruct them in Chronology. The Learned *Anthony Godean*,[2] Lord and Bishop of *Venice*, seems to have been sensible of this great Difficulty; for in his Learned Church-History, his Epitome from *Adam* to Jesus Christ, writing the Life of *Solomon*, he says, *he was twenty three Years old when he began his Reign.* Upon what Grounds, or from what Authority I know not; but this agrees better with the Age of *Solomon's* Son *Rehoboam*; but it doth not remove the Difficulty, so well as what I have said.

I come now in the last place to perform what I undertook, which is to prove, that the Scripture was not designed to teach us Astronomy, no more than Geometry or Chronology: And to make it appear that the two Texts cited by Father *Tacquet, viz.* that of Psal.19.4, 5, 6. and Josh.10.12, *&c.* are at least as much for *Copernicus* his System, as they are for *Ptolemy's*. The words of the 19th. Psalm are, *In them hath he set a Tabernacle for the Sun, which is as a Bridegroom coming out of his Chamber; and rejoices as a strong Man to run his Race, &c.*

That these words are Allegorical is most plain. Does not the Word *Set* import Stability, Fix'dness and Rest, as much as the Words *run his Race*, and *come forth of his Chamber*, do signifie motion or turning round? Do not the Words *Tabernacle* and *Chamber* express Places of

---

1 Jerome (c. 342-420), Biblical scholar and theologian, translator of the Bible into Latin

2 Bishop Antoine Godeau (1605-72), author of *Histoire de l'église, depuis Adam jusq'au 9me siècle* (5th edn, Paris, 1680)

Rest and Stability? And why may not I safely believe, that this makes for the Opinion of *Copernicus*, as well as for that of *Ptolemy*? For the Words of the Scriptures favour one Opinion as much as the other. The Texts of the Suns standing still at the Command of *Joshua*, are yet plainer for *Copernicus*, in *Josh*.10. and the latter part of v.12. the Words are these. *Sun stand thou still on Gibeon, and thou Moon on the Valley of Ajalon, &c.* [Josh.10.12]

The best Edition of the English Bible, which is printed in a small *Folio* by *Buck*, in *Cambridge*,[1] has an Asterism at the Word *stand*, and renders it in the Margent, from the Hebrew, *Be thou silent:* If it be so in the Hebrew, *be thou silent* makes as much for the Motion of the Earth, according to *Copernicus*, as for the Motion of the Sun according to *Ptolemy*, but not to criticize upon Words, consider this miraculous Passage, not only the Sun is commanded to stand still, but the Moon also, *And thou Moon on the Valley of Ajalon.* The Reason the Sun was commanded to stand still, was to the end the Children of *Israel* might have Light to guide them, to destroy their Enemies. Now when by this Miracle they had the Light of the Sun, of what Advantage could the Moon be to them? Why was she commanded to stand still upon the Valley of *Ajalon*? Besides, be pleased to consider, the Holy Land is but a very little Country or Province: The *Valley* of *Ajalon* is very near *Gibeon*, where *Joshua* spoke to both Sun and Moon together to stand still above, in Places so near each other, it is Demonstration, that the Moon was at that time very near the Sun; and by Consequence was at that time either a day or two before her change, or a day or two at most after new Moon; and then she is nearer to the Body of the Sun, as to appearance, so could not assist the Children of *Israel* with Light, having so little of her own: It was then for some other Reason that the Moon stood still; and for some other Reason that it is taken notice of in Holy Scripture. Both Systems agree that the Moon is the nearest Planets to the Earth, and subservient to it, to enlighten it, during the Night, in Absence of the Sun. Besides this, the Moon has other strange Effects, not only on the Earth it self, but upon all the living Creatures that inhabit it; many of them are invisible, and as yet unknown to Mankind; some of them are most appar-

---

1   brothers Thomas and John Buck (fl. 1625-70), printers to the University of Cambridge, who published various editions of the Bible during the first half of the seventeenth century

ent; and above all, her wonderful Influence over the ebbing and flowing of the Sea, at such regular Times and Seasons, if not interrupted by the Accident of some Storm, or great Wind. We know of no Relation or Corresponding between the Sun and the Moon, unless it be what is common with all the rest of the Planets, that the Moon receives her Light from the Sun, which she restores again by Reflection. If the Sun did move, according to the System of *Ptolemy*, where was the necessity of the Moon's standing still? For if the Moon had gone on her Course, where was the Loss or Disorder in Nature? She having, as I demonstrated before, so little Light, being so very near her Change, would have recovered her Loss at the next Appearance of the Sun, and the Earth could have suffered nothing by the Accident; whereas the Earth moving at the same time, in an Annual and Diurnal Course, according to the System of *Copernicus*, would have occasioned such a Disorder and Confusion in Nature, that nothing less than two or three new Miracles, all as great as the first, could have set the World in Order again: The regular Ebbings and Flowings of the Sea must have been interrupted, as also the Appearing of the Sun in the Horizon, besides many other Inconveniences in Nature; as, the Eclipses of the Sun and Moon, which are now so regular, that an Astronomer could tell you to a Minute, what Eclipses will be for thousands of Years to come, both of Sun and Moon; when, and in what Climates they will be visible, and how long they will last, how many Degrees and Digits of those two great Luminaries will be obscured. So that I doubt not but when this stupendious Miracle was performed by the Almighty and Infinite Power of God, his omnipotent Arm did in an Instant stop the Course of Nature, and the whole Frame of the Universe was at a stand, though the Sun and Moon be only named, being, to vulgar Appearance, the two great Luminaries that govern the Universe. This was the space of a Day in Time, yet can be called no part of Time, since Time and Nature are always in motion, and this Day was a stop of that Course. What is there in all this wonderful stop of Time, that is not as strong for the System of *Copernicus*, as for that of *Ptolemy*? And why does my Belief of the Motion of the Earth, and the Rest of the Sun contradict the holy Scriptures? Am not I as much obliged to believe that the Sun lodges in a Tabernacle? (as in *Psal.*19) Are not all these Allegorical Sayings? In the above-named Edition of the *English Bible* of *Buck's* at *Cambridge*, see *Isa.8.38.* where the Shadow returned ten Degrees backwards, as a Sign of King *Hezekiah's* Recovery, and there follow these Words, *And the Sun returned ten Degrees*; but on the Margin you will find it from the *Hebrew, The Shadow returned ten Degrees by the Sun*; and this is yet as much for *Copernicus* as *Ptolemy.* Whether God Almighty added ten Degrees or Hours to that Day, or by another kind of Miracle, made the Shadow to return upon the Dial of *Ahaz,* I will not presume to determine; but still you see the *Hebrew* is most agreeable to the new System of *Copernicus.*

Thus I hope I have performed my Undertaking, in making it appear, that the holy Scriptures, in things that are not material to the Salvation of Mankind, do altogether condescend to the vulgar Capacity; and that these two Texts of *Psal.19.* and *Josh.10.* are as much for *Copernicus* as against him. I hope none will think my Undertaking too bold, in making so much use of the Scripture, on such an Occasion. I have a Precedent, much esteemed by all ingenious Men; that is, Mr. *Burnet's* Book of *Paradise,* and *Antedeluvian World,*[1] which incroaches as much, if not more, on the holy Scriptures. But I have another Reason for saying so much of the Scriptures at this time: We live in an Age, wherein many believe nothing contained in that holy Book, others turn it into Ridicule: Some use it only for Mischief, and as a Foundation and Ground for Rebellion: Some keep close to the Literal Sense, and others give the Word of God only that Meaning and Sense that pleases their own Humours, or suits best their present Purpose and Interest. As I quoted an Epistle of St. *Jerome* to *Vitalis* before, where that great Father says, that *the Letter kills, but the Spirit enlivens*; I think it is the Duty of all good Christians to acquiesce in the Opinion and Decrees of the Church of Christ, in whom dwells the Spirit of God, which enlightens us to Matters of Religion and Faith; and as to other things contained in the Holy Scriptures relating to Astronomy, Geometry, Chronology, or other liberal Sciences, we leave those Points to the Opinion of the Learned, who by comparing the several Copies, Translations, Versions, and Editions of the Bible, are best able to reconcile any apparent Differences; and this with all Submission to the Canons of General Councils, and Decrees of the Church. For the

---

1   Thomas Burnet (?1635-1715), master of Charterhouse, London, author of the *Sacred Theory of the Earth* (1681), which argued that the earth's surface had originally been as smooth as an egg until "deformed" by the Deluge

School-men agitate and debate[1] many things of a higher Nature, than the standing still, or the Motion of the Sun or the Earth. And therefore, I hope my Readers will be so just as to think, I intend no Reflection on Religion by this Essay; which being no Matter of Faith, is free for every one to believe, or not believe, as they please. I have adventur'd to say nothing, but from good Authority: And as this is approved of by the World, I may hereafter venture to publish somewhat may be more useful to the Publick. I shall conclude therefore with some few Lines, as to my present Translation.

I have laid the Scene at *Paris*, where the Original was writ; and have translated the Book near the Words of the Author. I have made bold to correct a Fault of the *French* Copy, as to the heighth of our Air or Sphere of Activity of the Earth, which the *French* Copy makes twenty or thirty Leagues,[2] I call it two or three, because sure this was a Fault of the Printer, and not a mistake of the Author. For Monsieur *Des Cartes*, and Monsieur *Rohalt*,[3] both assert it to be but two or three Leagues. I thought *Paris* and St. *Denis* fitter to be made use of as Examples, to compare the Earth and the Moon to, than *London* and *Greenwich*; because St. *Denis* having several Steeples and Walls, is more like *Paris*, than *Greenwich* is to *London*. *Greenwich* has no Walls, and but one very low Steeple, not to be seen from the Monument without a Prospective Glass.[4] And I resolv'd either to give you the *French* Book into *English,* or to give you the subject quite changed and made my own; but having neither health nor leisure for the last I offer you the first such as it is.

---

1   "delate" in original

2   a league is roughly equivalent to three miles

3   René Descartes (1596-1650): French mathematician and philosopher; Jacques Rohault (1618-72): French physicist, author of *Tractatus physicus Gallice* (1682)

4   spy-glass or telescope

Works Cited and Select Bibliography

Alic, Margaret. *Hypatia's Heritage: A History of Women in Science from Antiquity to the late Nineteenth Century*. London: Women's Press, 1986.

Bacon, Francis. *Sylva sylvarum: or, A naturall historie, in ten centuries … written by the Right Honourable Francis Lord Verulam viscount St. Alban…* [includes *New Atlantis: a worke unfinished*]. London: 1635.

Battigelli, Anna. *Margaret Cavendish and the Exiles of the Mind*. Lexington: UP of Kentucky, 1998.

Behn, Aphra. See Fontenelle.

Birch, Thomas. *History of the Royal Society of London*. 4 vols. London: 1756-7.

Bowerbank, Sylvia. "History of Women in Science: Early Modern to Late Eighteenth Century." *The Women's Studies Encyclopedia*. New York: Routledge (forthcoming).

____. "The Spider's Delight: Margaret Cavendish and the Female Imagination." *English Literary Renaissance* 14 (Fall 1984): 392-408; reprinted in *Women in the Renaissance*. Ed. Kirby Farrell, Elizabeth Hageman and Arthur Kinney. Amherst: University of Massachusetts Press, 1990, 187-203.

Boyle, Robert. "Preface." *Experiments and Considerations Touching Colours*. In *The Works of the Honourable Robert Boyle*. 6 vols. London: 1772. I. 662-5.

Butler, Judith. *Gender Trouble: Feminism and the Subversion of Identity*. New York: Routledge, 1990.

Cavendish, Margaret, Duchess of Newcastle. *CCXI Sociable Letters*. London: 1664.

____. *The Convent of Pleasure and Other Plays*. Ed. Anne Shaver. Baltimore: Johns Hopkins UP, 1999.

____. *The Description of a New World, called the Blazing World*. London: 1668.

____. *Grounds of Natural Philosophy*. London: 1668.

____. *The Life of William Cavendish, Duke of Newcastle*. Ed. C. Firth. London: 2nd edn, n.d.

____. *The Life of … William Cavendishe, Duke, Marquess, and Earl of Newcastle…* London: 1667.

____. *Natures Pictures drawn by Fancies Pencil to the Life*. London: 1656

____. *Observations Upon Experimental Philosophy*. London: 1666.

____. *Orations of Divers Sorts*. London: 1662.

____. *Philosophical and Physical Opinions*. London: 1655.

____. *Philosophicall Fancies*. London: 1653.

____. *Playes*. London: 1662.

____. *Plays Never Before Printed*. London: 1668.

____. *Poems and Fancies*. London: 1653.

____. *A True Relation of My Birth, Breeding, and Life*. See *Natures Pictures*.

____. *The Worlds Olio*. London: 1655.

Cavendish, William, Duke of Newcastle. *La Methode Nouvelle et Invention Extraordinaire de dresser les Chevaux*. Antwerp: 1658.

Clucas, Stephen. "The Atomism of the Cavendish Circle: A Reappraisal." *The Seventeenth Century* 9.2 (1994): 247-73.

Dick, Steven J. *Plurality of Worlds: The Origins of the Extraterrestrial Life Debate from Democritus to Kant*. Cambridge: Cambridge UP, 1982.

Evelyn, John. *Diary and Correspondence of John Evelyn, F.R.S.* Ed. William Bray. 4 vols. London: 1857.

Fitzmaurice, James. "Introduction." to Margaret Cavendish, *The Sociable Letters*. Ed. J. Fitzmaurice. New York: Garland, 1997: xi-xxi.

Fontenelle, Bernard le Bovier. *Entretiens sur la pluralité des mondes*. Paris: 1686.

____. *A Discovery of New Worlds / from the French made English by Mrs. A. Behn*. London: 1688.

Gallagher, Catherine. "Embracing the Absolute: The Politics of the Female Subject in Seventeenth-Century England." *Genders* 1 (Spring 1988): 24-39.

Grant, Douglas. *Margaret the First*. Toronto: University of Toronto Press, 1957.

Harris, Frances. "Living in the Neighbourhood of Science: Mary Evelyn, Margaret Cavendish and the Greshamites." In Hunter and Hutton, 198-217.

Hunter, Lynette. "Sisters of the Royal Society: The Circle of Katherine Jones, Lady Ranelagh." In Hunter and Hutton, 178-97.

Hunter, Lynette and Sarah Hutton, eds. *Women, Science and Medicine 1500-1700*. Phoenix Mills, Gloucestershire: Sutton Publishing, 1997.

Hutton, Sarah. "Anne Conway, Margaret Cavendish and Seventeenth-Century Scientific Thought." In Hunter and Hutton, 218-34.

Jones, Kathleen. *A Glorious Fame: The Life of Margaret Cavendish, Duchess of Newcastle 1623-1673.* London: Bloomsbury, 1988.

Kahn, Victoria. "Margaret Cavendish and the Romance of Contract." *Renaissance Quarterly* 50 (Summer 1997): 526-66.

Kargon, Robert. *Atomism in England from Hariot to Newton.* Oxford: Clarendon Press, 1966.

Khanna, Lee Cullen. "The Subject of Utopia: Margaret Cavendish and Her Blazing-World." *Utopian and Science Fiction By Women: Worlds of Difference.* Ed. Jane L. Donawerth and Carol A. Kolmerten. Syracuse: Syracuse UP, 1994: 15-34.

Keller, Eve. "Producing petty gods: Margaret Cavendish's critique of experimental science." *English Literary History* 64 (Summer 1997): 447-71.

Keller, Evelyn Fox. *Reflections on Gender and Science.* New Haven: Yale UP, 1985.

Kristeva, Julia. *Black Sun: Depression and Melancholia.* New York: Columbia UP, 1989.

Letters and Poems in Honour of the Incomparable Princess, Margaret Duchess of Newcastle. London: 1676.

Lilley, Kate. "Blazing Worlds: Seventeenth-Century Women's Utopian Writing." *Women, Texts and Histories, 1575-1760.* Eds. Clare Brant and Diane Purkiss. London: Routledge, 1992: 102-33.

———. "Introduction." to Margaret Cavendish, Duchess of Newcastle. *The Blazing World and Other Writings.* Ed. K. Lilley. Harmondsworth: Penguin Classic, 1994: ix-xxxii.

Martin, Benjamin. *The Young Gentleman & Lady's Philosophy, in a Continued Survey of the Works of Nature and Art; by Way of Dialogue.* 2nd edn. 2 vols. London: 1772.

McKeon, Michael. *The Origins of the English Novel 1600-1740.* Baltimore: Johns Hopkins UP, 1987.

Mendelson, Sara. *The Mental World of Stuart Women: Three Studies.* Brighton: Harvester, 1987.

Mendelson, Sara, and Patricia Crawford. *Women in Early Modern England 1550-1720.* Oxford: Clarendon Press, 1998.

Merchant, Caroline. *The Death of Nature: Women, Ecology, and the Scientific Revolution.* San Francisco: Harper & Row, 1980.

Merrens, Rebecca. "A nature of 'infinite sense and reason': Margaret Cavendish's natural philosophy and the 'noise' of a feminized nature." *Women's Studies* 2 (Sept. 1996): 421–38.

Meyer, Gerald. *The Scientific Lady in England 1650-1760: An Account of Her Rise, with Emphasis on the Major Roles of the Telescope and Microscope.* Berkeley: University of California Press, 1955.

Nicolson, Marjorie. *Pepys's Diary and the New Science.* Charlottesville: The University of Virginia Press, 1965.

Ogilvie, Marilyn Bailey. *Women in Science: Antiquity through the Nineteenth Century: A Biographical Dictionary with Annotated Bibliography.* Cambridge, Mass.: MIT Press, 1986.

Pepys, Samuel. *The Diary of Samuel Pepys.* Eds. R. Latham and W. Matthews. 11 vols. London: G. Bell and Sons, 1970-83.

Phillips, Patricia. *The Scientific Lady: A Social History of Woman's Scientific Interests 1520-1918.* London: Weidenfeld and Nicolson, 1990.

Rogers, John. "Margaret Cavendish and the Gendering of the Vitalist Utopia." *The Matter of Revolution: Science, Poetry, and Politics in the Age of Milton.* Ithaca: Cornell UP, 1996: 177-211.

Rosenthal, Laura J. "'Authoress of a Whole World': The Duchess of Newcastle and Imaginary Property." *Playwrights and Plagarists in Early Modern England: Gender, Authorship, Literary Property.* Ithaca: Cornell UP, 1996: 58-104.

Sarasohn, Lisa. "A Science Turned Upside Down: Feminism and the Natural Philosophy of Margaret Cavendish." *Huntington Library Quarterly* 47 (1984): 289-307.

Schiebinger, Londa. "Margaret Cavendish, Natural Philosopher" and "Cavendish, a Feminist?" In *The Mind Has No Sex? Women in the Origins of Modern Science.* Cambridge, Mass.: Harvard UP, 1989: 47-59.

____. *Nature's Body: Gender in the Making of Modern Science.* Boston: Beacon Press, 1993.

Smith, Hilda. *Reason's Disciples.* Urbana: U. of Illinois Press, 1982.

Smith, Sidonie. "The Ragged Rout of Self: Margaret Cavendish's *True Relation* and the Heroics of Self-Disclosure." *A Poetics of Women's Autobiography: Marginality and the Fictions of Self-Representation.* Ed. S. Smith. Bloomington: Indiana UP, 1987: 84-101.

Shteir, Ann B. *Cultivating Women, Cultivating Science: Flora's Daughters and Botany in England, 1760-1860.* Baltimore: Johns Hopkins UP, 1996.

Stimson, Dorothy. "The Visit of the Duchess of Newcastle." *Scientists and Amateurs: A History of the Royal Society.* New York: Henry Schuman, 1948: 82-4.

Terrall, Mary. "Gendered Spaces, Gendered Audiences: Inside and Outside the Paris Academy of Sciences." *Configurations* 3.2 (1995). Special Cluster on Gender and Early-Modern Science: 207-32.

Tillyard, E.M.W. *The Elizabethan World Picture.* New York: Vintage Books, 1961.

Tomlinson, Sophie. "'My Brain the Stage': Margaret Cavendish and the Fantasy of Female Performance." *Women, Texts and Histories, 1575-1760.* Eds. Clare Brant and Diane Purkiss. London: Routledge, 1992: 134-63.

Williams, Gweno. "'Why May Not a Lady Write a Good Play?' Plays by Early Modern Women Reassessed as Performance Texts." In *Readings in Renaissance Women's Drama: Criticism, History and Performance 1594-1998.* Eds. S.P. Caesaro and M. Wynne-Davies. London: Routledge, 1998: 95-107.

Women's Writing: The Elizabethan to Victorian Period 2.2 (1995). Ed. Ann B. Shteir. Special Issue on Women and Science.

Women's Writing: The Elizabethan to Victorian Period 4.3 (1997). Ed. Emma Rees. Special Issue on Margaret Cavendish.

Yates, Frances A. *The Occult Philosophy in the Elizabethan Age.* London: Routledge & Kegan Paul, 1979.